Midnight

Amy McCulloch is the Chinese-White author of *Breathless*, an international bestseller, a Waterstones Thriller of the Month, and a *Sunday Times* Crime Book of the Month. She has also written eight novels for children and young adults. She has climbed two of the world's highest mountains, completed an ultramarathon in the Sahara Desert, and visited all seven continents, including Antarctica.

Midnight

AMY McCULLOCH

MICHAEL JOSEPH

PENGUIN MICHAEL JOSEPH

UK | USA | Canada | Ireland | Australia
India | New Zealand | South Africa

Penguin Michael Joseph is part of the Penguin Random House group of companies
whose addresses can be found at global.penguinrandomhouse.com

First published by Penguin Michael Joseph, 2023
001
Copyright © Tiger Tales Limited, 2023

The moral right of the author has been asserted

Set in 13.5/16pt Garamond MT Std
Typeset by Jouve (UK), Milton Keynes
Printed and bound in Great Britain by Clays Ltd, Elcograf S.p.A.

The authorized representative in the EEA is Penguin Random House Ireland,
Morrison Chambers, 32 Nassau Street, Dublin D02 YH68

A CIP catalogue record for this book is available from the British Library

HARDBACK ISBN: 978-0-241-53490-8
OPEN MARKET ISBN: 978-0-241-53491-5

www.greenpenguin.co.uk

For Chris – my partner in life's biggest adventure

Prologue

I watch as he scampers down the gangway, his fists clenched by his side. He avoids catching the eye of the distracted officer at the door to the ship, racing past the long line of passengers waiting to check-in for their voyage of a lifetime.

He looks so small through my binoculars. A tiny slip of a man. I wait, but the woman doesn't come after him. No matter. I had planned for that. Besides, this way is easier.

I've been watching them, waiting, biding my time. Every moment confirms what I already knew: these two deserve everything that's coming at them.

I look down at my phone, opening the message thread from a few minutes ago.

WE NEED TO TALK.

Not possible, *he'd replied.*

BE AT THE HOTEL IN FIFTEEN MINUTES OR ELSE THE VIDEO GOES LIVE.

He was too smart to ignore me. Especially with the screenshot I'd attached to the message. That would have made his blood run cold.

I set down the binoculars. Now I'm certain he's on his way, I have a few minutes to prepare the next stage of the plan. I take out the box with the syringe, making certain it's primed and ready. My bags are packed, waiting by the door for my getaway.

The hotel staff will give him a message, sending him to the room next to mine, so I double-check the adjoining door is unlocked and slightly ajar. I've already set up a laptop on the table in that room, facing away from the entrance.

I wait until I hear him enter. Then I call.

He answers on the first ring, so angry he's practically spitting. 'I gave you what you wanted. You said you would stop this.'

'It's not enough. Meet my demand, or else what's on that laptop goes live.'

'I told you. It's not going to happen. The ship sets sail in an hour. You've got your money. You can't just keep asking for more. Now it's time to leave us alone.'

'I don't think so. Why don't you turn it on and see for yourself the damage I can do?'

I wait for him to sit down at the desk. But it's a ploy. If there was proof, I wouldn't have to do this. Instead, while he's distracted, I step through into the room.

'What the fuck?' I hear him mutter as he double-clicks on the video file and nothing plays.

My footstep lands heavy on the hotel carpet, and the creak is enough to reveal me. He leaps to standing.

But it's too late. In the next second, I'm on him, plunging the needle into his neck. He barely has the opportunity to struggle. I'm too fast; it's too unexpected. And the drugs I've chosen work quickly.

As he sags to the floor, I search his pockets for anything I might need. I drag his body into the second room, the one I've booked for the next week. Then, I make sure the 'Do Not Disturb' sign is still on the outer knob, shut the door and start walking. I expect he won't be found for some time.

I'll be long gone by then.

After all, I have a boat to catch.

I

Twenty-four hours earlier

Huge, snow-capped mountains rise up behind the town, their jagged peaks piercing the bright blue sky. The Martial range cradled the southernmost town in the world – Ushuaia – and, with it, the gateway to Antarctica.

An icy breeze swirled around her body as Olivia stared out at the slate-grey sea. Half a dozen yachts were moored in the harbour and birds splashed in the surf, fighting over a silvery fish nabbed from beneath the surface. The waves were calm, lapping gently against the stone walls of the dock. For the moment there was no sign of the ferocious, stormy weather that this part of the world was notorious for.

She knew some people found comfort by being near water. Not her. For her, the sight of the water brought up a fear that caught in her throat, threatening to choke her.

She gripped the metal railing, took a breath and focused on the large ship docked in the port. The MS *Vigil*. Tomorrow, it would take her across one of the world's most perilous bodies of water – the Drake Passage – to the final continent. The ship was a converted icebreaker from Norway, designed to chop through icy waters and sail through polar storms with ease. She'd read up on the specifications for the ship and its captain's impeccable safety record. She knew she had nothing to worry about.

But the fear remained.

Movement on the dock caught her eye. Two men strolled down the gangplank from the *Vigil*. When she was sure one of them was her boyfriend, Aaron, she waved, glad of the distraction. Her palms stung as she let go of the cold iron.

She wasn't sure if he'd seen. If he had, he didn't acknowledge her. About halfway towards her, they stopped, speaking with their heads close. They shook hands before they parted, and Olivia watched as the second man stalked off in the opposite direction. She didn't recognize him from the meeting that morning, but that wasn't a surprise – she'd been introduced to so many people, and his face was covered by the fur-trimmed hood of his parka. He could have been anyone.

Olivia frowned, but then Aaron turned to her. His cheeks were flushed from being blasted by the freezing air, his normally perfectly set curly brown hair dishevelled in the wind. He gave her a wide smile.

'Feeling better, Livi?' he asked once he'd made it through the security gates separating the dock from the park. He kissed her firmly before she could answer.

No, she wanted to say. *I'm not ready. I'll wait for you here, safe, on land.* But she swallowed down her anxiety. She knew this was a make-or-break moment for them – in their relationship and their business. He'd put his trust in her again, even after how badly she'd messed up on the night of his big auction.

Still, he wasn't fooled. 'Once we're underway, I know you'll love it. The ship is incredible – it feels like a floating boutique hotel. You won't even know you're on the water.'

'Is everything ready?' she asked, looping her arm through his as they meandered back towards their hotel.

'Still a few last-minute niggles.'

Aaron had been on board overseeing the installation of a special showcase of work by his star artist – Kostas Yennin. Aaron had represented Yennin's work for years, steadily building his profile but never truly breaking him out in a big way on the art circuit. It was only after tragedy struck, resulting in Yennin's untimely death, that his star had had a meteoric rise – his pieces selling at auction for millions of pounds, demand from galleries and museums skyrocketing, even his social media following growing exponentially. But Aaron wanted to be careful. He'd seen so many gifted artists make a big splash but then fail to transition to blue-chip status – that top echelon of artists whose paintings consistently increased in value.

He wanted to create a lasting legacy for Yennin's art, and that required finding a way to make him stand out from the pack. Since Yennin's paintings had all been inspired by the beauty of the polar regions, Aaron had negotiated a deal to match artist with adventure. His work would be displayed exclusively aboard the MS *Vigil* and the passengers would have the unique opportunity to attend a high-end art auction at sea.

And if it was a success, the showcase format was going to be rolled out to the entire fleet of Pioneer cruise ships, turning Yennin into a worldwide household name and boosting the price of his artwork immeasurably – not to mention establishing Aaron as one of the premier art dealers in the world.

He'd start the Hunt Advisory off the back of it, to

search for the next Kostas Yennin. And, to her surprise, he wanted *her* to join him. 'With your brilliant financial mind to balance my creative vision, we could be unstoppable,' he'd said.

She hadn't known what to say. She thought she'd screwed up everything that night. Her career. Her relationship. Her mental health. But he'd offered her this lifeline and she'd grabbed it with both hands. This was her chance to rebuild.

'What's the issue?' she asked.

'The auctioneer from Art Aboard is going to be the death of me. Stefan Grenville. I wish we could have chosen our own person.'

It had been a frustrating but necessary compromise: Art Aboard had the experience of running auctions on cruise ships, so Aaron had agreed to partner with them. 'Next time, you will be able to. I really should have been there to help.'

Aaron squeezed her arm. 'You needed to rest. Besides, if all goes to plan, you'll be plenty busy on board – and when we get back. I need you in top form by then.'

She nodded, leaning against his arm so he couldn't read the expression of doubt on her face. Top form. When had she last felt like she'd been on her game? That version of herself was a distant memory, one she wasn't sure even existed any more. Did she even want to be that person again? Before she'd met Aaron, she'd had one goal: to qualify as an actuary as fast as humanly possible, make partner at her firm, and finally get the pay bump she needed to support her mother – who needed round-the-clock care. Every month, between her own rent and her mother's nursing home fees, she was barely scraping by. With every passed exam, she got a small pay rise, but it never seemed to be enough.

And so five a.m. wake-up calls, sixty-hour work weeks, late-night study sessions . . . that had become her norm. The thought of slowing down – of letting go of her vice-like grip on her career ladder – had seemed unthinkable. Even when she'd met Aaron, the thought of easing off on her laser-like focus on her goal had never entered her mind. In fact, she'd wanted it more than ever. He lived in a world so full of glamour and sophistication. She'd loved being part of it, but she wanted to match him – not rely on him.

On the surface, they'd been living a dream life.

The reality was: it was impossible to sustain.

That night, it all got too much. She'd broken down completely, with disastrous consequences.

She thought Aaron would never trust her again.

This was her rock bottom. She'd called her GP: anxiety and burnout, he said. On one hand it had been a relief to have it confirmed. On the other – she felt helpless. She knew she couldn't go back to the way she lived and worked before, but it was the only way she knew. Even taking a leave of absence from her job, going to therapy, trying to slow down and recharge, hadn't felt like enough.

All the while, things for Aaron had been skyrocketing. When he came to her with his plan for the Hunt Advisory, he'd thrown her a true lifeline. An opportunity to use her skillset, earn a good living and maybe even take some time to enjoy life too.

But it all would depend on the launch of the showcase in Antarctica. And that meant facing another fear of hers.

One she thought she could keep buried forever.

Why? Why did it have to be on a boat?

Her therapist had helped her to reframe it.

You won't be responsible, he'd told her, after she'd explained why she was so anxious about the trip.

And he was right. There was an entire crew manning the ship. An experienced captain. Top-of-the-line navigation equipment.

You won't have to keep watch.

She would just be a passenger, able to relax and enjoy the journey. It wouldn't be like last time.

You won't be responsible.

And then there was the destination: Antarctica. When she said the word out loud she expected to fall into a deep pit of grief. It had been a place that had achieved almost mythic status in her family growing up: the only continent her dad had left to visit before he died. But instead, she found herself smiling. Long-forgotten memories surfaced: how he'd spread maps out on their kitchen table showing her the various routes to the South Pole, how he'd sit on the end of her bed in the darkness and tell her about his desire to sail through the last truly untouched wilderness, past towering icebergs, spotting humpback whales and leopard seals, meeting penguins, and crossing over the Antarctic Circle to witness the midnight sun. His bookshelves had teetered under the weight of thick Shackleton and Scott biographies – had he been born in that era, she was sure he would have been one of the intrepid explorers himself. As a girl, she had absorbed his excitement, snuggling up to a cuddly penguin toy at night and dreaming of one day visiting 'the Ice'.

She'd been sixteen when he died. After that, her mother had banished his vast library to the rubbish dump, and scrubbed all mention of sailing, boats or exploration from their home.

Olivia had never questioned it. Why should she? After all, his death had been Olivia's fault.

She shook her head violently.

This time, you're not responsible. She took a deep breath. It was time for her to move on.

Besides, they'd come to the perfect place to start anew. Everything about the small town of Ushuaia felt fresh and crisp. It sat perched at the end of a rugged, wind-swept archipelago made up of thousands of sparsely populated islands called Tierra del Fuego. The name translated to 'Land of Fire' – ironic considering it was so cold. The town itself was a quaint fishing port with a mish-mash of houses with brightly coloured roofs and steep streets leading down to the water. A watercolour stroke of dark green forest led to snow-covered mountains rising up behind and circling the town, giving it an intimate feel, despite its frontier atmosphere.

'We have a couple of hours before dinner,' Aaron said. He grabbed her hand, squeezing it tightly. 'Shall we head back to the hotel?'

'Hang on – I want to get a picture.' Olivia stopped by a wooden sign, a few steps away from the water.

She looked around for someone she could rope in to take the photo for them. But the square was empty. Strange. When she'd walked past before, it had been buzzing with tourists, all clamouring to get a shot.

There was only one man in the park, leaning against one of the spindly, windswept trees. His black jacket was buttoned all the way to his chin, a hat pulled down low over his brow. But his gaze caught Olivia's, and she felt her heart leap into her throat. It was the way he was staring at her, at them.

She grabbed Aaron's arm, but at the same time he took the phone from her and held it up, his arm outstretched. 'Let's get a selfie, shall we?' He angled her phone so they could get both their faces in.

Olivia leaned in and smiled, putting the strange man to the back of her mind.

'Ushuaia: *el fin del mundo*.' Aaron read the sign aloud.

Olivia gave herself a shake. *The end of the world.*

And, hopefully, the start of a new chapter.

2

Olivia scrutinized the selfie, shaking off the sense of being watched. They looked good together, the cold air putting more colour in her cheeks than she'd had in months. She was so used to her complexion looking grey and tired, like too-weak tea. This was a photo worthy of her Instagram. Maybe Tricia would see it and stop sending her links to articles about 'burnout recovery' – pretty much the only communication they had nowadays. She knew her best friend was worried about her, but it wasn't necessary. She had everything under control.

Instagram had become a showreel of her recovery. Maybe if she posted enough pictures, the fantasy would become a reality. Otherwise, it was just wishful thinking.

A notification popped up on the top of her screen. 'Ah, it looks like our cold-weather gear is ready for pick up,' she said. 'Sara says we can drop by the office now.'

'Can't she get someone to deliver it? I've been running around all day. I'm shattered and with this dinner tonight—'

Olivia stood on her tiptoes to kiss his cheek. 'I'll get it. Your turn to rest.'

'Are you sure?'

'Of course. You've sorted everything on board the ship and I spent all morning relaxing in the hotel. It's the least I can do.'

He lifted her fingers and kissed them. 'You're too good to me. See you later.'

'I won't be long.'

He walked off in the direction of their hotel, his hands in his pockets. Olivia could read the tightness in his shoulders. She knew how important this exhibition was for him. Even though he was riding high now, the market was fickle. He was convinced it could go away as fast as it came.

That's why he needed to cement this deal. And Olivia wanted to do everything in her power to make sure it went smoothly for him and alleviate some of the pressure on his shoulders – just like he had done for her.

She plugged the Pioneer office address into her phone, where she was going to meet Sara – the cruise ship agent based in Ushuaia, and the woman who had made all the arrangements for their voyage. Olivia oriented herself on the map, the instructions leading her down the bustling main street filled with restaurants, outfitters and touristy tat shops, before turning on to one of the side streets.

She stopped in front of a prefab single-storey office building and knocked on the door. A small dark-haired woman greeted her with a warm smile. The walls of the travel agency were papered with images of icebergs, motivational posters featuring penguins, and postcards from the bottom of the world – thank-you notes from clients. '*Bienvenidos*, Olivia! How are things with the ship? Is Aaron happy?'

'I believe so,' Olivia said with a slight shrug to disguise her discomfort. She should have had a definitive answer. But the truth was, she didn't know if Aaron was happy or not.

Sara frowned. 'If there's anything I can do . . .'

'We'll be sure to let you know.' Olivia smiled now, in what she hoped was a reassuring way.

'Please do. In the meantime, you'll be wanting these.' Sara pointed to two pairs of insulated waterproof trousers, along with oversized fleece-lined mittens.

'Wow.' Olivia held up the mittens – each one almost bigger than her head. 'These are enormous.'

'Designed to keep you warm through the worst polar storms.'

'Not that we'll need that,' said Olivia with a laugh.

Sara smiled. 'Better to be safe than sorry. It will be a great trip. You have an incredible itinerary ahead of you. You've been on board already?'

Olivia shook her head. 'Only Aaron. I was too jet-lagged.'

'You're in for a treat. She doesn't look much from the outside, but the interior has been fully renovated – all the amenities and luxuries you can think of. It is one of the best ships for exploring the polar region.'

'I can't wait.'

'And I see you are signed up for the kayaking and camping excursions. Those will be once-in-a-lifetime experiences, truly. It's the perfect time of year for this kind of voyage, as after you sail across the Antarctic Circle, you'll experience the phenomenon known as the "midnight sun" – a sun that never sets.'

'Oh yes. That's the night Aaron has chosen for the big showcase auction.'

'A perfect choice. Then, when you land for your camping excursion, you'll get the chance to sleep under what's known as a "white night". It will never fully get dark.'

'Sounds magical,' Olivia replied. One of her burnout symptoms that she hadn't fully recovered from was severe insomnia. She had trouble enough sleeping in the dead of a dark night in a comfortable bed, so out on the ice at least her tendency to stay awake might be rewarded with a unique experience.

Throughout their conversation, Sara's desk phone kept ringing off the hook. Olivia glanced at it sideways. 'It's OK if you need to get that. I'll get out of your hair.'

Sara held up her hands in apology. 'Embarkation week is always frantic. Mr Hughes has demanded a full ship, so I'm busy sorting out cabins for some last-minute additional passengers.'

Olivia nodded sympathetically. She could imagine Cutler Hughes – the CEO of Pioneer Adventures – being a demanding boss. He was famous for it. 'I'm surprised anyone can get here at the last minute!'

'I have a waiting list a mile long for these cruises! There is no shortage of travellers with the flexibility to jump on board at short notice. We even have new crew starting this expedition. Antarctica is a big draw.' Sara sat down at her computer, her eyes frantically scanning the screen. 'If you or Aaron need anything, anytime at all before the ship leaves – get in touch with me. I'll be here all night long until your ship leaves the port tomorrow afternoon.'

'Thank you – I'll let him know.'

'If I don't see you before then, have a great trip.'

The gear was cumbersome but it was only a short distance back to the hotel. While not as luxurious as some of the places she and Aaron had stayed together in

Buenos Aires, Paris or Geneva, it more than made up for it with its expansive views of the wild coastline. From the vast windows of the lobby, she could see across to the harbour and the MS *Vigil*, the gangplank down and waiting for their arrival. Still, she couldn't help the visceral jolt of fear at the thought of climbing the wooden steps up to the boat – and then being trapped at sea for the next fourteen days.

You won't be responsible. She clung on to the phrase like a life jacket.

Aaron was sleeping when she snuck into their room. She wasn't surprised – between the jet lag and the intensity of preparing the showcase and auction, he'd been working nonstop. His hair sprawled across the pillow, and she felt a surge of affection for him. She thought he'd end things with her the night of the big Yennin auction. But instead, he'd brought her in closer, when she was certain she didn't deserve it.

They'd received instructions to leave their cases in the lobby, to be loaded on to the ship overnight. She wheeled the cases out, not wanting to disturb Aaron's rest with her packing.

Down in the lobby, she opened her case, squeezing the borrowed snow trousers and mittens into the already bulging main compartment. Then she did the same with Aaron's. Except that Aaron's dinner jacket was folded into the top of his case. He would be fuming if she sent it on to the ship before their big client meal.

She swapped it for his gear, resting the blazer over her arm. Something tumbled out of the pocket, sliding along the polished wooden floor.

She chased after it. A little velvet black box.

Her fingers trembled as she opened it. Inside was a platinum sapphire ring, the central stone a vivid blue, flanked on either side by smaller but no less sparkling diamonds. It looked vintage – and expensive.

An engagement ring.

She snapped the case shut, her heart racing, adrenaline flooding her system. Her fingers fumbled as she slid the box back into Aaron's jacket pocket and hurried to line their cases up with the others in the lobby.

It looked like everything was going to change in Antarctica.

3

Olivia swore everyone in the lift could hear her heart pounding as she returned to the hotel room. She'd smiled extra wide at the young couple who'd stepped in after her; they'd looked at her as if she'd lost her head. Oh well, she was happy. Aaron wanted to propose. Was he going to do it tonight, after their fancy dinner with all the VIPs on the cruise? It could explain why he was so nervous about it, and why he'd bought her a new dress for the occasion. Or was he going to wait until they were in Antarctica, out on the ice itself, surrounded by penguins?

It was so exhilarating. Wasn't it? Her stomach flipped and it didn't feel quite like excitement, but more like . . . fear.

She gave herself a shake. Not fear. Caution. That was far more likely.

After all, they'd been dating less than a year. When they'd first met, she could never have imagined it would last this long.

Their relationship had begun as a work assignment. Not a surprise, considering that's where she spent all her time.

'I have an exciting new project for you.'

Olivia had looked up from her morning cup of black coffee to see her boss Lisa standing over her desk, a thick folder of paper stuffed under her arm. Olivia prayed that wasn't part of the 'exciting new project'; she'd been up all night finishing the last project Lisa had assigned to her. If the bags under her eyes got any bigger, she could use them to carry her spare change. The price of pushing to be the youngest ever partner in her actuarial firm.

Still, a quirk in Lisa's smile had Olivia intrigued. 'You know we've been delighted by your work on the LUJO hotel group pension scheme. And by the looks of it, we weren't the only ones impressed. Do you want to come with me?'

Olivia jumped up to follow. Lisa was one of the senior partners at Pendle, and someone she needed to stay on the right side of if she wanted that promotion. She caught eyes with her best friend Tricia, Lisa's PA, who mouthed, 'What's going on?'

Olivia shrugged in reply.

Lisa's sun-drenched corner office looked out over the City of London, a sliver of the magnificent dome of St Paul's Cathedral visible through the office blocks. She pulled up a file on her computer screen, turning the monitor so that Olivia could see. It was a reproduction of a piece of artwork, instantly recognizable by the multicoloured skull painted in broad brushstrokes at its centre.

'Oh, Basquiat,' Olivia said. 'That sold for an astronomical sum, didn't it? The return on that investment was huge. I remember I shared the news on the team's WhatsApp.' Even her messaging apps were filled with work chat; it helped that most of her colleagues were nerds for financial news as well.

Lisa nodded. 'Which brings me to the assignment and Mr Lavaud's rather unique request. He's interested in acquiring art for investment purposes, and he's asked for you personally to consult.'

'Me?' Olivia blinked back her surprise. Pierre Lavaud was the owner of LUJO, the luxury hotel chain whose pension scheme Olivia had been working on for years. She never expected that the French billionaire would have any idea who she was, let alone ask for her by name. 'But why?'

Lisa shrugged. 'No idea. Maybe he heard about your interest in art?'

'I suppose so.' She'd visited one of his hotels in London for a convention and admired the Jeff Koons in the lobby. Maybe she had commented on it and he had noticed? 'Shouldn't we send one of the CFAs? Art investing isn't really part of my remit. He'd probably be better off with a financial advisor.'

'I agree, but he wants you. Like I said, you must have impressed him. A bit different from advising on the pension schemes, I know. And if he wasn't so important to us . . .' Lisa smiled, handing over the documents that had been under her arm. 'It's only a consult, but if you think it's too much I can assign someone else.'

Olivia shook her head. 'No, no, I can handle it.'

'Are you sure?'

'Of course.' Olivia took the file and plastered on a smile. She knew better than to refuse a request directly from Mr Lavaud. He was the firm's biggest client. And if she did a good job, she would have yet another string to her bow on her track to make partner. She only had one more exam left to pass in order to fully qualify as an actuary, and the partnership would be hers. The jump in salary would help her dig out from under the mountain of debt she'd found herself in – another bill had arrived from her mother's care home that morning, with an increase in fees.

'There is a little treat in there for you too – not just work,' said Lisa.

Olivia opened the folder. On top was an invitation to a gallery exhibition called *INTO THE UNKNOWN* in central London – Mayfair, according to the postcode – printed on heavy white card. The Hunt Gallery were presenting their artists of the future.

By the look of the embossing and gilded lettering, it would be a high-end affair. She would have to fork out for a new dress. Or at least, she'd have to do something about the dark circles under her eyes.

Lisa nodded her dismissal, and Olivia left her office in a daze. Maybe this was the opportunity she had been waiting for to make her mark.

'So, what's the word?' Tricia rushed over, hovering by Olivia's side as they walked back to her desk. In response, Olivia held up the tickets.

'Ooh, fancy. You're taking me, right?'

'Naturally.'

A few days later, and she and Trish had been on their way to the gallery.

She'd tugged at the hem of her plain black Zara shift dress, the nicest thing she owned. Despite her best intentions, she hadn't had time to buy something new – her next set of exams were rapidly approaching, and she'd fallen behind on her studies while she researched the art world for Mr Lavaud. The people queuing to enter the gallery were all in chic outfits by well-known designers, and Tricia looked fantastic in rented Hervé Léger. She'd understood the assignment, and Olivia wished she had half her friend's style. Trish had offered to lend her a dress, but there was almost a foot of height difference between them. Olivia towered over her friend – clothes sharing had never been one of the benefits of living together.

She wasn't here for fashion, she reminded herself. This was for her career. She needed to write up a comprehensive report for Mr Lavaud, to establish if any of them would be worth a potential investment.

All the facts stacked up in Olivia's mind, neatly arranged. She'd compiled recent auction sales over the past five years into a spreadsheet, trying to model a pattern for the investments. She tracked the major crashes too.

The financial models for art investment were complicated. Very few artists ever achieved blue-chip status with their work – meaning that they were likely to increase in economic value. It required all the stars to align. Not just producing an incredible piece. But also having the backing of the right gallery. The swirl of buzz from the media, acclaim from the critics. A heady cocktail of talent, luck and hype. Social media presence could help too. Flipping art for profit was a risky venture, but could be incredibly lucrative for the right buyer, with the right artist.

And it helped to have a feisty, motivated dealer to support you.

Everyone in the room was hoping to find the next Rothko or Hirst. Olivia craned her neck, trying to get a glimpse of the art on the walls, but the crowds were so dense, she could barely see – only glimpses of bright colour, interspersed among the cocktail attire and blow-dried hair.

'I'm going to find us some drinks,' said Tricia, who hadn't given the paintings a second look. She looked sensational, though, like she belonged.

Olivia wandered the gallery rooms, each sectioned off in a seemingly random fashion – a warren of art, each piece given its own dedicated space. The walls were so blindingly white it made her eyes ache. It didn't seem right that somewhere so bright could conceal so many secret corners – but she found it as easy to get lost in the blank spaces as in a darkened labyrinth.

Almost towards the very back of the gallery, she found a spot where a group wasn't already crowding the space in front of a piece, sipping champagne and making pretentious remarks. A slim red velvet rope sectioned off the room from the rest of the gallery. She checked over her shoulder before unclipping it and slipping inside.

For a moment, she found herself alone. The tension in her shoulders eased almost as soon as she entered the space, a soft hum vibrating over her skin.

A single canvas hung on the wall opposite, dominating the space. Olivia walked until she stood directly in front of the piece, transfixed.

She found herself transported back to visiting art galleries with her mum. Each time had been a treat, their chance to connect – whether learning about the grand masters in the Scottish National Gallery or checking out the latest installation at the Tate Modern on a rare weekend trip to London. Her mum had been an accomplished artist herself, painting from their cottage deep in the

Scottish wilderness. Olivia blinked. When was the last time her mum had picked up a paintbrush? It must have been years.

Her mother's talent lay buried under a mountain of grief, and now was lost to her disease – like so much of her personality and memories. Every visit, Olivia hunted for a way for them to connect again, a life jacket to throw out and rescue their relationship. Yet her mother only seemed to drift even further away.

Pinpoint the feeling. That's what her mum would say. Olivia took a step closer to the painting, trying to find the right word to describe her emotions. It was something like . . . wonder? Not quite.

Awe. Awe was closer. The sound seemed to wrap its way around her body, all while she was entranced by the image on the canvas: a stark, barren landscape made up of bold streaks of blue and white paint that almost seemed to glow from within.

It was a restless piece that seemed almost alive, like the paint was crawling across the frame, made of ants instead of oil. The hum in the background grew louder as she lost herself in the visuals, until she was bathed in sound. Finally she could wait no longer, and she scanned the piece with her phone, needing to know more.

nemiga by Kostas Yennin. A mixed-media piece. The hum was intentional, composed by the artist himself. She remembered the name from her research, but not much had come up about him – no social media presence to speak of, no major sales as of yet, represented by a young dealer with a lot of ambition but no real success yet. Aaron somebody.

She took a step closer.

Then a waft of cologne washed over her, the sense of it so strong, she felt it tingle her nostrils, something musky with a hint of vanilla sweetness. Expensive. Alluring.

She spun around, thinking of the velvet rope. 'I'm so sorry,' she said, skittering back from the artwork. 'I was just looking for some space and . . .'

But the man smiled. 'And what do you think?' He gestured to the canvas behind her.

She took a deep breath. With the white walls behind him, the man looked not unlike a painting himself – almost too perfect to be real. He looked so at ease in his expertly tailored suit but no tie, his hands resting in his pockets.

She used his words as permission to look at it again. 'It's astonishing,' she said.

He tilted his head. 'I personally think this is *the* piece to watch in this whole collection. The desolation of our planet's most remote landscapes inspires him, in particular Antarctica. Yet he takes something that's quite bleak and manages to find that spark of beauty too. His art speaks to the tension between isolation and peace, loneliness and purposeful meditation. A canvas devoid of life and yet full of emotion.' He lowered his voice.

'I've never seen anything like it,' said Olivia. 'But why aren't more people in here looking at it?'

'I roped off this piece so I could bring key VIPs to see it individually. But since you found it on your own, please – take your time.'

'I'm not one of your VIPs, though,' she said.

'Aren't you? Miss Olivia Campbell, isn't it?'

Olivia's eyebrows rose in surprise. 'Yes.'

'Then, as Mr Lavaud's representative, you certainly

are important to me. Aaron Hunter-Williams, curator.'
He held out his hand for her, and she took it, shocked by
how smooth his hands were – and neat, his nails trim
and cuticles tidy.

'Nice to meet you. So you represent this artist?'

'I have done for the past year. If it were up to me,
Yennin would be a household name. But it takes the
right buyer to recognize genius and appreciate it. Do
you think Mr Lavaud would be interested?'

'I'm not sure.'

'Well, how about you?'

She bit her lip, then stepped closer again, trying to
evaluate the painting through an investor's eyes. But
she couldn't do it. It wasn't about the quality of the
art – though, of course, it was exquisite. For her, it was
what her mother had talked about: the feeling the
painting evoked inside her. She thought the initial,
almost overpowering sense of awe she'd felt when she
first stepped into the room would fade as she stood in
front of the piece – instead, it only seemed to increase,
her eyes widening as she took in all the details. If she
could bottle it up and sell what she was feeling, she
would be a millionaire.

'If I could afford it, I would snap this piece up in an
instant,' she admitted.

Aaron smiled. 'Then you have most excellent taste.
Please inform Mr Lavaud that this one has attracted a lot
of interest. A Bollywood actress has her eyes on it. She
married a Saudi billionaire recently and they're thinking
about it as a wedding present . . .' He touched the side of
his nose, as if it was their little secret. 'It's good, though,
that we can enjoy it while it lasts. This painting is lucky.

It gets to breathe. It gets to be seen, as artwork is intended.'

'I guess whoever buys it will hang it in their home. You know, to be seen by their billionaire actor friends or whoever. Maybe their housekeeper.' She smiled – look at her, attempting a joke – but he didn't smile back. In fact, he seemed on the verge of tears.

'We can hope. Sadly I expect whoever buys this piece won't display it anywhere. It will sit in a storage vault somewhere, waiting.'

She shook her head. 'What do you mean? If they don't want it in their home, then it should tour the world's galleries. Or be donated to a museum. Do some sort of good with it. This needs to be seen.'

He nodded. 'I agree. But this is the art market nowadays. The hope is, it will gain more value if it disappears for a while.'

'What a shame.' She had the urge to grab *nemiga* and run away with it.

'I thought you would have understood the importance of growing an investment, given your job.'

'I do. I am very sorry, though. And if he loves the painting, that's one thing. But as a pure investment, it's not really something I would advise him to pursue. Not very safe.'

'Safe isn't always the most profitable, though, is it?'

'No, it rarely is. And if this was Mr Lavaud's personal wealth at stake, he could take a hit. But as part of the strategy for LUJO's pension scheme? Trust me, his employees would care if their hard-earned money was invested in something so volatile.'

He stepped towards her. 'Great taste in art and financial

prowess – I feel out of my depth around you, Olivia. I had been on tenterhooks waiting to meet his mysterious person that Mr Lavaud had sent along to the exhibition, but I can see now why he chose you to represent him. How about I take you to dinner later this week? I can explain to you more why I think Yennin is the artist of the future, show you my plans for building his presence in the art world . . .'

She coughed, thrown off balance by his question. Was it a business dinner? Or did she sense something more between them? Dating was normally the last thing on her mind. She didn't know whether it was the painting, the music or Aaron's intense gaze, but she found herself leaning towards him.

'Liv! There you are, I've been looking for you.' Tricia appeared on the other side of the rope, holding two glasses of champagne high in the air.

'Looks like we're not alone any more,' Aaron whispered. He placed his hand gently on her lower back, guiding her over towards the rope.

Tricia almost dropped the glasses when she took in who Olivia was with. She gave Olivia a sly grin. 'Sorry I interrupted . . .'

Aaron bowed his head, ever so slightly. 'I have to be showing this piece to some of my other guests, but it was lovely meeting you, Olivia.' He leaned over and kissed her, his lips lightly brushing the edge of her cheekbone, his hand warm against her shoulder.

And from that moment she'd been hooked.

So maybe it wasn't too soon for them to get engaged. After all, their relationship had been a whirlwind from the start, unconventional, electric and a mixture of business and pleasure. They made a great team; the showcase would prove that.

The lift doors swung open, and she clutched his jacket to her chest. She was grateful Aaron was still sleeping when she re-entered the room. She carefully hung up his jacket in the closet, running her fingers down the fine Italian wool sleeve. Next to it was her dress for the evening. There was so much riding on the cruise going well, and it was all going to start that night. She needed to get ready.

She stepped into the shower, allowing the searing-hot water to run over her body and calming the uncomfortable flipping sensation in her stomach. She was being ridiculous. Maybe it had been so long since something good had happened in her life, she'd forgotten what it felt like.

This wasn't fear, or even caution.

Anticipation. That was it.

It had to be.

4

The table was strewn with half-drunk glasses of red wine, the prickly shells of snow crabs and platters of barbe- cued meats; the VIP dinner at Ushuaia's most upscale Argentinian *parrilla* had been a huge success. Although she was sure most of the guests gathered would be more used to Michelin-starred dinners and fancy silverware, they were embracing the frontier spirit of the town. The mood was light-hearted and jovial. Aaron was at the far end of the table, sitting with Cutler Hughes – the CEO of Pioneer Adventures and owner of the MS *Vigil*.

Cutler was a larger-than-life presence. She'd never met him before, but she'd recognized him as soon as they'd arrived at the restaurant. More celebrity than CEO, he was a regular on reality TV, known for his fear- some temper and straight-talking management style (a bit of an aberration for a Canadian, though most people pointed to his Scottish roots), even fronting his own reality show – one of *The Apprentice* knock-offs.

His company – Pioneer Adventures – was known for off-the-beaten-track destinations and rugged expeditions. It seemed like an odd match for a high-end art show- case, but then Aaron had confided in her that Cutler wasn't going to be CEO of Pioneer for much longer. He was selling to a mystery buyer who wanted a more luxury operation, and adding the showcase to the list of his ship's amenities helped to attract a different kind of clientele. It was all part of the package – and if the show-case was profitable, the deal would go ahead.

Without it, the company might fold completely, with hundreds of employees out of a job.

Olivia would never have guessed Cutler was under so much stress from watching him this evening, as he held court with wild stories of his daredevil antics. He oozed charisma and a kind of brutish charm. She wished she could have appeared so at ease while her own life had been falling apart.

And judging from the buzzy, excitable mood of the evening, Cutler had nothing to worry about. Apart from Cutler and his wife, Ingrid, and Olivia and Aaron, the exclusive guestlist for the dinner had consisted of Robert and Aida Freedman, the founders of the online co-working company DoubleNet that had boomed during the pandemic; Tariq and Greg Akbas, a wealthy curator and art critic power couple; Delilah Constance, a young Australian fashion designer with an absent tech-industry husband who bankrolled her taste in art and her collection of high-end wigs (tonight, she had waist-length black hair); and Stefan Grenville, the auctioneer from Art Aboard Aaron had been complaining about earlier.

They were Cutler's inner circle, all eagerly awaiting their trip to the bottom of the world – and seduced by the exclusive opportunity to buy a Yennin painting. They weren't the only possible buyers on board, but they were the ones Aaron had identified as the most likely candidates, and he was working hard to woo them accordingly.

Though maybe not everyone was so eager. Beside her, Ingrid drained the remnants of her glass and shuddered.

'Can you take seasickness pills with alcohol?' she asked Olivia, her German accent thickening with every glass of red wine. They'd exchanged small talk throughout dinner, but this was the first moment Ingrid had let her glamorous, poised front slip and allowed a little vulnerability to seep through.

Olivia bit her lip in sympathy. 'Do you suffer badly?'

'Always. Can't say I'm really looking forward to this cruise. Especially the Drake Shake.'

'What's that?' Olivia asked, wide-eyed.

'It's what they call the Drake Passage when the conditions are bad. That stretch of water between here and Antarctica can be either the most dangerous ocean crossing in the world or it can be as smooth as glass. Hence it's either the Drake Shake or the Drake Lake. Ever fancied a spin inside a washing machine?'

Olivia cringed. 'Not particularly. They might have to sedate me for that.' She tried to pass it off as a joke.

But Ingrid didn't laugh. Instead, her pale complexion seemed to get a little greyer. She fiddled with the expensive diamond pendant at the end of her necklace. 'You get seasick too?'

Olivia shook her head. 'I had a bad experience on a boat once.'

'And you're going on a cruise? Is that wise?'

'Probably not.'

Ingrid raised a neatly pruned eyebrow. 'Well, if you ever need a drinking companion, you come find me.'

'I might just take you up on that.'

She glanced around the table. Most of the guests had left already, taking advantage of their last night of sleep on solid ground. She frowned, as she noticed Aaron

31

had disappeared from the table too. She muttered an excuse to Ingrid, picking up her coat from the back of her chair.

They had been sectioned off in a private dining room, all leather-backed chairs and wood panelling. But even in the main restaurant, Aaron was nowhere to be seen.

She stepped outside, quickly pulling her coat on – surprised at how cold it was. She could see her breath steaming out in front of her. The street was practically deserted, only one man lurking in the awning of a restaurant across the street. She only noticed him thanks to the orange glow of his cigarette tip, the hood of his jacket covering the rest of his face in shadow. She squinted, trying to get a better look at him.

Was it the same man from the harbour front?

It was hard to be sure. But it was the same feeling.

She edged back into the restaurant, shaking off her paranoia. That's when she saw Aaron standing in a hallway leading down towards the men's room. His back was to her, talking with Stefan.

'And does Olivia know anything?'

She stopped when she heard Stefan say her name, lingering just out of sight in the main restaurant.

'No, she's been . . . distracted lately,' Aaron replied, a bitter edge to his tone. He'd done a good job of keeping it hidden, but she knew he felt some resentment towards her for how she'd behaved over the past few months. What she'd caused. How could he not? But hearing it made Olivia's stomach flip with guilt.

'So you don't think we'll have any trouble.'

'The threat seems to have disappeared. It appears my last message worked.'

'Good. At least we're on the other side of the world. Besides, in two weeks everything will have changed . . .'

She stepped backwards. She didn't want to be caught eavesdropping – and besides, none of what they were talking about made any sense to her and was only making her more anxious. *What threat?*

Was there something else Aaron had been hiding from her?

She knew she'd spent the past few months in a dense fog, her mental bandwidth overloaded. But now she was on the mend, she'd have to ask . . . this sounded like a burden Aaron needed to share.

'Olivia, there you are. I thought you'd run away before I could say goodbye. See you on board?' Ingrid swept her up in a double-kiss, enveloping her in a cloud of perfume, still potent at the end of the night.

'Absolutely.' She plastered on a big smile, shaking off her anxiety.

'And remember what I said about finding me for a drink. Champagne fixes all problems.'

'Is my wife attempting to turn you into an alcoholic too?' Cutler thrust his arm over Olivia's shoulder. 'This one needs to keep her wits about her, Ingrid. She's the money woman. Aaron tells me she's some kind of financial genius.'

'I wouldn't say that,' said Olivia.

'She's being modest.' Aaron appeared from the hallway, took Olivia's hand and squeezed it. 'Until tomorrow, Mr Hughes?'

He unhooked his arm from Olivia and shook Aaron's hand. 'Two weeks of snow, ice and lots of sales, I hope.'

'Undoubtedly.'

They stepped out on to the street. Aaron was busy, saying goodbye to the remaining dinner guests individually, shaking hands and kissing cheeks.

'Who's up for another drink?' asked Delilah. 'There must be somewhere I can get a decent Martini in this tumbleweed town.'

'We'll join,' said Greg, looping his arm with Delilah. Tariq didn't seem quite as sure. Of the pair, he had been more reserved throughout the night, but a stern look from Greg made him yield.

'Why not? This is a vacation after all,' Tariq said.

'I don't think there are many options, but there looked like a nice wine bar further down the main street,' said Aaron. 'What do you think, Livi?'

'Maybe one,' Olivia said, forcing a smile. But she couldn't relax. From the moment they left the restaurant, she felt eyes on them, watching them. Aaron's words echoed in her mind. *The threat seems to have disappeared.* She glanced over her shoulder. A few people were lingering on the pavements, but no one specific to cause alarm.

She walked close beside Aaron as they headed in the direction of the bar. That's when she saw him. The same man was staring at them from beneath an awning.

He caught her eye and stalked away, moving briefly into the pool of light from a nearby street lamp. His hood fell back, revealing a close-shaven head, a small design etched above his ear. His ice-blue eyes never left Olivia's. She gripped Aaron's jacket tighter.

'Who is that?' She turned back to Aaron.

But when she pointed him out, the man was gone.

5

The next morning, they boarded the ship. It was every bit as impressive as Sara had made out. As they wandered from the dining room into the central lobby, Olivia could almost forget that they were on the water, pretending instead that they were in the foyer of some luxury hotel, far from any shaven-headed figures lurking in the shadows. A glittering glass sculpture rained down from the ceiling, echoing the same spiral as an impressive brass-railed stair-case, each piece hovering on a near-invisible wire to keep them suspended like ice splintering in the air.

'I wonder who the artist is,' said Olivia, leaning over the banister to get a closer look.

Aaron followed her gaze. 'It's inspired by Lasvit instal-lations. Cutler has pulled out all the stops on his redesign.'

'And it's working,' came a voice from behind them. Olivia turned to see a tall, elegant woman in a neat navy uniform and crisp white shirt, her blond hair pulled back in a sleek chignon. 'Mr Hunter-Williams? Miss Campbell? I'm Elisabet, the cruise director for the MS *Vigil*. I can't tell you how excited we are to have you on board.'

Aaron took her hand, shaking it firmly. 'Pleased to meet you.'

'Has the ship changed a lot then?' Olivia asked.

'A complete overhaul. New interiors, new safety features – we even had a helipad installed. It is a state-of-the-art expedition ship now, and one I am very proud to work on. Can I give you the tour?'

Aaron shook his head. 'I've been on board for the past couple of days. But I do have a few questions about the itinerary. I know the showcase is set for day six – will that definitely coincide with the Antarctic Circle crossing?'

'The captain understands how important this is, but he also has to keep the itinerary flexible. An Antarctic voyage is never predictable – weather, sea conditions, ice thickness – all those could affect our timings . . .' The two continued talking as they walked down the stairs towards the main reception desk. Olivia trailed behind, staring up at the installation. There was a small plaque at the bottom of the stairs naming the piece. *Ice Storm* by Perla Weinberg.

Olivia shivered, despite herself.

The lobby began to fill with people. The all-aboard time was set for four p.m. – still a couple of hours away – but many of the passengers boarded early to get settled in their cabins and take advantage of the lunch buffet. Olivia joined Aaron and Elisabet at the reception desk.

'Can I see the cabin list again?' Aaron asked Elisabet.

'Yes, of course.' She searched her desk for a sheet of paper listing all the guest names and their assigned cabins, before placing it in front of Aaron.

Their cabin was the one place Olivia hadn't been yet. They had boarded in the morning so Aaron could do his final checks in the onboard gallery, and they'd had an early lunch with Stefan. Aaron and Stefan had had an argument over what should be available for sale in the showcase. After Yennin's death, the Hunt Advisory owned the copyright to all his paintings, and in turn licensed the auction rights at sea to Stefan's company Art Aboard. Aaron had given them an original Yennin as the primary draw, but there were also a few limited-edition signed prints and sketches that would be extremely valuable, especially since getting his signature wouldn't be possible again. Art Aboard had also requested a slew of cheaper options – mass-produced prints, postcards, even a souvenir T-shirt – with Yennin's artwork on it. But Aaron didn't want to make the lower-priced items available. He was in charge of protecting Yennin's legacy, and it was a job he took seriously.

She admired his passion, and that he somehow never seemed to run out of energy. It was one of the things she loved most about him. But she soon learned it was something he expected of everyone in his life: artists, gallery owners and even girlfriends.

The months following their meeting in front of *nemiga* had been a whirlwind.

'Tell me everything,' Tricia had demanded, after Olivia had returned to their apartment from being whisked away on a European adventure straight after work on Friday. Trish had always wanted the details of Olivia and Aaron's dates, especially in those first few months. She'd curled her legs up on their Ikea sofa, glass of Pinot in hand, and looked at Olivia expectantly.

For her part, Olivia was willing to indulge; her relationship with Aaron was so different to any she'd been in before. She was exhausted from the travel, but she slumped into the shabby armchair opposite and told Trish as much as she could remember. Aaron had taken her to visit the Hunt Gallery's second location in the Swiss city. He needed to drum up interest in his next auction, exclusively of Yennin's work. Despite being reviewed well, *nemiga* hadn't sold at the *INTO THE UNKNOWN* exhibition, so he was giving it another chance.

It would be make-or-break for the artist, before Aaron would be forced to move on to promote someone else.

They'd then flown from Geneva to Vilnius, where Yennin was from. The artist had run away from his main studio in London, disappearing to his sister's home for a while. Their visit was for Aaron's benefit: to make sure Yennin's next pieces were progressing, and Aaron wanted to meet with Yennin's new social media manager, who was going to create new video content in the lead-up to the auction. Generate buzz a different way.

While Aaron had his meetings, Olivia had wandered the streets, taking in the medieval parts of the city, trying *cepelinai* – little potato meat dumplings – and admiring its grand cathedral. When they'd met up again in a small boutique art hotel, Aaron had no longer seemed so worried. 'You know these artist types. You can't rush them, so it's my job to tell their story while we await the next great masterpiece.'

Back in their small Brixton flat, she gratefully took the second glass of wine Tricia poured. 'It was amazing. I brought you home some chocolates, before you get worried I forgot about you.' She took a box out of her suitcase and laid it out on the coffee table between them.

'Oh, I see how it is. I get airport chocolate while you're living it up in fancy hotels. I have *severe* Instagram envy. Speaking of – what's your artist's profile? You said he'd set it up, right?' She had her phone out and was primed to follow him.

'His new social media person is launching it this week. I had no idea how important Instagram could be to building artists' profiles. But Aaron showed me what prices these new "red chip" artists are achieving at auction.'

'Wow, look at you using all the lingo. Aaron's really rubbing off on you. Does he have a friend for me?'

Olivia laughed. 'I'll ask.'

'Good, because I think I completed Tinder last week.' She unwrapped a chocolate and popped it in her mouth. She closed her eyes and moaned in exaggerated ecstasy – despite her protests, Olivia knew basic milk chocolate was Tricia's weakness. 'I don't know, I hang around Langan's and Hakkasan every weekend and can't score a date, but you go to one gallery opening and you end up with Aaron Hunter-Williams.'

Olivia picked at the edge of her fingernail. 'It's not all glamour, you know. He's under a lot of stress. I don't know all the details, but I have a feeling that if this Yennin auction doesn't go well, he'll be so disappointed.'

'Is he mad that you advised that billionaire guy against buying that painting?'

Olivia tutted. 'I didn't advise against it; I just stated the facts as I saw them. Besides, Aaron asked me to invite him to the auction, so I've done that.' From out of her laptop bag she pulled a stack of spreadsheets she'd printed out to look over. She preferred looking at hard copies; it helped her see things clearer.

Tricia raised an eyebrow. 'Whoa, what's all that? More work?'

'As always.'

'Which client? I can talk to Lisa if you want. She shouldn't be running you into the ground like this.'

'No, it's not for Pendle. Aaron asked me to take a look over his accounts.'

'Is that a good idea?' asked Tricia. 'It's almost exam time and you always go kind of mental . . .'

'I'll be fine,' said Olivia, feeling bruised by her friend's lack of faith. 'I can handle it. I'm just helping Aaron out a little.'

'You should put that on your Instagram. *It's not all cocktails at Annabel's and first-class tickets to Geneva. I have to look at spreadsheets too.*' Tricia flicked her hair.

Olivia threw a chocolate at her, which she caught with annoying dexterity.

'I just worry about you,' said Tricia, suddenly serious.

'I got this,' said Olivia.

Hindsight was twenty-twenty. Tricia had been exactly right. She'd taken on too much, her workload piling on top of her until she was buried by it. 'No' just wasn't in her vocabulary when it came to work. Her best friend had been the first one to see the signs, but she'd ignored her.

But it wasn't Aaron's fault. She'd only wanted to impress him.

She looked at him now, standing at the reception desk of the MS *Vigil*. This was his moment. She rubbed her hand along his back, and he jumped a mile, scrunching the piece of paper with the cabin list in his fist. His complexion had gone grey. He stepped back from the desk – and her touch – swearing under his breath.

'Everything OK?' Olivia asked, alarmed by his change in demeanour.

'Just had a message from London. There's been a crisis with Bertrand. I need a decent internet connection so I'm going ashore.'

'What, right now?'

'There's no time to waste. I'll head to the Pioneer office. I can video-call Jules at the gallery from there.'

'I'll come with you.' Bertrand was the next artist Aaron was wooing, and she knew he had been stressed about it. She gathered up her handbag, pulling it on to her shoulder.

'Don't be silly, Livi. I won't be long.'

She scanned his face. He was pale, a shimmer of sweat on his forehead. She hadn't seen him like this before. 'If it's an emergency, you might need help. I should be with you.'

'I'll be fine. Look, I mentioned your . . . discomfort with being on board to Elisabet and she's arranged for you to speak with the captain on the bridge before we set sail. He'll put your mind at ease. I'll be back before you know it. I've arranged a special delivery to our room so we can toast to a new start. For both of us.'

'If you're sure . . .'

'I have two hours until all aboard.' He kissed her on the cheek. 'Try to enjoy yourself. I mean, look around. Does it get much better than this?'

She drew in a breath, holding it in, pushing down the rush of words that bubbled to the surface – how she could imagine a lot better than this, many places that she'd rather be. Before they could come out, Aaron took her hesitation as acceptance. He rushed back up the stairs to the next level, where the gangway led to the dock, dropping the cabin list as he ran. 'Wait, Aaron!' She kneeled down to pick it up, but when she stood back up, he was gone.

She flattened the piece of paper against her thigh, scanning the names. Apart from the people she'd met last night, only one other name seemed to ring a distant bell. *M. Sadler.* She was sure she'd heard Aaron mention that name before, during one of her visits to the gallery. But that was a common enough surname. It was probably a coincidence.

'Miss Campbell?' Elisabet called out to her from reception. Olivia hesitated. But the moment passed, and she turned back to the cruise director, shoving the paper into her handbag.

'Yes?'

'I need your signature on a few forms and I can give you your cabin key. Then I will take you up to the bridge.'

Olivia nodded, crossing the few steps to the desk and signing the forms allowing their credit card to be used for incidentals.

A woman rushed up to the desk, knocking her into the polished walnut countertop. 'Hey!' Olivia cried out.

'I am so sorry,' said the woman, her voice breathless. A man jogged up next to her, placing his hand on her shoulder. Apology out of the way, she turned her attention to Elisabet. 'Please, we're really hoping you can help us. My name is Christa, and this is my husband, Jay. The woman at the Pioneer office got us these tickets at the last minute but in separate bunks in single-sex cabins. She said to ask on board for any potential upgrades? We're on our honeymoon and we'd really love to be together.'

'First of all, congratulations.' Somehow, even in the face of the woman's flustered monologue, Elisabet kept her cool. Olivia was impressed – but then Elisabet probably juggled a million customer service nightmares every day. 'I'm very sorry, but we don't have any double cabins left. The ship is completely full for this expedition. But my assistant Maria Elena can help you I'm sure.' A young woman with dark hair appeared from the small office behind the reception, summoned by a button on Elisabet's radio. 'Maybe some complimentary champagne for you to enjoy in our Panorama lounge?'

'Please, come with me,' said Maria Elena, gesturing for the two to follow.

'You handled that well,' said Olivia to Elisabet, as she stepped out from behind the desk.

'I wish I could have helped more,' she said in her clipped Scandinavian accent. 'But as I said, the cruise is at capacity. Sara has been working hard to make sure we don't have a single empty berth.'

'Must be a lot for you to juggle.'

'I am glad. It's been a hard industry to work in these past few years, but a full ship is a very good sign things are picking up.' She guided Olivia up several flights of stairs, past the level with the art gallery, gift shop and library, then the next with the Panorama lounge and the restaurant, before they reached the top, where there was a sky bar – and also the entrance to the bridge.

Elisabet knocked before signalling for Olivia to enter. 'I hope you don't mind, but I have to leave you here to make sure the boarding goes smoothly. The captain will ring down when it is time to collect you.'

'Oh, OK.'

Elisabet nodded, then she trotted down the stairs again, leaving Olivia alone to step into the bridge.

'Ah, Miss Campbell?' The captain had a melodic Italian accent and welcomed her in with a wave. His sun-kissed skin seemed to glow against the crisp whiteness of his uniform, and his thick black hair was slicked back from his forehead. 'I am Captain Enzo. A pleasure to meet you.'

'Please, call me Olivia.' There was something comforting about seeing the inner workings of the ship so outwardly on display. It felt reassuringly complicated – the masses of dials and buttons, the gigantic steering wheel in the centre, the thick volumes of binders and logs, the gentle beeps and flashing lights emanating from various bits of electronic equipment. This is what it should take to run a vessel through ice-infested and stormy waters. Anything simpler would have felt wrong. It was miles away from the cockpits of the yachts she used to sail in with her dad. While some of the equipment was familiar, she was happy to see not only the state-of-the-art electronics, but the multitude of people on the bridge monitoring it all.

And Captain Enzo oozed competence. Olivia recognized that immediately. She used to bristle at that word being used to describe her – competent – as if it implied that she was somehow boring or merely good enough. Nothing exceptional. But that wasn't true. It was a more valuable trait than she'd ever realized. Burnout had shown her that. It had stripped her of competency, leaving her feeling inept and useless, unable to perform the most basic tasks that had been asked of her. Now she wanted nothing more than a ship captain who was competent.

'Elisabet tells me that you suffer from a fear of water.'

Olivia winced. 'Well, actually it's a boat thing, rather than water itself.'

The captain raised one of his bushy eyebrows. 'Oh? Did something happen?'

'I used to sail quite a lot with my family. But there was an accident while we were on a yacht and . . .' The rest of the sentence choked in her throat, as she blinked back the memory.

The captain's voice softened. 'Well, as you can see, this is a very different kind of vessel to a sailing yacht,' he said. His gaze was steady on her, thoughtful and penetrating. 'Let me show you around. If you have some sailing experience, maybe it will be useful to know how things work.'

'I would appreciate that,' she said.

She was astounded by the captain's patience as he showed her around the various controls and introduced his crew. Much of it she knew already – she'd read the ship's spec a dozen times – but it was comforting to hear nonetheless.

As the captain showed off the electronic chart pilot, the first mate interrupted them. 'Excuse me, Captain, but we have an updated weather forecast. You might want to take a look at this system coming in from the Pacific.'

Captain Enzo nodded. 'If you don't mind, Olivia, I need to prepare for our departure. But we have an open-bridge policy on board. If you need anything, or have any questions, please don't hesitate to come back here.'

'You are too kind,' she replied. Before she could say more, the captain and his first officer stepped away, their heads together over the weather radar. Elisabet had returned – that woman must have a sixth sense for when things needed to be done on the ship, or maybe the captain had sent some kind of signal without her knowing – and gestured for Olivia to follow. But not before she caught wind of a few key words between the two men. *Storm approaching.*

She stared out of the window, away from the docile shoreline of Ushuaia, out towards the Beagle Channel, which led to the infamous Drake Passage. She thought back to Ingrid's words about the 'Drake Shake'. Maybe more than words – a premonition, perhaps. For now the waters still looked calm, the sky a muted grey peppered with cloud. No big dark storm clouds on the horizon. No monster waves.

Not yet.

Just as they were about to leave the bridge, the captain called out to the cruise director. 'Elisabet, are we set to sail?'

She unhooked her iPad from beneath her arm. 'We boarded the final passenger about ten minutes ago.'

'Excellent,' he said. He gave a signal to one of his officers, who jumped to his feet.

Elisabet touched Olivia's forearm. 'Come. I'll show you to your cabin.'

Olivia nodded, feeling her stomach churn. Seeing the bridge had been a kind idea from Elisabet – and the captain had been so generous with his time – but she could feel the physical symptoms of her fear beginning to take over as the officers on board began to prepare for departure, buzzing around the bridge like bees. Her breathing became shallower, her heart racing.

'Are you OK?' Elisabet frowned with concern when she noticed Olivia was trailing behind her, gripping on to the banister with white knuckles. 'I can take you to our medical bay . . .'

'No, the cabin is fine. You said everyone is now on board, right? I just need to see Aaron.'

'Of course. You are down on the fourth deck. Just a few more flights.' Elisabet led the way. 'Here's your cabin. Number sixteen.'

She pushed past her to open the door. 'Aaron?'

But he wasn't there. The large double bed was freshly made, undisturbed. A bottle of rosé champagne – her favourite brand – was in the corner, the pink foil poking out of a polished chrome ice bucket. Their suitcases were lined up neatly against the porthole, which Olivia avoided looking out of.

'I must return to the reception. Are you OK to be left here?'

There was a jolt and a shudder, and Olivia momentarily lost her footing. 'What was that?' she asked.

'The ship's engines,' said Elisabet. 'Looks like we're getting ready to go.'

6

Olivia took out her phone. The screen read 15:44. It wasn't quite all-aboard time yet. She dialled Aaron's number, grateful she still had reception, but the line rang out to his voicemail.

She typed out a message. *I'm in the cabin. Number 16 — where are you?*

Aaron was always glued to his phone. It wouldn't take long for her to hear back.

An announcement came over the tannoy, and Olivia recognized Elisabet's voice. 'Welcome, passengers of the MS *Vigil*. This is your cruise director Elisabet Eklund. On behalf of the captain and the crew, I want to thank you for your speed and efficiency in boarding this afternoon. As we are at full capacity ahead of schedule, the captain has decided to leave port early. We would like to invite you to the upper deck for hot drinks and our sail-away party.'

There was a good chance that was where she would find Aaron – he loved any excuse for a party, especially with so many people on board he needed to mingle with. At least, she hoped that was the case. The thought that he wasn't on board at all was too dreadful to contemplate. She pushed it away, determined to remain positive.

She left the cabin and made her way to the bow. While the interior was lush and designed for comfort, the outer deck had a functional green-painted weather-proofed floor – a reminder that this was first and foremost an expedition-class vessel. There were already plenty of passengers out enjoying the fresh air, wrapped up in their identical crimson Pioneer-branded jackets. Everyone on board had been given one – a gift to start their Antarctic journey. A table was set up in one corner, laden with lanyards divided by their room names. Under cabin sixteen, she spotted their name tags: Olivia Campbell and Aaron Hunter-Williams. So if he was on deck, he hadn't picked it up yet.

'Can I help you?' asked the crew member behind the desk. He had a strong Antipodean accent, a deep golden tan and a bemused expression as she dithered over picking up her name tag. 'I'm Liam, your excursion leader on board.'

Her cheeks flushed. 'I'm looking for my boyfriend, Aaron Hunter-Williams?' When Liam looked at her blankly, she continued. 'He's the one who's organized the showcase?'

'Oh, with you now! I'm afraid I haven't seen him. So that means you must be Olivia Campbell.' He picked up the lanyard and passed it across to her. 'Are you part of my excursions team?'

Olivia could hardly hear for the pit of worry that had opened in her stomach. Aaron wasn't there. She did, however, spot Elisabet standing on the deck above, clipboard in hand, like a general overseeing her charges. 'Excuse me,' she muttered to Liam without answering his question.

She took the stairs quickly, the spiked anti-slip metal digging into the bottom of her trainers.

49

'Elisabet, have you seen Aaron?'

'I'm sorry, Miss Campbell, I've been in my office since I left you at the cabin.'

'Can you tell me if he came back on board? I'm worried that I can't find him.'

'It's a big ship; I'm sure he's here somewhere.' Elisabet smiled, but Olivia noticed a quavering in between her brows. The cruise director was staring down at her iPad, her fingers swiping across the screen. Her smile widened when she found Aaron's name. 'Yes, look.' She turned the iPad around so Olivia could see. 'We have Mr Hunter-Williams logged in as on board.'

Olivia put her hand on her chest. 'Oh, thank goodness. Can you tell me what time he returned?'

'He boarded at ten thirty-four a.m.' Her voice drifted as she came to the same realization as Olivia.

'That's when we arrived this morning. He left again this afternoon.' Olivia's mouth went dry.

Elisabet remained ever the consummate professional. 'Come with me. We can do a ship-wide announcement and ask him to meet us at reception. He knows so many people on board; he probably got swept up in conversation.'

'I'd appreciate that,' she replied through gritted teeth, barely holding on to her mask of politeness. Underneath it, she felt like she was breaking down.

'It's the least I can do.'

But fifteen minutes after the announcement, and there was still no sign of him. She kept looking at her phone, willing it to ring, or for a message to pop up. Her nails were bitten down to the quick.

When she couldn't wait any longer, she accosted

Elisabet at the desk once again. 'Can you try the Pioneer office in Ushuaia? That's where he said he was going,' said Olivia.

'Absolutely,' replied Elisabet, already picking up the phone and dialling.

But when Sara answered, she swore she hadn't seen or heard from Aaron since the previous morning.

Panic well and truly set in, her nerves afire. *What could have happened?* She could imagine Aaron's alarm at the sight of the ship pulling away from the harbour. Watching his hard work disappear into the horizon. His potentially life-changing deal down the drain. She shook her head. There was no way he would miss it intentionally. That meant . . .

She glanced down at her phone for what felt like the millionth time. Already the signal was down to a single bar – soon she would be cut off completely. She'd been looking forward to that aspect of the trip. No phone, limited Wi-Fi, just her and Aaron and the artwork.

Now it was a nightmare.

Then there was the fact she was on a ship heading out to sea for the first time in almost fifteen years. And she was alone. She pushed that thought to the very deepest recess of her mind.

Elisabet had disappeared into her office, and the moment she returned to the desk, Olivia jumped forward. 'Any luck?'

She shook her head. 'I'm so sorry. I contacted the hotel as well. They did see him this afternoon but he collected a note from behind the desk and then left. They haven't seen him since.'

'He wouldn't miss this on purpose,' Olivia said,

repeating herself for what felt like the hundredth time. 'Something must be wrong.'

Elisabet nodded, her head tilted to one side in sympathy. 'I understand. I've asked Sara to let us know if she hears anything in town. I will try another announcement in a few minutes, in case he missed the first one, and I have also put an alert out to all our staff to radio me if they come across him.'

Olivia's hands were shaking. She couldn't believe this was happening. She wished she had gone with him. 'Wait. If he didn't get on board, he'll be doing everything possible to get here. The ship has a helipad, right? Could Aaron fly here to rejoin the ship?'

'If he gets in touch within the next couple of hours, before we enter the Drake Passage, there is a short window for flying in to us. After that, it's not safe.'

'What about me? Can I fly back to Ushuaia? I don't want to be here if Aaron's not.'

Elisabet reached out and touched Olivia's arm. 'I know this is an awful position to be in. But you're on the ship now. We'll be back in Ushuaia in two weeks, and you can be reunited with your boyfriend. This is supposed to be the adventure of a lifetime. Besides, who will help to run the showcase in his absence? But I think he will still turn up on board. Why don't you go up on deck, have a cup of tea . . . I'll have someone find you immediately if I hear any news.'

'Look, I don't want tea. I want to find my boyfriend. My phone doesn't have much reception, but can I use yours to call the gallery back in London? That's where the emergency message came from. Maybe they know something.'

'Yes, of course,' Elisabet's voice was annoyingly calm for how frustrated Olivia was feeling. 'You can do it from my office – it might be more comfortable for you.'

She led Olivia behind the desk to a small but cluttered room. It was Olivia's first glimpse of what the ship might have looked like before the renovation – with more clinical linoleum flooring and plastic worktops. There were lists and spreadsheets everywhere – it almost took her back to her day job. There were lanyards hanging from hooks above two computer screens, chargers for radios, and two desk phones.

'The phone should work using our Starlink connection. It will give you a decent line back to London. Please take your time.'

'Thank you so much.' Olivia sat in one of the high-backed office chairs and pulled the number of the gallery from her contacts list on her phone. It took a few moments to connect, but eventually someone picked up.

'Hunt Gallery, Mayfair, how can I help you?'

'Hi, Yelena. Is Jules around? It's Olivia.'

'I think he's in a meeting . . .'

'I need to speak to him urgently. Please can you get him on the line? Tell him it's about Aaron.'

'Just a moment.'

After a few more rings, Olivia was put through to Jules, one of the gallery curators. She sat up straighter when she heard his deep voice. 'Yes?'

'Jules, have you heard from Aaron?'

'Isn't he with you, off on his polar adventure?' There was something in his tone that Olivia couldn't interpret.

'Well, a few hours ago he got a message from you that there was an emergency to do with Bertrand. I just need to know how long your video call lasted for, and if you know where he was when he did it.'

There was a pause on the other end of the line. 'There's been no emergency here – except that one of our curators has run off to the end of the world taking one of our top-performing artist portfolios with him.'

'But—'

'I'm sorry, I haven't heard from Aaron today – or for the past few months, in fact. Anything else?'

Olivia was so stunned, she couldn't summon words to speak. 'Um, well, I don't think so. If he gets in touch, will you let me know?'

'Of course. But I wouldn't hold your breath.' And then the phone clicked off.

Olivia sat back in the chair. Aaron had lied to her. There had been no emergency. No reason for him to leave the ship at the last moment. She thought back to the last time she'd seen him, as they'd been standing in the lobby of the ship beneath the sculpture. He had looked pale, sweat on his brow. Discombobulated.

Something had spooked him.

If it wasn't Bertrand, then what?

She thought back to the cabin list, scrunched into his fist just before he left. Could that be it? She pulled out the paper from her handbag and scanned it. Only that one name stood out to her. *Sadler.* But she couldn't figure out why it was familiar.

Then there was the conversation with Stefan yesterday in the restaurant. Talk of a *threat.* Remembering it turned her blood cold. She knew who she had to speak to next.

'Did you manage to get through?' Elisabet returned to the office, standing in the doorway.

'I did.' Olivia swallowed, her hands feeling numb. 'They don't know what's happened to him. Any word from the staff?'

Elisabet shook her head. 'No, I am sorry.'

'Looks like he missed the boat then. I can't believe this.' As the reality sank in, Olivia wasn't sure whether to be angry, worried or scared.

The result was an unsettling mixture of all three.

'Do you know where I can find Stefan?' Olivia asked.

Elisabet smiled, a tinge of sympathy in her eyes. 'I think I saw him on the bow. You Brits are like magnets for the tea stations. And the internet should be up and running in the library in a few hours.'

'Do you have Wi-Fi I can use on my phone?'

'We do, but I suggest using one of the computers if you want the most reliable connection.'

Olivia nodded, leaving the office in a daze. She walked up the stairs, checking her phone at the same time. The signal had died completely now.

The deck was still full of passengers and crew, but Olivia couldn't spot Stefan. The crew member, Liam, who had been manning the name-tag desk had moved to the tea station. 'Excuse me, have you seen Stefan Grenville, the man who works in the gallery?'

'The gallery is closed until tomorrow.'

'Oh, I know. But he's a friend. I need to speak to him.'

'Let me get him on the radio. Why don't you make yourself a cup of tea in the meantime?'

'Um, OK.'

She picked up a mug, filling it with hot water from one of the carafes.

'He's resting down in his cabin, but he said to come and meet him in the gallery after the muster drill.'

'But it's really urgent that I speak to him.'

Liam gave a nonchalant shrug.

She couldn't let it go. 'Please, can you get him on the radio again?'

He looked down at his watch. 'The muster will begin any minute. We're on our way to Antarctica. What could be so urgent?'

She gritted her teeth, annoyed at his dismissive attitude. But in a way he was right. She couldn't do anything more at that moment if Stefan wouldn't see her. She took her mug and forced herself to walk to the prow of the ship, dodging large metal winches and complicated-looking mechanisms for the anchors. She stood a little way back from the railings, staring back at Ushuaia as it pulled away into the distance. The ship sailed past innumerable islands and hidden bays, the coastline jagged and fragmented. Seabirds gathered in flocks on the rocky outcrops, squawking and disappearing into the slate-grey waves. A flag with a single star fluttered on the prow.

Aaron was somewhere over on that vast continent. Was he OK? Was he worried about her? Was he trying some other way to get to the ship?

Then there was the matter of the showcase. What would happen now? Best-case scenario: Aaron would get in touch via email with a full explanation for his absence and a detailed guide she could follow until they returned to port. It would be up to her to make sure everything went smoothly. She clenched her fists, letting the wind whip her hair and steal away the sob that had risen in her chest. She couldn't believe he'd abandoned her.

And she was angry. Worried. Afraid.

There had to be more she could do. But what?

She turned away, unable to look at the water any more. Instead, she focused on the crowd of passengers. She knew a few of them already from the dinner party. They weren't exactly the type she could confide in or commiserate with. She'd have to keep up her professional veneer. But remembering them at least kept her mind from jumping to the worst-case scenarios.

She wasn't great with people at the best of times. She'd spent most of her career studying and creating financial models in front of a computer screen. Networking didn't come naturally to her.

That had been what she'd relied on Aaron for. He could sweep her into any group at a party, introduce her, state some interesting fact that would spark a talking point and away he would go – on to the next client or friend who he'd spotted nearby. When he'd come to her work parties, she knew she could leave him in a room with anyone and he would charm them. He had the kind of charisma that drew a crowd, his personality like an oil masterpiece on display for all to enjoy. She was interesting too, but getting to know her required a bit more effort. Her stories had to be excavated like mosaics under soil, and not everyone could be bothered.

'Why don't you show other people all the things I love about you?' he'd asked her once, after they'd collapsed into bed following an overly long dinner party.

She'd rolled over, stroking a lock of his hair off his forehead. 'I don't need anyone else to see. As long as you do.'

She spotted the Hughes family walking up on to the deck. Cutler seemed to part the crowd like Moses through a sea of red jackets. He and Ingrid had brought their two young boys aboard too, giving them the adventure of a lifetime. The younger of the two had truly embraced the Antarctica spirit, with penguin stickers decorating his jacket.

She thought she saw Robert Freedman talking the ear off the expedition leader Liam. That would mean Aida was probably nearby too. Even easier to recognize was Delilah – even though her hair was bottle-blond and the last time Olivia had seen her, she'd been a brunette. Her fashion line was known for its bright neon colours, flashy prints and silky fabrics, and she'd accessorized her oversized waterproof jacket with an electric-blue neck scarf. She wasn't drinking tea; she already had a glass of champagne in hand.

As she scanned the crowd, she locked eyes with a man in a blue crew jacket. He turned away from her almost as soon as she caught his glance, disappearing back inside. But it was enough for her to catch sight of his shaved head. A chill ran down her spine.

It couldn't have been the same man she'd seen in Ushuaia. She was being paranoid. She was shivering now. She needed to find a warmer jacket, but going back to the cabin would only serve as a reminder that she was alone.

Totally alone.

At that moment the ship's horn sounded, signalling a goodbye to the mainland. They'd sailed well into the Beagle Channel, the low buildings of Ushuaia disappearing from view.

The trip to Antarctica had begun, and there was nowhere to run.

7

The wind picked up on deck, driving most of the passengers inside. Olivia headed for the ship's library – where she could access the internet and see if there was that wished-for email from Aaron.

The library was open but empty, tranquil after the busyness of the sail-away party. It was decorated with polished walnut wood panelling and shelf after shelf of books – Antarctic history, geography, travelogues, memoirs and hundreds of novels – mostly the crime and thriller variety. There was a quadrangle of laptops in the middle, the keyboards firmly screwed into the desk – she wondered if that had more to do with the potential for bad weather, as opposed to any worries about thieves on board.

She booted up the computer and on the log-in screen she had the option to pay for two hours of usage for a princely sum. A warning underneath the screen emphasized in bold letters that the signal could drop at any time, so she'd have to be efficient. She plugged in her credit card details and waited, watching the cursor move with almost malignant slowness. Gmail finally opened but in plain text, not loading any of the graphics.

There were a slew of new messages in her inbox. But skimming the names, it was mostly junk; there was not a single message from Aaron.

She double- and triple-checked, making sure she didn't

miss one between marketing emails from The Outnet and subscription requests from actuarial newsletters.

She groaned in frustration, logged off, stood up from her chair, and the ship pitched forward, making her bump her thighs hard against the desk edge. She cried out, steadying herself against one of the bookshelves. Her shaking fingers closed around a little brass rail designed to stop the books from tumbling off the shelves and on to the floor. The books were protected. But what about her?

They were about to cross one of the most notorious stretches of water on Earth, potentially facing the worst kind of roiling sea. When it came to facing her fear, she really had thrown herself in the deep end, and she wasn't sure how she would cope. Not without Aaron.

When she was sure she could walk again, she headed back to reception.

There was a different woman behind the desk – younger, with dark curly hair. It was the person who had spoken to the honeymooning couple. Her name tag read 'Maria Elena'.

'Excuse me, is Elisabet available?' Olivia asked. 'I need her urgently.'

'She's just taking a break—'

'Please.' Olivia's throat was so tight, the word came out as barely a croak. Her desperation must've been written all over her face, as the woman nodded and disappeared into the office behind.

Elisabet emerged, wiping a crumb from the corner of her mouth. 'Did you hear from Mr Hunter-Williams?'

'Not yet. How long is it until we hit the Drake Passage? I want to get details to Aaron via email, so he can arrange a helicopter to meet the ship. Or maybe another boat? Can the captain radio the authorities on shore to let them know to expect him?'

Elisabet's professional veneer waivered; she struggled to hide the grimace on her face and the pity in her eyes. 'I just had an update from Captain Enzo – he's already been in touch with the port authority in Ushuaia. The weather has changed and the wind is too strong for a helicopter to fly and meet the ship.'

Olivia closed her eyes, taking a deep breath. 'I heard something about that on the bridge. So, is a storm coming? Is it going to be bad?'

Elisabet tensed. 'Captain Enzo is extremely experienced. His plan is to get us through the Drake Passage quickly, so we miss the worst of it. Why don't you relax in your cabin, get unpacked . . . I promise you will still have a wonderful adventure ahead of you. And a whole cabin all to yourself – what a luxury.'

Olivia shuddered. She didn't want to spend two weeks in a cabin on her own. She'd known coming on this trip would unlock fears she'd buried for almost fifteen years, but she'd convinced herself she could handle it with Aaron by her side.

But without him? She felt like she might drown.

She couldn't be alone.

She swallowed. 'Is that couple who were here earlier still in separate cabins?'

'The honeymooners? Yes, all our double cabins are full, except—'

'Except for the fact Aaron didn't make it on board. They can have our cabin.'

Elisabet raised her eyebrows. 'Are you sure? You'll be with three other women. It won't be as spacious.'

Olivia nodded. Her apprehension at being alone overwhelmed any concerns about missing out on luxury. It would be good to have others around. A distraction.

'Very good. I will page them to meet us in the lobby and we can arrange the swap. This is very generous of you, Ms Campbell. I know they will be incredibly grateful. I'll send one of the crew to transfer your luggage.'

It didn't take long after Elisabet put a call-out for the honeymooners. Christa was practically sprinting when she reached the desk.

'I have good news,' Elisabet said. 'Miss Campbell here has decided to give up her cabin to the two of you.'

Christa enveloped Olivia in a hug. 'You have made our vacation! Thank you so much.'

'A real lifesaver,' said Jay.

'The other women in the cabin are really nice,' Christa continued. 'You'll have a lot of fun. We'll have to thank you somehow.'

'Thank me by stopping by the art showcase. That's why I'm on board.'

'Is that the Yennin guy? We saw one of his paintings through the window of the gallery. It looks amazing. You're a part of that?'

'My partner is the curator,' Olivia said, forcing a smile. 'I handle the finance side of things.'

'Well, we'll definitely stop by on auction night. How exciting. And you'll have to have dinner with us.'

Christa had such a beaming smile, Olivia felt vindicated in her decision. She would be no good to anyone if she was locked up with fear. She was angry at Aaron for not being there, but she still wanted to make him proud. He'd done so much for her. This way, she could show him she could step up when he needed her to.

'Here you go – your new key cards.' Elisabet handed the credit card-sized piece of plastic to each of the women. 'Miss Campbell, you'll now be in cabin twelve. It's just down the first set of stairs, towards the bow of the ship. I'll send someone to move your luggage. Take your time, settle in, meet your cabinmates, and soon we'll do a muster station practice.'

'I had taken the top left-hand bunk,' said Christa. 'But I hadn't done any unpacking yet.'

'No problem,' said Olivia. 'Enjoy your new space.'

Following Elisabet's directions, she made her way to the opposite end of the ship to her original cabin. The elegant interior continued, with smooth wooden railings hanging off both sides of the narrow hallway. On the walls, old-fashioned maps of the North and South Poles were hung in gilt-edged frames. She didn't stop to admire them, but instead concentrated on the brass numbers hanging on each door, until she came to cabin twelve.

She jammed the key card against the black reader, then used her hip to open the door.

By comparison to the suite, the cabin was tiny – and almost immediately she regretted her decision to swap. Two bunk beds framed a small porthole with a side table in between. Just inside the cabin door, there was a tiny en suite bathroom and enough wardrobe space to hang a few jackets. She had no idea how four women were supposed to spend two weeks in that cramped space. There was barely enough room to swing a backpack.

It didn't help that four huge suitcases dominated the room. On the left-hand side, one was labelled

C. Bellweather, so Olivia moved it to the front so the crew could easily take it to her new berth.

She almost jumped out of her skin as she realized she wasn't alone in the room. The suitcase had blocked her view of a woman curled up asleep in the bunk below the one she was about to claim.

The door behind clicked open. 'Honey, we're hooome!' came a booming voice with a distinct North American twang. Olivia wasn't well travelled enough to take a stab as to where exactly. 'Janine? Christa? Are you two decent?'

Two women stood in the cramped doorway. The older woman was slightly in front, wearing a bright yellow shell jacket, black leggings and a bum bag, like it was the 1980s. She had lurid pink lipstick on, accentuating her wide smile, which faltered only for a moment as she realized Olivia was in the room. It was only a split second of surprise, though, before she was back to her warm self. A true pro. 'Oh, hello. Did we accidentally break into the wrong cabin?'

Olivia gestured to the sleeping form in the bottom bunk, and the woman cringed, holding up her hands before backing out into the hallway. Olivia followed, shutting the door with a quiet click.

'No, you have the right cabin. I'm Olivia,' she said, stretching out a hand. 'I switched with Christa so that she could share a cabin with her new husband.'

'Oh, you are such a doll! She seemed so bummed not to be with him. I'm Patricia, but call me Patty,' the woman said. 'And this is Annalise. We're from Toronto. What about you?'

'I'm from London.'

'Oh, London! Annalise is doing her MBA there near that famous market. What's it called again?'

'Covent Garden,' said Annalise.

'Right! Is that near you?'

Olivia shook her head. 'Not exactly. I live on the other side of the town – a place called Chelsea.'

'Sounds so fancy when you say it in your accent.'

Olivia couldn't help but laugh. She'd never thought of her gentle Scottish accent as 'fancy', but she supposed it could be true. It still felt strange to refer to Aaron's Chelsea home as her own. She'd only moved in a month ago, and his gorgeous Georgian conversion was a world away from her flat share with Tricia in Tooting.

'What university are you studying at?' Olivia asked.

'LSE. But right now, I need to get in there,' Annalise said, scowling. She was different to Patty – at least a decade younger, rail thin and in dark jeans paired with a Led Zeppelin T-shirt and leather jacket, her hair dyed box black.

'Someone's sleeping . . .' said Olivia.

'That's Janine,' said Patty. 'Poor thing is suffering from terrible jet lag. Add in a bit of seasickness and I guess she's conked out.'

Annalise shrugged and entered the cabin anyway.

'Don't mind her,' said Patty. 'A once-in-a-lifetime trip to Antarctica and she's still grumpy. So you gave up your own private cabin? Do I need to take you to the medics? You must be a loon!'

'I hope not. Just didn't want to be here on my own! My partner, he . . . had a work emergency and missed the boarding time.'

'Oh, honey.' Patty enveloped her in a warm embrace.

'What an idiot. Is he normally like that? No, you don't look the type to date someone simple-minded. But we all do dumb stuff from time to time. And he's a fool for missing this. I wish my Karl were here too, so we can mope around together.' Patty tutted, then clapped her hands together. 'Instead, I'm stuck with that sourpuss. But I can't complain – I'm here on the company dime.'

'You're here for work?'

'Well, my branch was the top performer in sales for Pioneer this year,' said Patty, red blooms appearing in her cheeks. 'And Annalise was my top sales gal before she jetted off to London to do her studies. This is a kind of thank-you present from Mr Hughes, I suppose. A spot on the maiden voyage of the newly refurbished ship. And the art auction should be exciting. That was a big draw for our customers.'

'That's why I'm here too. The auction is my partner's baby. He's the art dealer who set it all up.'

'No way! Well, I am extra glad to have you with us. You can get us into the VIP events, right?'

'Of course.'

Patty glanced at their cabin door. 'Look, I'm sure Janine won't mind if we get on with a bit of unpacking. She had those fancy headphones in and an eye-mask – I'm sure she's out like a light.'

'You go ahead. My bag's not been transferred yet so I might have a look around the rest of the ship. Give you guys a bit of space.'

'I wouldn't worry about that, my dear. We've got two weeks together, the four of us. We'd better get used to being in close quarters.'

8

Close quarters. On that, Patty couldn't be more accurate. Olivia needed to find somewhere less claustrophobic to be.

She could picture the look Aaron would give her when he found out she'd changed from a suite to a shared cabin. Total disbelief.

Dating him had been eye-opening: watching him slide over a Coutts Silk card to pay for their dinners out, seeing him wearing a different tailor-made Savile Row suit to every event, owning several Swiss watches and having daily shoe shines. In his business, having the right look made his clients feel like they were in a safe pair of hands. The first night she spent in his Chelsea pad made her truly understand the gulf between them: not an Ikea flatpack piece in sight, no mismatched mugs, no roommate to split the cost of rent. Aaron operated in a different stratosphere of wealth than she'd ever known. Sometimes she wasn't sure how he afforded it all, especially before the Yennin sale. But the investment he'd made in himself and his image had paid off. He could have anything he wanted now.

Looking at the floorplan of the ship posted by the lifts, her most likely bet to find some space was the Panorama lounge on one of the upper decks. And it lived up to its name, as she arrived at a huge semicircular lounge with wraparound floor-to-ceiling windows. The ceiling was painted to depict the aurora, swirls of bright teal, green and purple studded with tiny lights that sparkled like stars. There was comfortable booth seating in soft blue leather and a couple of fancy coffee stations, laden with a variety of espresso pods, hot chocolate, teas and an abundance of biscuits.

'Pretty rad views from in here.'

Olivia jumped. It was the expedition leader, Liam, again – wearing a Pioneer-branded navy fleece. He was laying out stapled pieces of paper on all the tables.

'What are those?' she asked.

'It's a loose rundown of our itinerary, provided by the captain. He's going to go over it after the muster. You can get a sneak preview.' He handed one to her.

'Thanks.' She scanned the page. They weren't due to arrive at their first anchorage – Barrientos Island – for three days. After that, it was another two days at sea until they crossed the Antarctic Circle. That meant six days until the auction. Then they had stops scheduled at Neko Harbour, Paradise Bay and Deception Island before heading back to Ushuaia. 'There's a lot of time at sea.'

He nodded. 'We've got a lot of water to cross if we're going to get to the Circle and back. Most cruises don't go that far south. But it's worth it. Are you OK? You look a little green.'

'I'm fine,' she replied.

'Did you find your boyfriend?'

Olivia frowned. 'How did you . . . ?'

'Not much stays a secret on board. Especially when someone that high-profile is missing. I was manning the gangway when we closed it off, so I feel extra bad that I didn't realize he hadn't made it back.'

Olivia blinked. 'Wait, you were in charge of logging people in and out?'

'Yeah, but I was focused on the passengers coming on board, not leaving. That's very rare.'

'We still had twenty minutes before the official all-aboard time. If his absence had been noted, we wouldn't have left early. We would have waited.'

'That is a bummer, I'm sorry.'

'You're sorry?' Olivia's jaw clenched. She felt like she was about to explode. At least he had the decency to look abashed. But his mistake had cost Aaron his place on the cruise ship. 'How could you—'

Several beeps sounded over the PA, interrupting her impending rant. 'Ahoy, passengers and crew of MS *Vigil*. This is your captain speaking. If you could please return to your cabins to get your life jackets and make your way to the muster stations, we will aim to complete our safety drill in record time so you can get back to enjoying this wonderful – if windy – cruise out of the Beagle Channel. In a few moments you will hear five blasts of the ship's emergency whistle. This is a practice muster so that you know what to do in the event of an emergency.

'Since we have seventy-nine passengers aboard, we will all be mustering in the Panorama lounge, on deck five. Please take a note of the group letter on your life jacket and make sure that you stay with that group. We'll be taking attendance, so it's important that you are present. After the muster, I'll do a briefing of the itinerary to come, and you can pick up schedules for the week.

'Captain out.'

'For what it's worth I truly am sorry. You don't have to go back to your cabin – I have a spare life jacket you can use for the drill.'

Olivia felt her anger deflate. She wanted to rant and rave, but she knew Liam wasn't to blame for her problem. 'Thanks,' she replied.

'I'll check which muster group you're in. Hang on.' He turned around, picking up his clipboard from off one of the low tables. 'What cabin are you in? Number sixteen?'

'Actually I switched after Aaron didn't make it on board. I'm in twelve now.'

'Great! Then you're with me. I have here Patricia, Annalise, Janine and Christa.'

'Christa – that's the woman I've swapped with.'

Liam crossed her name off his list, scrawling Olivia's in its place. 'All sorted. I'll let my colleague Melissa know about the change – she would've been your original muster leader. You OK here?'

'Yes, fine. I'll wait.'

It didn't take long. The lounge began to fill up with people, some of them wearing their life jackets already. Delilah Constance arrived, a lurid blue cocktail in hand to match her scarf. She seemed to have enlisted a younger male guest to carry her life jacket for her. Olivia kept an eye out for the honeymooners, but they were nowhere to be seen.

'Olivia! There you are.' Patty's booming voice sounded over all the commotion in the lounge. 'Is this our muster point?'

'I think so.' She shuffled down the sofa to allow Patty and Annalise to slide in.

'Right, ladies, so you're all on Team Liam!' The expedition leader perched on the edge of the sofa, clipboard in hand.

Patty leaned over and growled, 'If I was thirty years younger,' waggling her eyebrows at Annalise and Olivia.

They were joined by cabin twenty – Yara and Helena, two social media stars who Annalise recognized immediately.

'I hope you give this Pioneer cruise a good write-up,' Patty said with a wink.

'They do video content, Patty, not written journalism,' muttered Annalise.

'Oh, right, you're inspirers!'

'Influencers,' corrected Yara.

Patty slapped her palm against her knee. 'That's the one.'

Helena smiled. 'This is our first visit to Antarctica, so I'm sure there will be loads of interesting travel content. And Yara here has a following with the TikTok art niche, so she's going to follow the auction. That's how we got the invite out here. Hashtag gifted!'

Olivia turned to Yara. 'I can give you a tour of the gallery if you want – like a showcase preview?' She knew that if Yara had been specifically invited to create videos about the art, then Aaron must have had a hand in it.

'That would be great! I love, love, LOVE Yennin's work. It's so tragic that we won't see any more from him.' Her brown eyes watered with tears.

'Hang on, this is such a moment.' Helena scrambled for her phone, and the two of them repositioned themselves so Yara was framed by the window, the roiling sea outside contrasting against her tear-stained cheeks as she narrated her emotions to camera.

Olivia scanned the rest of the crowd. She could spot about twenty navy blue fleeces in the room, but while there were a couple of people with shaved heads, none of them gave her the creeps like she'd felt on deck. She supposed there might be more crew below who wouldn't be at the muster.

Her eye caught on one man sitting across the lounge near Cutler Hughes and his family. He looked vaguely familiar. Not threatening but just . . . she was sure that she'd met him before. He caught her staring and nodded back a greeting.

The name from the cabin list sprang into her mind.

Sadler. And the 'M' initial stood for Maxwell. She'd seen him hanging around the London gallery; she was sure of it. She hadn't realized he would be there. Why hadn't he been at the VIP dinner? She tried to remember what she knew about him. He was in finance — an investor of some sort.

Her train of thought was interrupted by the alarm ringing again, which also hushed the chatter in the room.

After the final beep, Captain Enzo stood at a microphone in front of a lowered projector screen. As if on cue, a map of the Antarctic Peninsula appeared on the screen behind him, a thick red line displaying their projected route. So far, everything had been very slick on board — clearly no expense had been spared in kitting it out.

'Hello, sailors on the MS *Vigil*! I am your captain, Enzo Giuliani. As you can probably tell from my accent, I am from Italy. Sardinia to be precise.

'Welcome on board — a full-service adventure to one of the most magnificent places on Earth. Our first duty is to make sure you are safe, and then we must protect the Antarctic environment. This is a bit different from the type of cruise you might have been on before, on a tour of the Caribbean perhaps. There is no rescue in the Antarctic. No hospitals or police. We're going to territory that has still only been visited by half a million people in the course of history. Although that number is growing fast.

'Some of you may have done a muster drill before, but this is going to be different. I need to stress how serious it is that everyone on board understands what to do in the event of an emergency. No one will leave this room without knowing how to find a lifeboat, so one by one, each group will be led outside by your crew leader. I leave you now in their capable hands.'

At his cue, Liam clapped his hands together. 'All right, Team Liam, let's go! The sooner we're outside, the sooner we can get back in. Hope you're wrapped up warm – it's chilly out there.'

He led them downstairs and through heavy fire-proof doors to the outer deck. He was still talking and Olivia tried to concentrate, but she couldn't tear her eyes from the roiling grey sea and the clouds on the horizon.

'OK, everyone, get those life jackets on,' Liam shouted as he walked them out towards the lifeboats, two large orange vessels suspended from the deck.

Olivia shrugged the life jacket on over her jacket, glad for that extra bit of warmth. It was huge, orange and bulky, packed with hard foam and a long inch-wide strap that needed to be fastened around her waist. It took some fiddling for her to untangle the strap, one side of it catching on something, and she ended up lagging behind the group. She half bent over, wrenching her arm around her back to find the missing end.

Another set of passengers pushed through the heavy double doors, following their muster leader. It was Delilah, now leading a group with cocktails still in hand, and by the volume of their conversation it seemed like they'd been at it for some time.

They barely noticed her as they jostled past, knocking her forward so she had to brace herself against the railing to avoid bashing her forehead. She was about to snap at them, when she felt a tug around her neck. The wayward strap of her life jacket tightened, pressing her windpipe.

She couldn't breathe.

She dug her fingers underneath the strap, trying to loosen the hold. She looked behind her, seeing the bulk of another person, but then she was yanked backwards so forcefully pain burst behind her eyes. She let out a strangled cry and her arms flailed, her fingernails clawing at her neck. The front of the life jacket lifted as she fell, making it harder for her to grip the strap.

She was being dragged, even as she dug the heels of her trainers into the deck to try to stop it. She felt her vision blacking.

Then – relief. She dropped to her knees, coughing and spluttering, pulling the jacket over her head and tossing it aside. It spun across the polished decking, stopping by the railing. She turned to look for the culprit, but Elisabet was standing in the way, the door open behind her.

Whoever had tried to choke her was now hidden. She scrambled to try to see around the door, but there was no sign of anyone on the deck behind. Her neck throbbed with pain.

'Are you OK?' It was Elisabet. 'I saw you struggling – did you catch the strap in the door handle?'

Olivia shook her head, massaging her neck. 'No, someone grabbed it.'

'Seriously?' Elisabet shut the door, looking from side to side down the now empty deck.

'Everything OK here?' Liam jogged up to them. 'I noticed you weren't with the group and came to find you. Come on, let's get you to your feet.'

The two crew members linked under her arms and pulled her up. She stared behind her at the empty deck, no one in sight. But she'd felt the tug. The strap hadn't caught on a door. Someone had tried to kill her.

But why had they stopped? Had Elisabet's arrival spooked them just in time? Or was it a warning . . . ?

Whatever it was, there was no doubt in her mind now. There was a threat on board. And she knew exactly who she had to speak to next.

9

'Those people shouldn't be drinking,' muttered Elisabet. 'Don't they realize we're in the middle of a safety drill? This is serious.'

Liam was still holding Olivia's arm. 'You sure you're OK?'

'Not really.' Now the shock had subsided, her eyes welled up with tears from the pain. Liam fetched her life jacket but she didn't put it on, clutching it against her chest instead. He led her back to the group.

She kept touching her neck with her fingertips. She wondered if it would bruise.

Patty wouldn't leave her side, sticking to her like glue as they walked back into the lounge. But as Liam talked, going over an Antarctica-specific safety briefing and something about not touching the penguins, Olivia's mind raced. She couldn't concentrate. When she blinked, she felt the strap around her throat. She wished she'd never come on board. If she had kept her head, they would be together. How was she supposed to just relax and enjoy this cruise? What if something had happened to him? The niggle of the word 'threat' hung in her mind.

What if someone was now targeting her?

As soon as the muster was over, she needed to find Stefan the auctioneer, and demand he tell her what he and Aaron had been talking about in the restaurant. If 'the threat' had followed her on board, that meant it had been in Ushuaia too. If someone had targeted her – and Aaron – then the police needed to know about it. All the same, she was tempted to lock herself in her cabin and not come out until they were back in Ushuaia.

Some of Captain Enzo's words seeped through her haze of fear. Despite the fact that all visitors to Antarctica agreed to abide by rules put in place by the IAATO (the International Association of Antarctica Tour Operators), it was essentially a place without government. There were no laws here or law enforcement. There was no rescue, no phone signal, limited internet – and no way to turn around and get off. Knowing that only deepened the pit in her stomach.

When all the groups had reassembled in the lounge, Captain Enzo took the microphone once more, explaining more safety features of the ship and what to do in the case of inclement weather. He made them all repeat the same mantra: *one hand for oneself, and one for the ship.* Essentially? They needed to remain prepared for rough seas at any time, which meant always having at least one hand free to grab a railing or a banister.

Out of the huge panoramic windows towering banks of cloud were building on the horizon over the grey sea. The waves looked manageable, the ship navigating the swells with ease. She could still see tiny outcrops of land, smudges of green and slate-grey rock. Birds congregated in swarms, shags, skuas and cormorants feasting in the krill-rich waters. She tried to concentrate on that. Nature was soothing.

You can learn so much from watching the birds. Suddenly her dad's voice sounded in her mind. A memory of him:

standing on the prow of their little sloop, heavy black binoculars around his neck. They'd been trawling the Isle of Mull's coastline and hadn't seen more than a couple of seagulls – but they had been treated to all seasons of weather in a single day. She'd whined and moaned, grown increasingly tired, wet and cold, begging to turn around and go home – until he had pointed at an obscure spot in the cliff. She looked through the glasses and realized he'd spotted a golden eagle. It sprang off the cliff as they were watching, opening its wings and soaring overhead.

Hard work, suffering and, yes, sometimes fear, were the price you paid to see the world's hidden wonders. She wished she could sit back and enjoy it.

'Are you all finished, Captain?' Cutler was making his way to the microphone. 'Mind if I say a few words before you dismiss us?'

'Please.' The captain gestured to the makeshift stage and took a step back, standing with his hands behind him, as rigid as a board.

A hush descended on the crowd, as most eyes turned to the front of the room. Olivia felt Patty tense beside her, the older woman leaning forward, her hands tightly clasped on her lap. She caught sight of Annalise behind her, who rolled her eyes but then turned her attention closely to the CEO.

'Welcome, one and all. For those who don't know, I am Cutler Hughes, CEO of Pioneer Adventures. This is a very special cruise, the inaugural voyage of our newly revamped ship. This has been a very difficult year for the travel industry, and I am delighted that Pioneer is at the forefront of reinvention. Central to that is our wonderful art showcase, which will take place when we cross the Antarctic Circle. Please make a special mark in your diaries. This is the only place in the world you can buy a Kostas Yennin to take home – an artist whose work has made serious waves in the art world, especially in the wake of his tragic death.' He paused, lowering his gaze for a solemn moment. Then he smiled again. 'Above all, though, this is a celebration. A celebration of you, of this year and of the travel industry not just getting back to normal – but progressing.'

'Hear, hear!' someone said.

'And as a special welcome to everyone, please join me now in a glass of champagne.'

A few more crew appeared from the galley, with trays of golden fizz. Immediately the atmosphere in the lounge shifted, as people got to their feet to take a glass. As the server approached, Olivia hesitated. She wasn't in the mood for celebrating after her ordeal. But it would look too conspicuous to miss out, so she took one for herself.

'We deserve this,' said Patty, downing her glass and then waving the server over to take another. 'Especially Annalise. He said that artist made waves, but so did she. My husband and I have owned our branch for thirty years, and she's the best of the best.'

A hint of colour appeared on Annalise's cheeks, and she drank to cover her embarrassment.

Olivia took a sip of hers, the fizz slipping down easily. But her neck still throbbed from the feeling of the strap tightening around it.

She could see Cutler looking around, and she got the sense he was searching for her. He probably wanted an explanation about Aaron's absence. And he was owed one. But not now.

Not while she could still feel pain from the strap around her throat.

She had to talk to Stefan.

10

Emboldened by the champagne, she knocked on the door of the gallery, ignoring the 'CLOSED' sign hanging at the entrance. It was not meant to be open to passengers until their first full day at sea. But Stefan had said he'd be there after the muster drill. Through the frosted glass she could see a shadow moving, so she knocked even louder.

After a few moments a man approached the door. 'I'm sorry, we're closed until tomorrow!'

'Stefan? It's Olivia.'

'Oh hello! I didn't realize it was you.' He unlocked the door to let Olivia in.

The gallery space looked incredible. She'd seen it that morning, with Aaron by her side (her heart panged at that memory – was it only a few hours ago that they had all been together?). But even seeing it again now took her breath away. She was transported back to when she'd seen a Yennin for the first time – and when she and Aaron had met. Here Yennin's signature piece – the only original on sale – was hidden away. But even the prints were striking, the stark, spare canvases contrasting with the opulence of the ship's design.

'Has Aaron sent his better half to convince me to back down? I told him, everything is in motion now. He signed this deal putting me in charge – he has to trust me. He doesn't know this clientele like I do.' Typical for

81

an auctioneer, Stefan let his mouth run before Olivia could get a word in. He was a slight man – shorter than Olivia – and he styled his rail-thin frame like a fancy French gentleman – patterned scarfs, silk shirts and tailored trousers – even though he was really from Liverpool. It was all a grand act, but he was undeniably charming. He locked the door behind Olivia.

'Wait, what are you talking about? You're changing the plan?'

'Tell Aaron to talk to me himself if he has an issue—'

Olivia shook her head. 'That *is* the issue. Stefan, Aaron didn't make it on to the ship.'

Now she managed to render him speechless. In fact, he seemed properly dumbfounded, the muscle above his left eyebrow twitching. 'Say again?'

'He left the ship after we had lunch. He said it was a work emergency. He wasn't logged out of the ship's system and didn't make it back on board before we left. I haven't been able to get hold of him since.'

'You're joking. This is a joke, right?'

Olivia shook her head.

'Well, this is outrageous! How on earth did this happen?' He rushed to the nearest window, as if Aaron would be speeding up in a boat at just that moment to catch them up.

'I don't know. Like I said, I haven't been able to get hold of him. So I take it this means you haven't heard from him either?'

'Of course not – I mean, I just assumed . . .' He sat down on the plush velvet-covered window seat. 'This is a situation.'

'That feels like a bit of an understatement.' She took a deep breath before continuing. 'I know he wouldn't have missed the boarding time on purpose. Something must have happened to him. So we need to talk . . . about the threat back in London.'

Stefan stared at her for a second, his eyes narrowing. 'What do you know about that?'

She didn't reply. Instead, she held Stefan's gaze, waiting to see what he would reveal. He sighed, rubbing at his brows. 'Unfortunate business. But Aaron assured me that he had sorted it out.'

Olivia was dying to ask more questions, but Stefan already seemed on edge. She came and sat down next to him. 'Do you agree? It sounded scary but I don't think I got the whole story . . .'

Stefan blew out a long breath. 'Well, scary is one way of looking at it. Aaron had received a few nasty letters and emails. Social media slander, that type of thing. All baseless accusations, of course.'

'Oh my God. But why?'

Stefan frowned. 'Because of Yennin.'

'I don't understand.'

'The way he died. Some people had questions.'

'Do you know who?'

Stefan shook his head. 'Aaron didn't say. I'm not sure he knew really. It was all done anonymously – he shared a few of the emails with me. They were unpleasant, but he has a good legal team. I don't think he thought it was anything really credible.'

'I don't understand. Yennin died in a car accident. The police didn't deem anyone responsible. It was a tragedy.'

'I suppose not everyone was convinced.'

'But . . . Aaron was nowhere near the car when he died. I don't understand how anyone could blame him. It makes no sense.'

Because if anyone was partly to blame, it was her. Her own memories of that night were shrouded with guilt. It was supposed to be Yennin's big evening. The auction of his work. But the artist was notoriously shy, introverted. He hadn't wanted to attend.

Aaron had insisted, as close to begging as she'd ever seen him. But Yennin would only get in a car with someone he'd met before. Aaron was far too busy on the day to pick him up, so he had asked Olivia to do it. He had made her promise.

But he hadn't known how fragile her state of mind had been. That day she'd reached rock bottom with her mental health. She'd walked out of her job and forgotten her obligation to Yennin.

When she had shown up a half-hour after the auction had been scheduled to begin – she was still a mess. She already knew she'd let everyone down – her work, her friends, her family – and now Aaron and his prized artist. Yet she'd been surprised to see guests still mingling and sipping champagne in the lobby. Many of them were engrossed in their phone screens. She would have found it amusing – all those people in tuxedos and ball gowns staring at their glowing phones – if she hadn't been so worried about how Aaron would react to her lateness.

She slipped through to the back, where she hunted for Aaron. Huge paintings were propped up against the walls, waiting their turn on the auction floor. In front of the potential buyers, they'd be handled with white gloves and extreme care. But back here? It was almost painful to see them treated so casually when she knew each one was potentially worth millions. But just how much, the auction itself would determine.

She found him in a small room, where other dealers, journalists and critics were mingling, watching the action unfolding on a small television. The guests were taking their seats, and large screens on either side of the auctioneer would display live updates of the bidding once it began.

'Thank God, Livi, there you are. Where the hell is Yennin?' Aaron asked. The moment she got close to him, she saw the sheen of sweat on his brow.

'He's not here yet?'

'No! Wait – didn't you bring him?'

'I . . . I couldn't. I got swept up at work. I came straight here.'

'Shit. The auctioneer only gave us half an hour's grace. It's going to start without him. I can't believe this . . .'

'I am so, so sorry . . .'

One of the journalists in the room hissed at them to be quiet. Aaron turned to the screen, his complexion pale. His hands were shaking. The auction for *nemiga* was beginning.

Aaron tapped his foot as the auctioneer accepted bids, energy fizzing off him like freshly poured champagne. Here, away from the judgemental eyes of his clients, he could be more himself – let the polished veneer slip just a little. She caught a glimpse of the boy underneath and realized how much was at stake. He was so good at hiding the risk, even from her.

'Holy Christ,' said the journalist in an overly loud whisper to his companion. 'Have you seen these tweets?'

Olivia looked over her shoulder, where two men were huddled over their phones. Now she was really confused.

'Is it confirmed it's Yennin?' the other one whispered back.

She looked up at Aaron, but he was entranced by the auction, lost in his own world.

She took her phone out and opened Twitter. She typed in Yennin's name. There were a few tweets about the auction, but one caught her eye: *BREAKING NEWS: Fatal car accident closes down a street in Mayfair.*

But it was the tweet in reply that was most concerning: *I think it's that artist. Kostas Yennin.*

Olivia blinked, unable to believe her eyes.

A car accident. It couldn't be true. She nudged Aaron's shoulder, but he refused to look, his eyes glued to the screen.

She gripped his hand and he held it tight. Bids started to appear in rapid succession, many coming in over the phones and from online buyers. The numbers crept up and up, head-swimming sums.

Then – the hammer fell at three million. It was an astronomical sum, several times the reserve price. A silver-haired man in an expensive sailing jacket had been the final bidder. Her billionaire client, Pierre Lavaud.

The room emptied out around them, as the journalists rushed to get an interview with Pierre. Olivia, though, was only looking at Aaron. He looked devastated.

'Aaron, what's wrong? You did it. Yennin is going to be a superstar,' she said to him.

Now, he looked down at his phone. 'I think I have to talk to the police.'

As it turned out, for once, the social media rumours had been correct. Yennin had been involved in a fatal car accident that evening, mere minutes from the auction house. But Aaron had been inside the entire afternoon, hundreds of witnesses could testify to that. Nowhere near the site of the incident.

It couldn't have possibly been his fault.

But as for her . . .

Stefan shrugged. 'You can't change what some trolls online think, but I know it made his life a bit difficult.'

'You don't think whoever it was took it further than just letters and emails, do you? That someone might have attacked him?'

'It would be a bit of a jump from sending an anonymous tweet to following someone to the bottom of the world.' He sank back against the cushions.

Seeing him visibly relax helped put Olivia at ease too. It didn't seem like Stefan was worried the 'threat' had turned physical. Maybe she had got the strap of her life jacket caught in the door? If there was anything she'd learned about her mind this year, it was that it couldn't be trusted. Sure, she was on a path to recovery, but she was a long way from being at full mental capacity.

'So Aaron really isn't here.' Stefan rubbed at his chin, his eyes darting around the exhibition. His mood had shifted. Olivia didn't know him well enough to understand what was happening, but it put her on edge. 'I suppose it will be up to you to take over Aaron's duties. The selling is really up to me, you know – so you don't have to worry about that. But Aaron's job was continuing to seed the excitement on board. Talk up Yennin, of course. Yet, more than that, making sure the guests are having a good time, making sure they want to buy the artwork. He was going to do all the excursions available – the kayaking, sleeping on the ice, that sort of thing. Then the VIP drinks the night before the auction. Keeping clients happy. You up for that?'

Olivia nodded. 'Absolutely.'

Stefan slapped his knees with his hands. 'Excellent. Then I think we can make this work after all. Fancy missing the boat, after everything he's put himself through to get the deal this far. Now if you don't mind, I have a bit more admin to do before we reach the dreaded Drake Passage. The crew cabins are so much less comfortable than the beautiful stateroom you have.'

Olivia debated telling him that she'd moved cabins, but then realized – like Aaron – he wouldn't understand her decision. She stood up, making her way to the door. 'You'll let me know if you hear from him?'

'Of course.' Stefan stopped her just before she left. 'Oh, Olivia. It may not just be the clients you have to worry about keeping happy. Cutler Hughes has a lot riding on this going well. We need to demonstrate a strong, repeatable model for profit on our return – it's a key feature of his package to the mysterious buyer of his cruise ships.'

'You don't know who it is?'

Stefan shrugged. 'That's not up to me. I'm surprised *you* don't know.'

Olivia felt her cheeks turning red, annoyed with herself that she'd revealed some of her ignorance. 'I'll make sure Cutler feels reassured. You just make sure the auction is profitable.'

'On that, I no longer have any worries.' He ushered her out of the door, clicking it shut behind her. He couldn't hide the ghost of a smile on his lips.

Olivia thought he looked just a little too happy that Aaron was no longer on the ship.

11

By the time the bells chimed for dinner, they were out of the shelter of the Beagle Channel and into the Drake Passage proper, where three great oceans met. They appeared to be having an argument, the waves lashing up against their porthole window, drenching it with spray.

All the passengers ate together, in a spacious dining room on the second-to-top level. By the time Olivia arrived, it was mostly full, passengers laughing as they tried to stop their glassware from tipping over. She felt like a new girl in school, unsure of where to sit. Stefan's words rang in her ears: she needed to keep the clients happy. She was about to approach Delilah's table when she heard her name.

'Olivia, over here!' Patty waved to her, directing her to a table that was filled mostly with their group from the muster. By the looks of things, they'd come straight from drinks in the lounge. She smiled back – schmoozing could wait until the next day – and made her way over.

Patty pulled out the chair next to her and Olivia sat down gratefully.

'Did you get hold of your auction friend?' Patty asked.

'Yes, thankfully – I explained the whole situation to him.' On the plate in front of her was a menu for a three-course meal. At least she wouldn't go hungry. After she'd given her choices to the waiter, she turned back to Patty. 'So you said you've been a travel agent for thirty years?'

'We prefer the term "travel consultant" nowadays,' said Patty with an exaggerated wink. 'But, yes, my husband and I, we own the branch together. Karl lives and breathes travel. He's been to so many countries, I lost count, but never Antarctica. He so would have loved coming down here.' Patty looked a little rosy, colour high in her cheeks, and she was already signalling the waiter to top up her glass of red wine and fill Olivia's. The glasses seemed to have exceptionally heavy bases, and even as the ship rose and fell, not a drop was spilled. 'Anything from your boyfriend?'

Olivia shook her head. 'The internet's not great.'

'They were talking about this in the lounge after you left. Apparently the storm isn't helping,' said Yara. 'I haven't been able to upload to my TikTok since we got on board.'

'Trust me, a little bit of separation could be a good thing,' said Patty. 'You'll have something to talk about once you've been married for twenty-three years. You'll be yapping his ear off about penguins until death do you part – so help him!'

'Where's Annalise?' Olivia asked.

'She's helping Janine down to the medical bay to get some anti-seasickness medication. Poor chick didn't seem that prepared for a trip to Antarctica. I wonder if this was a last-minute decision, like that honeymooning couple.' Patty craned her neck to look around the room. 'Speaking of whom, I don't see Christa in here either. Maybe she and her husband are also down with seasickness – or taking advantage of that double cabin you gave up.' She waggled her eyebrows salaciously.

Olivia couldn't help but laugh.

When their first course arrived – a variation on a prawn cocktail – Olivia took her opportunity to look around. The loudest voice in the room was easily Cutler's. He and Ingrid sat at a long table at the head of the dining room, alongside Robert and Aida, and some others that Olivia didn't recognize.

'Must be a bit intimidating to have your boss on board,' said Olivia, as she noticed Patty's eyes trained on Cutler.

'I'm lucky to have been given the opportunity. I'm hoping to get a chance to thank him properly,' she said, before taking a forkful of prawns. 'Pioneer has been my whole world, and yet I've only met him in person once, years ago. I'm sure he has no clue who I am.'

'But he invited you?'

'I think Annalise might have more to do with that than me.' Patty took a long sip of wine. Olivia sensed she might have hit on a sensitive topic, and she tried to think of something else to move the conversation on.

The boat lurched and she didn't have to worry any more. Plates slid along the dining table, and somewhere nearby a glass salt shaker smashed to the floor.

Olivia squeezed her eyes shut, waiting for the swell to pass. When she opened them again, her heart hammering in her chest, she saw Patty's concerned look.

'I'm not the biggest fan of boats,' Olivia said, trying to relax her hands from their vice-like grip around her cutlery.

'You poor thing. Want to go down to the medical bay to get some Dramamine? I can take you . . .'

Olivia shook her head. 'I don't think it's seasickness. But I'm not sure I can eat much more.'

'I'll take your portion,' said Patty. 'Something about international travel always makes me starving.'

The ocean swells continued to rise throughout dinner, and Patty decided to turn in at the same time as Olivia, skipping the first scheduled lecture. The poor glaciologist – one Dr Arthur Vance – was down to give a talk called 'Ice, Ice, Baby' about the variety of icebergs, and by the sounds of things was going to have a pretty empty audience.

Olivia was grateful to see her suitcase had arrived. Aaron's presumably had been taken into storage – there was no room for it in the tiny cabin.

Olivia clambered up the precarious ladder. That's when she noticed that someone had been in to turn down the beds. Or not turn down exactly. They had placed a bolster along each edge of her bunk, so that the mattress curled up on both sides, like she was sleeping in a half-pipe. It took a large swell for her to realize why: it was so that she didn't roll out of the bed.

Outside their porthole, the thick cloud had built up so it obscured the sky, turning it an unsightly sallow yellow. The waves were capped with white, like foam at the mouth of a rabid animal. The storm the captain had mentioned. She dragged across the blackout curtains, obscuring the view, and huddled down under the blankets. Olivia willed herself to sleep. But it was impossible with the crashing of the waves. The lurch that accompanied every swell. And the occasional bang as unsecured items – a camera, Patty's glasses case, a toothbrush holder in the bathroom – tumbled to the floor. Picking the top bunk had been another mistake. The rocking had to be worse up here. Plus she had to stay rigid, her

93

arms and legs stiff by her side, because if she rolled out of the bolsters she would have a nasty fall. Not to mention that now she was in bed, all the thoughts she'd kept at bay came crashing in, her mind unable to stop racing over the events of the day.

Why hadn't she gone with Aaron?

Why hadn't he been in touch?

Was he OK?

Who had tried to attack her during the muster?

She flipped over, trying to tuck in as close to the wall as possible. The ship lifted and her stomach with it. She squeezed her eyes tightly shut again. But when it didn't work, she opened her eyes and tried to fixate on a point in front of her. She thought about yoga, controlling her breath, regulating it.

This was shock and fear. Like those first few steps into a freezing-cold loch. She blinked in surprise. She hadn't thought about that in years, another memory she had suppressed. Her dad had swum every morning when he was at home or at sea, rarely missing a day. When Olivia was on school holidays, she'd join him, squealing as she jumped in but loving it once her body had adjusted to the cold. Then they'd get out and snuggle up into robes, sipping hot chocolate before getting dressed again and heading back out into the wilderness. Sailing on the loch they'd swum in. Or kayaking or going for a hike.

Thinking about him calmed her down. He'd always believed in her. Always thought she was capable. And she'd thought more about him in the few hours she'd been on the way to Antarctica than she had in the past decade. The trip could be worth it, if only to recapture those memories of him. And his memory could inspire her to be strong.

There was bound to be a reasonable explanation for Aaron's lack of contact. Reasonable. Logical. Cool under pressure. Those words had always described her, and she clung to them now, as if they could weigh down the panic that made her want to cry and scream and demand to be flown back to Ushuaia immediately.

She made herself a promise. If she didn't hear from Aaron within the next twenty-four hours, she would ask Captain Enzo to radio the Argentinian police. A concrete plan. That's what she needed. And while she was on the ship, she had to focus on the job at hand: making sure the showcase was a success.

Her stomach roiled. She hadn't eaten much at dinner and nausea rose in her throat. She'd never had much seasickness as a child, but clearly the years had stolen away her seaworthiness. She decided she couldn't stay in bed any longer. Maybe it would be easier to get some medication – a patch or some tablets from the medical centre – than to suffer in bed. It might also be enough to send her to sleep.

She waited for a pause in the rise and fall, then swung her legs over and crawled down the ladder.

She paused at the bottom, trying not to disturb the others. But somehow they were still managing to sleep.

Again, timing it with the swells, she crossed the cabin floor. She opened the door carefully, making sure it didn't make a sound as it shut. The hall was deserted.

She kept one hand on the brass railing that ran along the edge of the hallway, gripping tightly in case the ship made an unexpected move. Somewhere down the hall was the cabin she would have shared with Aaron. They would have laughed and clung to each other as the waves did their worst, and when she was scared, he would have comforted her. She hoped the honeymooners were appreciating their time together.

As she thought of them, someone in a navy Pioneer-branded polo stepped out of cabin sixteen, wearing a pair of white gloves. A cabin steward. He had a mostly shaved head apart from two straight lines of hair above his ear.

There was no denying it this time. He looked exactly like the man who had been watching them outside the restaurant in Ushuaia.

She let out an involuntary gasp. He looked up sharply. She caught sight of his eyes – a pale, watery blue. They narrowed, and he strode towards her.

Her bravery deserted her and she fled back down the stairs, taking them two at a time. But as she released her hand from the banister to cut the corner of the landing, the floor disappeared beneath her feet. The ship lurched and bucked, and she was thrown. Her foot missed the next step, skidding instead against the edge and sending her flying backwards, arms wheeling.

Her head cracked against the rail.

'Don't move, Olivia,' the man growled.

She winced, clawing at the back of her head. She opened one eye, then cried out with fear.

He was staring down at her, his hand raised. This was it. He'd been searching for her in the wrong cabin and she'd stumbled right into his path. Now she was at his mercy. She kicked out, scrambling backwards, but the stairs blocked her. There was nowhere to go.

'Hey! Are you OK?'

She tilted her head back and saw Liam leaning over the railings in the stairwell. At the sound of his voice, the other man growled, before fleeing through a 'CREW ONLY' door.

Liam's warm brown eyes filled with concern as he raced down the stairs to help her. 'Did you fall?'

'Th-that crewman,' she stammered out. 'Do you know him?'

'Hmm, sorry. I couldn't tell from the top of his head.'

'He chased me. He caused me to fall. He was going to attack me.'

Liam frowned. 'A member of the crew? I don't think so.'

'He's about six foot tall, bald – with these two strips of hair above his ear. I saw him in Ushuaia as well.'

Liam chuckled. 'Sounds like my roommate. A "hair tattoo" he calls it. He's quite meticulous about it. What a

97

muppet. But you wouldn't have seen him in Ushuaia; he's just come off another sailing and we didn't have much time on shore.'

'Then why did he run?'

'He's not supposed to be on the guest floors during his duty. He probably saw I was coming and let me take over rather than risk a bollocking from Captain Enzo.'

Olivia chewed on her lower lip, but she couldn't drop it. 'All right, then tell me how come he knew my name?'

'We're all given binders with passenger information. He probably recognized you from that.'

She blinked, the information taking a while to sink in. Maybe that was the man from Ushuaia, but more likely not. In the end, all he had really done was tell her not to move – probably good advice given her potential head injury. As the adrenaline faded, the pain came back in full force. She groaned.

'That was quite the fall you took. Shit, and you're bleeding. Can you stand? Come with me.'

'I'll be OK—'

'The medical centre isn't far. I want to make sure you didn't do any real harm.'

She leaned on his arm and he led her down the stairs to the medical bay on the lower deck. She found it hard to open her eyes fully due to the pain. 'What were you doing up and about the ship so late?' he asked.

'Actually I was aiming for the medical bay. I was hoping to get some seasickness pills.'

'Dr Ranjeed can get you those. You'll be right. Remember, you've got to have one hand on the ship at all times.'

He knocked on the door for her, waiting a few seconds until it opened.

The doctor looked frazzled, his dark hair askew. He had the kind of deep brown skin that even a season in Antarctica couldn't shake the vibrancy from, with warm creases around his eyes. She wondered what his story was, how he came to find himself on a boat to Antarctica.

He muttered at her to come in and gestured for her to hop up on the bed. 'What's the problem?'

'She took a fall down the stairs,' said Liam. 'Hit her head. Might need stitches.'

The doctor nodded. 'I'll get some Steri-Strips.'

'I'd better continue my rounds or else *I'll* be the one experiencing Captain Enzo's wrath. I'll see you in the morning, yeah?' Liam said to Olivia. She gave him a small wave as she gingerly clambered up on to the examination-room bed. What must he think of her? This was the second time that day he'd had to come to her rescue.

Maybe she could convince the doctor there was a medically necessary reason for her to be flown back to Ushuaia. She stared at the doctor's back as he rooted around one of the cupboards. What would it take? Severe concussion? A broken limb? Maybe a psychotic break?

Before she could formulate a plan, the doctor turned back with a bandage and some antiseptic wipes. He wiped away the blood from her forehead and examined her wound, doing a few checks of her brain function by asking her to follow his finger. He gave her a sharp nod. 'It looks bad but you won't need stitches. You're lucky. This has been an unfortunate crossing.'

She frowned. 'Have other people been hurt?'

'Ranj?' A woman's voice came from the adjacent room. Olivia tried to turn her head to see who was speaking but a stab of pain stopped her.

'Yes?' He handed her an ice pack to put against her forehead, which she took gratefully.

'I really need your help in here.' The voice quivered with desperation. They must be overwhelmed with patients. Maybe that was no surprise. The ship was being battered by the storm, a rough introduction to cruise life. There was no porthole in the medical bay, but she could easily imagine the swell outside, thirty-foot waves slamming the side of the boat, tossing it around like a toy. She tried to pretend they were back on land and not surrounded by steel-grey ocean that could swallow them up whole, never to return.

'I have to help my colleague. Don't go anywhere,' he said, pressing on her shoulders to guide her to a lying-down position on the bed.

She closed her eyes to try to manage the pain, resting the ice pack against her skull – and her entire body tensed as the ship rocked precariously once again. Would she ever get used to the motion? How long did the captain say the Drake Passage crossing could last? Two days? In bad weather, it could take much longer . . .

Voices drifted to her. Dr Ranjeed had left the door slightly ajar behind him, so although she couldn't see them, she could overhear their conversation.

'What are we going to do?' the woman hissed. She had a slight Slavic accent that turned her Ws to Vs, intensified with panic. Another doctor? 'We left port less than twenty-four hours ago,' she continued. 'We have to send them back on the chopper.'

'In this storm? No way,' replied Dr Ranjeed.

'Then we need to turn the boat around! This is serious, Ranj.'

100

'The captain will never allow it. Not with Mr Hughes on board.'

'And if it really is poison? What do we do then?'

Olivia sat bolt upright in the bed. She couldn't have heard properly. *Poison?* The ship rose up beneath her, and the door clicked shut.

The voices were cut off. Her entire body had gone cold. Surely if someone had been poisoned, they wouldn't be continuing to sail. They would be turning the ship right now, heading back to port. She must have been confused by the woman's strange accent, and the pounding in her head, distorting, distorting.

This has been an unfortunate crossing. Well, at least she now understood the doctor's grim statement.

She was snapped out of her morbid thoughts by Dr Ranjeed's return. The adrenaline rush from overhearing the conversation had pushed the headache to the back of her mind.

He blinked at her, and she forced a smile. He smiled back, but she thought it wavered at the edges ever so slightly.

'What was that about?' she asked.

'My colleague needed a hand with some paperwork. It's always complicated when someone gets ill on board. Insurance claims and all that rubbish. We'll be out of the rough seas soon enough. You don't have any signs of concussion so I'll give you a little something to help with the pain so that you can get some sleep, and some seasickness pills in case the weather stays bad. If you still feel bad in the morning, come and see us again.' He gestured to the door.

'Wait, please. I heard you two talking. I heard something

about –' she could barely bring herself to say the word – 'poison.'

She watched for it and there it was: a moment's hesitation. 'You must have misheard. We had someone come in with gastroenteritis – in other words, your garden-variety food poisoning. It's a pretty typical problem on cruise ships; we were just sorting out how to advise the captain on doubling down on sanitation protocol and possible quarantine for affected passengers.' He passed her a small cup with pills at the bottom. She took it, and her fingers trembled. 'I'd better get back to it,' he said. He helped her to her feet and led her to the door.

She didn't protest any more. The words swirled in her mind as she swallowed the pills dry and headed back to her cabin – not letting go of the railing for an instant. Food poisoning. She felt like such an idiot.

Back in the cabin, the ship swayed, rocking her like she was in a crib. The motion was much less violent than it had been a few hours ago. Maybe this meant that the storm was abating. Her head still pounded, but the medication began to take hold.

She closed her eyes, and finally managed to drop off to sleep.

13

When she woke, it was still early, her digital watch showing just after six a.m. She blinked, finding it hard to
register her surroundings. For one thing, the ship had
stopped swaying entirely. It almost felt like they were
hardly moving at all. Maybe they'd turned around in the
night and gone back to Ushuaia? She half expected to
look out of the porthole to see mountains on the horizon once more.

Her head still throbbed, her eyes swollen and sore.
She stared up at the ceiling, touching her throat gently.
Stefan hadn't seemed to be worried about the 'threat'
moving from online to the real world. But what had happened with her life jacket had felt so real. She'd seen
someone behind her, hadn't she?

Then there was the man with the shaved head. Was it
possible he was the same man she'd seen in Ushuaia?

She was being paranoid. But was that such a surprise?
She was on her own, in an environment she hated. The
only thing she had to hold on to was her plan: if there
was no word from Aaron today, she would demand
the captain radio back to shore and alert the authorities.

She wished she had someone to talk to. Anyone who
could make her see sense. Patty had been nice enough,
but her loyalty to Pioneer meant Olivia couldn't be too
honest about how she was feeling. Stefan might be on
her side when it came to the showcase, but there was

something about him that put her on edge. She needed a friend.

She sat up in the bed, wincing as the pain in her head intensified. Thankfully, within a couple of seconds of her eyes being closed, it subsided. She pushed her hand into her hair, at the edge of her forehead, and felt the lump there — along with the butterfly stitch. Ouch.

A series of three bells chimed in the cabin. The captain's voice sounded over the PA. 'Good morning, *Vigil* crew and passengers, this is Captain Enzo. My first words to you all should be congratulations for making it through the Drake Passage. However, I had a few worrying reports from the medical bay overnight. Please remember to always have one hand free to hold the railings around the ship. Try not to walk around looking at your phone or holding your camera — you're on a moving vessel, and although we've made it past the worst of it now, you never know what we may confront.

'On to some more pleasant news: despite the rough seas, we have made good time through the passage and we may even make our first landfall as early as tomorrow morning. To prepare, I've asked our superlative crew to work extra hard on getting us landing-ready, so, after breakfast, expect to be going through the safety drills and selecting your gear a bit earlier than we anticipated.

'I also invite you to look around our very special art gallery, which opens today from ten a.m. for a preview before the auction. This is a once-in-a-lifetime opportunity to purchase a unique piece from one of the most acclaimed artists of his generation — but our gallery specialist, Stefan, can tell you more, so please visit him on deck four. Have a great day at sea, everyone.'

'Are you feeling better now, pet?' Patty asked the woman in the bunk beneath Olivia.

'Still a little fragile,' said Janine.

'You look a bit less seasick now. Not so green around the gills.'

'That's good. I'll just get up to brush my teeth.'

'Oh please, me first,' said Patty, and without waiting for a reply, dashed towards their shared bathroom.

Olivia could feel the woman shifting on the bed, slowly stretching on her mattress, the tips of her fingers appearing over the edge of the top bunk. Then she stood up and spun around.

The ship lurched as she moved, and the woman stumbled backwards, bashing against the other bed and falling to the floor.

'Oh my God! Are you OK?' Olivia scrambled out of the top bunk. She helped the other woman back to standing.

'Not got my sea legs yet, I guess,' she muttered, her voice soft. Her copper hair was frizzy from where she'd slept on it. Then she blinked, staring quizzically at Olivia.

'Goodness, I'm being really rude. We haven't met yet. I'm Olivia.' She extended her hand.

Janine shook it, a small crease between her brows. 'Sorry – between the seasickness and the jet lag, I've lost my mind a bit – I thought I was sharing a bunk with someone called Christa?'

'Yes, you were. But we switched cabins so she could be with her husband.'

'Oh, I see. That makes sense. I'm Janine. Nice to meet you.' She smiled.

Patty exited the bathroom, looking flustered and hot

in her thermal underwear. 'Jeez, these things are tight. Oh good, you two have met at last!' said Patty once she clocked Janine. 'Cabin twelve is complete!'

There was an excited squeal from the bunk opposite. Olivia was shocked it came from Annalise, who had barely cracked a smile since she'd stepped on board. 'Look at that!' She leaned over the small desk in between the bunks, pushing back the curtain from the porthole.

Through the wave-splashed glass, murky with dried sea spray, they stared at the vast swell of the ocean. It was like they were floating on mercury, grey and molten, the sea was the same colour as the sky, and everything seemed almost unnaturally calm.

There was something out there, on the horizon. A shadow. Another ship? Were they already approaching land? Olivia rubbed her eyes.

As she stared, the cloud lifted off the grey slate tile of the ocean, and her breath caught in her throat. An iceberg – her first sighting – a triangle of stark white snow bulging from the ocean's surface. Her immediate reaction was visceral terror – she hadn't realized she would feel that way, but there was something about icebergs, the thought of how much more bulk lurked beneath the depths. Too many *Titanic* rewatches maybe. It brought home that she was on a ship in an ocean cold enough to sustain a floating island of ice and that if they were to sink, death would be slow, painful and inevitable.

She took a step back from the window to allow the others to take a closer look. Annalise snapped away with her camera, intent on capturing it from every angle. It was the most spark Olivia had seen from her since they'd met. People were like icebergs, weren't they? Only allowing the tips of their personalities, their histories, to rise above the surface. Everything else was hidden beneath, masked from view.

Olivia had never let anyone beneath the surface. Not even Aaron, she realized with a start. It was below that she carried the memories of her childhood. Of her dad – watching him at the helm of a yacht, cruising through the turquoise waters of the Caribbean, learning to tie knots or how to paddle a kayak. Of her mother, who had been so different back then too – always carrying a sketchbook with her, disappearing for hours into her shed-turned-artist-studio to paint. She'd been so vibrant and carefree. Olivia hadn't seen that person in a long time. Even before her mother's illness had stolen her memory, that side of her had been locked away.

'Our first iceberg. Wow,' breathed Annalise.

'Let's go out on deck,' said Patty.

'I think some fresh air would do me some good,' said Janine. But then her expression changed as she looked at Olivia. 'Oh my God. You're bleeding,' she said, her brows knitting together.

'What?' Olivia lifted her hand to her forehead. 'Oh. My bandage must have come off. I had a trip to the medical bay last night. I took a tumble on the stairs,' she explained.

'You went out last night? In the storm?' Annalise raised her eyebrows.

'Honey, no!' said Patty. 'I could barely walk straight – I'm not surprised you fell. We'll take you down to get you a new one.'

For the first time since she got on board, Olivia felt a weight lift from her shoulders. Changing cabins had been the right decision. She might even come out of this with some good friends. It had been a long time since she'd made friends – and not pushed them away. With a pang, she thought of Tricia.

Their last conversation had not been good.

She'd have to write to her, explain why she'd acted so out of character. Maybe when she got back to London, they could laugh about it.

'I'll be fine,' Olivia said.

As they stepped outside the cabin, Annalise began to walk in the opposite direction.

'Aren't you coming outside with us?' asked Patty after her.

'No. I'm going to the library. I have some work to do.'

Olivia stopped in her tracks. 'Mind if I come with you? I need to see if there's been any word from Aaron.'

'Whatever.' Annalise shrugged.

'Well, have fun, you two,' said Patty. 'I for one am going to avoid the internet all this vacation. Have a proper switch-off. Come on, Janine.'

As they walked to the library, Annalise chewed her lip, deep in thought.

'What are you working on?' Olivia asked, to break the silence.

'What?'

'You said you need to be in the library for work . . .'

'Oh, my dissertation for my MBA.'

'Wow. What's it on?'

'The travel industry post-Covid 19.'

'Sounds fascinating!'

But Annalise didn't elaborate any further. Olivia took the hint and hung back, letting her get a few steps ahead.

'Weird about your boyfriend,' Annalise said over her shoulder. 'How is it even possible to miss the boarding time? Did he just forget?'

Now it was Olivia's turn to feel defensive. 'That's why I need to get online.'

In the library, Olivia sat down at the laptop she'd now adopted as her own, while Annalise sat down at one opposite.

Thankfully the login went much smoother this time, so it seemed that the internet – while still glacially slow – was at least functioning.

As her inbox loaded, Olivia audibly sighed. Still no emails from him.

She opened a new draft.

Aaron. I don't know what's going on or why you're not contacting me. I'm praying that you're OK and nothing bad has happened. But if you're reading this somewhere, then you have to know: I'm scared. I keep seeing danger everywhere, jumping at shadows – I even thought the guy who was hanging around outside the restaurant in Ushuaia was on the boat. All I need is some reassurance from you that things are OK. That we're OK.

Your Livi xx

Then she knew it was time to get in touch with someone else.

Tricia.

The last time they spoke properly had been the day she'd found out she'd failed her final actuarial exam, a couple of weeks before the Yennin auction.

Results day was always huge at Pendle, and ordinarily Olivia would be excited. The results got posted at five p.m., the entire office gathering around a single computer screen – normally Tricia's, as she was impartial, being one of the admin team as opposed to an actuarial candidate.

Tricia would have the list of exams printed out, marked with who had taken what. Then she'd load up the results and announce the pass/fails out loud to the whole office – to cheers or boos. Once all the results were given, they'd go out as a company to a nearby bar and celebrate – or commiserate – with each other.

This time, when Tricia had reached the page for Olivia's exam, there'd been a hushed silence. Everyone knew this was the final pass she needed before she would be a fully qualified actuary. She hadn't failed one yet, making her somewhat of a unicorn of the actuarial world, where the pass rates for each exam hovered at around thirty per cent.

Her luck – and her manic workload – had caught up with her. She hadn't just failed the exam – she'd bombed it.

Tricia had moved on quickly, but not quickly enough.

Olivia had disappeared to the bathrooms. She'd sat down on the closed toilet seat, her head in her hands. When she sat up again, in her palm was a clump of her auburn hair. She stared at it in disbelief.

There was a knock on the bathroom stall door. 'You OK in there?' came Trish's voice.

'Fine,' she replied too loudly. She dumped the hair in the toilet and flushed it, making a show of pulling toilet paper from the roll.

When she exited the stall, Tricia was still standing there, waiting for her with her arms crossed.

'I'm going home,' said Olivia.

'Hang on. We don't have to go to the bar if you don't want to. But we could go somewhere else, just the two of us? Have a nice cocktail and catch up?' Tricia played with the bracelets around her wrists. 'I've been meaning to ask you about something . . .'

'I really don't have time. Aaron will be waiting for me.'

'Please, Liv – it won't take long.'

'Sorry.'

But she barred the door with her hands. 'Look, I'm worried about you. I think you need to speak to someone.'

'I fail one exam and you think I've lost it? Thanks for the vote of confidence.'

'If it was just about one exam, I wouldn't be saying this. You know it. You have to get some help before it's too late. I've been reading about burnout and exhaustion. You've taken on so much recently. Side projects for Pierre Lavaud, helping out Aaron, and I saw the latest bill come in for your mum. I think you need to slow down . . .'

'You've been looking at my post?'

'You left it open on the kitchen counter . . .'

'So you saw that, know the pressure I'm under, and your advice is to slow down? Oh, please – do inform our landlord that I won't be able to make rent this month because you advised me to take it easy.'

'That's not fair.'

'You know what's not fair? The fact that I have to wait months until I can take that exam again and make part-ner. Months I don't have.'

'Talk to Lisa. There must be a way for you to regain some balance. Or maybe Aaron can help?'

'Not all of us pin our hopes and dreams on landing a sugar daddy,' Olivia snapped.

'Fine. See if I care.' Tricia turned and walked out of the bathroom, but not before Olivia saw the hurt in her eyes.

Olivia ran cold water over her wrists, waiting for tears to come. Waiting for some emotion to hit. She and Trish had never fought like that before.

But she felt nothing.

Feeling something would mean acknowledging how precarious the Jenga blocks of her life had become. Her career, on top of her qualification, on top of her relationship, on top of his work, on top of her friendships, on top of her mum – all of it threatening to come tumbling down if she stared too hard at the gaps appearing in the foundation: her health, both mental and physical.

Burnout.

Obviously Tricia had seen the signs long before she'd been willing to admit it to herself.

Their relationship hadn't recovered from that fight. Even when Olivia had finally got signed off from Pendle, she rarely heard from Tricia – except for those occasional links to burnout-recovery articles. She'd moved out of their shared apartment into Aaron's place and Tricia had blocked her on social media.

That had felt like the end.

Now Olivia wished she'd tried to reconcile. Maybe it wasn't too late? Tricia spent eight hours a day in front of her computer, and many more on her phone. She at least could be relied upon to reply quickly. She felt a flash of guilt at using her friend to test whether her emails were getting through. But it wasn't only that.

Hey Trish – I know it's been a long time. Too long, and I'm really sorry about that. I want you to know that I'm feeling much more myself again, and I owe a lot of that to you.

I'd suggest meeting up for a coffee, but you'll never guess where I am. On a boat to Antarctica! It's pretty remarkable. There's a cute guide here that you'd be interested in. When we get back to proper Wi-Fi, I'll send you a photo. Tell me how you've been! I miss you.

OJC x

Email sent, she tried to search her emails for her last communication with Aaron about the Pioneer deal. But the screen froze, the connection faltering.

Olivia took that as a sign. She logged off, stood up from the desk and stretched. She glanced up at a clock ticking above the door. It was still early, only nine a.m. She'd give it until three p.m. to hear back from Aaron. The countdown was on.

Annalise was still typing away on her computer, and Olivia walked around to look at the shelves behind her. Annalise slammed her laptop screen shut. 'Do you mind?'

Olivia blinked, taken aback. 'I was just looking at the books. But is your connection still working? Mine failed.'

'It is.'

'OK. I'm going to try again.'

She edged back around to her computer, logging in and opening her email one more time.

To her surprise, a new message did appear in her inbox. The timestamp showed it had been sent about fifteen minutes before.

It was from Aaron.

Her heart pounded as she opened it.

Dear Olivia,

I'm so sorry I missed the departure time. I've been scrambling to arrange a helicopter to come and join the ship, which is why I haven't been in touch before, but I haven't been able to get a flight.

I know this is a complete disaster, but I don't want you to worry about me. Have fun. Go on the excursions. Look after the art for me. I know you can do it.

I'll see you on the dock when you return.

Love, Aaron

Relief flooded her system. 'Oh, thank God for that,' she said, leaning back in her chair and running her hands through her hair.

'What's happened?' asked Annalise.

'It's Aaron. He's been in touch finally. Finally! He's OK.' She took another look at the email, reaching out and touching the screen with her finger, as if she could connect to him that way. She double-checked the email address that it came from, still unable to believe that it was him. But it was. She wouldn't have to go to the captain after all.

Only there was something about the email that bothered her. She read it again.

Dear Olivia . . .

But she gave herself a shake. He was OK. Then she felt heat creep into her cheeks. Why had it taken him so long? She clicked on the button to reply, but when she tried to type anything, the cursor moved in an infuriating circle. Then the connection cut out altogether.

She took a deep breath, worried she might be tempted to break the keyboard otherwise. 'I think I need some air. You coming?' she asked Annalise.

'Later.'

Olivia shrugged, then walked out of the library and towards the bow of the ship, where some crew members were serving coffee. The wind was still strong but no longer so aggressive, and while the waves were big, the ship was managing to cut a path through the water without too much disruption.

She picked up a cup, drinking it black. She spotted Patty and Janine, but she still needed a moment to herself. As the realization that Aaron was OK settled, she felt another emotion replace the relief. Anger. *Have fun. Go on the excursions*, he'd written. Have fun? How dare he? How could he do this to her? How could he abandon her, leave her hanging for an entire day, all alone on an expedition ship to Antarctica? She'd been so worried that something terrible had happened to him.

Now that she knew he was fine? There was no excuse for him to have missed the departure.

Then Olivia heard a noise that made her heart skip a beat. The belly-deep thwack of helicopter blades. She ran to the railings, leaning out to try to see where the helicopter was coming from. Had Aaron managed to find a way to her after all now that the weather was clearer? Was the email a decoy to surprise her? She searched the sky, but in among the clouds she could see no sign of it.

Then a gust of wind hit her, and she finally saw the heli. But it wasn't arriving.

It was leaving.

14

Olivia watched the helicopter as it circled the ship, then flew off – presumably in the direction of Ushuaia. Her heart sank as it disappeared from view.

Her last opportunity to get off the ship was well and truly gone.

She jumped as someone put a hand on her back. It was Patty. She, Janine and Annalise were together now. 'I wonder what happened?' she asked.

'They use the chopper for medical emergencies,' Olivia replied. 'Elisabet told me that.'

'Probably one of the old people on board. Hope they had life insurance.' Annalise shrugged, then headed inside to the dining room without waiting to see if the other three would follow.

'That's terrible,' said Patty. 'Imagine if you'd paid all that money to come all this way to Antarctica and had to be airlifted back home after one terrible night at sea. Olivia, what's wrong?'

Only seeing Patty's look of concern made Olivia realize how shocked she was. 'Oh my God. I just realized. I wasn't the only one in the medical bay last night. I overheard the doctors talking about someone else. They were discussing whether to use the helicopter or not. I guess things got so bad, they had to.'

'Did they say why?' Janine's eyes opened wide.

'All I could hear was snippets.' She didn't want to share

her paranoia with the two other women, but they were both staring at her so intently, she caved. 'Someone said the word "poison" but when I questioned Doctor Ranjeed, he clarified they were talking about food poisoning.'

'Common enough ailment on a cruise ship,' said Patty. Her grey curls shook when she shivered. 'But bad enough to warrant an airlift? I've only ever heard of that for cardiac distress or head trauma. Maybe a badly broken limb.'

Janine raised her eyebrows at Patty, who shrugged. 'I've helped a lot of my clients with insurance issues. Happens more than you think on board a cruise ship. Come on. Let's go get some breakfast. Despite all this talk of poison and illness, I'm famished. Plus, Annalise tells me you heard from your boyfriend? You must be so happy! I want to hear all about it.'

Olivia's stomach growled too. She never thought clearly on an empty stomach. Food had been something else she'd neglected when she'd been in the worst stages of burnout.

She knew all too well it wasn't possible to run on fumes. She nodded, and Patty took her arm, drawing her inside. She kept thinking about the helicopter. She had to find out what happened.

The dining room was jam-packed and noisy with excited chatter. A chef was frying bacon and eggs to order, the buffet laden with cereals, juices and freshly baked pastries.

She scoured the options with her plate in hand, piling up a stack of pancakes drenched in maple syrup, whipped cream and fresh fruit. There was a decent-looking coffee machine too, so she made herself another extra-strong cup. She needed it.

Cutler entered the dining room, and Olivia watched him as she waited for her espresso to drip into the cup. He was with Robert, one of the VIPs from the dinner in Ushuaia. Then he caught her eye, and to her surprise, made a beeline straight for her. Robert followed close behind.

'Olivia! I looked for you yesterday but couldn't find you. What's this about Aaron not being on board?'

Olivia gripped her coffee mug. She knew this conversation had been coming but she had hoped to find him in a more private environment. Behind him, Robert was frowning. But maybe this was better. Get the word out faster.

'I'm afraid he was called away on urgent business in Ushuaia.'

'More urgent than this? I find that hard to believe.'

'But that's why he made sure I was here in his place. Stefan is perfectly qualified to answer any questions about the art, and I can talk through the financials of the investment. I'm part of the Hunt Advisory as well.'

Cutler nodded. 'See, Rob? What did I tell you? There's no need to worry. You're in very capable hands here.'

'You have to forgive me for being worried,' said Robert. 'This art investing is all new to me, but your man Aaron knows how to talk a good game. Without him here . . .'

'I can tell you anything you need to know,' said Olivia. 'Why don't we talk about it a bit more over dinner? I'd be happy to share with you some of the benefits of buying on board this trip.'

'Let's do it,' said Rob. Behind him, Cutler caught Olivia's eye and nodded.

She waited till Cutler had moved Robert towards the buffet before breathing a sigh of relief.

The others were still choosing their breakfast options, so Olivia picked an empty table in the middle of the room, far from any of the windows.

'How you going? Seen your first iceberg yet?' The voice made Olivia jump. It was Liam, the expedition leader. She quickly swallowed her mouthful of pancake, dabbing at the corner of her lips with her napkin in case there was maple syrup there. His objective attractiveness made her self-conscious.

'Yes, I did. I thought it was another ship at first.'

'That's going to be the first of many.' He slid into the chair next to her and began shovelling scrambled eggs into his mouth. She watched him carefully, but he didn't seem to display any caginess. He didn't look like someone who had been told a passenger had been poisoned, anyway. He was the only one wearing short sleeves – even though the dining-room temperature was plenty warm enough, almost everyone else was layered up in their thermals in preparation for time spent outdoors. The hair on his forearms was dark against his tanned skin.

'How does the captain navigate through them?' she asked.

'We're not on the *Titanic* with a lazy watchman; don't worry!'

Olivia almost choked into her coffee at Liam's words, her mind immediately leaping to her dad. She covered her mouth, trying to supress the sudden jolt of fear and guilt she felt in her stomach.

'Captain Enzo has decades of experience in icy waters.

He also has an open-bridge policy, so you could head up there and ask him yourself.'

'I went up there yesterday,' she said, grateful her voice wasn't shaking. She needed to change the subject. 'Hey, do you know why the helicopter left this morning?'

'Medical evac, I assume.'

'Something bad?' She held her breath, waiting for the answer.

Liam shrugged. 'I'm just an excursion guide; we don't get briefed on that sort of thing unless we were directly involved. Speaking of, though – your head OK?' He frowned. 'I was worried about you last night.'

'Much better now, thank you.'

'Glad to hear it. Want you fit for the kayaking tomorrow.'

'Kayaking?'

'I'm the guide. Your name is down on my list for the excursions – kayaking and the outdoor camping.'

'Oh, that sounds fun! Can I join?' Janine sat down opposite Liam.

'Hmm, last time I looked there was a bit of a waiting list. I'll see if I can pull some strings.' He winked at Janine, who blushed. 'Do either of you have any experience?'

'Not me,' said Janine. 'But I'm a quick learner.'

'No problem, we can teach you everything you need to know. What about you, Olivia?' He nudged her shoulder, which made her tense.

'Dad, seriously, do I have to?' In a blink, she was back at Loch Lomond, the mist rising on the calm waters. This time, it was a good memory of her father. Even in midsummer, he used to make her dress in a full wetsuit, because the Scottish weather could turn from sunny to *dreich* at any moment. He'd taught her how to roll in the water if anything happened to them, and made her do it every time they went out.

'No,' he had laughed. 'I trust you on the water. I just think there's no better start to the day than with a good old wet exit.'

'So you tricked me!' She'd splashed water at him with her oar.

He was better at it, and soon they were both drenched but laughing their heads off, all their teeth showing. 'Paddle ready?' he'd ask, and she'd check herself over before tapping her helmet, giving him the OK. 'Let's dive in.'

She didn't think those skills had left her. Like the other things her dad had taught her – how to tie a bowline, navigate with a compass, start a fire with flint – she felt them in the foundations of her being. She might have tried to bury them under a mountain of maths and statistics, turned away from adventurous activities to keep the promise to her mother, but those skills remained. Part of her DNA.

'I have a little,' she replied, realizing she hadn't answered Liam's question. 'But that was before . . .' She drifted off, not knowing how to explain how her relationship to the water had changed. 'I don't know how I'll handle a kayak on my own.'

Liam nodded. 'I'm sure we can refresh any gaps in your knowledge. And you won't be alone. Most of you will be in double kayaks.'

She took a deep breath. The thought terrified her. But there was more at stake here than her own fear. It was her future. There was her promise to Stefan, to entertain the art clients by going on the excursions. Aaron had told her to enjoy herself. 'OK, I'll try it.'

'Mega. Don't worry, I'll take good care of you. Both of you.'

Olivia grimaced. She wasn't so certain. She decided to change the subject. 'So, excursion leader in Antarctica? What a job! Have you been on this ship long?'

'Since the start of the season, which makes this my fourth cruise? I lose track, honestly. I spent last summer guiding white-water rafting trips down the Salt River in Colorado and then was supposed to start a ski patrol job in Banff when I got the call that this random Antarctica job I applied for had been approved. Never thought I'd be spending my winters on the water too . . . but down here it's summer. Reminds me of home.'

'Wow – so where is home?'

'New Zealand. Queenstown. Always knew I was going to spend my life searching out rad adventures. This is definitely up there with the most incredible. Every expedition brings its own new challenges. A whole new set of people. A whole new set of weather conditions. And generally a whole lotta new ice.'

'Sounds interesting!' said Olivia.

In truth, it sounded inconceivable. The transience of his life was totally antithetical to how she lived. The instability. Never knowing where your next pay cheque was coming from. She couldn't live like that. After studying maths at uni, she'd chosen the most stable career she could with her degree. Regular pay cheques, regular pay rises. That was the goal.

Liam's life, chasing the sun – or the snow – sounded

123

idyllic in its own way, but it also meant never feeling secure. Never making ties or building any sort of home. Where did he store all his stuff? She thought of her piles of textbooks, her hundreds of scented candles, her favourite charity shop knick-knacks. Her home was her sanctuary, the place she could shut the rest of the world out. Even her coffee maker she considered to be a prized possession.

Liam wouldn't be able to keep much more than he could carry on his own back – unless he had family willing to store his belongings. Olivia wasn't sure that she could live like that. She needed a comfort zone.

'Have you ever been to New Zealand?' Liam asked Olivia.

But Olivia's attention had been caught by something else. A woman in a bright blue crew fleece had entered the dining room, making a beeline for the captain. Her blond hair was tied back in a braid that was fraying at the edges, dishevelled. Straining to hear, Olivia couldn't make out the words, not exactly. But mostly because the woman was speaking with a very strong Slavic accent.

If anyone knew why the med evac had been called, it would be the doctor who'd been in the other room.

15

She mumbled an explanation to Liam and Janine about needing the toilet before running out of the dining room.

'Hey, excuse me!' Olivia called out.

The woman hesitated for a moment – Olivia was sure that she had heard her – just the way that she had tilted her ear in her direction. And in the quickness of her steps as she picked up speed.

'No, wait, please . . .' Olivia followed her down the stairs, speeding up to catch her along the hallway.

The woman stopped at a 'CREW ONLY' door and was fumbling around for her pass. It gave Olivia an opportunity. Just enough.

'Excuse me, are you a doctor?' Olivia said. 'I was wondering if you could help me with my scrape from last night? I think my Steri-Strip came off.'

Her name badge read 'Dr Tove', and Olivia felt vindicated in her chase. The doctor looked pale, the skin under her eyes a sickly blue-green, as if she'd been awake all night.

Dr Tove gave Olivia's forehead a cursory glance. 'You're fine.'

'Well, maybe you can ask Doctor Ranjeed . . .'

'He's pretty fucking busy right now,' the woman snapped.

Olivia blinked back her shock but didn't say anything, searching the woman's face. The doctor's eyes caught something behind Olivia. She turned to see Elisabet walking behind with one eyebrow raised in their direction.

The doctor rubbed her brows with her fingers. 'I . . . I'm sorry. I apologize. I overreacted. I shouldn't have sworn at you – it's been a long night and I haven't had my rest yet. You know how it is. Bad Drake crossing and the medical staff are up all night, as if we don't get seasick too.' She put her hand protectively over her stomach.

'Oh, gosh, I completely understand,' said Olivia. 'That's why I wanted to talk to the doctor from last night, but when I saw you I thought maybe you could help? But that's so selfish of me. You go ahead and get your rest. I think I have some plasters back in my cabin.'

'No, no. I will help you. Let's go and take a look.'

They walked in silence down the stairs to the medical bay. Olivia's heart was beating so hard, she felt sure the doctor could hear it too. She hadn't thought through what she was going to ask, or why she had chased after the doctor, interrupting her much-needed rest.

Once they were inside, Olivia sat back on the bed. She had more of an opportunity to take it in now. There were rows of locked cabinets, packed with bottles of pills, bandages and boxes of face masks and gloves. A defibrillator was strapped to the wall, along with oxygen and an external pacemaker. They seemed pretty well equipped to handle most on-board crises.

But poison?

She had to find out.

Dr Tove came up and shone a small torch into her eyes. She asked Olivia to follow her finger, checked her reactions – the same checks that Dr Ranjeed had done.

'No signs of concussion. That's good. You haven't been sick at all?'

'Just nauseous but that started before my fall, so I think that was genuinely related to the storm – not my head.'

'Good. OK. Your wound looks as if it might bleed still, so I'll put another strip on. More painkillers – I can give you that. I've got a stronger anti-emetic as well that you can try for when the seas get rough.'

Dr Tove got up and went to one of the cabinets, sorting through the myriad pill bottles. Olivia swallowed, staring at the door to the next room.

'So was it an unusually rough crossing for injuries?' Olivia asked.

The doctor's shoulders stiffened beneath her fleece jumper. 'What do you mean?'

'The helicopter. We watched it take off this morning.'

'Oh yes. But I'm afraid I can't discuss the medical condition of other patients.'

Olivia needed to press if she was going to get to anything resembling the truth. 'What about the poisoning?'

Dr Tove shut the medicine cabinet door quietly, then turned. Her features were blank – her clinical professionalism taking over. Olivia recognized that expression. It was the same one she'd had on her face when the market crashed, and she'd been forced to explain to her client why their investments were worth half what they had been the day before.

Cool. Calm. Collected. Nothing wrong. Or at least – it's all in hand. 'I don't know what you are talking about.'

'I heard you talking last night. Dr Ranjeed confirmed it with me after.'

Her blank expression waivered. She was tired – no,

more than that, exhausted, her body quivering with it. Olivia almost felt guilty taking advantage. 'He was the one who told me it was poison,' Olivia reiterated.

'He shouldn't have said that,' said the doctor after a moment's pause. 'Not until we know the full results of the autopsies.'

Olivia's breath hitched, though she tried her best to keep her expression neutral. *Autopsies.* That meant . . . Her mouth went dry. 'You seemed pretty sure last night. If someone has been poisoned, are we in danger?'

'No,' the doctor said sharply. 'We believe they brought the substance on themselves – they had a champagne bottle in their cabin but our ship doesn't carry that brand. If I had to guess, it was a party drug overdose gone wrong, but until we get the results back, we won't know for sure. Cabin sixteen has been quarantined. You have my assurance.' She stepped forward and applied the bandage to Olivia's forehead. 'All done. I'm afraid I really have to go now. There are other patients on board that I need to check up on.'

'Wait, did you say cabin sixteen?' asked Olivia.

'Goodbye, Miss Campbell.' Dr Tove ushered her out and shut the door in her face.

Christa and Jay. The honeymooners. She hadn't seen them at breakfast. The doctor's words continued to spin in Olivia's mind, so much that she had to take a seat on the carpeted floor.

Some*one* hadn't been poisoned.

Two people had. The couple from cabin sixteen. The cabin she and Aaron had been assigned. She'd seen a bottle of champagne in there before she'd switched.

And now they were both dead.

16

Three bells chimed from the loudspeaker. There seemed to be no end to the announcements they were expected to listen to.

Olivia's head was spinning. She thought of the champagne, the bottle wrapped in opaque pink foil. Her favourite brand. Maybe Jay and Christa had thought someone had left it as a gift for their honeymoon.

It had been intended for her and Aaron.

She needed to tell him. Ask him if he had any idea what might be happening.

'Greetings, everyone!' It was the chirpy voice of their cruise director Elisabet. Olivia could hardly focus enough to hear. 'Following on from the captain's announcement earlier this morning, we're going to do your kit testing, disinfecting and briefings so that we face no delays once we reach our first anchor. In your cabins you'll find your assignments. If you're part of the kayaking or camping groups, please head to the mudroom now for your briefing.'

Olivia picked herself up off the floor. She had to get to the library. If this was deliberate, then . . .

A door opened at the end of the hallway, a few feet from where she was standing. 'All right, keener?' Liam popped his head out of the room and grinned at her.

Olivia blinked. 'I'm sorry?'

'You're the first to arrive. You were looking for the mudroom, right? For the briefing.'

'But . . .'

'It's mandatory, so you might as well come in.'

Still, Olivia hesitated. But it didn't look like she had much of a choice. Besides, if she was with Liam and the rest of the kayaking group, she wouldn't be in any immediate danger. She nodded and followed Liam into the room.

Black-rubber matting covered the mudroom floor, and it bounced as she walked over it. All around the perimeter of the room were low wooden benches with pegs above, like an old-fashioned locker room. A shelf stacked with pairs of mid-calf-length black wellington boots was at the far end, along with rows of kayaking paddles.

She walked over to the paddles, running a finger down a plastic stem. Could she do it? Paddle in the polar water? It had been years.

The next person to walk in was a tall Black woman with a cap over her braided hair. Her name tag read 'Melissa'. Even though it was chilly in the room, her crew jacket was wrapped around her waist. Her arms were bare, showing off well-muscled shoulders. She would be strong with a paddle.

'All right, Liam?'

'Decided to show up finally, did you? We need to get these drysuits sorted by size.'

'My orientation with Elisabet overran,' the woman replied curtly, getting down to work by wiping down each drysuit as she arranged them in order.

Olivia waited along the back wall as other passengers began to filter in. She looked out for Janine but couldn't see her. Cutler and his family came next, along with more of the VIP guests she'd met at dinner. It seemed like they were participating in all the excursions, getting the full service treatment. Naturally Robert was there – he had been bragging about his experience, and she was certain he'd never miss an opportunity to show off his outdoor skills. But Greg and Tariq – the art critic and curator – didn't exactly seem like the type to relish physical exertion. Greg especially was eyeing the drysuits with wary scepticism. She was conscious these were some of the people she needed to schmooze, but for the moment she hung back, watching.

The room gradually filled, until there were about twenty of them standing, shivering in the chilly room. The final couple to enter the room included the man she thought she'd recognized the day before. Maxwell. Next to him was a tall, slim woman with jet-black hair tied up in a bun – his girlfriend presumably. They shook hands with Greg and Tariq, confirming her suspicion that Maxwell was the same man she'd seen back in the art gallery in London. It was too much of a coincidence otherwise. Finally Olivia spotted Janine standing off to one side.

Liam clapped his hands together. 'Welcome to all our extra-adventurous expeditioners. Let me tell ya, I've been doing this for several trips now and it never gets old. If you're out with us on the kayaks, you are gonna get up close and personal with the world's most wild and untamed landscape. This is nature as you've never seen it before. For those of you camping on the continent next week, you are in for a proper treat.'

'Sounds fantastic, Liam. Now how about you get us suited and booted? We want to be first out tomorrow.'

Of course it was Cutler who was taking the lead, most of the others nodding in agreement. Greg looked vaguely alarmed, whispering something in his partner's ear.

'You got it. If you check out the shelves around you, you should find your cabin number. Under that cabin number are your boots. Then come and see me or Melissa, here, and we'll get you sorted with a drysuit. Once we've figured out all the kit issues, we'll get you all to disinfect your boots, so they're ready for tomorrow morning. Keep. Them. Here. Anything that goes on shore needs to be vacuumed and disinfected, to make sure that we don't drag any of our rest-of-the-world contaminants on to the pristine peninsula. The rules are in place to keep us all safe.'

Olivia nodded. This felt comfortable to her. After all, her life was all about rules. She understood their importance. It was one of the reasons she loved the finance industry – there were regulations to abide by, lines people couldn't cross without serious repercussions. As a child, she'd watched her dad check, double-check and triple-check his equipment, running his hands over any ropes they might use for signs of fraying, making list upon list so he didn't forget a step. He'd ask her questions (she knew it was a quiz, but she didn't mind – she'd always thought that was where her love for a good exam came from) and she would dutifully answer. But for her dad, the meticulous process – the checks and balances – were the structure within which wild – but safe – adventure could take place. Some people felt rules were stifling. But because of him Olivia found them comforting.

But rules only kept you safe as long as everyone

obeyed them. She looked around at her fellow passengers. Would they all listen?

After she had chosen her kit and disinfected it, she set it all to one side in a cubby that had been marked for her.

'Excuse me, Olivia?'

'Yes?' She turned to see the familiar man standing behind her, along with the beautiful dark-haired woman, both smartly dressed in expensive merino wool layers.

'Maxwell Sadler. This is my girlfriend, Lucinda.' He extended his hand, and Olivia took it, and then Lucinda's. The woman had to be at least a decade – or maybe more – younger than him.

'Oh, it's very nice to meet you both.'

'And you. I've heard a *lot* about you.' He put a strong emphasis on *lot*, making Olivia blush. 'So is what Cutler tells me true? The Hunt Advisory man himself isn't here?'

'I'm afraid so. You'll have to settle for me. But I'm sure I can answer any questions—'

Maxwell tutted. 'Well, that's just typical. I was going to surprise him at your special dinner in Ushuaia, but our flight was delayed. Didn't get to the hotel until almost midnight. So did he see my name on the passenger list and run? Of course he didn't want to come and face the music.'

Olivia frowned. 'Face the music?'

'Your husband and I go back a long way. I knew him when the debtors were banging down the door and he was begging us to extend his credit. He never had much luck with an artist until Yennin. I know he's turned things around with that auction sale – he got lucky there. He was probably a day away from total bankruptcy. I hope he thanked whoever it was who introduced him to that French billionaire. Now he's just got to sustain it. I suppose Yennin's untimely death has helped too.'

'Max! Don't say things like that.' Lucinda slapped her partner's chest. 'Yennin's work is remarkable. His success has been a long time coming and it's a travesty he isn't alive to bask in all the praise.'

'On that I agree,' said Olivia.

'Lucy here is a big fan.' Maxwell pulled her towards him, and it looked like she winced just a bit, although maybe Olivia was imagining it. 'She was the one who convinced me to come on this cruise. I'm more the relax-on-a-hot-beach-in-Ibiza type than freeze-my-balls-off-in-Antarctica, but whatever Lucy wants, she gets.'

'As it should be,' Lucinda replied.

'This Yennin guy is a big deal back in her country. I tried to get Aaron to give me a good deal, but he said the only way to purchase a piece was to come on this cruise, so, here we are.'

'You're from Lithuania?' Olivia asked Lucinda.

'Yes,' she replied, although she glared at Maxwell.

'I've been once,' Olivia said. 'To Vilnius. It's a beautiful country.'

'Thank you. I miss it very much.'

'I've stolen her away,' said Maxwell. 'It cost me a premium berth on a luxury cruise but she's worth every penny.'

Olivia smiled, but she was worried about what Maxwell had said right at the beginning of their conversation. He was right: Aaron *had* left after seeing the passenger list. He'd lied about the Bertrand emergency. So was the list the trigger?

A day away from total bankruptcy.

She tried to remember how Aaron had been acting on the day of the auction. Had he been worried? Afraid? He'd been nervous, sure – but jitters on auction day were completely normal. And then, of course, there'd been Yennin's absence and the rumours flying around about the accident. That would've been enough to put anyone on edge. She hadn't been in the right headspace to notice either way. It had been her worst day too. She'd been moments away from – well, from a consequence of burnout that she couldn't have recovered from.

Then the auction had happened, and she'd been swept away into a new life.

She'd always been impressed – overwhelmed even – by Aaron's lifestyle, ever since they'd started dating. He spent money like it was water, never seeming to worry about price tags or budgets, and she knew how important it was for him, in his industry, to project the right image. It sounded like Maxwell was suggesting it was more than a projection. Instead, it was a total delusion. There was so much she didn't know. Hadn't been bothered to know. She'd just been a passenger in her own life.

She had to step up and take control.

'Max, that lecture we wanted to attend is about to start. Shall we make a move?'

'Of course.' He leaned over and kissed her cheek.

'I'll see you at our first kayaking excursion, if not before,' said Olivia, relieved the pair were leaving. She didn't like the way Maxwell was continuing to stare at her, a strange rictus grin on his face. She wanted to get back to the cabin, maybe look over the passenger list again.

But Maxwell blocked her exit, waiting for Lucinda to walk away. When she was out of view, he gripped Olivia's arm, his fingers digging into her bicep. She looked up at him in alarm, her eyes wide. 'So did he give it to you?'

'G-give me what?' Olivia stammered.

Maxwell snarled, releasing Olivia from his grip. 'When you hear from Aaron, you tell him he's ruined everything,' he hissed at her. 'And he still owes me.'

17

'Are you OK? That looked serious,' Janine asked Olivia after Maxwell stormed off. 'Want to talk about it?'

Olivia shook her head, but a shiver ran through her entire body. 'I'm going back to the library. I . . . I have to reply to Aaron.'

'That's a good idea actually. I'll come with you,' said Janine. 'I wanted to send an email to my parents anyway. They're probably desperate to hear from me.'

'Have you been travelling long then?' Olivia asked as they made their way back up the stairs from the mudroom.

'A few months. It's what I do – I travel and document my trips online.'

'Wow, this trip is full of either art aficionados or travel influencers. I'll introduce you to two others I met yesterday – but you might know them already.'

'Probably only by their handles,' Janine said with a laugh. 'I was thinking about doing a video on the art stuff on board. That might interest my followers. Is the artist himself on board too? I should do an interview.'

'Sadly not. He passed away a few months ago. But his legacy is in good hands with Aaron.'

'Such a shame he couldn't make it. Maybe I can interview you?'

'I doubt anyone will be that interested in what I have to say. But I can introduce you to the auctioneer, Stefan?' Olivia asked.

'Perfect! And I know it's not nice to be on your own, but at least we can stick together.'

'That would be great,' Olivia said. And she meant it. It was nice to have someone to talk to who wasn't directly connected to the art world.

When they arrived, they weren't the only ones inside. Annalise was reading in one of the armchairs, her legs up over the side.

'I wouldn't bother,' she said without looking up from her page. 'It took about twenty minutes just to open a search engine.'

'I have to try.' She cursed herself as she sat down at the laptop, while Janine browsed the bookshelves behind. She should have replied straight away, instead of playing a stupid game by making him wait. Her encounter with Maxwell had been terrifying. What could Aaron still owe the man?

But Annalise was right. Olivia burned through several minutes of internet time with nothing but a frustrating wheel under the cursor spinning around and around.

Eventually she gave up, slapping down the lid of the laptop.

'Told you.'

Olivia closed her eyes. 'Guess you did.' She sighed, then sat down in one of the chairs opposite Annalise. 'Reading anything good?'

'Still studying.'

'I've been studying what feels like my whole life, so I know how you feel.'

Annalise looked up. 'But you're not at university still, are you?'

'I'm working towards my actuarial qualification. So

even while I've been working, I've been taking exams. It's never-ending.'

'Oh wow. I looked into doing that but an average of seven years to qualify sounded like a nightmare. Do you like it?'

She bit her lip before replying. 'Hard to say. I kind of fell into it, being good at maths and needing a secure job. I'm sort of taking a leave of absence from that. I'm now helping my boyfriend with his art advisory.'

Annalise nodded. 'That sounds cool. Business is in my blood, especially the travel industry. I've worked for Pioneer for the past three years. Not quite as long as Patty, but still.'

'She's quite the force of nature.'

'I mean, she's literally spent her whole working life at Pioneer. She and her husband worked their butts off building the Toronto branch from the ground up. Poor guy. Who even uses travel agencies any more? Especially after Covid? I think a serious shake-up is coming. Take all the money Pioneer spent on this ship. Cutler ordered a total refit. Why?'

Olivia frowned. She knew why. Cutler was trying to sell the cruise ship arm of his business to a mystery buyer, for a large sum – the showcase was part of the package, something unique to draw passengers to the line. But Annalise didn't appear to know anything about it, and it wasn't Olivia's place to say.

Annalise continued. 'To be honest, I was kind of dreading coming on board. I don't exactly relish spend-ing this much time in close proximity to him.' Olivia wasn't sure who she was referring to, but there was a bitterness in her tone that made her wary to ask. Then

Annalise shrugged. 'Still, Patty is like my second mom. It's nice to be able to support her. And so far it's been cool.' She nodded out of the porthole, at the ice drifting past their window.

'Quite literally. Shame Patty couldn't bring her husband on this trip.'

At that, Annalise winced.

Olivia frowned. 'What did I say?'

'It's not really my place. It's still really raw and I don't think she's dealing with it that well. But her husband passed away a couple of months ago.'

'But the way she was talking about him made it seem like . . .'

'I know. Like I said – she's not doing well. Probably not great to bring it up.'

'Jesus. I had no idea,' said Olivia.

Annalise put her finger to her lips as Patty walked into the library.

'There you guys are! I've been looking for you.' Patty dropped into one of the armchairs, as Janine perched against one of the computer tables. She looked closely at Olivia's forehead. 'I see you got your bandage replaced. Did you find out why they needed the chopper?' Patty leaned forward, her eyes sparkling with curiosity.

'We're not all about to catch some terrible variant of norovirus, are we?' muttered Annalise.

Olivia hesitated. She didn't want to become the source of a rumour that could spread throughout the ship, seeding panic. But she didn't want to lie to her cabin-mates either. She glanced around her. They were the only ones in the room; there was no one to overhear. 'No, it wasn't food poisoning. But I do know it was two people affected. The honeymooners. They were flown back to Ushuaia so the cause of their . . . illness could be investigated.'

Patty's expression became more sombre. 'Oh dear. I hope they're OK. Christa was such a sweetheart.'

'At least they dealt with it quickly,' said Annalise. 'It would be a PR nightmare if there was an outbreak of some virus onboard. Remember the "poop cruise", Patty?'

She grimaced. 'How could I forget?'

'I studied that whole incident for my dissertation.'

'So they're OK? They just needed medical assistance?' asked Janine.

Olivia didn't trust herself to say anything, so she just nodded.

'Well, lucky for them that it happened so early, while there was a chance of rescue. The further south we get, that would become impossible,' said Patty.

Rescue. Olivia didn't want to correct Patty. You couldn't rescue people who were already dead.

'I wonder what happened?' Annalise mused.

'They think maybe the couple brought something on board themselves that they ingested,' said Olivia.

'Like drugs? God, some people,' muttered Patty. 'She didn't seem like the type but you never know these days. If anyone was going to bring drugs on board, I would have expected one of those rich art types. Am I right, Olivia?'

'Think the cops will get involved?' asked Annalise.

She skirted around Patty's question and only answered Annalise. 'No idea. I guess it will depend whether the Argentinian authorities have jurisdiction in these waters.'

141

'I'm sure the doctors back in Ushuaia can help.' Patty reached over to pat Olivia's knee. 'Don't be too worried. I mean, maybe that's why they were so insistent on being together? You never know.'

'Oh my God, what was that?' Annalise dropped her book, ran to the window, then to the door to the outside deck.

The tone of her voice made Olivia's heart rate speed up, fearing the worst – someone overboard, an iceberg too close to the ship.

She followed, the others not far behind. She pushed through the heavy double doors, the wind blowing her hair back off her face. Annalise was leaning out over the railing, up on her tiptoes. Olivia rushed over, grabbing the back of her shirt.

'Don't—' she cried out.

'Look!' said Annalise, her finger pointing out into the depths of the dark grey waves. Olivia swallowed, following the line. She could see nothing but a froth of white cresting at the top of each wave.

Just as she was about to turn away, Annalise grabbed her arm. 'There,' she whispered.

And, right at that moment, a penguin leaped from the wave, like it had been shot from a cannon.

It was so unexpected, so novel, that she laughed. They continued to watch the waves, delighted shrieks punctuating every time another penguin performed an acrobatic manoeuvre.

The deck doors opened behind them, making them all jump. 'Liam, you scared us!' said Patty.

The expedition leader shrugged in apology, then turned his gaze to Olivia. 'The captain is asking for you.'

18

The bridge was calmer now, with only a skeleton crew manning the controls along with the captain. Olivia knocked on the door, hoping that she looked more at ease than she felt. She gripped her fists at her sides to stop them from shaking as the captain invited her in.

'Ah, Miss Campbell – thank you for coming.'

'Is everything OK?' she blurted out.

'Please, let's talk in my office.' He ushered her into a small room at the back of the bridge. The shelves behind were stacked with books, maps and manuals. He shut the door behind Olivia. 'Have you heard from your husband?'

'Boyfriend. We're not married. Actually, yes, I did receive an email finally this morning. He'd been trying to arrange a helicopter but hasn't been able to . . .'

The captain nodded, rubbing at his chin. 'That is good that you have had word, and I'm sorry we weren't able to facilitate that connection. But I've asked you here as I have been asked to pass a private message on to you. It was from a –' he looked down at a note on his desk – 'Monsieur Pierre Lavaud?'

Olivia blinked. It was the last name that she had been expecting. Her old client from Pendle, the billionaire who had set her on the path to meeting Aaron. She'd only met him a handful of times – mostly in the context of her actuarial work, and once at the Yennin art auction, after he'd spent a record-breaking amount of money on *nemiga*. What was he doing contacting her in Antarctica?

She sucked in her lower lip. Maybe *this* had been the work emergency that Aaron had been spooked by. If Pierre was having trouble contacting Aaron, maybe she would be his next port of call.

'Yes, I know him,' she replied, trying to keep her voice steady.

'Here.' The captain handed over an envelope.

She slipped her finger under the lip of the envelope and tore it open. There was a printed message inside.

OJC

He'd used her initials; it was how she signed off emails at Pendle.

I've been trying to get in touch with Aaron but cannot reach him. I have received some concerning news and I want to make sure you and he are both safe.

PL

Olivia stared at the note, reading it several times. But she only ended up with more questions. *Concerning news?*

And why wasn't Aaron responding to Pierre? It was unlike him to ignore his most important customer. Dread filled her belly, so overwhelming she had to steady herself against the captain's desk.

'Everything OK?' he asked.

Olivia shook her head. 'Can I get a message back to Pierre?'

'He contacted the ship via our satellite radio. That is highly unusual. But we try not to use that for passenger messages, especially if they are not urgent. I realize our internet signal has been intermittent, but our engineer is working on it and the email will be up and running shortly. Please, try to enjoy yourself on this cruise.'

Olivia frowned. Enjoy herself? That seemed like the last thing she'd be able to do. 'What about this line? About wanting me to be safe?'

'If you want, I can introduce you to our head of security, Pedro, but I can assure you, you are perfectly safe on board.'

'What about the deaths yesterday?' she asked, annoyed by the captain's patronizing tone.

The captain's expression changed immediately, his eyes losing all their previous warmth. 'Who have you been talking to?' he asked gruffly.

'I was in the medical bay at the same time as the couple,' she said, taken aback by his tone. 'The doctors couldn't hide it from me. They were too worried.'

'And have you told anyone on board?'

'No,' she said quickly. 'But have there been any updates? Are the police involved?'

'I'm not at liberty to discuss this with you. What I can say is there is no need for all these questions. The couple involved are recovering in hospital in Ushuaia.'

'So they're not dead? There's no autopsy?'

'No. I hope that puts your mind at rest.'

Was there something warning in his tone? Olivia couldn't quite tell. 'There is one more thing . . .'

'Yes?' He was moving towards the door, obviously ready to usher her out as quickly as possible.

'That night, I saw someone exiting their cabin. Cabin sixteen. I was on my way to the medical centre to get seasickness medication. It was a member of the crew. I described him to Liam – he said it sounded like his roommate.'

The captain nodded. 'Ah, right. And then you hit your head?'

'Yes . . . but I didn't tell you that, did I?'

'I am informed of every incident that happens on board my ship. It just took me a few moments to piece it together. That crew member had been sent in to fetch the couple's passports in preparation for the helicopter flight.' He leaned forward. 'Olivia, I know this is a difficult journey for you. You are uncomfortable on boats, your partner is not on board, the pressure of the showcase on your shoulders. I am sure you have much to worry about. But as far as your safety on this ship is concerned, rest assured, you are in good hands. Our barometer shows that we have clear skies and good weather ahead. Please, try to keep any dark thoughts from your mind. It won't do you any good on the ship – or on the shore.' At that, he spun on his heels and walked out of the office. There couldn't have been a clearer dismissal, and yet she felt distinctly uncomfortable.

Someone was lying to her. But she remembered the tone of Dr Tove's voice last night, the fear lacing her words. That wouldn't be so easy to fake. The captain was most likely trying to keep her from panicking.

She thought now that she'd heard from Aaron, she would be able to take the captain's advice and relax. But instead, the questions just kept on mounting. Between the dead honeymooners, Maxwell's threat and Pierre's warning . . .

Olivia had never felt more on edge.

19

The next morning, Olivia stood in the mudroom, watching through a porthole as the *Vigil* sailed to its first Antarctic mooring, off the coast of Barrientos Island. It wasn't the vast expanse of snow and ice that she had been expecting but instead something far more stark and inhospitable: a jagged shard of rock protruding from the dark water, rising up behind a semicircle of shingle beach. The sky had a distinctly grey pallor, the colour of smoke from a smouldering bonfire, haze hanging thick in the air. There was a strong smell wafting from the land too, thanks to the vast colony of gentoo penguins nesting and squawking in their hundreds.

She was already fully kitted out in her drysuit and kayaking jacket, breathing into the inner linings of her gloves. Beneath the suit, she had on multiple layers of clothing – thermal undergarments, another jumper and her thickest fleece-lined leggings. Tucked into her pocket, she carried a small digital camera, locked in a waterproof case.

'You look like you could use some of these,' said Liam. He handed her a set of handwarmers – the kind you shook to activate. She took them gratefully, stuffing them into the lining of her gloves.

'It's colder than I expected. And we're not even that far south yet.'

'Trust me, when you get out on the water, it will be

worth it. Never gets old for me, no matter how many times I lead a trip. Kayaking in the Southern Ocean!'

She offered a weak smile. 'It's pretty wild.'

'Normal to be nervous. You'll be in good hands with Melissa.'

'Yes, thank you for arranging that.'

'She's new, but she's good.'

'New? To kayaking?'

Liam laughed. 'No, not to kayaking! To the ship. This is her first voyage with the *Vigil* after the last guy got a better job offer at the last minute. Now I have to spend my time training as well as looking after all the pax.'

In truth, she was glad for the distraction of the kayaking. She'd spent most of the night waiting for the internet to connect, missing dinner. Eventually she had to give up in favour of a few hours' sleep, and even then she had tossed and turned.

Melissa came over to double-check her clothing was fully sealed, then went over her suit with the vacuum to pick up any lingering contaminants. 'Ready?' she asked.

'I think so.'

'Liam explained about your fear. I think it's really brave of you to be coming out again.'

'I . . . thank you,' said Olivia.

'But he also said that prior to that, you had some experience in a kayak? You've done a wet exit? You know how to sweep and draw?'

Olivia nodded.

'Then you're way ahead of most people here,' she said with a wink, making Olivia smile. She caught eyes with Janine, who had a grim look of determination on her face. As Melissa moved on to check the others, Olivia moved closer to Janine.

'Who are you kayaking with?' she asked.

'Some guy named Robert. I think he's a fancy businessman as he's been heads together with that CEO man this entire time.' She shivered. 'Apparently he's done this sort of thing a lot, but I still wish I was in the boat with you.'

'You're right, Robert is one of the VIP guests, but he's also pretty adventurous. I'm sure you'll be fine. I don't even know how I'll be out there.'

As she spoke, Cutler and Ingrid started arguing – about what, Olivia didn't care to listen. The husband and wife were sharing a boat too, but it didn't look like it was going to be a pleasant experience.

Melissa signalled for her to wade through a shallow pool of disinfectant and towards the outer door. Melissa banged on it twice before swinging it open – and there, in front of them, was the water. It pulsed, as if it had its own heartbeat, lapping against the ship, threatening to spill inside. It took Olivia's breath away just how *dark* it was; it was thick and almost tarry from her vantage point.

She wondered whether it really was wise to make this her first-ever sea-kayaking adventure since the incident. Then her dad's voice came to her. *Let's dive in.* It didn't matter what the activity was: going for a walk, a wild swim, a kayak – or a sail.

It was too late to back out now. She was tackling her fear head-on. She took a deep breath and lowered herself into the kayak Melissa had brought forward.

She settled into the cockpit, making sure the neoprene skirt was secured. It was amazing how quickly her body adapted back into the skills she'd honed as a teen, and the gentle bobbing of the boat relaxed her. Melissa clambered in behind. Once they were settled, she gave a thumbs up to Melissa, then slipped the blade of her paddle into the water and pushed away from the ship.

And, just like that, they were free.

Olivia closed her eyes and tried to control her breathing, which had become shallow and rapid. She gripped her paddle tightly. What was she doing? This was too much, too soon. Only Aaron understood the depths of what she had been through, and he wasn't here.

'Can you do a forward stroke for me?' Melissa asked from behind.

But Olivia was paralysed. She shook her head, not wanting to even open her eyes.

'Olivia? Forward stroke.' Her voice was firm but gentle.

She opened one eye a crack, then placed the blade in the water. Even though her hands were shaking, she pulled the blade towards her. Then she did the same on the other side. The kayak slid through the water.

'Good. Excellent. Now reverse stroke to slow us down – I have to make sure everyone is in the water first.'

Olivia did as she was told and was amazed to find that she had the control – she asked the kayak a question with her paddle, and it responded as she intended.

It was a small win, but it was a win all the same.

The *Vigil* towered over them. She could see every rivet and mark in the blue paintwork. Higher up, some passengers in red jackets looked down at them from the deck. One lifted her hand to wave – Patty, Olivia thought, although it was hard to tell from that angle.

'No sudden moves, but look to your left,' said Melissa in a low voice.

Olivia turned just in time to see a leopard seal poking its head above the steel surface of the water, Antarctica's sentinel. It stared them down with its glassy eyes before ducking back underneath, the glossy sheen of its body curling back beneath the waves.

She let out a long breath, then a laugh. 'It was so close!'

'Likely hunting penguins. But that's the benefit of being in the kayak. It's the closest you can get to the wildlife here.'

Seeing the seal had made her forget herself – and her fear – for a moment.

Another kayak pulled up alongside them, pushing the nose of their boat. Cutler was snapping pictures with an enormous telephoto lens.

'Where'd it go?' he demanded.

'Under the waves,' she replied. She looked over her shoulder at Melissa, who rolled her eyes but gave a small smile.

'If you let us take the lead, I'll show you some of our favourite wildlife-spotting places,' said Melissa. She waved her oar in the air, trying to get the attention of all the kayakers, signalling for them to follow her. With a few deliberate strokes, she steered the boat in front of Cutler and Ingrid.

'OK, Olivia, let's see what you can do. Traditionally I would steer from the back of the boat, but I have to keep an eye on the other passengers. So if you could steer us around the back of this island, that would be great.'

Olivia took a deep breath, trying to remember her skills. Even though Melissa said she was watching everyone else, she knew she was also being assessed – to check her competency levels, see how worried she needed to be about her fear taking over. She shifted in the seat, sitting upright and strong. Making sure her grip wasn't too firm on the paddles, she picked up the pace, turning her torso in time with the strokes. The kayak skimmed the surface like a water beetle, and she felt powerful, not afraid.

Away from the *Vigil*, the wildness of the continent was so much more apparent. On the ship, wrapped up warm, hot chocolate in hand, watching with feet firmly planted on the polished wooden deck, she felt detached from the landscape – like she was watching a super-high-definition movie. But out on the water, with the waves lapping the kayak's hull, freezing droplets splashing on her cheek as she raised her paddle, the cries of the birds overhead, knowing that leopard seals lurked under the waves – she was immersed. It felt very real.

'Great job,' said Melissa. 'You're a natural, even in these conditions. I don't often get to paddle with people with so much skill.'

Olivia blushed. 'I was lucky to be able to learn from my dad. How did you get into this?' she asked over her shoulder.

'I grew up near the water, but honestly my mum thought I was crazy to always want to be out either swimming or surfing. She ran a holiday let in Dorset, so I had the whole of the Jurassic Coast as my playground.'

'Oh, I've sailed around there. It's beautiful.'

'Seriously? I rarely meet anyone who's been there.

Anyway, then I took a summer job in teaching sailing and supervising watersports. But I wanted something wilder.'

'What does your mum think now?'

'That I'm still as mad as a hatter. But she sees how happy I am and she shuts up. I mean, she'd still prefer I was working as a nurse or something, but she lets it go for now.'

'Liam said you were new on the *Vigil*. What were you doing before?'

'Oh, this and that. Mostly private charters. OK, hang on, let's slow down the pace—'

There was a cry behind them, and both Olivia and Melissa put their paddles in the water, applying the brakes. Cutler appeared to be in the centre of the action again; this time, his kayak somehow seemed tangled with Janine and Robert's. They were close to a rocky promontory where two seals were lounging, and Cutler had his camera out.

Janine wasn't helping matters, her paddle was flailing around in the air, almost making contact with Ingrid's head. Her kayak was tilting dangerously, the nose caught underneath the other's.

Melissa was shouting at them to calm down, while also trying to signal Liam. Finally he spotted the issue, and in his nimble solo kayak he powered his way towards the kerfuffle.

Janine looked panicked, clawing at the skirt of the kayak, then at the thin ropes criss-crossing the hard plastic nose, as if she wanted to get out. The boat began to rock violently, and Olivia's heart leaped into her throat. She turned to Melissa. 'You have to help her!'

Melissa was already on the radio, asking for one of the Zodiacs – the big inflatable boats used to tender passengers from the ship to the mainland – to come to the rescue.

Olivia kept paddling until they were near enough for her to talk to Janine – but not close enough to get in the line of fire. 'Janine! Breathe for me; you're having a panic attack.' She tried to keep her voice calm.

Janine was gasping for breath, in between begging to get out of the kayak. It looked like she was trying to stand. Robert was red-faced from yelling at her – not the way to help.

Finally Liam reached them. He grabbed hold of their boat and took the paddle from Janine. He shoved Cutler and Ingrid's kayak away so that it was no longer attached to Janine and Robert's. When they were stable, the Zodiac pulled up alongside and Liam helped her out of the kayak and into the safety boat.

A whistle sounded, signalling them back to the *Vigil.* Their kayaking excursion was over.

'Let's make our way back, shall we?' said Melissa, her voice surprisingly even after all that action.

For her part, Olivia was breathing hard, sweat gluing strands of her hair to her forehead. But she nodded. She glanced over at Janine in the Zodiac, hugging her knees up to her chin.

She knew exactly how she felt.

20

'Janine, are you OK?'

Olivia caught up with her in the locker room and dropped down next to her on the bench.

'I don't know what happened,' she said. Her copper hair had gone frizzy from being stuffed into a woolly hat, and her complexion was still pale.

'I think you had a panic attack. I understand completely. I went through the same thing not that long ago.'

'What the hell were you doing, girl?'

They both looked up to see Cutler standing over them, Robert just behind him.

'Hang on a moment,' said Olivia.

'She almost got me killed out there,' said Robert. 'If she doesn't know what she's doing, she shouldn't be on the excursions.' His face was glowing red.

'Um, you were the one steering us!' Janine snapped back.

Olivia leaped to her feet. 'I think we should just take some space. Robert, it was Janine's first time in a kayak.'

Cutler looked as if he were about to explode. 'She had her phone out! That was the problem.'

Olivia shot him a warning glance. 'Janine won't put anything about the incident on her social media, will you?' She looked over her shoulder at Janine, who shook her head.

'Fine,' he said through gritted teeth. 'Come on, Rob,

let me buy you a drink. I made sure they had some top-shelf whisky on board.' The two of them stomped away in their heavy boots.

'What a jerk,' Olivia said, turning back to Janine.

'Isn't that one of your clients?'

Olivia shrugged. 'I can still say he's a jerk. You couldn't help it. It was scary out there.'

'I don't want to think about it any more.' She shivered.

Olivia frowned. 'Are you OK? We should get you warmed up.'

Liam overheard. 'We have a sauna just here. Perfect way to destress if you need it.'

Janine shook her head. 'I think I want to get out of here.' She turned to Olivia. 'What are you going to do now?'

'I'm all yours,' she said. 'What about seeing the gallery? I can give you a tour if you did want to film it. I can give you an exclusive I won't even give that other influencer.'

'That sounds brill. I did get some good footage out on the kayak, before all the drama. I'm sure I can piece something together about the excursions based on that. I'm not sure I'll make it out again. Plus, I'm excited to see what you're a part of on the ship.'

'And I get to see your work too.'

'Just don't judge – I'm still learning. I actually started out in digital marketing so I'm more used to the corporate side of social media. Then when I wanted to travel, it made sense for me to try to start my own thing. Help me pay for some of this.' She gestured to the ship.

'That's so impressive. Do you have a big following?'

Janine shrugged. 'In my niche, I do OK.'

'Sounds like false modesty.'

'When we get back, you can follow me and see for yourself.'

Olivia smiled. 'I will. I'm terrible at social media, though.'

'I doubt that. Your life seems kind of amazing from what I've heard. Art galleries and fancy trips . . . I'm sure you'd pick up a lot of followers.'

'It's the disconnect for me. I went through kind of a rough patch these past few months, but if you looked back over my social media, you wouldn't know anything was wrong. Sure there are some beautiful pictures. But I was too numb to feel anything, and no one understood because it looked like everything was perfect.'

'I can relate to that. Never let them see the cracks.'

'Even if those cracks are Grand Canyon deep,' muttered Olivia. 'Only my best friend saw through it. And I was too far gone to listen to her.'

On the way to the gallery, they passed a small gift shop with a vast array of Antarctica-branded ornaments, clothing and souvenirs. Tokens from the very bottom of the world. They stopped to browse, looking over penguin-themed magnets and bookmarks, along with books about Antarctica, postcards and notebooks.

She took a woolly hat to the nearest mirror, but then screamed and dropped it when she saw a face in the reflection, standing in the hallway outside the shop staring at her.

The crewman with the shaved head. Liam's roommate, who'd chased her until she'd fallen and cracked her head.

'What is it?' Janine asked.

Olivia spun around, but the crew member was gone.

157

She placed her hand over her racing heart. 'It's stupid.'

'No, tell me. A problem shared, and all that.'

'Really, it's nothing. I think it's being on the boat, without Aaron . . . I'm all jumpy and confused.'

Janine raised an eyebrow, leaving Olivia to fill the silence.

'OK, so I keep seeing this guy with a shaved head following me. It happened first when I was out to dinner with Aaron in Ushuaia. It looked like he was staring at us. And then I've seen him on board a couple of times . . . like right before I fell down the stairs. It sounds ridiculous, I know.'

'No, it sounds scary. But I bet it's just men with similar hairstyles.'

'I think you're exactly right. My mind is playing tricks on me.'

'Hey, I would never tell you not to trust your instincts. You never know. Obviously your gut is telling you something, so you might be right to keep your guard up.'

They moved on to the gallery. At the end of the long hallway, Stefan had hung an enormous painting – the original on board. Not *nemiga*, the painting she had fallen in love with, but another – *šviesa* – a burst of sunlight from behind a cloud, over a world covered in ice. Although the painting was essentially made up entirely of shades of white, it seemed to glow with inner light.

But she narrowed her eyes, staring at it as they walked closer. She felt the urge to turn to Aaron, as if he was standing beside her – he would know immediately what was wrong.

Before she could question it in her mind any further, there was a loud noise – a shout – from inside the gallery.

Janine and Olivia exchanged a look of concern, and Olivia picked up her pace.

'This is outrageous!' came a woman's voice.

'Please, calm down . . .' Olivia heard Stefan reply.

A woman came into view, her hands thrown high in the air. It took Olivia a moment, but she recognized her as Lucinda, Maxwell Sadler's girlfriend. 'Get away from me,' she snapped. 'You shouldn't be able to get away with this.'

She stormed out of the gallery.

'You go ahead,' Olivia said to Janine. 'I'd better make sure she's OK.'

'Sure?'

Olivia nodded, then walked back down the hallway in the direction Lucinda had gone. She didn't know exactly what she was going to say, but it was part of her responsibility to make sure the potential art buyers were happy, and Lucinda had looked anything but.

She worried she'd missed her, but then saw strands of long dark hair flying out on deck. She tugged on the heavy exterior doors and stepped out on to the balcony.

'Hey,' she said tentatively.

Lucinda looked up, then wiped her face. 'Oh, hello. Olivia, right?'

'Yes, that's right. I'm sorry, I couldn't help but overhear what went on in the gallery.'

'You're part of this, aren't you? This art auction business.'

Olivia nodded.

'Well, you should have a talk with that auctioneer.

That's not an original Yennin hanging at the far end of the gallery.'

'I'll discuss that with him, absolutely.'

'It's not right. After everything that Kostas went through in his life, he doesn't deserve to have his memory tarnished like that.'

'I understand.'

'I hope so. Or else it won't just be Stefan that I have a problem with.'

The wind picked up, the coldness of it stealing Olivia's breath away. Lucinda pulled her jacket closed and headed back inside.

Olivia waited a beat before she followed. Her instinct had been right. There was something wrong with the painting in the gallery. It wasn't an original, and she had to find out why.

21

When she returned to the gallery, Stefan was regaling Janine with his well-rehearsed spiel. 'This exhibition is exclusive to this ship, but it's going to be rolled out to the entire Pioneer cruise ship fleet. Yennin's art captures the beauty and magic of Antarctica far better than any photograph. He was obsessed with the polar regions, especially the light in these parts of the world. When we cross the Antarctic Circle and you see the midnight sun, you'll truly see why he is one of the few artists on the planet who has managed to capture the magic of the region. There's a dangerous edge to his artwork – wild and lawless, a bit like the continent itself. You might say he was trying to hide the darkness inside him with the explosions of light and snow in his painting. But eventually the darkness won.'

'Amazing,' cooed Janine. 'Are these all originals?'

'Oh no. The originals are worth far too much. His first work sold for millions. But these limited-edition prints have his original signature and they will only increase in value. What a story to tell your friends and family back home – that you bought a masterwork on board. After all, it's not as if he's producing any more.'

'I'm not sure I can afford any of it,' said Janine.

'Don't be so sure. We have some incredible deals on board for Yennin original sketches, also signed by the artist. Things that could become good investments.'

'Really?' She arched an eyebrow.

'Of course! At least you could come away with a post-card.' He led Janine down the gallery, and Olivia hung back to stare at *šviesa*. She took a step closer, unease growing in the pit of her stomach.

Once Stefan had given Janine the tour, he returned to the front while she continued to film some pieces to camera.

'Stefan, I thought this was supposed to be an original Yennin piece?'

'What do you mean?'

'You just told Janine we weren't selling any originals.'

The man coughed. 'Well, of course.'

She frowned. 'But isn't that the whole point of this showcase? I'm sure Aaron said—'

'Aaron emailed me and told me he'd changed his mind.' Stefan's tone hardened. 'I'm in charge of the sales decisions, and he agreed with me it was the right way forward.'

Olivia was alarmed. Why hadn't Aaron told her? It didn't make sense with what they had discussed prior to the cruise. Aaron had always talked about preserving Yennin's legacy, making sure to keep the value high.

It didn't feel right.

'Can I see that message?' she asked.

Stefan rolled his eyes. 'If you must.' He took her back to his office and turned on his computer. Olivia noted that the internet was just as slow for Stefan as it was in the library. When it connected, he called the email up on the screen. It seemed legitimate. Once again, she felt out of the loop. But maybe he had written to her too, while she'd been out kayaking.

'Do you mind if I check my inbox while I'm here?'

'Fine.'

She opened her Gmail but there were no new messages from Aaron. She chewed on her bottom lip, trying to hold back the swell of emotion rising in her chest. Why wouldn't he keep her informed?

She stood up from the computer. 'I've got some things to do. Would you mind telling Janine that I've gone back to the cabin?'

'Sure. And, Olivia, try to loosen up. Maybe drink some champagne.'

Olivia's eyes widened. 'What did you say?' Was that a threat? A reference to the champagne that had been meant for her and Aaron? But before she could question Stefan further, he had already walked off, back towards Janine.

She fled back to the cabin, glad to find it empty. She needed some time to think, to get her mind around what had happened over the past two days. Had it really only been that? It seemed like she'd be on the ship for a week.

She dragged out the suitcase and carefully folded her clothes away into the drawer that she had been assigned. She didn't need much – there wasn't great cause for dressing up on board, but she needed to find her best outfits to put together for drinks with the VIPs the following night – an evening earlier than planned since they made such good progress through the Drake Passage.

Her coats and fleeces she hung up in the wardrobe. She noticed Aaron's jacket was in her small day bag, somehow mixed in with her clothes from their last dinner in Ushuaia. She brought it close and breathed in his cologne. She ran her hand down the front, but there was no sign of the ring box any more – Aaron must have it with him. But as she straightened it to place it on a hanger, a piece of paper fluttered to the floor.

I know what you did. And I'm going to make you pay.

22

Olivia snatched up the note and balled it into Aaron's jacket pocket as she heard someone coming into the cabin.

It was Annalise. She stopped in her tracks when she caught sight of Olivia's face. 'You OK? You look like you've seen a ghost.'

'It's nothing.' Olivia hurried to put Aaron's coat on a hanger, then squeezed it into the tiny wardrobe next to her things. 'Just had a reminder of home as I was unpacking.'

'You're shaking.'

Olivia hadn't realized. Now that she was aware of it, she could sense her breathing tightening inside her chest, her vision squeezing at the edges.

Aaron was in trouble, and she couldn't help.

'I think . . .' But her mouth was so dry it took a moment for her to string the rest of the sentence together. 'I'm having a panic attack.'

Annalise moved into action swiftly, helping Olivia over to the bed and grabbing her a glass of water from the bathroom. Olivia lay back down on the mattress, trying to count her breaths until the feeling passed.

'Do you want to talk about it?' Annalise asked. 'Is it the boat thing?'

Olivia blinked. It made sense that Annalise thought that was the trigger. But she hadn't told the story of what had happened to her dad to anyone in a long time – even Aaron only knew the bones of it. Tricia knew everything, of course.

But maybe talking about it with a total stranger would help. Get it out in the open, so she didn't have to be scared of the memory any more. At the very least it would be a distraction from the note.

She sat up in the bed, sipping from the glass Annalise handed to her. 'It might be hard to believe, but I spent my entire childhood on the water.'

'Oh yeah?'

'My dad used to work as a yacht captain. Well, once I came along he didn't do it full-time but he'd made a few good connections and so was often trusted with moving people's boats from one port to the next – you know, from the Mediterranean in the summertime to the Caribbean in winter. Or from Australia up to the Pacific Islands. Whatever the owners wanted. He'd do the transitions solo, then Mum and I would fly out to meet him for a holiday on the boat for a week or two.'

'Honestly that sounds pretty idyllic.'

'It was, for a long time. And he taught me a lot about sailing, of course. We had our own little boat up on a loch in Scotland. By the time I was sixteen, he trusted me with handling myself in pretty much any situation on the boat. But then—' Her voice cut off with a choke. 'We were in the Caribbean, off the coast of St Lucia. We were on this really fancy yacht, just the three of us. It was called –' she hadn't said the name out loud since the night it had happened, even though she'd often seen it in her dreams – 'the *Clarissa*. We'd had an amazing time, and Dad was really starting to trust me. But Mum was

166

feeling under the weather and needed some rest. So he asked me to stand watch on our final night.'

She closed her eyes. The sound of the water lapping against the porthole took her right back to the moment.

That had been the only sound in the darkness during her watch. How she'd longed to put her headphones in and blast out some tunes, but that was against the rules of keeping watch. She needed all her senses sharp.

She leaned forward against the polished wooden railing, her eyes straining to spot any pinpricks of light on the horizon. But there was nothing. Even the sky was starless. She picked at a callous on the palm of her hand, newly raised following a few days at sea, pulling at ropes and tying knots.

The hard work showed on her hands. Earlier that day, she'd smiled about it. Now, digging into the callous with the sharp edge of her nail was the only thing keeping her awake.

Keep watch.

That's what her dad had asked of her. She knew the rules. It was her responsibility to alert him if she noticed a change in the wind, heard something out of the ordinary or spotted any lights at all. But it was almost midnight, and she'd been up for hours. She thought of her bunk downstairs, how she'd grown used to the gentle sway of the ocean rocking her to sleep. It was their last night at sea. Tomorrow they'd be back on land.

Her eyelids felt heavy, so she pinched herself harder.

But even the chill in the air couldn't keep her awake.

167

She sat back in her perch, tugging a heavy woollen blanket over her lap.

Keep watch.

She closed her eyes for just a moment.

Too close, a light winked into view. And she hadn't been awake to sound the alarm.

'In the night, we collided with another boat. A little speedboat but big enough to do some damage. I thought both my parents were asleep, tucked up in their bunks. But it turns out, Dad was up and getting ready to take over from me. He went overboard.

'It was all my fault.'

She was the reason he'd died. There was no getting away from it. After that, she'd vowed to stay away from boats forever, for the sake of her mum. And now the only reason she could break that vow, was because she'd basically lost her mum as well.

'Damn,' said Annalise. 'Your dad trusted you and . . .'

'And I ruined it. Haven't been on a boat since.'

She jumped as the ship blasted its horn, signalling that they were leaving their anchor at Barrientos Island, to head to the Antarctic Circle.

'You going to be OK?'

Olivia shook her head. Annalise stood up and headed into the bathroom.

Olivia lay back on the bed. In a way, it felt good to have told the story, if only because it put into perspective how she could change things this time. She'd been given the responsibility to look after the Hunt Advisory's first major deal.

The *Vigil* was not the *Clarissa*.

There were so many details of that time of her life

that she'd forgotten. Buried deep. But today she'd got in a kayak. She'd told someone the full story of what happened on the yacht that night. She could move forward.

She could keep watch.

Starting with the auction.

She made sure the next full day at sea was productive, since there were no kayaking excursions to go on, no land to visit. The internet was back up and running. She was disappointed not to have received anything new from Aaron, but she emailed him anyway, asking for a full list of instructions for what he wanted out of the showcase now he'd changed things with Stefan, and told him about the cryptic message from Pierre. She wrote to Pierre as well, to acknowledge that the captain had relayed his message to her.

She spent extra time going back over some of Aaron's emails to her from their relationship, scouring them for any clues as to what might be going on. But instead, she found herself drawn back into memories of the early stages of their relationship. How exciting, how lucky she had felt back then.

The first email from him was seven months ago. Seven months – in some ways it felt like they'd been together for years. But the truth was, things had moved fast. Way faster than she'd realized. That was another consequence of burnout. She'd allowed herself to be swept away on a wave of Aaron's charm and sophistication.

But was that such a bad thing? There was real affection and romance in his emails to her. *My darling Livi . . .*

She was allowed to have something go right in her life.

She opened up his final email to her again. There was

something strange about it. She narrowed her eyes at the screen, biting her bottom lip. When was the last time he'd called her 'Olivia'?

A message popped up on the screen. *TWO MINUTES OF INTERNET CONNECTION REMAINING. PURCHASE MORE?*

She rubbed at her eyes. It was almost time for her to get ready for the VIP drinks. She needed to have some time to prep. She logged out and closed the laptop.

She caught a glimpse of a large iceberg out of one of the library windows and shivered. They'd left the volcanic Aitcho chain of islands, of which Barrientos had been one, and were heading further south towards the Antarctic Circle. As they sailed, the icebergs were getting bigger. Each one seemed so dangerous, like some sort of mythological beast, able to take down a behemoth. But the *Vigil* was built for this environment, to cut through great swathes of sea ice. The icebergs wouldn't bother them – no matter what they might be hiding under the surface.

She stepped out on to one of the outer decks, wrapping her jacket close around her body. She needed some fresh air to clear her head. Her eyes followed each mountain of ice as they passed by. It was hard to keep her eyes from the wildlife that abounded too – the petrels that rode on the wind and the occasional penguin.

'Know what that's called?'

She turned around to see Liam coming through the open deck doors.

'Porpoising,' he continued. 'They do it to confuse predators. Zippy creatures, aren't they?'

'Amazing,' said Olivia.

171

'So . . . that was quite the morning on the kayaks yesterday, wasn't it? Hope your roommate is OK.'

'She was a little shaken up, that's all.'

'And how did your meeting go with the captain? I wanted to ask you about it before but it was all so hectic.'

'Oh, that. He had a message for me from the mainland.'

Liam nodded. He put his hands on the rail, his knuckles turning white as he leaned forward. 'Makes sense. That all? I know you were curious about the helicopter . . . I wondered if you'd asked about that.'

Olivia nodded. 'I did ask about it. Well, more specifically, about what happened to the two people who had been in my former cabin.'

'What did he say?'

'That I had nothing to worry about. Which is weird, because I'd spoken to the doctor who implied that they had . . . well, that there needed to be an autopsy.'

'Shit. Those people *died*? Ranj told you that?' Liam said, his words garbling together, his Kiwi accent getting stronger in his panic.

'Not Dr Ranjeed – Dr Tove. But shouldn't you know more than me?' Olivia folded her arms across her chest, confused by Liam's change of tone.

'Nah, they didn't brief us all – need to know and all that – just that the chopper was for a medical emergency.' He ran his hands through his hair, but it was more of a nervous twitch than a rakish gesture. 'She say what happened?'

'Poison. She mentioned their champagne bottle as a possible source, but I guess it's all got to be investigated.'

Liam clenched his jaw, a hard look in his eye. Suddenly

she was aware that she was all alone on the outer deck with Liam – someone much bigger and stronger than she was. The boat was moving at speed, the wind rushing past. If she went overboard, would anyone notice?

She took an involuntary step back. 'But I should be clear, the captain said they were recovering in Ushuaia.'

Liam frowned. 'Whoa, hang on a tick. So which is it? Are they dead or are they OK?'

'The doctor mentioned an autopsy. The captain said different. But I don't know. I'm just a passenger. You're the crew.'

'Yeah, well. This is a very important cruise and I'm sure whatever it was, Cap doesn't want to make a big scandal out of it.'

Olivia thought back to what Annalise had said, about all the money they'd invested in renovating the ship, how it was a keystone of the Pioneer relaunch. She could imagine the PR firestorm if it got out that people were dying on board, even if it wasn't the ship's fault.

'If you find anything else out, would you tell me?' he asked.

'Will you tell me?' she shot back.

'Blimey, yes. Yes, of course. I appreciate it, Olivia.' He reached out to touch her arm, but she stiffened.

'I have to go.' She turned, moving quickly towards the heavy metal door. She placed a hand on the handle, then looked back at Liam. 'I also told the captain about seeing your roommate that first night coming out of cabin sixteen. I don't know what he'll do with that information, but I wanted to let you know.'

She didn't wait to hear a reply. Instead, she hurried

down to the cabin. She had to get out of the jittery head-space Liam had put her in and prepare for the drinks.

Ingrid Hughes waved her over to her table, where she was sitting sipping a Martini with Cutler. Olivia handed her coat to Maria Elena, who had created a makeshift cloakroom in one corner of the bar, smoothed down her dress and plastered on a smile.

'Ready for this?' asked Cutler. He snapped his fingers at the young woman behind the bar, signalling for another round of drinks.

'It's such a shame that Aaron isn't here. I really liked him,' said Ingrid.

'Of course you did,' muttered Cutler. Then he perked up as two people walked into the room. 'Ah, Maxwell, come in. Good to see you. And Lucinda – looking gorgeous as always.' He shook Maxwell's hand and kissed Lucinda on each cheek. 'When are you going to make an honest woman of her, eh?' Cutler slapped Maxwell on the upper arm.

At the sight of Maxwell, Olivia stiffened. She could still feel his grip on her bicep, from when he had accosted her in the mudroom. But she knew she had to smooth things over with him, especially after her chat with Lucinda on deck – for the sake of the showcase. She didn't want to be the reason they missed out on a potential buyer. 'Mr Sadler, I wanted to apologize once again for Aaron's absence.'

Surrounded by people, the fierceness she'd seen from him earlier didn't return. 'Oh, there's no need. We've had our differences in the past. But he has nothing to worry about now.'

'He doesn't?'

He glanced sideways at Lucinda. She obviously wasn't aware Maxwell had threatened her last time. 'As far as I know, once the deal goes through to roll out Yennin's art to all the Pioneer cruise ships, that should clear all of Aaron's remaining debts. I hope you're not here to tell me that's not the case . . .'

Olivia shook her head. 'No, nothing like that at all. Everything is going smoothly with the deal.'

'That's excellent news. I've always liked Aaron. Being an art dealer is a risky business. You never know what's going to take off. Like I said, he got lucky. Or, you both did, I suppose is more accurate to say.'

When Lucinda was pulled away into a conversation with Ingrid, Maxwell leaned in close, so that no one else could hear. 'Things could have been pretty nasty otherwise.' He clinked his glass against Olivia's and drained it.

Olivia covered up a shiver by taking a long sip of her drink.

Delilah walked in next, chatting with the art critic Greg. They both looked chic: Delilah wore a flowy animal-print kaftan, her hair in waist-length braids, while Greg was dressed in a cream-silk shirt under a navy-wool blazer paired with tapered trousers.

Olivia took a couple of cocktails over to the pair.

'You're a doll, thank you,' said Delilah. 'Greg was just saying what a treat this is. To see where an artist's inspiration truly came from.'

'I'm glad you're enjoying yourselves,' replied Olivia.

'Yes, this art showcase concept is intriguing,' said Greg. 'A twist on the art auctions you normally come across at sea. I appreciate the focus on a single artist – it does allow the viewer to immerse themselves fully in the paintings. You met him, didn't you? Kostas Yennin?'

'Yes, in Vilnius,' said Olivia.

Lucinda joined them, having left Ingrid deep in conversation with Maxwell. 'That's quite the privilege,' she said. 'He was very private and secretive, along with the rest of his family. You are lucky that you got that chance, especially as no one ever will again.'

'I'll never forget it,' said Olivia, placing her hand over her heart. 'Delilah, Greg – please meet Lucinda. She's from Lithuania too, like our artist. Delilah is a fashion designer from Sydney and Greg—'

'I cover the art world for various publications. I did a profile on Yennin in *Vogue* last year. I know *all* about how private he was,' said Greg. 'After he died, my editor tried everything to get an interview with someone close to him – his sister or his girlfriend. Hell, even his social media manager. But no one would talk.'

'Girlfriend?' Delilah asked.

'Oh yes. I think he kept her hidden to keep up his elusive artist image, but she's been on the scene for years.'

Olivia nodded, trying to keep her expression neutral. But the conversation made her realize how little she really knew about Yennin.

'Or maybe it was her choice. Not one for the spotlight,' said Lucinda.

'What do you think he would make of this?' Delilah gestured around her.

'It doesn't seem very much like Kostas,' replied Lucinda.

'Did you know him too?' Olivia asked.

'I think it's every artist's dream,' interrupted Delilah.

'You know I was at the auction that night? I don't think I've ever been to a buzzier sale in my life. It's put all others to shame! That's why I couldn't miss out on this cruise. I'm not having the chance to own one stolen from me again.'

'You were the underbidder!' said Olivia.

'You forgot?' Delilah feigned horror. 'How is that possible?'

'I'm so sorry . . .'

She pushed her braids over her shoulder. 'Honestly, I think I'm owed some kind of consolation prize. I was bidding all that money and I didn't know a thing about his accident! I just loved his art.' She leaned in. 'I think Pierre was tipped off somehow. About Yennin's death. Maybe he's got an inside man. I mean, he practically tripled his investment in one night because of what happened. Still, at least I can buy one now. It's still early enough to catch him on the up and up. Right, Olivia?'

'Absolutely.'

'I'd rather he was alive,' said Lucinda, putting down her glass, still half full. 'Excuse me.' She turned to leave, but not before Olivia spotted the grimace on her face. The look of disgust.

Olivia debated going after her, but Delilah stopped her, her long fingernails digging into Olivia's forearm. 'Don't bother. Because of what happened, Yennin has what every artist wants.'

'What's that?' Olivia asked.

Delilah licked her lips. 'Immortality. You can't put a price on that. Isn't that right, Greg?'

He leaned in. 'Right. Although from what I heard, he was off his face on drugs. Not exactly an accident if you're driving in that condition. Someone should have given him the number of a good taxi service.'

'No!' Delilah clasped at her necklace. 'Olivia, is that true?'

Olivia swallowed. 'All I know is what the police said. That it was an accident.' That wasn't entirely true. The police knew he had been under the influence of MDMA and who knows what else. But she didn't want to repeat that to anyone – especially not a journalist and a potential buyer. She looked up as two other VIPs, Robert and Aida, walked into the room. 'Please excuse me while I greet our other guests.'

'Any more cocktails?' Delilah asked.

Olivia nodded. 'I'll have another round sent over.'

Instead of walking over to the Freedmans, Olivia went to the far corner of the bar, downing a glass of water as she attempted to compose herself. All the people she was supposed to schmooze were in this room, but she couldn't stop thinking about how much she wished Aaron was with her. She wasn't sure she was cut out for this kind of networking. She was shaken by the look she'd seen on Lucinda's face. She wished she could return to her cabin, to the friendly atmosphere of her cabinmates.

Anything not to continue to be reminded of the night that Yennin had died, and her part in it.

As far as she was concerned, the evening couldn't end fast enough.

24

When the next day dawned, it was clear that they had arrived in true Antarctica. Vast white cliffs rose out of deep blue water, towering above even the highest decks of the *Vigil*, making her seem like a toy boat bobbing in a bath.

The Aitcho Islands had been mere specks of dirt adrift in the ocean compared to what they were seeing now, sailing through the Gerlache Strait. She'd expected the change in landscape, having listened to a lecture after breakfast. The glaciologist on board, Dr Vance, had given his postponed talk about the varieties of ice they would encounter. Brash, pancake, bergy bits – all names for different types of sea ice. He told them to expect terminal moraines plunging into the water, to watch out for the glaciers sloughing ice like a second skin. These 'calvings', had changed in nature over the past decade, and with the increasing global temperature sometimes the continent shed chunks of ice as large as their ship. Over eighty per cent of the glaciers in Antarctica were in retreat, the calvings a far too regular occurrence. It sounded bloody terrifying but impossible to fathom; her mind couldn't wrap itself around the scale of the problem.

Everything felt foggy. Muddled. She hadn't slept well after the party, unease swirling in her stomach. In fact, she couldn't remember the last time she'd had a full night's sleep. It reminded her of the very worst points of her burnout. But tonight they were due to host the special showcase – on the evening they were going to cross the Antarctic Circle and see the midnight sun. At least there hadn't been any further direct attacks.

She focused on the view. It was spectacular. The sun made the water sparkle like multifaceted diamonds, the ice impossibly blue where it was scraped by the waves.

The captain had to be careful as he navigated through. The passage was surprisingly narrow, the cliffs – and the mountains behind – giving the place an intimate feel. Wildlife was still abundant here. It was no longer uncommon to see whale backs breach the surface, plumes of water from their blowholes misting in the air.

She was too cold now. It came on so quickly, even through her layers. The bright sunshine was deceptive, making it feel like she should be warm. Instead, she felt her fingers stiffening inside her thin gloves, the moisture on her eyelashes and the inside of her nostrils starting to crystallize. She moved back inside.

She remembered the hot drinks station in the Panorama lounge. Tea. Tea would be good.

The room was almost deserted; most people were eating lunch or resting in their cabins. She made herself a steaming cup of Earl Grey tea, loading it up with far more sugar than she would back at home. The coffee was tempting, especially combined with the lack of sleep, but she knew that too much caffeine would increase her jitters. She was on edge enough as it was.

She looked out of the enormous windows, scouring the waves, looking for more penguins – or maybe the tell-tale puff from a whale spout, but for the moment the water was quiet. But she knew the ocean was a living, breathing thing, with its own whims and desires. When they had crossed the Drake Passage, it was angry with them, wanting to punish. When they were kayaking, curiosity got the better of it, and creatures popped up to say hello. For now, it was shy, hiding rather than displaying its wonders. The ocean was an artist, shifting its canvas according to its mood.

She used to think it was the water that she was afraid of. It was the water that had taken her father. But the truth was, the ocean was too vast to be blamed. Maybe one day she could even look at it and feel calm again.

She wished that for her mother too. Neither of them had been the same since they had stopped going to the water. It was hard that something that had been so integral to their lives, so core to their beloved family memories, had become so cursed.

She couldn't help but wonder if her mum could visit the ocean again and feel a sense of peace . . . Maybe that would help. Something that had once been a source of pain could become a place of relaxation, maybe even fun, again. It might be possible.

She thought back to the last time she'd visited her mum. It had been after Yennin's death. After she'd been forced to leave Pendle. She'd delayed visiting the care home, avoiding the conversation about how she would continue to afford it without a job. But then Aaron had invited her to join the Hunt Advisory, starting with the trip to Antarctica. She had been worried her wariness of boats would prevent her from agreeing, but it was a solution to her money issues.

From Victoria she'd taken the train out to the care

home in Oxted where her mother was living. The home was on a leafy street, with views out to the rolling green North Downs countryside.

She was led through to the sunny conservatory. It was too cold to sit outside on one of the benches – her preference – but with fairy lights and tinsel dressed over the windows, it was cheery enough.

She walked over to the wicker sofa, where her mum was taking tea. She bent over her, giving her a kiss on each cheek. 'You look nice today,' she said.

'Did you bring my iced buns?' Her mum looked up, her brown eyes lacking any recognition.

Olivia's heart sank. She'd hoped that it would be a good day.

'It's me, Olivia, remember? How are you, Mum?'

Her mum grimaced.

'I wanted to let you know that I'm taking some time off work. I think I might go on holiday – maybe even to Antarctica. Do you remember how dad always said he wanted to take us there? I could visit his final continent.'

'It's too dark and cold.'

Olivia laughed. 'It's not too dark. It's their summertime now. And as for the cold, I've got lots of layers.'

Her mum shivered. 'I don't like the dark. It's dark in here.' She pulled her shawl closer around her body. 'I want to go to my room.'

Paige – her mum's main caregiver – scurried over. Olivia felt a tiny pang of disappointment at the way her mum lit up once she saw Paige's face. But at least she was in good hands. 'It's all right, Mrs Campbell. Maybe time for a rest?'

'Yes, dear. That sounds good.' She stood up. She

looked down at Olivia still sitting in the armchair, searching her face.

Olivia sat up a little straighter, sensing something in her mother's eyes – recognition maybe?

'You don't look well. Can I suggest sleep and a good eye cream?'

Olivia sighed. She slumped back on the sofa.

'Miss Campbell?'

She sat up. Paige was looking at her expectantly. 'Yes?'

'I couldn't help but hear about your trip. Sounds fun.'

'I'll visit again as soon as I'm home . . .'

'Don't feel bad. I'm glad you visited. But you may want to see something – your mum had been excited to show you.' Paige crooked her finger, and Olivia got up to follow her, intrigued. They walked down a long hallway, and Olivia did a double take at the art on the walls. She recognized the places depicted in the paintings. The landscapes of Scotland, the vast and gloomy mountains, the mist rising up over the lochs. And sailing scenes. Yachts gliding over choppy waters, boats lined up in busy harbours.

'These . . .' She couldn't finish her sentence. Her eye hooked on the signature in the corner. *L Campbell.* Laura Campbell. Her mum.

'She's a talented woman. There's even more in here,' said Paige, gesturing towards a small room filled with canvases, some finished, some in progress.

Olivia walked around the room, rendered speechless by her mother's skill.

One final painting caught her eye. It rested on an easel, covered by a piece of white fabric. She lifted it and took a step back, her fingers to her mouth. She recognized the loch in the Trossachs and the season – a wintry morning, the trees such a deep green they looked nearly black, and the grey mountains behind dotted with snow. In the water was a small sailing boat, two figures perched either side of the tiller. One in a bright pink hat. Her dad's woolly hat, his favourite. He'd bought it for her but she refused to wear it for being too girly. So he wore it every time he went sailing after that, with or without her.

She reached out and touched the dab of pink paint. A patch of vibrancy. That's the role her dad had played in their lives. Their bright spot. The world without him had been far more monotone.

Her mum had never spoken about those times. She'd locked those memories up tight, shutting down any mention of sailing with a fierce bark. Now she looked blank whenever Olivia mentioned his name. But here was proof that her mother still thought about him.

There was love in the way she had depicted the yachts too. Mum had always loved those holidays. Did she dream about being out on the water again? Of them working together as a family, whether that was sailing out on the loch or in some of the most magnificent ports in the world? Did she want to be out in the sun, under a big wide sky, chasing the wind?

Olivia didn't know. But it didn't look as if she still clung on to the same resentment that had plagued her for the past fifteen years.

In that moment, she decided she would go to Antarctica with Aaron. She was going to face the water again.

She rushed back to her mother's room, but when she got there, she was already asleep. She gave her a kiss, stroking her hair back off her forehead. 'I'll be back soon. I promise.'

The sound of a fist banging against a table broke her daydreaming; she was no longer on her own. She unfolded her legs, leaning forward so she could see around the corner of the U-shaped room, to where the noise was coming from. She was surprised to see Cutler and Annalise at one of the tables, although Annalise jumped up.

'You can't be serious?'

'Keep your voice down,' said Cutler.

'So it was all for nothing. You lied to me!'

'I didn't lie. I did it for you. For us.' He reached out and touched her arm, with a tenderness that shocked Olivia. She pulled away, not wanting to see any more, feeling second-hand shame.

Now it became clearer why Annalise had been chosen for the trip. It seemed a bit bold to bring your mistress on a cruise with your family. She could hear an even louder kerfuffle, and she caught sight of Annalise's dark hair as she stormed past the lounge windows.

Olivia felt a pull in her stomach, as she looked at how stricken her roommate appeared. She put down her tea and followed her out of the lounge. But it wasn't Annalise she saw. It was Patty. She was on the outer deck, staring at the passing waves.

'Everything OK?'

'Oh, just being an old softie. Missing Karl. He would have loved to be here.'

She moved to stand next to her, leaning against the railing. 'Annalise told me about your husband. I'm very sorry.'

Patty sniffed. 'He worked too hard. To the bone. He didn't go to the doctor until it was too late – the cancer was too widespread. He's in a better place now, but our Pioneer branch was his baby. It's been a tough few years but Cutler won't let us go adrift; I'm sure of it. Look at the job he's done with this cruise ship. I'm already looking forward to selling it to my clients.'

It won't be owned by Pioneer then, thought Olivia. But then maybe that didn't matter. If that's what was needed to save his company and keep the branches open, then he was doing the right thing.

Olivia thought about what she'd just seen between Annalise and Cutler. Whether Cutler always did the right thing, she wasn't so sure.

'You seem to be feeling better,' Patty said. 'Got more colour in your cheeks now.'

'Yes, it's easy to forget your troubles when you're surrounded by scenes like this.' She gestured at the landscape slipping past the ship.

Patty nodded. 'And no more scares, like after that first night?'

She shook her head. 'Nothing so far. I wish Aaron would email again.'

'He probably doesn't want to interrupt your fun.'

'Hmm.' But he wasn't the only one. Pierre hadn't replied, nor Tricia. Pierre, perhaps that was to be expected. But Trish? Had she really messed up their friendship so badly that Tricia wouldn't even reply to an email from the bottom of the world?

She'd gone to the library to try again that morning.

Trish – I am very sorry for what happened between us before I left. I was in a very dark place, but it's no excuse for how I behaved.

I didn't tell you in my last email, but Aaron isn't here with me. He missed the boat somehow – he got caught up in a work emergency. Don't worry, we will have words when I get off the ship.

The internet is apparently going to get even worse the further south we get – we should be crossing the Antarctic Circle tomorrow.

I miss you. Truly. And once again – I'm sorry.

OJC xx

She had tried to picture what Tricia would be doing when she received the email. It would have been late afternoon UK time, and Trish had probably come in from her lunch break, tackling tasks for Lisa. Trish always worked hard but maintained a balance. Why had that been so hard for Olivia?

She'd been so afraid of letting go of her vice-like grip on her career. Qualifying, making partner, gaining financial independence – it had loomed so large in her life that giving it up had seemed impossible. She realized now how ridiculous it had been to hold on so tightly to a workload and job that had almost killed her.

The truth was, she hated letting people down. Her boss, her clients. She absolutely couldn't let her mum down. She'd flaked on responsibility once in her life, and the consequence had been catastrophic.

Patty tapped her hand. 'I bet there's an issue with the internet. Even Annalise said she was having trouble. I don't know how all those young influencer types cope with it,' said Patty. 'Even Janine looked like she was so frazzled she couldn't get online to post; I had to buy her a drink just to calm her down! But you must be excited for the showcase and midnight sun party tonight?'

Olivia nodded. 'I am. It's my one big responsibility on board. Then maybe I can sit back and enjoy, well . . .' She threw her arm out, gesturing at the view.

'Precisely. You deserve it.'

'And you'll be there too, right? I don't want my cabin-mates to miss out.'

'You bet. I'm not one to turn down some free drink, even if I know nothing about art. Still, I bet this is going to be a story to tell my clients. I wouldn't miss it for the world.'

25

'Stefan, I really don't think Aaron meant for these pieces to be on sale too.'

She was back in the gallery a few hours before the showcase was due to start. She'd been shocked by the change in the layout since she'd last visited – she'd been so busy that she hadn't come by every day to check on the actual gallery itself. But instead of the elegantly sparse display of his artwork, meant to create the biggest impact for each piece, the selection adorning the walls had multiplied.

In particular, she was standing in front of a crowded display of Yennin's pencil drawings and drafts, pieces she knew Art Aboard had requested, but had no idea had been actually printed. Beneath was a selection of postcards, unsigned prints and even a T-shirt with his artwork on it.

'I told you, Aaron and I agreed that I am in charge of what goes on sale. This is my area of expertise, remember?' Stefan brushed past her, straightening one of the prints that had been knocked off its line.

Yennin sketch, read the plaque. *Official reproduction.*

She narrowed her eyes, looking at it. 'I know, but it's very clear that Aaron wanted to roll these pieces out slowly – to start out with a buzzy, exclusive art auction to keep the value high. If we suddenly sell everything . . .'

'If he has an issue, he can take it up with me afterwards.

You're the numbers woman, right? If you're unhappy with the numbers at the end, then you can talk to me.'

'Rest assured, I will,' said Olivia. She glanced down at her watch. She needed to go and get changed. She wasn't going to have any luck changing Stefan's mind. She'd just have to explain things to Aaron when they got back to Ushuaia – and hope that he understood her position. 'I'll be back just before six o'clock, in time for the guests' arrival.'

'See that you are.'

She rolled her eyes at Stefan's back as she left the gallery, a flush of heat prickling the back of her neck. But she could hardly argue with Aaron's emails. She only wished he'd bothered to reply to her with a proper explanation. *Dear Olivia* . . . maybe it was a brush-off, and his affections had turned.

She couldn't think about it now. She just had to do the best job she could, and deal with the consequences when they returned to Ushuaia.

Back in her cabin, she changed into one of the few nice outfits that she had brought with her: a simple burgundy lace dress from LK Bennett, which she wore with her only pair of heels. She put on a bit more make-up too, lining her eyes and swiping on lipstick. With all the people filming, this was going to be a major PR event, and she wanted to represent the advisory well.

Janine walked into the cabin. 'You look nice. Going to the auction?'

'I'll head up there in a few minutes. You're coming too, right?'

'Wouldn't miss it,' said Janine.

Patty came in next, her cheeks flushed from being outside. 'Ooh, I didn't realize we had to dress fancy.'

'You don't. I'm sure most people will be in their fleeces.'

'So I'm OK like this?' she said, gesturing to her thermal leggings and Antarctica-branded hoodie that she'd bought from the gift shop.

'Of course. I'm glad you're all coming. I'm going to need the moral support.'

'I'm sure Janine will give it a fabulous review, won't you, darling? We might not be able to afford any of the art, but at least we can drink some free wine.' She leaned in and lowered her voice. 'It *is* free, right?'

Olivia laughed. 'Yes.'

'The drunker people get, the more they spend, is that the idea?' Annalise muttered. 'Capitalism at its finest.'

'Come on, don't be sour,' said Patty, throwing her arm around her colleague. 'We've got to sell this to all the VIPs who want to go on a Pioneer cruise. This could be the bestseller for our branch next year, don't you think?'

'If you really think that, then you're more naive than I thought. There are bigger forces at play here and, trust me, they don't give a fuck about anyone but themselves.'

'Annalise!' Patty gasped. 'What are you talking about?'

'I gotta go,' she muttered, shrugging off Patty's arm and leaving the cabin.

'But the auction?' Patty moved to go after her.

'I'd give her some space,' said Olivia. She also felt thrown by Annalise's words – and the fact that her eyes had flicked to Olivia's when she talked about bigger forces.

There was real anger in that look.

Patty, Janine and Olivia walked up to the gallery together, and when they arrived there was already a healthy buzz of excitement. There were chairs set up facing a small stage at the front of the room, a traditional gavel and plinth for Stefan as auctioneer set off to one side. It didn't feel like the modern, sophisticated auction she'd attended in London, but, once again, she had to trust Stefan to know his audience.

As the guests began to arrive, Olivia felt – once again – underdressed. Delilah wore a full-length glittering ball gown, Aida and Lucinda were in designer cocktail dresses, and both Robert and Maxwell were wearing tuxedos, incongruous with the bright sunlight pouring through the windows. Even the crew had made an effort. Elisabet had styled her hair in an elaborate updo, the captain was resplendent in his full uniform and even Liam seemed to have dug out a blazer from somewhere.

As the guests entered, they were offered a small white paddle with their cabin number on it.

'So who are these people?' Janine leaned in to ask.

'The big clients are the ones over there, standing with Cutler and Ingrid,' said Olivia. 'We're expecting purchases from Robert and Aida Freedman – they're a business power couple from the US. Then Delilah Constance, the one with the bottle-blond wig, is an Australian fashion designer, she's a known collector and was the underbidder at the London auction. Greg Akbas is an art critic – he writes exhibition reviews for *The Times*, *Vogue* and the BBC, and has a popular podcast. His husband Tariq is a curator and tastemaker. There was a rumour that when he bought a sculpture from this unknown artist in Seattle, the artist's next piece was commissioned by MOMA. Then there's Maxwell Sadler and his girlfriend Lucinda. He's an investment banker – one of Aaron's backers. And Lucinda is a big fan of

Yennin's artwork – she's also from Lithuania, like the artist.'

Janine's eyes widened. 'Maxwell Sadler?'

'You know him?' Olivia asked, surprised.

'Not really. I read an article about him once. He's the one who intimidated you down in the mudroom, right? Scary guy.'

'Tell me about it,' said Olivia. She dreaded to think what kind of trouble Aaron had been in. *Might still be in*, she reminded herself. Maxwell obviously felt Aaron still owed him something. But she couldn't think of that now. This evening had to go well. Everything else could wait.

Cutler waved her over. 'Olivia! Nice to see you. Looking lovely as ever.' Olivia turned to introduce Janine, but she had escaped into the crowd to find Patty and Annalise.

A gong sounded at the front of the room. The auction was beginning. Stefan clapped his hands and stepped on to the stage.

She took a spot towards the back, not wanting to take a seat from someone who might be purchasing. She could see a glow from several phones, their cameras trained on Stefan.

'Welcome, one and all, to this very special early-evening event. Yes, later on we will have the Antarctic crossing and witness a midnight sun. But, right now, you have the chance to experience something almost equally as rare. The chance to claim a piece of history – an artist, cut down in his prime, whose value is only going to soar as his legend grows around the world.

'Take his social media presence. Maybe this is ironic, seeing as the man himself rarely posted, but his Instagram grew to over a million followers in the wake of his death, before it dramatically went dark a few days later. Collectors, curators and art lovers alike have been clamouring to get the chance to own a piece of Yennin ever since. But the only way to do it – except by being a billionaire, of course,' he added with a wink, 'is to buy one right here in this very room. Before he died, he authorized a very limited run of prints, which he personally signed, and which only we have access to. There will never be an opportunity to buy one of these again. This is Banksy at the ground floor. And with the restricted audience here, you're sure to land a bargain.

'But enough from me. I know you've all been dying to see the main event.'

He stepped back, and with a flourish opened the white curtain to reveal the first exclusive, limited-edition signed print that would be on sale – *šviesa*.

The audience made appreciative oohs and aahs. It wasn't the original, but in that moment no one seemed to mind.

'Let's open the bidding, shall we?'

Olivia felt like she was holding her breath throughout the bidding. But maybe Stefan was on to something. There was a lot of interest – the bids flooded in from all corners of the room. Delilah was keenest – and the price rose to over $100,000.

Stefan's hammer finally fell at a cool quarter million to Delilah. There was a loud round of applause and she flushed with happiness, and Cutler sent over more champagne in her honour.

The success of the first sale had warmed the crowd, and as Stefan ran through the rest of the items the bidding racked up for every lot. Sure, it wasn't the same heart-pounding tension as during the auction that had seen *nemiga* sell for over three million. But if this was something that could happen regularly, on multiple ships, several times a year . . .

Maybe Stefan did know what he was on about. And could it be such a bad thing to get Yennin's name out there, to get more people to see his masterpieces? They had lost something in ditching the multimedia component, the experience of viewing his art was less immersive, but it was still stunning. Especially with the Antarctic landscape floating past the window – the place that had so inspired him during his travels – bringing a special magic to the auction.

Her head was swimming. She needed to tell Aaron. Let him know what a success it was. She checked her bag for her phone so she could take a photo of the showcase in action, but realized she'd left it charging in the cabin.

She snuck out of the back as the auction wound down and nipped back to their room, amazed how the layout of the ship had become second nature, the hallways much more familiar. But as she approached the cabin, she frowned. Something wasn't right. Their door was ajar, light from their porthole spilling into the hallway. She thought the others were still in the gallery.

Her heart hammered as she spotted the hem of one of her shirts poking out from beneath the door. A shirt that had been folded neatly in a drawer when she'd left the room.

She placed her palm on the door and pushed.

Then she gasped.

Their cabin had been ransacked.

26

Someone shouted her name. She was standing in the doorway, paralysed. Was the perpetrator still in the room? Maybe behind the door of the bathroom?

She didn't want to step inside to find out.

'Olivia!'

Finally she turned to see Patty and Janine at the end of the hallway. Patty was the one who'd called her name. 'What's wrong?' she asked. 'We saw you leave the auction and thought we'd make sure everything was—'

But Olivia didn't need to answer. The pair caught up and could see the destruction for themselves.

'Oh my God.' Patty's hand flew to her mouth.

'Shit,' said Janine. 'Has anything been taken?'

Olivia finally managed to speak. 'I don't know. I just found it like this. I haven't been inside yet. I don't even know if there's someone still in there . . .'

Patty took hold of Olivia's hand. 'We'll go in together. Come on. Janine, go tell a crew member. We need them to know we've been robbed.'

'Sure,' said Janine, jogging back up the hallway.

Olivia leaned down and picked up her shirt from the floor, the one that was blocking the door, and hugged it to her chest. Patty took the lead, firmly stepping through. 'Hello? Anyone here?'

There was no answer, and she walked further in, picking her way across the strewn clothes, books and electronics.

'It's not so bad,' she said, scooping some clothes off the floor. 'Olivia, is this yours?' She held up a cardigan.

'Yes,' she replied, surveying the wreckage. Cupboard doors were thrown open and her suitcase lay on its side, the lining ripped and torn. Her mattress was on its side, the pillow on the ground. 'It's . . . all mine.'

'Oh, honey.' Patty put her arm around Olivia's back, squeezing her tight. 'I'm so sorry. I think you're right.'

'Holy shit.' Annalise appeared in their doorway. She leaped straight to her bed, but her laptop was under her pillow where she had left it. She breathed a sigh of relief. She turned to Olivia. 'Anything missing?'

'I don't know.' With the help of the other women, she picked up all the clothes from the floor, folding them into the drawers. Still in the pocket of her suitcase, she found her passport. 'I just don't get it. It's not like I have anything expensive with me.'

'You're a major part of the art showcase. You heard the money being thrown around out there. Maybe someone assumed you'd have something valuable?' Patty said.

'Well, they were wrong.'

Olivia hugged her arms around her waist. In her cabin, with these three women who had become her friends, she had felt safe. But now that space had been violated.

There was a knock on their cabin door that made them all jump.

'Didn't mean to scare you, ladies. What's happened?' It was Liam.

'He was the first crew member that I came across,' said Janine by way of explanation.

197

'I radioed Elisabet too, so she'll be here soon. The auction just ended,' said Liam. 'Blimey. What a mess.'

'Yes. And it looks like it was just my stuff that's been taken.'

'Oh, really?' asked Janine.

'Double-check for yourself, but I think so.'

'Anything missing?' Liam asked.

Olivia shook her head. 'I don't know what they were looking for.' In the wardrobe, all her jackets and zip-up fleeces were crumpled on the floor. She picked up Aaron's coat and placed it back on the hanger. Her eyes pricked with tears when she saw the sleeve was torn.

'Honey, sit down. You've had a shock.' Patty took Olivia's hand and guided her to the bed.

'Who would do this? I had nothing worth stealing.'

'What about your camera? Your phone?' asked Liam.

'Accounted for,' she said, gesturing to the side table, where her little digital camera sat. 'My phone . . . hang on, that's what I came for.'

'It's here,' said Janine, picking up the phone from where it had slipped between the mattress and the bed-side table, where it had been charging. She passed it over to Olivia. She turned it on, but of course there was no signal.

Liam picked up the camera and flipped open the cover for the memory stick.

'What are you doing?' she asked, frowning.

'Just checking it's properly intact. You never know, maybe they were looking for something on your stick.'

'I think you've been reading too many spy novels,' said Annalise.

'OK, well, let me make sure Elisabet is on her way and she'll liaise with you about what to do next.'

'Thank you, Liam,' said Patty, ushering him out of the door. She closed it behind him with a click. 'Looks like it was just a lot of bad luck for you, my dear. Some opportunist thinking they'd stumbled on a rich woman with some jewellery or something.'

'Next time we'll direct them to Cutler and Ingrid's cabin. I bet that woman brought diamonds galore with her,' said Annalise.

'It really sucks,' said Janine, sitting down next to Olivia. 'Do you think it could be –' she lowered her voice – 'that man you were talking about? You know, the one you thought had followed you from Ushuaia?'

'Who's that? Who is she talking about?' asked Patty.

Olivia sucked in her bottom lip before replying. 'I thought I was just being paranoid but I keep seeing this guy around the boat. He has a shaved head with a strange sort of hair tattoo design above his ear.'

'That's terrifying!' said Patty. 'And you think maybe he was trying to rob you?'

'I guess it's possible . . .'

The next knock on the door was Elisabet, along with a beefy-looking man who Olivia recognized as Pedro, the ship's head of security. She didn't hold out much hope that anything could be done. There was hardly a CSI team on board. 'I am very sorry that this has happened,' said Elisabet. 'But I will go through our records to see who used their key card to enter your cabin last. And Pedro will change the lock code on your door and reset it.'

Instinctively Olivia felt in her pocket for her key card.

But it wasn't there. Was this all her fault? Had she dropped it somewhere, or left it in the gallery? She swallowed. 'My key card. I don't know where it is,' she managed to say.

Pedro glanced at Elisabet. Olivia knew what they were thinking. How stupid could a person be?

'What about CCTV?' Olivia asked.

'There are a few cameras in the hallways. We'll check the footage for this time too,' said Pedro. 'During the auction you said?'

'Yes.' She looked around at her other cabinmates. 'We all left together for the auction, and then I returned a bit early as I was hoping to grab my phone to take some photos. That's when I discovered . . . all this.'

'Don't worry, we will get to the bottom of what happened,' said Elisabet. 'And, Olivia, Captain Enzo would like to invite you to his table to have dinner tonight. Hopefully it can take your mind off this unfortunate incident.'

Elisabet and Pedro left them to finish tidying up.

'*Unfortunate incident*,' Patty scoffed, 'that's putting it mildly. If you were one of my clients, I hope you'd be on the phone to me complaining straight away. I'd get you more than a captain's dinner as recompense. You should get that jacket fixed on the house at least.'

Olivia went to the wardrobe to examine the damage and see if it could be fixed. As she ran her hand down the slice in the sleeve, she felt inside the pocket. But the note had gone.

27

'I think we all deserve a strong drink, don't you? At least tonight is the midnight sun party. Let's put this unpleasantness behind us and focus on that. Crossing the Antarctic Circle – that's a once-in-a-lifetime experience. Don't you think?'

Patty's energy was intense. Olivia could only nod. They'd straightened up the cabin and it didn't appear that anything other than the note was missing.

The ship was due to cross the Circle a little before eleven p.m. Before that, Olivia had the captain's dinner. She was hardly feeling up for it. She carefully reapplied her make-up, but the strain showed clearly on her face, the bags under her eyes an uncomfortable shade of mauve that several layers of concealer couldn't hide.

Pedro reappeared with their new key cards. He had disappointing news about the data from the computer. The last registered card to open their door before the auction had been Olivia's. Considering she didn't know when she'd lost it, her only hope was that someone had been caught on one of the cameras.

She insisted on going to watch the CCTV with him. It was strange seeing herself on screen as she and her cabinmates walked to the auction. Pedro sped up the footage showing the following couple of hours. The cleaning crew came down the hallway, but apparently they weren't doing the interiors of the cabins at that time – only vacuuming the carpets and polishing the rails. There were only two other sightings of people walking past – both had come in from outside, so they were wearing either hoodies or woolly hats that obscured their faces. She squinted, wondering if one of them could be the shaven-headed man. But with no camera covering their cabin door, it was impossible to tell if anyone had entered during the auction. Useless.

Pedro muttered his apologies and assured her that nothing like this ever happened on board normally, that they would monitor the situation, and then she'd left.

Back at the cabin, Olivia shared the disappointing news that the culprit wouldn't be caught.

'Don't worry,' Janine said. 'We'll all be together. We're not going to leave each other alone.'

'That's a promise,' said Patty. 'Right, we'll implement, like, a buddy system.'

'I'm in,' said Janine.

'Annalise?' Patty prompted again.

'I don't see what the fuss is all about. It's not like anything was taken. No harm, no foul, right?' Annalise faltered under Patty's intense glare. 'Yeah, OK. Whatever. I'm in too.'

Olivia smiled gratefully. She knew it was all for her benefit and it made her feel better. 'I really appreciate it, all of you. But I'll be fine—'

'Nonsense! It's a done deal. We won't leave each other alone.'

'Starting with this captain's dinner.'

'I think that was just an invite for you—' said Patty.

'The captain can make room,' said Olivia. 'In the meantime, I have to get out of here. It's too cramped.'

As she pulled on her warm clothes, she wondered what the final totals were for the auction. She'd have to get an update from Stefan as soon as possible. Since she hadn't been able to get a photograph herself, she thought of asking Janine to share some of her footage.

When she was ready, she stepped out on to an outer deck.

It was ironic after how much the water had panicked her a few days ago that now the only place she felt any solace was outside.

But getting the freezing wind in her hair, watching the Antarctic landscape shift in front of her eyes – it was the only thing that worked to clear her mind. Every hour the continent changed. Earlier the glacial cliffs had seemed so close to the ship that she could almost reach out and touch them. But now they'd sailed much further south, the coastline was flatter, more expansive. The water was thick with ice, so much that you could hear the crunch of it against the bow. The icebergs were no longer formless masses bobbing in the sea, but great natural sculptures, showcasing every shade of blue imaginable.

After they crossed the Circle, the ship would spend some time exploring the poetically named Crystal Sound before heading to their next landing site, Neko Harbour. Then they'd sail to Paradise Bay, where some of them would camp on the continent itself. A final stop at Deception Island for the infamous 'polar plunge'. Then it would be back through the Drake Passage to Argentina – and she could finally reconnect with Aaron.

She was literally counting down the days now.

Behind her, she heard the exterior doors slide open. Immediately she felt on edge, only relaxing when she saw who walked outside. Lucinda.

'Quite something, isn't it?' Lucinda leaned on the railing, staring out at the view.

'It's breathtaking. I could never imagine how beautiful it could be.'

'So was your showcase a success?'

'Absolutely.' Olivia forced a smile, not wanting to give away how terribly her evening had gone. That was personal. As far as she knew, from a business point of view, things had gone well. 'I'll catch up with Stefan to get the full picture tomorrow, but I think it went above and beyond expectations.'

'And now Yennin's artwork will be rolled out across the cruise ships.'

Olivia nodded. 'I expect so.'

'Even without originals for sale.'

'That will be made much clearer for future cruises, I promise. But hopefully that means the originals can go to the world's top museums and galleries – be seen the world over.'

'I hope so. It sounds like you need it to be a success from what Maxwell has told me. It's a shame that I never got to meet your partner. I've been told a lot about him.'

'I do miss him very much.' Emotion rose in Olivia's chest, threatening to overflow. She needed to change the subject. 'How did you and Maxwell meet?'

'Oh, at Soho House in London. I was over doing some work a few months ago, and we've been flying back and forth between London and Vilnius ever since. He is very good to me – if a bit intense.'

'He seems very devoted.'

'On that front, we feel the same. He has supported me through some very difficult times, even in our short relationship. He's very protective of me. In fact, I think he would do anything I asked of him.'

Olivia swallowed as Lucinda clapped her hands together. 'I suppose we should get ready for this midnight sun party.' She stepped away from the railing, opening the door and gesturing Olivia through. 'What deck is your cabin on?'

'Deck five.'

'Then this is where I leave you. See you up there?'

Olivia nodded.

Back in the cabin, Annalise and Janine were taking shots from what looked like small vodka bottles snatched from an aeroplane or hotel minibar.

'Want to get into the "midnight sun" spirit?' asked Janine, waggling the bottle at Olivia.

She shook her head. 'Not for me.'

'Sensible.' She leaned in close, and Olivia could smell the alcohol on her breath. 'Just don't let me get too drunk and do something stupid.'

'Or some*one*, right, Janine?' Annalise laughed.

Janine threw a pillow at her. 'Definitely not that. I'm not ready for that yet.'

'Bad break-up?' Olivia asked.

'Something like that,' Janine muttered.

'Amen,' said Annalise, raising her shot glass.

Olivia thought about Ingrid and Cutler in their suite.

She took Janine's hand. 'You promised to look out for me. It's the least I can do for you as well.'

Janine smiled. 'Then it's a deal,' she said, before knocking back the rest of the bottle.

They didn't have to wait long for dinner. The captain had agreed to have the entire cabin at the table, but, as a result, she was sitting about as far from the captain as it was possible to be. But Olivia didn't care. She had retreated now into the company of her cabinmates, keeping a watchful eye out for the man with the shaved head – but there was no one who roused suspicion.

At least the food remained top-notch. And the drinks were flowing. Patty took a sip of her cocktail – an Antarctic Sunrise, made (allegedly) with real glacier ice. She was already several drinks deep – at this rate, Olivia wasn't sure any of her cabinmates would make the midnight sun party. Plenty of activities were planned for that magical moment they passed 66° 33' south, starting with a champagne toast, live music at the bar and a fancy-dress party.

Even now, it was impossible not to be transfixed by the view outside the dining-room windows. Even though they were finishing dinner and the hour grew close to ten thirty p.m., it was light outside, the sun sitting low on the horizon. It cast shadows on to the icebergs, turning them a light shade of golden. Tonight the sun would never fully set beneath the horizon. They would get to experience the phenomenon of the midnight sun.

The familiar three bells rang over the intercom, and Patty gripped Olivia's arm. 'It's happening!'

'Greetings, crew and passengers of the *Vigil*, this is Elisabet. I hope you all have enjoyed the showcase, a nice meal and the rest of your evening at sea. But soon we will come to the point that we have all been waiting for. In approximately fifteen minutes, we will reach 66° 33′ south. Or, as it's more commonly known around these parts, the Circle. If you would please make your way on to the deck for a special surprise when we cross over . . .'

Leaving them hanging on that cheerful tone, the tannoy switched off and immediately there was a burst of excitement from the dining room.

'Come on, it's time,' said Patty.

They pulled on their jackets and joined the rest of the passengers, a sea of red flowing out on to the forward deck. They all looked so similar, indistinguishable with their hoods pulled up to ward against the cold, and Olivia felt comforted by the sense of anonymity. If she was being targeted – and after what had happened at their cabin, surely it couldn't be denied now – she couldn't be distinguished.

The crew came out in costume. They were wearing brightly coloured leis around their necks, oversized sunglasses and swimwear on top of their blue jackets, all to celebrate being in peak 'summer' – even in the freezing cold.

Each of them held a tray of fizz, the liquid almost looking like it was steaming from the flutes. Olivia shook her head. She couldn't think about drinking champagne on board any more. She wasn't sure she'd ever drink it again. Instead, she took a glass of apple juice. The non-alcoholic option.

The captain stood on the upper level, with one eye on his bridge. The moment the ship sailed over the line, he would sound the signal. He looked up and gave the ten-second countdown, as everyone joined in.

Then the captain set off a foghorn, and cheering erupted on deck.

There was no magic flash, no bump, no flag or post – just miles and miles of sea-ice shards strewn across the water. As she clinked her glass against Janine's, standing shoulder to shoulder with the other passengers in red, she felt tears swim in her eyes, her breath stuttering in her chest.

There was something undeniably moving about crossing over to this part of the world where few people ever got to travel. They'd truly come all the way to the ends of the Earth.

Yet despite all the warmth and joy on the deck around her, Olivia found herself shivering.

The sun wasn't going to set on the ship. There was someone on board who was targeting her. And that meant there was no place to hide.

28

As Olivia's watch ticked past midnight and towards one a.m., the party was still raging.

After what had felt like an impossibly long day, she wanted nothing more than to retreat to bed, but her stomach churned with anxiety at the thought of going back to the cabin – especially alone. Her cabinmates weren't ready to leave yet. Janine was tossing back shots with Liam, who had wrapped his multicoloured lei around her neck and was liberally pouring from an electric blue liqueur bottle, his hand on Janine's knee. Annalise was deep in conversation with Lucinda and Greg, while Patty was cutting a rug with Captain Enzo on the dance floor.

The bar at the top of the ship had a small outside deck. Olivia stepped through the sliding doors, glad to leave the noise and stale air of the bar. Immediately she felt the blast of freezing air creep into the collar of her jacket, but she breathed it in deeply.

The midnight sun. One of the few places in the world where it was visible. It wasn't like daylight, per se. The sky had an indigo, purpling quality, a bruise spreading behind the clouds. The sun itself hugged the horizon, shrouded in a haze. The light reflected off the icebergs, making it difficult to distinguish ice from cloud, water from sky.

She thought she would miss Aaron being there, but instead she found herself thinking of her parents. Her dad's dreams of Antarctica. Her mother appreciating the stillness and unique quality of the light, maybe getting her paintbrush out.

She took out her phone to take a photo. Even if she had no one to share it with, at least she could show her mum once she was back home.

'It doesn't even look real,' said a voice from behind her.

Olivia turned to see Janine walking through the sliding doors. She hadn't brought her jacket with her, and she was only in her sparkly tank top and jeans.

'He would have loved this,' she said, standing beside Olivia and leaning out against the railing.

Olivia winced for her, thinking how cold the metal was even through the thick material of her jacket. 'Are you talking about your boyfriend?'

Janine nodded. Tears welled up in her eyes. 'Ex-boyfriend now, I guess you would say. It's just hard.' She swayed ever so slightly, her cheeks flushed.

'I'm so sorry,' Olivia said. 'You've spent so long listening to my problems and I've never asked you about him. Do you want to talk about it?'

'We were supposed to be doing this trip together, but it's history now.' She shivered.

'Are you OK? Let me grab your jacket from inside.'

But in the next instant Janine's tears were gone, so quickly that Olivia thought she must have imagined them. Instead, the girl gave herself a shake and winked. 'Yeah, you're right. I'm going to freeze my tits off out here. Hey, so that Liam is really cute, right? Should I go for it?'

'Janine . . . remember what you said to me earlier?'

'Oh, that? No, it will be fine. I'm fine. No better way to get over someone, right?' She waved at Liam, who was holding up two more shots and gesturing for her to come back in.

Olivia bit her lip. 'Look, you must be feeling so vulnerable . . .'

'I think you're just jealous,' she said with a wink, then sashayed back into the bar.

Olivia followed her in, sitting in an empty armchair next to Patty. Through the crowd she could still see Janine and Liam, especially Liam's arm casually thrown over the girl's shoulder.

'That man's going to find himself kicked off the boat if he's not careful,' muttered Patty. 'I'm not sure fraternizing with the passengers is allowed.'

'It's a bad idea. I'm worried about her.'

'She's a big girl; she can look after herself.'

'I don't know . . .'

Patty touched her on the knee. 'I know it must be a change to worry about someone else as opposed to who's making your life miserable on this boat. But you have to let people make their own mistakes . . .'

'She asked me to look after her. She needs it,' Olivia continued. Then she looked back up at the bar. But Janine was nowhere to be seen. And neither was Liam. 'Oh God. Did you see where they went?' She stood up, scouring the bar. No sign of them. 'We have to make sure she's OK.'

'Oh, honey, we *know* what they're doing,' said Patty, taking another swig of her wine – which almost fell out of her hand as Olivia pulled her to her feet. 'Hey!'

'Sorry, Patty, but you have to come with me. I don't want to search the ship alone.'

Patty hesitated. 'Fine. But only because of what you

went through today. But once we find Janine and see that she's OK, we're going back to the cabin.'

'Deal.'

'Let's get Annalise.'

Annalise refused to come with them. 'I'm not the paranoid one here. I'm fine on my own, seriously.'

'Are you sure?' asked Olivia. But Annalise turned her back on them, waving them off with her hand.

They searched each deck, public room by public room. Some were locked – like the library, gallery and dining room – but the lounges were open. The couple was nowhere to be seen.

'I bet Liam knows all the hidden places on the ship to take a woman,' said Patty.

But Olivia wasn't going to give up so easily. They passed a door marked 'CREW ONLY', the one she'd stopped Dr Tove from going through. Liam wouldn't have . . .

Before she could second-guess herself, or let Patty stop her, she pushed against the door. Locked. No – there was a little black box where she'd need to swipe for entry. She slapped her palm against the door in frustration.

'Oh, let's not give up that easily,' said Patty. 'Where's the reception area? I get so turned around.'

'It's just down here. But I don't see how . . .'

'Hush. This isn't my first time on one of these things, you know.' They hurried back towards the lobby.

Patty reached over the desk and lifted the latch. 'Now let's see what we have here . . . I wouldn't expect to have any luck usually, but on a party night like tonight? Maybe someone might have got a bit lax . . .' She was opening drawers and rifling through the shelves. Then she held up a lanyard, a key card dangling at the end, her eyes spark-ling. 'Come on, let's go see if we can find our cabinmate.'

The crew door swung open, leading into the bowels of the ship.

'Well, this is a bit less appealing, isn't it?' Patty said.

Olivia had to agree. Like when she'd been allowed into Elisabet's office, the difference between the crew and passenger areas was stark, the plush carpeting and polished wood replaced with easy-clean linoleum floor-ing. No fancy artwork on the wall here.

There were other differences too. Lists of rules and regulations were pinned up on boards, schedules high-lighted in bright colours and bold type. They passed the crew mess, which was in utter disarray – mugs of tea and empty beer bottles piled high, but then most of the crew were partying upstairs. Tidying up probably wasn't high on the priority list. Most striking of all, though, was the lack of natural daylight. She'd been so used to the light streaming in from the huge windows on the upper decks that its absence was sorely felt.

'We're never going to find them down here,' said Olivia. 'They could be anywhere.'

Patty held up a finger, and she fell quiet. Music and laughter flowed from down the hallway. 'I think we have a direction.'

Voices came from behind them as well, from the hall-way they'd just walked. They picked up speed so they wouldn't get caught. Patty almost had full-on giggles now, so much that Olivia had to prop her up. It was absurd the two of them sneaking through the crew quar-ters, trying to find a cabinmate who probably didn't want to be found. But Olivia had to try to keep her promise.

Janine had been so earnest. So sure and clear-eyed. With the amount of alcohol she knew must be coursing through the girl's system, she couldn't be thinking straight. She at least had to confirm it's what she wanted.

'Hey, what are you doing down here?'

Olivia spun around to see Melissa approaching them.

'Oh crap,' said Patty. 'We've been rumbled.'

'You really shouldn't be down here. We could get in a lot of trouble . . .'

'Please, Melissa. It's our cabinmate, Janine, the one who freaked out in the kayak? Liam brought her down here and we just want to make sure she's OK, then I promise we'll leave.'

Melissa looked from Olivia to Patty, her arms folded across her chest. Then her expression softened. 'Liam is such an idiot. Come on, this way.'

The music grew louder as Melissa led them through the labyrinthine corridors, towards the crew cabins. The doors were open, crew members she'd never seen before lounging against their bunk beds with beers, speakers playing loud techno music. 'To another crossing!' said one of them. Patty and Olivia practically had to run to keep up with Melissa's long strides.

'In here,' she said, stopping at one of the cabins. The door was slightly open.

'Janine?' Olivia called out.

Patty repeated it, louder.

Janine emerged from the room. 'Oh my God! You guys! You found me.'

'Bugger,' muttered Liam from behind her. 'You can't be here.'

'Maybe you shouldn't have taken her to your cabin,'

said Olivia. She turned to Janine. 'Are you OK? You said—'

'Yeah, I remember. You're right; I shouldn't be here. Let me just grab my things and we can go back.' She stumbled and Olivia leaped forward to catch her, at the same time as Liam did.

'I think you should back off,' said Olivia to the expedition leader. She leaned down to Janine. 'Where's your coat? I'll help you.'

'What were you thinking?' Melissa said to Liam as Olivia and Janine scrambled into the cabin. There were two low beds, two desks and a wardrobe – similar in size to their cabin upstairs, except with no porthole. Liam's side of the room was filled with personal touches – souvenirs from home, photographs, thank-you notes from previous clients. The other side was much barer. The bed was neatly made, the sheets tucked in with military-like precision. The only mess had come from Janine – her bag tossed on to the man's desk. Olivia gathered it up, disturbing a small black-velvet box that had been lying underneath.

She picked it up with trembling fingers and opened it. She couldn't believe it. Inside was a platinum ring with a large deep blue sapphire at its centre, flanked by two sparkling diamonds. Vintage. Distinctive.

Olivia picked it up, turning it over in her hands in disbelief.

'What is it?' Patty asked.

'It . . . it's my engagement ring.'

29

She sat in Captain Enzo's office, having gone over her story for what felt like the thousandth time.

Her possessions had been the only ones disturbed in the cabin raid.

She hadn't noticed the ring missing initially as she hadn't realized that it had been among the few pieces of Aaron's belongings she had in the cabin – she had assumed he'd kept it with him.

Liam claimed he'd never seen it before. That meant they had to track down his roommate. When he arrived at the crew cabin, Olivia had immediately tensed, hardly daring to breathe.

There was no denying it. It was the man she'd seen outside the restaurant in Ushuaia, and the man who she'd seen leaving cabin sixteen that first night.

Patty and Janine stood protectively on either side of her.

'What's going on?' the man asked gruffly.

'Sergei, mate. You need to wait here. The captain is on his way.'

'We found the ring,' said Janine, her voice overly loud from alcohol. 'We know what you did.'

'You stole from Olivia,' said Patty.

'No, this is a mistake. Miss Campbell, please . . . you don't understand,' he said, his ice-blue eyes locked on to her. 'You are in danger.'

'What are you talking about?' Olivia asked, her voice wavering. There was a confidence in his expression that made her doubt herself. 'From who?'

But that's when he hesitated. 'I don't know exactly . . .'

'We know. From you,' Janine said, taking several steps back from him, dragging Olivia with her.

'Look, don't talk any more,' said Liam, putting himself as a barrier between the women and Sergei. 'Pedro and the captain are on their way. Talk to them.'

'Ask Pierre what I'm doing here.' Sergei spoke over Liam's shoulder, his eyes locked on Olivia. 'He's in Ushuaia. He will explain.'

Then Patty and Janine led her out to the hallway, and Liam closed the door to the cabin.

Olivia's mind raced. *Ask Pierre?* Since Pierre's message from the captain, she hadn't heard anything from the billionaire – no more radio messages, no more emails.

All the evidence pointed to Sergei being a thief. He'd been watching her since before she got on board – targeting her, learning her background. Of course he would try to throw suspicion on someone else.

After a few moments, Pedro showed up, asking all of them to make their way up to the bridge. He asked Patty and Janine to wait outside, while Olivia, Sergei and Liam joined the captain inside his office.

'Sergei, can you explain yourself?' asked Captain Enzo, when they had all arrived. 'Where were you between six and eight o'clock this evening?'

'I've been down in the engineering room on my shift, Captain.'

'And this ring? How did it get in your cabin?'

'I've never seen it before. I have no idea how it got here.'

'You're new to the *Vigil*, so I understand you might not understand the protocol. But you are not to be on guest floors unless specifically assigned.'

'I saw him that first night,' said Olivia again. 'What if he'd been looking to steal from me then too, but found out I had changed cabins? How do we know he's telling the truth? Was there anyone down there with him?'

Sergei remained tight-lipped, while the captain rubbed at his eyebrows. He turned to Olivia. 'I'm very sorry for what has happened to you, Miss Campbell. We will confine Sergei to a different cabin, where he will remain under guard while I investigate further. I'm afraid we don't have many options until we return to port. Then there will be a full police investigation. I will inform the Argentinian forces so they are primed and ready when we dock.'

She nodded.

'I hope now you can put this unfortunate business behind you and get some rest. We should have a beautiful sail up to the Lemaire Channel and Neko Harbour later today.'

'Thank you, Captain.'

When she left the office, Janine and Patty were sitting on a bench just outside, along with Annalise. They leaped to their feet when they saw her. 'How are you? Everything OK?'

'They're going to keep that man locked up for the rest of the trip.'

'Oh, thank God for that,' said Patty. 'I think this has to be the most eventful cruise I've been on in my whole life!'

'Same,' said Annalise.

'As long as it doesn't cause Pioneer a PR nightmare when we get back. Can you imagine the calls we'll have to field?'

'I don't think that will be an issue,' said Annalise.

'Why's that?' Patty asked, frowning.

Janine pulled on Olivia's arm, letting the other two go on ahead. 'While they're talking business, I just wanted to say thank you for coming to get me.'

'Of course. I made a promise and Sergei would still be stalking the ship if I hadn't. Strange how things work out.'

'And how great that Aaron wants to propose to you! You must be so happy.'

Olivia blushed. 'Yeah. Although I'd have preferred it if he had made the boat instead of the ring.'

'But you have to admit, your life is kind of amazing. You've got a great job, this glamorous art-world boy-friend who loves you, travel to far-flung places . . . I want to be like you. You know, in a few years.'

Olivia let out a bitter laugh. 'I don't think so.'

'What do you mean?'

Ask Pierre. The words still rung in Olivia's ears. Pierre said he'd had some concerning news. Did all this have something to do with why Aaron wasn't on the boat?

Olivia shook her head. 'I'm sorry. I'm just feeling shaken up.'

'Understandable. I think we all need to get some sleep. Hopefully now you can rest easy.'

'Yeah.'

'And then tomorrow night, we get to camp on the snow! That's going to be so cool. My parents won't believe me when I tell them. Have you heard any more from Aaron?'

Olivia shook her head. 'I'm not even sure if my emails are getting through. I haven't had a reply from anyone.'

'At least you know Aaron is OK. I'm weirdly enjoying being cut off. I can't send any drunk texts at least. Kinda feels like we're the only ones in the world. Just us and the penguins.'

And a potential killer, Olivia thought, remembering the couple in cabin sixteen. But Sergci was locked up. The danger contained.

She had to believe that.

30

For once, cabin twelve slept in. By the time they woke up, they were moored in Neko Harbour, an enormous bay shaped like a whale's tail and surrounded on all sides by towering glaciers.

Now that Sergei was locked up, Olivia was determined to enjoy the rest of the cruise. She double-checked the engagement ring was locked inside the safe in their wardrobe.

Looking at it now, stunning as it was, she didn't know what her answer would be if Aaron did go ahead and propose when they got back. There were so many questions she had for him, not only brought up by his absence, but also by the conversations she'd had on board – with Maxwell, with Lucinda, with Stefan. Even the one with Sergei. Pierre was clearly more than just Yennin's first major buyer. There had to be a reason Sergei had brought him up, a reason why he would say the billionaire was in Ushuaia.

The kayakers were called to meet down in the mudroom. When she and Janine arrived, Liam was busy preparing the life jackets. She hadn't seen him since the captain's office, and when she caught his eye, he looked away.

'Can you help me with my drysuit?' Janine asked. Dark roots were beginning to show in her dyed-copper hair, and with her eyes wide she looked even younger than her early-twenties age.

She turned around to allow Olivia to do up the zip in the back, then she helped hoist the PFD – personal flotation device – on to her back.

Olivia waited a beat. 'I'm glad you're trying this again.'

'I'll be better in the kayak this time. Maybe we can go together?'

She was about to say 'of course!' when Melissa stepped in. 'I'm afraid not. You'll be in my boat. Olivia here will be in one of the solo kayaks. If you're OK with that?'

'Really?'

'From what I saw last time, you'll have no issues.'

Olivia smiled. Her old skills hadn't deserted her. Melissa trusted her with her own boat. If that wasn't a vote of confidence, she didn't know what was.

'Don't worry, I'll make sure you see all the cool stuff first,' Melissa said to Janine. 'And if you have another panic attack, I can get you straight to the Zodiac and you can go ashore with the rest of the passengers.'

Eventually Janine nodded. Decision taken, they made their way to the door, where Liam was pulling up the kayaks one by one. She settled into the seat of her solo kayak, making sure her camera was easily accessible.

Once everyone was in the water, Liam took the lead with a few powerful strokes. Olivia decided to show what she could do too, slicing the blade of the paddle into the water, pulling strongly so the front of her kayak shot forward, leaving Melissa and Janine's kayak in her wake. She loved the feeling of her bright yellow vessel skimming across the water, like she was more sea creature than human.

Neko Harbour was the picture-postcard view of Antarctica. The weather was perfect – the sun high and bright in the sky, the snow glittering under its rays, the pale glacial cliffs cracking to reveal hints of deep blue from within. A phrase from one of her dad's books sprang to mind – 'many glaciers beryl blue *most beautiful* contrasted with snow' – and she knew exactly what Darwin had been talking about.

The water was mirror-still; it was almost a travesty to be disturbing the surface with their boats and paddles. With the sun beating down on her face, she didn't even feel cold – and the air filling her lungs with every breath had never felt so pure.

She passed Cutler and Ingrid, their children together in another boat, then Robert who was steering a double kayak with Helena in front this time. She had a fancy mount for her smartphone that kept it steady as they were paddling. Lucinda was in a boat with Maxwell, and she kept glancing over at Melissa and Janine, frowning. Maybe she was anxious Janine would cause a capsize.

Liam guided them close to the granite-grey shore, where the basalt cliffs were bare of ice. They saw Wilson's storm petrels perched against the rock, their bright yellow feet breaking up the monochrome of the surface, little slivers of silver fish in their beaks – a tasty breakfast.

Olivia didn't know where to look; there was such an abundance of riches. She double-, then triple-checked her camera was recording, imagining putting a little video together for her mum. Something they could watch together at her next visit. She kept scanning the water around them, hoping to capture a video of one of the humpback whales that were rumoured to be lurking in the bay, but the surface for the moment was still. She hoped that they would kayak back out into the Lemaire

Channel, maybe attempt some more remote locations, only accessible in their little boats.

After some time watching a group of penguins waddling up in single file on the mainland, like commuters on an icy highway, she finally got her wish. Liam led them out of sight of the ship, the kayaks moving easily and quickly through the calm water.

Away from the ship, the motorized Zodiacs and the chatter of the other passengers, the true serenity of the surroundings revealed themselves. Now the only sounds were of their own paddles dipping beneath the water, the occasional squawk of a seabird and the waves lapping the cliffs.

Liam led them directly through an iceberg, beneath a glacial arch, her breath stolen away by the diamond hardness of it. She was stunned at how intensely blue the ice was. She'd seen pictures, but no photograph could do it justice – not until she saw it with her own eyes. It wasn't just any blue. It was so rich it could be cobalt, the depths of it reminding her of the sapphire engagement ring tucked away in the safe.

It couldn't have been the plan for him to abandon her, not if he was thinking of their future so seriously. Whatever he was dealing with, it had to be big. She was sure he would be pleased by how the auction had gone, however. As soon as they were back from kayaking, she would get a proper update from Stefan.

They wound their way through more icebergs, passing huge Weddell seals lounging on the ice floes like sunbathers. On another floe, they spotted a new breed of penguins, the Adélies, with their all-black faces and beady eyes.

Then they saw another iceberg, this one more bulbous than the others. The top of it seemed to be stained red with blood. It made Olivia's stomach turn to look at it, wondering what animal had lost its life there.

But then it didn't quite look like blood. As she stared, she saw that the red seemed embedded in the iceberg itself, almost as if the sides were painted with crimson stripes.

Melissa and Janine pulled up alongside her. 'What is that?' Olivia asked Melissa.

'Hmm, not a great sign. That's microscopic algae. Unfortunately the more algae that spreads on the ice, it prevents sunlight from reflecting away, resulting in more meltwater. We call it blood snow.'

Olivia shivered.

'This looks like the berg has flipped – it must have broken from shore only recently.' Melissa looked up at the glacier. 'This coastline has become more and more unstable with every crossing.' She shook her head. 'I'm not sure how this place is going to survive.'

Olivia moved her boat away from the creepy 'blood ice' berg and towards the open water. That's when she saw a whale spout exploding from the waves. She thought she saw a glimpse of a slick black fin slicing through the surface. Orca.

Her heart pounded with excitement. This was one of the special moments she could only hope to witness down here. She thought of her dad urging her onwards, willing her to push through her fear for the experience of a lifetime. She fumbled for her camera, attaching it to her life jacket so she could use it hands-free.

She steered the boat so it took her around the other side of the iceberg, separating her from the group.

The orca was moving away, fast. Realizing another spout meant there might be a whole pod of them, Olivia increased her speed, but the brash ice around this side of the iceberg was thicker and crunched against the plastic hull. She needed to work harder to move the kayak.

The ice shifted for her bow. She was amazed. From the deck of the *Vigil*, it looked like the ice was still, locked into position – like grass rooted on a watery field. But when you were down close to it, it was clear how fluid the ice was. Every time she blinked, it shifted. And the ice here was far heavier and thicker than in the shelter of Neko Harbour.

She glanced behind her. The group was distracted; they hadn't seemed to notice the potential whale sighting. Cutler was shouting at his son to get his paddling sorted, his frustration apparent. Then Ingrid was screaming at him that 'he's only twelve, leave him alone'. Melissa was trying to get in the middle, but it was difficult for her with Janine in front.

The whales seemed to change direction. She knew better than to follow the pod further out into the open water, but she hadn't realized how close she'd come to the enormous glacier. It towered up beside her, the striated surface like it had been raked towards the sky. She spun the kayak back around to face the group but kept the camera trained on where she'd last seen the whale.

Something else caught her attention further down the channel. Another boat? It was much smaller than the MS *Vigil*, with broad cream sails – a yacht of some kind, although she was too far away to tell. She was impressed. It would take real guts to sail down here, but she was sure they would be rewarded with magnificent remote anchorages – maybe even places that no man had ever set foot on before. She pointed her camera at it, hoping to show the others on video.

But then her patience was rewarded. A black silhouette curved from the water, revealing its white eyepatch and a glimpse of pale underbody, followed by the blade of its dorsal fin slicing up from the inky waves. Her heart pounded inside her chest as she watched, mesmerized, then squealed with delight as a smaller fin appeared alongside – a mother and her calf, swimming together.

The others needed to see this. She swung her head around and saw Liam powering towards her, his arms swinging, propelling the kayak forward and gaining on her. Her heart dropped. She'd drifted too far from the group. Feeling guilty that he had been forced to come and get her, she began to paddle hard towards him.

'Olivia, look out!' Liam shouted.

There was an enormous crack like a gunshot, and she grabbed the lip of the kayak seat. She looked up at the wall of ice hanging up above her. Then her jaw dropped as the ice seemed to shift in front of her eyes. No, not shift but calve, slipping down the wall. The ice was breaking away, crumbling like someone had hacked at it with a gigantic axe.

The first blocks collided with the surface and for a moment, it was as if time stood still. The rest tumbled afterwards, a chunk the size of a small car. She was holding her breath, waiting to see what the impact would be. She braced for it.

It wasn't enough.

The water rose up where the ice had disappeared, rippling and bulging almost in slow motion. Then it rushed towards her, faster than she could escape it.

The wave crashed against the side of her boat. The kayak overturned and she plunged into the icy waters.

31

'What the hell were you thinking?' Liam stood over her, his knuckles on his hips.

She took a sip of the hot tea, loaded with sugar, that had been thrust into her hands.

'I'm sorry,' she said, when she was finally able to speak without stuttering. 'I was following this pod of whales and I didn't realize how far I'd gone . . .'

'Thank Christ Melissa was keeping an eye out for you. The Hugheses were at each other's throats and I thought it was going to be Cutler who ended up in the water, they were rocking their boat so much. You really are trying to get me sacked, aren't you?'

'I think you're doing a pretty good job of that yourself.' She pulled the towel closer around her body. Her hair was dripping on to the black plastic floor, making a tiny ticking sound. The locker room stank of seawater and sweat. All she wanted was to go back to the room, shower, get herself back into some fresh clothes. She wondered if her camera had survived the dip. It was supposed to be waterproof, but who knew.

The shock of the cold had stolen any logical thought from her brain and her eyes were squeezed tightly shut. Luckily her body had remembered how to wet exit the kayak, and because of the drysuit she wasn't soaked to the bone. She'd surfaced, gasping and flailing in the water. Melissa had held out her oar, shouting clear and calm instructions, and Olivia had managed to grab hold of it and they were able to get her into a Zodiac.

'I've been guiding for over a decade and never had a single capsize,' said Liam, still shaking his head in disbelief. 'Look, that's it. No more kayaking trips for you.'

'I deserve that.' She took another sip of the drink, wrapping her fingers tightly around the cup.

'Here, this might help more.' He reached under the bench and removed a small bottle of whisky from the floor. She nodded. He poured a small measure into her tea. When she sipped it this time, she felt the whisky warm through her fingers and bring colour back to her cheeks. She actually audibly sighed, which made Liam smile.

'Better?' He took a swig as well.

'Much, thank you. And . . . I am sorry. I don't know what got into me.'

'Trust me, not even a breaching whale is worth a dip in Antarctic waters. If you had been closer to the cliffs when that glacier calved, or if an iceberg had tipped . . . we might have lost you.'

'I really appreciate your concern.' She paused. 'How were things after . . . what happened last night?'

Liam shrugged. 'They can't get rid of me right now; I'm the most qualified exped. leader and Cutler wants to keep everything running smoothly. I got a bollocking from the captain but it's OK. He's all mouth and no trousers.'

'And Sergei?'

'He's pretty miserable, yeah. Still claims he had nothing to do with it. Says it will all become clear when we get into port. Well, now he doesn't say much at all. Clammed up completely.'

'I'm glad he's locked up until then. And there's been no more news about that couple?'

Liam's expression turned dark. 'Nothing yet. I keep pestering Dr Ranj. He'll tell me as soon as he hears anything.'

'Let me know.' She stood up, then almost immediately sat back down again, her head falling into her hands.

'Maybe *you* should go see Dr Ranj.'

'No! No, I really don't want to go back there.'

'OK, if you're sure. Even though you can't kayak, you're welcome to go on shore with the others in a Zodiac later.'

'Thanks, but I think I'll stay on the ship for the rest of today. I need to go and speak to Stefan – find out how the auction went.'

Just outside the locker room, Janine was waiting. 'I didn't want to leave you alone. You know – our pact?'

Olivia smiled at her. 'Thank you. Although I feel much better now that guy is locked up.'

'I guess my little almost-hook-up had some benefits. What was Liam talking to you about?'

'Oh, just telling me off for not listening to him out on the water.'

Janine grimaced. 'As if he can tell anyone off for not obeying rules.'

Back in the cabin, Olivia dried her hair and changed into warmer clothes. Janine was flipping through the pictures she'd taken while out on the kayak.

'So did you get a picture of that whale after all?' Janine asked, when Olivia emerged from the bathroom.

'I'm not sure. Let's take a look, shall we? See if that polar plunge was worth it.' She grimaced. She flipped over the camera's viewscreen, playing the last video on the memory stick.

An involuntary shiver passed through her body as she saw the glacier appear on screen – the one that would calve and capsize her boat a few moments later. The view panned out towards the open ocean. 'There!' Olivia said, as the nose of the orca pierced the top of the waves. An iceberg came into the frame as the camera tracked the whale.

'What's that?' Janine asked.

'Hmm?' Olivia paused the video. Janine pointed at a small splotch of blue on the screen. 'Oh yes – I saw another boat while I was out there.' She paused the video and zoomed in. 'See, it's a yacht, I think.'

'Wow, they're brave.'

She played the rest of the video, watching the boat now instead of the whale. It slipped in and out of view behind an iceberg. It looked like quite a sophisticated sailing vessel, with a sleek navy hull and those broad cream sails she'd spotted from the water.

Just as she was about to fall in the water, the camera panned over the yacht one final time. She paused and zoomed in as far as the camera could go. The horizon was tilted but she got a view of the name of the ship.

CLARISSA II.

She dropped the camera like it was on fire.

'What's wrong?' Janine asked.

But Olivia couldn't answer.

Her worst nightmare had followed her to the bottom of the world.

32

Her mind was whirring, going over the video footage. Janine had been worried about her, fretting and pestering her about why her mood had suddenly shifted. Olivia claimed it was shock from her capsize. She used it as an excuse to crawl back into bed.

Eventually Janine left her alone, and Olivia could sink into her thoughts.

They were dark ones. *Clarissa.* That was a name she would never be able to forget.

She could clearly remember the excitement she'd felt at sixteen years old on arriving in St Lucia with her mum. They'd been apart from her father for three weeks at that point, as he'd soloed the *Clarissa* across the Atlantic, moving it from its summer mooring in Lagos, Portugal. The yacht's owner wanted to spend the winter exploring the turquoise-blue waters of the Caribbean, but didn't want the hassle of moving it himself.

As was often one of the perks, her dad was allowed to take his family out for a little holiday at the end of the crossing, making sure the yacht handled well and didn't need any sort of repairs before handing it over to the owner. Those trips had formed some of her favourite childhood memories – whether it was on a small thirty-two-foot sailing boat in Greece or a far more luxurious super yacht in Bermuda – it was a chance for them to escape into a different life for a week as a family. Both she and her mum were competent sailors, with Dad entrusting them as his worthy deckhands.

She was older this time, capable of handling more responsibility. She was looking forward to it. She'd pored over the schematics for the *Clarissa*, always interested in the numbers and logistics. Perhaps a foreshadowing of her later career. She'd known this was one of the higher-end sailing vessels, one capable of handling long ocean voyages and navigating rough seas. A week pootling around the crystal-clear Caribbean waters would be like taking a Ferrari for a spin around a car park. The forecast had called for calm seas, a light breeze and endless sunshine. They'd been all set for a perfect voyage.

Whoever owned it had spared no expense. The interior looked more like a penthouse apartment straight out of *Selling Sunset* than your basic nautical interior design. Her mum had oohed and aahed over the artwork on the walls, the fabric on the sofas – even the soft damask pattern of the wallpaper.

It wasn't a large yacht, but she was beautiful. Even her name, *Clarissa*, had sparkled in fresh gold leaf against the bright white hull. For the first six days, it had been truly idyllic: dropping anchor in secluded half-moon-shaped bays with white-sand beaches, snorkelling over pristine coral reefs, spotting clownfish and moray eels, taking the rubber dinghy to restaurants overlooking the water.

Until. Until.

That final night. Her father's last words to her: *Keep watch*.

The trust he had in her, that she had betrayed.

The aftermath had been a blur. The boat had been

towed back into harbour by an ugly fishing vessel. The smell – of gasoline and burnt metal – stuck with her, stronger than any other memory from that time. Then there was the investigation. Being questioned by the police in the early hours of the morning. The gash in the side of the hull, marring her perfect finish, from where the speed-boat had collided with them. *Clarissa* was mangled.

A fleet of boats went out looking for her father's body. He had been a well-known, popular figure at the St Lucia Yacht Club in Gros Islet, and she was amazed by the number of people who came to their aid. They worked in coordinated grids based on the data recov-ered from the *Clarissa*. But they never found him.

Her mother, wrapped in a blanket, was drowning in shock. Unable to take care of herself, let alone Olivia. Olivia had taken the lead, liaising with the lawyers and the police, figuring out how to get her and her mother home.

Accidental death. That had been the ultimate ruling. Her mother feared every day that they would be held respon-sible for the damage to the boat, but no letter of demands ever came. They never heard from the owner of the yacht at all.

But one thing she did know, absolutely. It hadn't been an accident. She had caused it.

It had been her responsibility. And maybe the owner of the *Clarissa* knew it.

Once they were home, life got even more compli-cated. Their savings had barely covered the move and her mum's new substitute teaching job just about covered their day-to-day living expenses after that. They'd scraped by until Olivia had been old enough to go to university, where again, somehow her dad had set money aside to make sure she could complete her degree. She'd been surprised her dad had been that forward thinking – and even more so that there was a secret account she hadn't known about – but her mum wouldn't accept any questions.

Then there had been setbacks that no one could have anticipated, not even the most advanced forward planner. Her mum's health began to deteriorate almost the moment Olivia left for university. Early-onset dementia had been the diagnosis. Pretty soon, she knew she'd have to find a job that could pay for her mum's care. She'd looked up all the options and the starting salary for actuaries was one of the highest for new graduates, along with excellent earning potential; if she could fully qualify in good time, she might just be able to juggle care costs on top of her own living expenses.

She'd landed a position on Pendle's graduate scheme and the rest was history. She'd blocked sailing, the yacht, the whole trip from her mind.

But now, seeing another yacht with the name *Clarissa* had shaken her to her core.

It couldn't be a coincidence. But what on earth could it mean?

She had to see the yacht again or speak to someone who might know about it.

Bells chimed, informing passengers that Zodiacs for the mainland would be leaving shortly for anyone who wanted to go ashore.

Olivia jumped up. This was her chance.

She went back down to the mudroom, carefully dressing in her big waterproof trousers, jacket and boots, making sure to step through the disinfectant. She settled down into the big rubber Zodiac, along with a few other passengers she didn't recognize.

'Hold the boat! You can't go on shore without us.' Olivia heard Cutler's big booming voice and closed her eyes. *Please don't be in my boat, please don't be in my boat,* she silently begged. She wasn't in the mood for small talk.

'Not with your kids this afternoon?' asked their Zodiac driver, Dr Vance, the glacier expert from a few nights before.

'They decided to go for another trip in the kayaks after this morning's disaster.' Once Cutler settled in the boat, he noticed Olivia. 'And there's the culprit! Not going to tip this boat over too, I hope?'

Olivia's need to respond was swept away by the wind as the Zodiac sped away towards the shore.

The Zodiac was a remarkable vessel – while it was basically an oversized inflatable dinghy, she was surprised by just how stable she felt nestled down in that bucket of rubber.

They sped through the harbour, passing small rocky beaches separated by cliffs of ice that rose from the blue waters, glacial moraines terminating at the sea. She was glad to be far from them. Behind them lay enormous mountains covered in snow and a pure white landscape that stretched beyond the horizon.

The icebergs seemed to multiply as they approached the shore; there were floating islands and thicker brash ice to navigate that crunched against the rubber of the boat.

'Is this normal?' Olivia asked Dr Vance, gesturing to the ice cluttering the bay.

'Normal?' He shrugged. 'It's hard to say. The continent is shedding ice far quicker than any scientist's predictions. The whole coastline is unstable. But maybe that is our new normal.'

'That's scary.'

'It is. I worry every trip down here that the continent shrinks. It's hard to make people care unless they see it with their own eyes. That's why you should take pictures, share your memories of this remarkable place when you get home. So that it still exists for the future generations.'

He cut the Zodiac's engine, allowing them to drift on to the landing beach. 'Please be careful when disembarking – and, remember, use the sailor's grip when you get off.'

As she was waiting her turn to disembark the Zodiac, Olivia leaned over to look in the water. There was life there too. Wafts of seaweed floated by – even a couple of sea anemones clung to the rock. Whatever lingering perception she'd had of Antarctica as barren and lifeless evaporated.

'Careful,' said Dr Vance, the glaciologist, taking her arm above the wrist and helping her on to shore. She stumbled – vertigo from the sensation of going from a constantly moving boat to solid ground.

'It'll take a few steps to get your legs back after being at sea.'

'Actually I'm just wondering. Where can I go to get some good views?'

He looked down at his watch. 'If you're up for it, you can follow that path up to the head of that trail there, leading to the top of the hill. You should get a pretty amazing view back over the harbour. Just make sure you're back within two hours.'

'Thank you.' She squinted as she looked up at the mound of snow. Already a few people were making their way up, wrapped in their red jackets, dotting the pristine landscape.

She trudged on, but a flash of movement by her feet caught her eye. She looked down – by her boot clucked a little gentoo penguin, young and fluffy. While she knew they weren't allowed to approach the wildlife, there were no rules preventing *them* approaching *her*. She moved slowly, gently removing her camera from her pocket while trying not to frighten the penguin away. But actually the penguin was completely unflappable. If anything, her movement drew it closer to her, ever curious. It even pecked at the hard silicone of her boot as she snapped photo after photo.

She took a step forward, though reluctantly. It quirked its head at her, and she thought she could read annoyance in its face. 'Sorry, little buddy, I've got a mountain to climb.'

The cold stung her cheeks as she walked, and she tucked her chin into the collar of her jacket, pulling the hood up over her head for an additional layer. She was grateful for her sunglasses; the sunlight reflecting off the snow was almost blinding.

As she walked higher, the snow crunched beneath her boots. It was quite steep, and she passed a few people huffing and puffing – including Cutler. His wife was faring better, a few feet ahead. 'Tell me, how is Annalise doing?' Cutler asked as Olivia passed.

Olivia narrowed her eyes. 'Why?'

'I care about my employees.'

'Right. Your employees,' Olivia muttered.

'What?'

Olivia paused. 'Nothing. She's doing fine. As is Patty.'

'Oh yes. Poor woman. Decent travel agent but should've moved on a long time ago.'

'Moved on? She seems to really love the business. It's rare to see anyone speak so passionately about their job.'

Cutler grunted.

'At least the auction went well yesterday,' said Olivia, changing the subject.

'Yes, I think it did. Although that reminds me – I meant to speak to Stefan today about getting a final tally. I want to make sure the deal is ready to sign the moment we get back to the mainland. Have you heard from him?'

'Not yet. I was going to find him this morning after the kayaking but then I had to get warm . . .'

'Then let's go together. Might as well hear it at the same time.'

After a few more steps, they reached the pinnacle of the small hill, where there was a crowd of passengers already. Looking inland, the continent of Antarctica stretched out for miles. For most of the trip, the ship had been glued to the coastline, and the interior had remained a mystery. It was truly epic, in all senses of the word – huge towering mountains leading to a vast desert of snow. One of the mountains had a cross at the very top of it.

'It honours two scientists who died at one of the nearby bases,' said Elisabet. She'd been standing at the top of the hill, waiting for the passengers with a clipboard, and followed Olivia's gaze up to the cross. 'They went out to climb a mountain, and never returned.'

Olivia shivered. For all its beauty, this was a brutal,

inhospitable landscape. And out beyond the mountains, it was impossible to fathom how big the continent was, just snow and ice for thousands of miles, flowing in waves of sastrugi – windswept snow formations reminiscent of sand dunes. Once people were lost out there, that was it. Gone forever.

She pulled her gaze away, turning back to face the water. From this vantage point, the ship seemed so small – like a toy boat with its blue painted hull and bright red stripe, floating in a sea of glass. Despite knowing it was a hardened icebreaker, it looked fragile, dwarfed by the vastness of the landscape all around. She could see the yellow kayaks like little aphids, clustered together. The way the sea ice was broken up on the dark surface of the water made it seem as if there was a whale's tail pattern etched into the ocean.

It was so still. So calm. So peaceful.

'Excuse me, Elisabet?'

'Yes?'

'Can I borrow your binoculars?'

'Of course.' Elisabet unleashed the strap from around her neck and passed the binoculars over to Olivia.

She pressed them to her eyes, wincing at the cold. She cast her gaze around the bay. She focused the lenses on the kayakers, trying to make out Liam or Melissa. She spotted Liam on a double kayak with one of the Hughes boys. They were staying well away from any danger. She felt a twinge of guilt at being the reason the excursion was likely more risk-averse than normal.

She turned her attention further away from the boat. She scanned the coast, seeing nothing but miles of glacier and icy black water. She couldn't even spot a whale spout misting the air, or a seal lounging on one of the icebergs. Definitely no sign of the *Clarissa II*.

She heard fingers clicking in her direction. 'Pass those binoculars over. I want to spot the kids,' said Cutler. He'd finally caught up with her. His wife trudged on, exploring some of the top of the hill.

'Oh, um, sure . . .'

Just as she passed them over her head to give to him, there was an enormous crack like a thunderclap. A chorus of screams came from the nearby hikers. Olivia turned in the direction of the sound – back towards the far shore glacier.

A huge chunk of ice calved away from the glacier as if in slow motion. It tumbled into the water as if it had been cleaved with a knife, a plume of ice and snow rising as it hit the surface. Seeing it from here was almost as terrifying as watching it from below.

Almost, but not quite.

The impact was immediate. The water swelled from where the glacier had fallen, a wave rippling out from the impact. It grew in intensity, and the worried shouts began again.

Ingrid was one of the loudest voices. 'Matthew! Nate!' she screamed, as if her sons had any chance of hearing her.

The wave created by the calving was heading straight towards the kayaks, threatening to swamp them. Olivia could imagine the frantic shouting, the instructions to try to turn the boats in the direction of the wave, Liam coming into his element, taking charge and making sure everyone was safe.

Olivia held her breath as the first kayak rode the swell

and none of them appeared to capsize. Beside her, Cutler blew out his cheeks and held his wife, who he was propping up, her knees gone weak. All the kayakers had raised their paddles, signalling that they were OK. They all then seemed to slap them together in a paddle high five. They looked like they were laughing. Having fun. Olivia smiled.

'What the hell was that idiot Kiwi doing steering them so close to the glacier again? Doesn't he know we're trying to *avoid* disaster for the rest of this trip?'

'It's always about the scandal to you! The cost to the business, your deal – what about my boys?' Ingrid let out a stream of curses in German.

Olivia took the binoculars back from Cutler, who hurried back down the hill, chasing his wife. Her hands were gesticulating wildly – presumably still furious.

But now that the wreckage from the glacier had cleared, the sea calming again, she thought she spotted something odd. One of the kayaks appeared to have been separated from the group, slipping off behind one of the icebergs. It was just a flash of orange, but she was sure that was the case.

She pointed the binoculars at Liam, but his focus was on returning the group to the boat, his back to the rogue kayak.

She followed the movement all the way to a small alcove, hidden from view from the ship – and from most of the shoreline. Only from this vantage point, high above the harbour, could Olivia see the tip of a yacht.

The kayaker was heading to a different boat. To the *Clarissa II*.

A horn sounded, letting the passengers on shore

know that their time was up. She needed to get back to the ship. She was the only one left high up on the hill. Even Elisabet had gone, presumably distracted by the commotion with the Hugheses. She felt a sudden chill, as the threat and terror of being left behind took root. She had nothing but the clothes on her back – not even a granola bar in her pocket. That was stupid. Everything she had been told about this trip so far was that while it *looked* like a luxury cruise, this was actually an expedition. They were in dangerous, unpredictable terrain.

If she got into serious trouble – if she had an injury while out on the ice, if she got lost or missed the deadline and they left without her . . .

She would be on her own.

33

She slid her way down the hill, and when she found it tricky to stay on her feet, she dropped to her bum. There was a channel through the snow she used as a glissade, dragging her hands to maintain control as she gained in speed.

The Zodiac was full, and the professor was staring at his watch. She raced to the boat, her boots splashing in the water.

Dr Vance looked up, his mouth set in a grimace. 'Olivia, you just made it.' He reached down to grab his clipboard, putting a tick next to her name.

She leaned down on her knees, struggling to catch her breath. 'You need to call for help.'

'What?'

'I was watching the kayaks returning to the ship and I saw one of them get separated from the others.'

The professor frowned. 'Are you serious?'

'Positive.' She held the binoculars up from around her neck.

'I'm sure you're mistaken . . .'

'What if it's our boys?' Ingrid said, standing up abruptly in the Zodiac and making the sides wobble. The other passengers gripped the safety ropes tightly.

The professor nodded, rubbing at his chin. 'All right. Let me radio the ship.'

Olivia breathed a sigh of relief, glad she was being taken seriously, and clambered aboard the Zodiac.

She settled down on to the seat, arranging her life jacket around her neck. She kept her eyes trained on the professor as he listened to his radio. He smiled at her. There was a patronizing edge to it. 'No need for anyone to worry – all the passenger kayaks have been accounted for. You may have seen one of the crew doing a recce.'

He turned away to start the engine, and Olivia frowned. She stared out across the icy ocean towards the cove where she saw the kayak disappear. There was no sign of anything amiss – no *Clarissa II*, no rogue kayak, nothing but ice and water and . . .

There was a gasp from next to her, as a fin breached the water not far from the Zodiac. It was timed with the professor getting the small motorized boat moving, so he steered it towards the whale. All around her, people were snapping photos, their long lenses leaning out over the side.

But she couldn't bring herself to feel excited. She was a bundle of nerves. She didn't want to return to the ship. She felt safer on the peninsula.

Beside her, Cutler gave her shoulder a nudge. 'What's wrong? Not interested in the wildlife any more?'

'I'm a bit on edge,' said Olivia through gritted teeth.

'You'll feel better once we've heard from Stefan. I'm so glad this cruise has gone off without a hitch.'

'Without a hitch? What about cabin sixteen?' she blurted out.

She wasn't sure if he had heard her against the chatter of other passengers, the buzz of the Zodiac motor or the ice cracking against the rubber as he turned his broad-set shoulders away from her.

On board, he stomped away, not even bothering to

remove his boots. Dr Vance tried to stop him, but eventually dropped it. He wrote something down on his clipboard, presumably to follow up about the boots later on.

A hand grabbed her arm, swinging her around. It was Ingrid – Cutler's wife. She gestured for her to follow with a sharp tilt of her head. Intrigued, Olivia obeyed. The woman led her through a wooden door, then closed it firmly behind them.

A prickle rose on the back of her neck. Her eyes flicked around the small enclosed space. The panels of cedar, benches and bucket of water were a dead giveaway. The sauna. Thankfully it wasn't on, but it was still warm with residual heat.

Sweat began to bead on her upper lip.

'What have you heard about what happened to cabin sixteen?' asked Ingrid in a low whisper.

Olivia unzipped her jacket, but the thermals she was wearing underneath were trapping the warmth. She debated how much to say. 'I was in the medical centre at the same time as the couple.'

Ingrid peeled her hand off the door and started pacing the room. Olivia tugged at the neck of her undershirt, running her hand through her hair. Sweat glued strands to her forehead.

'You knew them?' Ingrid asked.

'Not really. We met at check-in. They were on their honeymoon: Jay and Christa.' She was about to say she'd swapped cabins with them, but stopped herself. She didn't want to reveal her suspicion that maybe she was the original target.

Ingrid continued pacing the small space. 'My husband

always tells me not to worry, that he has everything under control, but . . . I heard something I shouldn't have.'

'What did you hear?'

'You tell me! You know what happened. I know you must or else you wouldn't have asked my husband about it. I saw how he reacted.' She fumbled at her necklace as she spoke, one of the many pieces of expensive jewellery she had on. The diamond pendant looked almost wet in the humidity of the sauna, as if it had been dipped in the ocean.

Olivia took a deep breath. 'OK. I know that they were flown back to Ushuaia by helicopter so that there could be an investigation into why they were ill. I don't know how or why we didn't turn the ship around, but I assume the captain had a good reason. But that's all I know, I promise.'

Ingrid sat down on the bench. 'That's what you heard? That they were ill?'

'That's what the captain told me. But when I asked the doctor, she thought it was much more serious.'

'That they had died?'

Hearing it out loud, from someone else, made Olivia's blood turn cold. 'Yes,' she replied, but the word barely came out.

'But how? I don't understand . . .'

'Poison, the doctor thought. Maybe drugs?'

'No wonder Cutler has been so worried. I expect he is the one who convinced the captain to carry on with things as normal. There is so much resting on this trip for us . . . he does not need the PR firestorm if it came out that two people died on board.'

Olivia sat down next to her, gripping her hand. 'Why can't you ask him to confirm it?'

'He wouldn't tell me. He thinks he is trying to protect me.'

'Protect you? What do you mean?'

Ingrid laughed, but the sound was bitter. 'When we first got on board, we were shown to cabin sixteen. But I didn't like it. It didn't have an adjoining door with the boys, like the one we are in now. I asked that we move, and so we did.'

Olivia swallowed. 'That was meant to be your cabin?'

Ingrid nodded. 'I can't help but think . . . what if that was meant to be us?'

'But . . . why? Why would anyone want to do that to you?'

Ingrid's eyes went wide. 'I can't say. I've said too much already.'

Olivia felt faint, unsure whether it was Ingrid's words or the heat and claustrophobia. She needed to get out of the sauna.

She stood up and pushed on the door. But it didn't budge.

She searched for a handle. There was a wooden one but there was no lever or lock. She rattled the door again – but it still didn't seem to budge.

'Did you lock this when you came in?' She turned to Ingrid, who was still sitting on the bench.

The older woman stood up. 'No. I didn't think you could lock a sauna.'

'You shouldn't be able to.' Olivia pressed her face up against the small glass window, rubbing the steam away. But she couldn't see anything. She peered down and it looked as if something was jamming the door – but she couldn't be sure.

She slapped her palm against the wood. 'Hello? Can anyone hear us? We're trapped in here.'

Ingrid stood up now too, grabbing the handle and yanking hard, as if Olivia might not have been strong enough. But it wouldn't open for her either. They exchanged a panicked look, and Ingrid added her voice to Olivia's shouting.

From behind them, there was a hiss, as if someone had poured water on the heated stones inside the sauna stove. Steam began to fill up the room, and as the temperature rose – so did Olivia's panic. She turned her palm to a fist and began to pound on the door.

'E-emergency button,' she managed to stammer out. 'We need to find it.'

But the steam thickened, making it difficult to see her own hand in front of her face, let alone where the emergency stop button was. Her head began to throb. And her voice was getting more faint by the moment.

It was so hot; it was getting hard to breathe. Ingrid's fingernails dug into her upper arm as the woman clung on tight. 'I have a heart condition . . . I don't know if I can take much more of this.'

As if on cue, she clutched at her heart and began wobbling at the knees, her hand sliding down Olivia's arm. Olivia tried to guide her safely down to the bench, but she was feeling light-headed as well.

The humid steam was suffocating.

As Ingrid panicked, so did Olivia. They were trapped. And no one had any idea they were inside.

Except the person who had locked them in there.

34

'Holy shit, what are you doing?'

Olivia blinked open her eyes at the sound of the voice. She was crumpled up on the floor of the sauna, Ingrid moaning beside her. She instinctively crawled out of the now open door, gasping for the fresh, cool air.

Liam helped her, then Ingrid, out of the sauna and on to one of the mudroom benches. 'What happened?'

When Olivia gained back her breath, she tried to explain. 'We were trapped! The door was locked – or something blocked the door from the outside and we couldn't get out.'

Liam's eyes widened. 'Hey, it's OK. You're safe now.'

'What was blocking it?' asked Ingrid.

Liam shook his head. 'I couldn't see anything. And there's no lock on the door. Far as I could tell, you could have walked out at any time.'

Olivia groaned, her face dripping with sweat. Sitting in the mudroom, she shivered. She wondered if she was cooling down too quickly. Beside her, Ingrid looked pale, her once carefully applied make-up now dripping down her cheeks. 'We tried. We both did. We couldn't get out.'

He put his hand on her knee. 'Mate, I believe you. Why don't you head upstairs, get yourself water and food, then try to rest. You've both had a bit of a trauma. I'll take Mrs Hughes up to her cabin.'

Olivia's heart was pounding. She was certain someone had tried to kill them.

But Sergei was locked up.

If she'd been wrong about him, that meant the true culprit was still out there.

'Come with us,' said Ingrid, grabbing Olivia's hand. 'I don't think you should be alone.'

Olivia followed Ingrid and Liam to one of the higher decks, to the Hugheses' cabin. It was on the same floor that cabin sixteen was on, and the sight of the door haunted her.

The Hugheses' cabin was lavishly decorated with things Cutler and Ingrid must have brought from home – velvet bed coverings, silk sheets and plush towels. There was an open adjoining door to another cabin, as Ingrid had mentioned.

'Boys, are you there?' Ingrid stuck her head around the door, and sighed with relief when they weren't in. 'I didn't want them to have to see me like this. I'm going to clean up,' she said, before disappearing into the bathroom.

Olivia slumped down on one of the two plump sofas and dropped her head into her hands.

Liam kneeled down to the mini-fridge, rooting through the options. Eventually he handed her a bottle of sparkling water. 'Not great, but better than nothing.'

She took a swig. 'I thought with Sergei under lock and key, I wouldn't have to worry about stuff like this happening any more.' *You're in danger.* That's what Sergei had said. Was he right, and someone else was behind this?

Liam grimaced, shifting from foot to foot. Olivia narrowed her eyes. 'What is it?'

'Sergei wasn't locked up this arvo. He asked to talk to the captain while we were at anchor. Whatever he said convinced the captain to let him out.'

'You're kidding me.'

''Fraid not. He works below deck so maybe Cap thought you wouldn't find out.'

'Until I get locked in a sauna and almost die.'

Liam looked about to reply when Ingrid came out of the bathroom, her face freshly washed and a towel around her neck. He passed her the second bottle of sparkling water, which she took gratefully.

'We have to tell the captain what happened,' said Olivia.

'No,' said Ingrid. 'We need to talk to Cutler first of all.'

'What? We can't just pretend like this didn't happen . . .'

Ingrid looked up at Liam. 'Would you be a dear and get us something to eat from the galley? I feel like we need something solid after that.'

'Oh, sure. And I'm going to get Dr Ranj to come and look you both over.' He quirked an eyebrow at Olivia before leaving the cabin.

Ingrid fell back on the bed.

'We have to tell the captain,' Olivia repeated.

'Coming on this trip was a mistake,' said Ingrid, ignoring Olivia's statement. 'He wanted one last hurrah on a Pioneer ship before they're all sold off and we close all the branches for good.'

'What?' She'd known that Cutler had made a deal to sell off the Pioneer ships. But all the travel agency branches too?

'Oh, it's going to be all over the news when we get back into port but Cutler is retiring. Pioneer's going to be online-only. But only if the deal goes through. If not, then it's gone completely.'

'Wait, but – do the Pioneer employees know?'

'Not yet. But I think someone caught wind – and that's why we're being targeted.'

Olivia's mind raced. She thought of Patty and the branch she'd built with her late husband, of Annalise and her career dreams, thinking they were here for a relaunch celebration when they were on board for a farewell voyage. It was so unfair. Even though she knew full well that brutal decisions were sometimes necessary in business, how some divisions could be cut with ruthless efficiency to make financial savings, it was impossible not to feel for the people affected.

But hearing the news also made Olivia feel a small jolt of relief. If all the bad things that had happened were connected to the Hugheses, maybe she wasn't the target after all. She had simply been in the wrong place at the wrong time.

That doesn't explain the Clarissa, she reminded herself. *Or what Sergei said about Pierre.*

'I am sorry that you have been caught in the middle of this.'

'Ingrid, if you think you're in danger, you have to tell the captain. Otherwise . . .' The lock on the stateroom door clicked open.

Cutler stormed in, his face red with exertion. He stood in the open doorway. 'Ingrid, put that down.' He grabbed the bottle, so fast it spilled on to the duvet.

'Cutler!' Ingrid squealed, as water poured over her lap.

'Who gave this to you?' he asked her.

'Liam did!'

'What did I tell you?' He stormed over to the bath-room and poured the rest of the bottle down the sink. 'You're not to drink anything in the cabin that we didn't bring on board.'

Ingrid's eyes widened as she looked from Cutler to Olivia, then back to her husband. Cutler blinked, as if seeing her for the first time. 'Never be too careful,' he muttered.

'Olivia knows,' said Ingrid. 'About the champagne, the deaths, your retirement – everything. She and I were trapped together in the sauna, and if it hadn't been for Liam we would have suffocated in there.'

'Ingrid, my God—'

'She wants to tell the captain.'

Cutler turned to Olivia. 'No, you can't. Every incident will be recorded and passed on to the new buyer. He's already breathing down my neck as it is. A scandal like this – a malfunctioning sauna – could ruin the deal.'

'Excuse me, but we almost *died* today. Two people already have. You don't think that's more important than some deal?'

'I'm handling it,' said Cutler through gritted teeth. 'And you are both alive. For now, let's focus on the positive. Like going to see Stefan. Since you're here, we should go and find out what the final numbers were.'

'This is ridiculous. Liam will report the incident to the captain anyway.'

'I can deal with Liam. So can I rely on your discretion?'

'I—'

'Remember, the Hunt Advisory has as much riding on this deal as I do.'

Olivia stared at Cutler. The epitome of a man used to getting his own way. But she knew if she went to the captain without Ingrid's back-up, she would sound even more paranoid. He already thought she was a bit of a lunatic. 'I won't tell the captain – for now. But if anything else happens, it won't be the captain I go to. I'll demand to talk to the police.'

35

Olivia was still fuming as they made their way to the gallery. The 'CLOSED' sign hung on the door; the gallery shut while they were at anchor.

Cutler strode ahead, knocking on the door. As he waited for Stefan to open up, he turned back to Olivia. His brows were knitted together in concern, but she felt cagey. 'Look, I know what happened must have been scary. But my wife is prone to hysteria – I promise you, no one on board is out to target us. I'm just sorry that you got caught in the middle of it. And the couple in cabin sixteen – I have been getting daily updates from the captain. You want the truth? They both ingested liquid MDMA from inside the champagne bottle. They couldn't have ordered the champagne on board, so they must have brought it themselves. Maybe they wanted to have a bit of extra fun and it got out of hand – who knows? – but it's been ruled as suicide.'

Olivia shivered. 'It's not just that. One of the crew members robbed me last night.'

'What? I hadn't heard about that . . .'

'They took the engagement ring Aaron had bought for me. So you have to forgive me that I'm a bit on edge.'

'A ring? Well now. Understandable,' said Cutler, still keeping up his act of concern. 'But hearing Stefan's news will cheer you up, I'm sure. Where is that man?' He knocked again, even harder.

Olivia leaned past Cutler and tried the handle. It opened. 'Was he expecting us?' she asked.

Cutler shrugged.

Olivia's fingers went cold, dread filling her stomach. She could feel her heart beating inside her ears. She allowed Cutler to take the lead, his bulk and confident take-charge attitude comforting in that moment.

They stepped into the gallery and everything appeared normal. Yennin's prints still hung on the walls, although most were marked with little 'sold' stickers. The pictures looked surreal hanging in between the floor-to-ceiling windows now showing off the stunning Antarctic landscape outside. To Olivia, it only served to show how well Yennin had managed to capture the beauty and sparseness of the environment without losing any of its vibrancy. Like the pulsating water outside the window, the paintings seemed rich with their own beating heart and life. Even as prints, they astounded her.

'Stefan?' Cutler called out, but the gallery was empty. He turned to Olivia. 'I think he has an office in the back. Maybe we caught him napping.'

The ominous feeling in the pit of Olivia's stomach opened up again. Something wasn't right. She wanted to turn around right then and there. But she was just being stupid. She needed the report from Stefan, as much as Cutler did.

Cutler knocked on the office door, but once again there was no answer. He took the lead in opening the door this time, Olivia standing just behind.

As the door swung open, she couldn't help the scream that sprang from her throat.

Cutler turned, taking Olivia in his arms, trying to shield her from the sight inside.

But it was too late. She had seen Stefan hanging from the window bar over his office window.

He was dead.

36

The captain and Cutler were locked in the captain's office, along with the two doctors – Ranj and Tove. Olivia sat in the bridge, a blanket draped over her shoulders, her hands gripping a scalding-hot cup of tea – not that she was drinking it. The sensation helped stop her hands from shaking.

Liam came and kneeled down in front of her. 'Can I get you anything else? Maybe something to eat?'

She shook her head.

'I can't believe it. To have someone die on board? That's awful. I'm so sorry you had to be the one to find him.'

Olivia felt numb, like she was in shock. Stefan was dead. Apparently by his own hand – that's what all the ship's crew were saying, even if that felt wrong to her in the depths of her bones. There had been no signs Stefan had been suicidal. Still, she knew all too well that a person's mental state couldn't be judged by their outward actions. Maybe he had been struggling and no one had realized. Yet in the context of what had happened to her already on this voyage, Stefan's death did not sit right.

Pedro and Elisabet were scouring the CCTV, but the gallery had been shut all day, most of the passengers out on the water on their Zodiac tours or on shore. Apart from the usual flow of people moving from the dining room back to the cabins past the gallery, there was no sign of anyone lingering or acting suspiciously.

Cutler came out of the captain's office and Olivia leaped to her feet. 'What are we going to do?' she asked.

Cutler shook his head, and it was the captain who answered. 'Unfortunate, very unfortunate.'

'What about Sergei? Where was he in all of this? Liam told me that you set him free, and now there's been another death? That can't be a coincidence.'

'I can assure you, it wasn't Sergei,' said Captain Enzo.

'How can you possibly know that?'

'Because Sergei is no longer on board the *Vigil*.'

That stopped Olivia's protest in her tracks. No longer on board? That meant . . . maybe he had been the one in the rogue kayak, heading to the *Clarissa II*. Where else could someone go, in the middle of Antarctica?

She was just about to ask the captain, when he continued to speak. 'The helicopter is gone, so we can't fly him back to the mainland. We've been in contact with Art Aboard headquarters, who are going to be in touch with his family. Our ship has space to keep him in the medical centre until we get back.' He took a deep breath in. 'However, we have decided to continue the itinerary as planned on the cruise, for the sake of keeping things as normal as possible for our passengers on board – we'll just keep the gallery shut. We will continue to sail to Paradise, and, Liam, you will continue to run the excursion tonight. Then we will begin our journey back to Ushuaia as planned.'

Olivia's jaw dropped. 'You can't be serious? We have to turn back now.'

The captain shook his head. 'This is not a decision I have made lightly. There is another storm front moving through the Drake Passage this evening. If it's safe to do so, we will miss out on Deception Island, save a day, but

261

it will be more dangerous for us to cross while a storm of that magnitude is in the area. In Paradise Bay, we will be sheltered from it.'

She opened her mouth to protest again but knew it would be fruitless. If there was a storm big enough to create chaos in the Drake Passage, she could see the logic in not putting the entire ship through that again. And keeping the excursions running as normal meant avoiding a panic on board.

The only person the captain had to worry about panicking was her.

'I have to go back to the cabin. I need to lie down.'

'I'll take you,' said Liam.

She was glad to leave the stuffy air inside the bridge. She took a shuddering breath.

'Look, I know you've had a terrible day. I can't even imagine.'

'Just . . . in shock, that's all.'

'Not a surprise after what you've been through. But I've been meaning to ask . . . have you heard any more about that couple?' Liam's tone was casual, but Olivia could see the tightness in his shoulders, his jaw clenching.

Olivia hesitated. She'd seen him barely keeping control once before. Could she really trust him? What did she really know about him?

'You do know something,' said Liam, reading into her stalling.

Her brain was too tired; she couldn't think on her feet. 'They're dead,' she said, barely above a whisper.

'Fuck!' Liam's hand balled into a fist, and he whipped around, punching the wall so hard the plaster cracked.

Olivia ran.

37

'Wait! Olivia, hang on.'

She was running, flying down the stairs as fast as she could manage. If she could get back to the cabin, she could lock herself inside and not come out for the rest of the cruise.

It seemed like the safest – maybe the only – option.

Liam's anger terrified her. He didn't seem stable.

He'd found them in the sauna. He'd also been wandering the halls the first night of the voyage. What if *he* was the one trying to scare her? The ring had been found in *his* cabin.

He was quicker than her, stronger too. He grabbed her arm, pulling her sideways. She felt a blast of cold air as he dragged her through heavy double doors and out on to deck. The ship was moving now, heading to its next anchor point in Paradise Bay. She struggled against him, frantically searching for something she could use to stop him from doing whatever it was he planned.

'Please, I'm not trying to hurt you.' He finally let go, and she wrenched her arm back.

'What the hell?'

'Listen to me! Jesus Christ. I'm sorry. This is important. When we were in Ushuaia, I went out with the crew. I got properly munted. When we're in port it's our time to let loose, you know? Anyway, I ended up hooking up with this girl . . .'

'Liam, I really don't want to hear this.' She couldn't even look at him. She didn't understand how what he was saying connected with anything – all she knew was that she felt afraid.

'Please,' he begged. 'She found out I worked on the *Vigil* and she asked me to do her a favour. Deliver a birthday gift to one of the cabins. A bottle of champagne.'

Olivia stopped in her tracks. 'What?'

'Yeah. Exactly. Clearly not a good idea, right? But she gave me ten grand to do it. That's like almost double my wage for this cruise – just to put a bottle of champagne in a room.'

'And that amount of money didn't make you suspicious?'

'You don't understand – that much money . . . it could change things for me. I don't want to be fucking about any more. I want to find a job that actually means something to me – and this would give me the time to do that. I couldn't see any downside. I'm a fucking idiot.'

She didn't need any guesses to know which cabin. 'So *you* brought the poisoned bottle on board?'

Liam hissed a breath in through his teeth. 'I didn't bloody know it was at the time. Just looked like a fancy bottle of fizz wrapped in pink foil. Not my normal style, but whatever. Then I spoke to Ranj. He said the liquid looked weird – brownish red and had a kind of aniseed scent. They sent it back with the couple in the chopper. If the police do any sort of investigation . . . my fingerprints are all over that bloomin' thing.'

'Liam . . . it was liquid MDMA. Cutler told me.'

His face drained of colour. 'Shit. I swear, I didn't know anything about it. I thought I was just doing some

264

chook a favour. If I end up in Argentinian prison . . . I can't even think of it.'

'What do you remember about the woman who asked you to do this?'

'Not much, to be honest. Like I said, I was wasted, but when I woke up, the champagne and the money were on the table. She had dark hair, really long. About your height.'

Olivia's mind raced. First Sergei, now a woman involved? An accomplice?

'Do you think she's on board? Would you recognize her?'

He winced. 'I was properly out of it. I can barely remember anything from that night.'

Long, dark hair. There were a few women on board who matched that description. Or it could have just been someone wearing a wig as a disguise – someone who must have known Liam was desperate enough for money that he would accept an offer like that. An easy target to frame for the deaths. Liam had told her that Sergei was new on board – so maybe he was in place to make sure the plan was executed properly. And when things immediately went wrong, Sergei had been forced to act . . .

'Jesus, Liam. Why are you telling me this?'

He frowned. 'You said you were the intended target for the champagne. Since it was your cabin originally.'

'Or the Hugheses'. Ingrid seemed to think so. They were given cabin sixteen as their first choice.'

'Fuck. What are we going to do?'

Olivia stared at him in alarm. '*We* aren't going to do anything. How can I trust you? You could be making all this up!'

'Why the heck would I do that? You could go to the captain now and tell him that I did it and I'd be locked up like that.' He snapped his fingers. 'But I think we can help each other.'

Olivia searched his face. He was right – he didn't gain anything by confessing that he put the bottle in the cabin, except to gain her trust.

'So who do you think is behind it?' Liam asked.

'I have no idea . . .'

'Come on, you must know something.'

She hesitated. 'At first, when Aaron didn't make it on board, I thought it was a genuine mistake. But . . .'

'But?'

'Just before the cruise, I'd overheard him and Stefan talking about a threat he'd been facing. Someone had been sending him threatening emails accusing him of having something to do with the artist – Yennin's – death. Then I found a note in among his clothes, kind of accusing him of the same thing. He'd been in a lot of debt too, that the profit from this deal was going to clear. I just wonder if it all caught up with him. But then there's the fact that Ingrid thinks there's pretty good motive against her and Cutler too. He's planning on retiring and closing down his entire business. What if it has nothing to do with me and Aaron at all?' She sighed. 'But then there's the yacht . . .'

'The yacht?'

'Did you see it while you were kayaking? It has a dark blue hull – the *Clarissa II*.'

Liam nodded. 'The captain alerted us all to her this morning. Some rich guy wanting adventure – we had to coordinate to make sure our landings don't cross over to abide by IAATO rules. What does that have to do with this?'

'I don't know. Maybe nothing.' She didn't know how to explain her connection to that particular boat name. 'But if Sergei is no longer on board the *Vigil*, where did he go? Did he go to the *Clarissa II*?'

'OK, listen. Take this.' He passed her his radio. 'I've got a second one. If you feel any kind of threat, any concern at all, radio me. Then tonight we'll be on the continent.'

'No way. I'm not doing that now, not after what happened to Stefan. I'm just going to lock myself in the cabin and wait it out.'

Liam frowned. 'But your cabinmates are all on the excursion with me, right?'

'Um, yes.'

'So if they're all with me, you'd be left totally on your own. I don't think that's a good idea.'

Olivia sucked in her bottom lip, then nodded. Liam was right. Being alone did not sound very appealing. Though neither did being on the ice. She didn't know which was the lesser of two evils. Maybe she didn't have to choose just yet. She took the radio and slipped it inside her jacket. It did feel better to have it on her.

'C'mon. I'll take you back to your cabin and make sure you're not alone before I leave you.'

'Thanks, Liam.'

'Whatever happens, I'm going to keep you safe. I owe you that much.'

38

Patty and Janine were in the cabin when Olivia opened the door. Liam touched her arm. 'Stay safe. And remember.' He tapped at his chest pocket, the place where she'd tucked the radio in her own jacket.

She nodded.

Patty stopped mid-fold of a thermal top into her backpack. After Liam left, she let out a low whistle. 'What's going on there then?' she asked.

'It's not like that,' said Olivia. She glanced at Janine, not wanting her to get the wrong idea.

But she looked concerned – not jealous. 'You OK?' asked Janine. 'You look a bit shaken up. I went looking for you but couldn't find you anywhere.'

'Oh, um.' She scrambled to think of the right thing to say, knowing she had agreed to keep Stefan's death quiet – for now. 'I've been up with the captain. The sauna malfunctioned while I was in there.'

'What? You're joking,' said Patty.

'Liam found us before it got too bad. That's why he was telling me to stay safe.'

'Us?' Janine asked.

'I was with Ingrid Hughes.'

'I didn't realize you guys knew each other,' said Annalise, piping up for the first time. 'How is she?'

Olivia paused, eyeing Annalise. It seemed like she was trying hard not to look *too* interested in how Ingrid was doing, but she was waiting for Olivia's answer with bated breath. 'She's fine too,' said Olivia. 'Liam and I took her back to her cabin.'

'Ooh, honey, I'm afraid we need details,' said Patty with a grin. 'What's their cabin like?'

'A lot bigger than ours,' said Olivia.

'I'd hoped we'd be offered a tour of some of the bigger cabins. It would be good for me to be able to describe it to my customers. Do a bit of upselling.'

'Was Cutler there too?' asked Annalise.

'He was,' said Olivia.

'Their marriage on the rocks yet? Cutler can't even bring up his own kids, let alone somebody else's,' said Annalise, folding her arms across her chest.

'Wait, those aren't his sons?' Olivia was shocked.

'Nah, he and Ingrid only got hitched a year ago. I placed a bet that it wouldn't last eighteen months.'

'I've got to return this,' said Janine, holding up a thriller she'd taken from the ship's library.

'I'll come with you,' said Olivia. She wanted to look up information about the *Clarissa II*. After her dad's death, she hadn't managed to find out who the owner of the original *Clarissa* was. But this was fifteen years later. There wasn't any central database of yacht names and owners, but if Liam was right and it was owned by someone really rich, there might be some press mentioning the boat online.

Out in the hallway, they both jumped, as the radio that Liam had given her began to bleep and chatter. 'What was that?' Janine asked.

'This.' Olivia took the radio out from inside her jacket and turned the dial down. 'Liam gave it to me after the sauna.'

'I see. You two have been talking quite a bit, huh?'

Olivia reached out and squeezed Janine's arm. 'Oh, please don't worry. He's only interested in you. Trust me – I'm *way* over here, worrying about my fiancé-to-be.' She outstretched her arms.

'You sure?'

'I promise. The radio is because I'm a big old mess at the moment. I think he's just trying to make me feel better. Especially since the captain let Sergei go.'

'What? The thief? You're kidding me! How could they do that?'

'Apparently he convinced the captain he was innocent.'

'No wonder you're freaked out.'

In the library, Olivia sat down at a computer while Janine returned her book. She opened her emails – no longer even surprised that there were no new replies – just the normal junk mail. She couldn't understand why Pierre would send her that warning and then not reply to any of her emails – especially the one she'd sent asking about Sergei.

She opened a separate tab with Google, typing the name of the yacht into the search engine.

The page of results appeared slowly, but because it was a relatively common name, there didn't seem to be anything that corresponded to a yacht, let alone who owned it.

Olivia sighed.

'Everything OK?' asked Janine.

'You know that yacht we saw on my camera? I was curious if I could find out who owns it. I wondered about the type of person who would sail down here.' It didn't sound like a particularly plausible excuse to Olivia's ear, but Janine nodded.

'Let me? I have amazing Google-fu.'

'Sure thing.' She stood up from the chair so that Janine could sit down.

Janine typed a long string of text into the search engine, using all sorts of symbols – quotation marks, colons and hashtags. She was able to refine the search so that only relevant articles popped up.

'Where did you learn to do this?'

'This is what I do for a living. Or did, I suppose. Alongside the influencer stuff. Digital marketing, SEO, that kind of thing. When you have super-slow internet like this, it really helps to be specific in your filters. And . . . look!' said Janine. She'd struck gold – an article about the *Clarissa II*. There was an image at the top, which froze midway through loading. But the caption underneath it was clear.

Olivia gasped.

Janine looked up at her in alarm. 'What is it?'

Pierre Lavaud stands in front of the latest addition to his fleet: the ice-class expedition yacht Clarissa II.

'*I can't wait to explore some of the most unseen parts of our planet,' says Mr Lavaud. 'I name all my ships after my daughter, who we lost far too young. This way, I feel like she explores with me.'*

Olivia's stomach turned, her mouth suddenly as dry as the Sahara.

Pierre was the owner of the *Clarissa II*. Had he known her dad all those years ago? Had he known about her?

'Olivia? You're shaking.'

'I know the owner of that boat,' she said, barely above a croak.

'You do?'

'He was a client of mine. He bought the Yennin that kicked off this whole venture for Aaron and me.'

'So he's come to check on his investment?'

Olivia blinked. She hadn't thought about that. 'I guess so.' She thought about Sergei urging her to talk to Pierre about why he was on board. Maybe he was supposed to be Pierre's eyes and ears for the showcase?

'Tell me what you're thinking,' said Janine.

'My mind is a mess. It's just . . . Sergei mentioned Pierre. Maybe he was working for him?'

'So why raid our cabin and steal your engagement ring? I don't know. Something seems off about all this. Are you *sure* Pierre doesn't have a different motive? Didn't you mention something about Aaron being in debt? Maybe Sergei is collecting . . .'

Olivia swallowed. That was a distinct possibility too. She didn't know who she could trust. The fact that Pierre might be connected to her dad . . . it was all too much. What did it mean that he was down here? Was it all about Yennin? Or did it go further back than that?

Janine grabbed Olivia's hand. 'Whatever it is, you don't have to be scared on your own. You have friends here. You have me, you have Patty and Annalise, you have Liam. We can look out for you.'

The unexpected level of fierceness in Janine's tone made Olivia smile. 'Thank you,' she said.

There was a loud knock on the glass door of the library. Liam burst into the room, his eyes wide. 'Jesus, I've been looking for you everywhere. Why haven't you been answering your radio? I thought something awful had happened to you.'

Olivia pulled it out of her jacket pocket. 'Sorry. I

wasn't even thinking. I turned it down – I thought it was more if I needed to contact you. What is it?'

Liam's eyes flicked from Olivia to Janine. 'It's OK,' said Olivia. 'She knows about the situation.'

'We're almost in Paradise Bay. The moment we anchor, you're coming on shore with me.'

39

Olivia held her breath as she watched the two Zodiacs filled with passengers leave the MS *Vigil*. She'd spent the last two hours helping Liam and Melissa ferry equipment from the ship to the shore, stacking it up in neat piles ready for the overnight camping. There was a surprising amount for how many were coming ashore – fifteen additional passengers, plus three staff.

Cutler and Ingrid were coming, of course, although their children were too young – they'd be staying with a nanny and camping on the deck of the *Vigil*.

Robert and Aida. Greg and Tariq. Maxwell and Lucinda. Delilah, in a long dark wig this time. That was almost all the VIPs – hardly a surprise, considering the spaces were extremely limited for the exclusive experience. Three spots were her bunkmates from cabin twelve: Patty, Annalise and Janine. The rest were people Olivia hadn't really interacted with on board. Like Yara, one of the influencers, carrying Helena's drone. (Helena was feeling too unwell to make the excursion.) And a sweet older couple, who'd introduced themselves to Olivia as Dave and Kathy from southern California. They spoke excitedly about the 'investment' they'd made in a Yennin piece. This was the point of the showcase . . . so that even non-art lovers would hear of him and spread the word.

The other crew member was Arthur Vance, the

glaciologist, who was going to explain Antarctic phe-nomena to them – although Olivia kind of wished it was Dr Ranjeed. Having a medical doctor with them seemed like good sense.

They had to keep the excursion numbers small to minimize the impact on the environment, and it was part of the treaty to vow not to take external food or waste on to the continent, so they ate beforehand, and were only allowed water to drink. The plan was for them to sleep outside, under the open air in oversized sleeping bags known as bivvy sacks fitted with thermal mats.

The hard physical work unloading the bivvies and barrels meant she wasn't constantly thinking about poor Stefan, or what had happened to her and Ingrid, or about the *Clarissa II* somewhere out there with Sergei on board. She instead focused on the landscape. Para-dise Bay certainly lived up to its name. For most of the afternoon, the sky had been an intense cobalt blue. The sun sparked against the pristine white landscape, an almost agonizingly bright glow. The mountains hugged the bay, making it feel sheltered and protected. There was a cluster of red-painted buildings near the far edge of the shore – Almirante Brown Base, a scientific out-post run by the Argentinian government. Arthur had told her there were no personnel there; the base was shuttered for the season.

As the evening drew on, the sun dipped lower in the sky, casting a more gentle, serene glow across the bay.

'Look at this – it must have washed ashore after a recent calving,' Arthur said, picking up a block of ice so clear, deep and black, it was like a piece of onyx. 'Aren't glaciers amazing?'

Olivia kneeled down next to him. 'What is it?'

'This is history. The air bubbles within this glacial ice could have formed millions of years ago. And now I'm holding it in my hands.' He placed it carefully back down on the shore. 'It's also a shame. That we're the ones to see it. Every time I come here, the continent has changed. Glaciers shift and move. I expect that. That's in their nature. But it's happening quickly. Way too quickly.'

He stood up abruptly, staring off at the icy cliffs.

Olivia stood up next to him. 'Are you waiting to see if it will happen again?'

'Inevitably it will. Just hopefully not while the Zodiacs are unloading.'

'I also don't recommend being in a kayak at the time.'

'That was you?'

She nodded, and he laughed. 'Well, you're an Antarctica crew legend now. A capsize on an excursion is everyone's worst nightmare but as rare as Ice VII.'

She wanted to ask more but was wary of setting him off on another lecture about the different kinds of ice. There was only so much ice talk she could take.

A strong breeze swirled around their boots, lifting her hair. She expected the wind to come from the ocean, like when she had been standing in the harbour at Ushuaia. But this wind came from the interior. Everything was topsy-turvy here.

It was only a few more days until the trip was over. Then she could go to the police and find out what was happening.

The first Zodiac pulled up on to the stony beach, and Liam leaped out. He held out a hand to Cutler, who ignored it.

'I don't think I can do this,' declared Ingrid. She still looked pale from their terrifying sauna experience. Olivia spotted Annalise rolling her eyes, and she wished she could tell her what she and Mrs Hughes had gone through. Then Annalise would understand.

Unless she had been the one to give them the scare . . .

'I want to be back with my boys.'

'I'll take her,' said Melissa, who had just pulled up in the second Zodiac. Liam did a double take as one of the passengers swung her legs on to the shore. Delilah. His face drained of colour.

'You OK?' Olivia asked Liam under her breath.

'That woman . . . she looks suddenly familiar.'

Olivia thought back to the story he'd told her, about the person who had bribed him to bring the champagne aboard. 'You don't think it's . . .'

Liam shook himself. 'It can't be.' Then he turned to the rest of the group, the colour back in his cheeks. 'It'll be easiest if you stay in pairs – try to buddy up,' he said. 'Make sure you have a shovel and a bivvy sack.'

Olivia swallowed, glancing over at Delilah, who had paired up with Yara, the influencer. Delilah had been the underbidder at the London Yennin auction. She was a woman used to getting what she wanted. Did she really feel like Pierre had been informed of Yennin's death in advance of the official news? Would that be enough to drive her to get payback in the form of poisoned champagne? Olivia felt herself shiver.

'Excuse me.' Ingrid pushed past Olivia to clamber into Melissa's Zodiac. Melissa then steered it back towards the boat.

'I think that's another divorce incoming,' said Anna-lise out of the corner of her mouth.

Olivia hadn't realized that all her cabinmates were around her.

Patty elbowed her in the side. 'That's not nice.'

'What? There's clearly no love lost there,' muttered Annalise.

'She's been through a lot today,' said Olivia.

Janine picked up one of the big shovels.

'Let me give you a hand with that,' said Olivia. But Janine had already swung it over her shoulder.

'Don't worry, I got it.'

'See? This is why we need young people around – to do all this heavy lifting,' said Patty with a laugh.

'Come on – we'd better catch up,' said Olivia.

Liam was dragging a long red plastic pulk behind him, laden with emergency supplies. He led the group single file along the ice shelf, up a short hill to a plateau that had a clear view across the bay to the ship. From that vantage point, the blue-hulled boat seemed so small, surrounded by the majesty of the big white continent.

Olivia took a moment to catch her breath and take in the view. The sky was a deep indigo, the sun dropping ever lower. At this latitude, the sun would set for a few minutes, hovering just below the horizon. But ambient light would linger in the sky, never fully extinguishing. A white night.

There were wisps of cloud tinted yellow. She gripped the handle of the shovel tighter. Some movement close to the boat caught her eye. Melissa was steering the Zodiac back to shore. Olivia squinted. It looked as if someone was in the boat with Melissa. It was hard to tell if it was another person or just a large sack of supplies in a black duffle. Black – not the regulation red parka or the crew blue.

She scoured the bay, wishing she had binoculars. She couldn't see anything except the gentle white caps on the waves and the towering icebergs floating. No sign of the *Clarissa II*. Still, just because she couldn't see it, didn't mean it wasn't there. There were so many inlets and crevices where the glaciers jutted out on to the charcoal-black water. So many places where a yacht could hide.

She turned back to look at the group on the little plateau. It was hard to tell who was who with everyone wearing the same red Pioneer-branded jackets. They were like a crèche of crimson penguins. Only Liam, Melissa and Dr Vance stood out.

'Are they trying to tire us out before bedtime or something?' Patty huffed from behind. She dropped the shovel she'd been carrying with a thud.

'I'll help you with that,' Olivia said, picking up the handle and dragging it along the ground.

'Can you believe this? That we're here? Karl would have given his left arm to camp on Antarctica. He'd have loved it.' Patty took a deep breath.

Olivia touched her shoulder. 'Was he adventurous?'

'Oh, always. But what he loved most was getting to share that with other people. The look of excitement on his face when he booked a client on a trip and knew what a life-changing experience they were about to have . . . It made him so happy.'

'He sounds like an amazing man.'

'He was. When he passed, our business suffered too. I had to use all his life insurance and remortgage the house to keep it going during Covid and the downturn. But we're steadily getting back on our feet now. Annalise really stepped up to help. She might be taciturn, but she's whip-smart. I wouldn't be surprised if she ran Pioneer one day.'

Olivia kept her head down, tugging her hot pink hat lower down over her ears. There wasn't going to be a Pioneer Adventures for much longer if Cutler went through with his plan.

Liam stopped in the middle of the plateau and dropped the rope of the pulk. 'All right, everyone, this is where we're going to camp for the night. Time to take out your shovels and dig yourselves a hole long enough to lie down comfortably in. The sides of the hole will offer you shelter from the wind. Try to remove any stones or hard chunks of ice that might stick into your back – or else you might find it a very long night.'

'No one told us we had to do hard labour,' muttered Cutler. He didn't look like a man used to doing his own digging.

Olivia set down Patty's shovel. 'Don't worry, I'll help you first.'

'You shouldn't do that, honey. You know the plane rule – put on your oxygen mask before helping somebody else.'

Olivia laughed. 'This is hardly an oxygen-mask situation. Let me help you.'

'Well, of course I will. But you shouldn't make a habit of this, you know. Or before you know it you'll have spent your whole life helping other people and you won't have left any time at all for yourself.'

Olivia's laughter died away. She gave Patty a tight smile instead, then thrust the shovel into the ground. In the meantime, Patty shook out their bivvy sacks.

She found it strangely comforting to dig, listening to

the crunch as the metal slid through the snow. Sweat beaded on her forehead, her muscles aching, and she felt tired – but it wasn't fear or worry or stress driving it for once. It felt good.

'That's about the right depth,' Liam said, over her shoulder. 'Just need it a bit longer so you can stretch out.'

'Thanks. This one is for Patty. Must be annoying having to oversee us amateurs. And manage that.' She gestured with a tilt of her head over to Cutler, who was barking at Melissa – the one doing most of the work digging out his bed for the night.

'That's sort of what I was talking about before. My dream is to land a permanent gig on a small expedition ship. Maybe even a yacht like that one you were talking about – the *Clarissa II*. I can't believe Melissa traded private charters for a big corporate cruise line; she's nuts. Some companies offer mountaineering and skiing experiences in Antarctica. I could be climbing Mount Banck right now.' He gestured towards the mountain rising up behind Brown Base. 'More bespoke adventure. More money too. Time off to go back home for the summers. Maybe run my own business. That would even give me an opportunity to find someone, start a family, while still doing what I love.'

'Sounds perfect.'

'It's the dream.' He tilted his head towards the light, absorbing the sun's golden glow. 'But more likely I'll take whatever guiding job's available, get paid fuck all, and then get suckered into doing stupid things that get me into trouble. Like with that bottle.'

Olivia cringed. 'No, I wasn't going to say that. It sounds wonderful. Just totally out of my wheelhouse. I picked a career with a really set path, exams to pass – we even have a code of conduct we have to abide by.'

From a short distance away, Cutler swore at Melissa. Liam looked over his shoulder and cracked his knuckles. 'I'd better go make sure everything is OK. I've got a code of conduct too. Or else that guy wouldn't keep running his mouth.'

She watched him retreat, thinking of everything he had to deal with – all the responsibility. Her job was hard work too, but ultimately she shied away from leadership. There were always checks and balances in her role. Always someone else to look over, verify and confirm her work.

Ever since that night on the yacht, when her father had trusted her with the night watch, she'd feared responsibility. He'd trusted her and she'd failed.

The consequence had been the worst thing she could imagine. That night on the *Clarissa* had defined the rest of her life.

Above her head, a skua circled. She thought of the little gentoo penguin chicks that swarmed along the shoreline, hoping they'd all survive the night. The lights of the ship reflected on the still water of the bay, looking so warm and comforting, like a Christmas tree. It didn't look as if someone dangerous was on board.

A fierce gust of wind hit her back. Her foot slipped on the edge of the hole she'd dug out for Patty. She cried out, tumbling backwards into the snow.

'Are you OK?' Patty cried out.

Olivia winced, but she moved her legs gingerly; she wasn't hurt. She sat up and caught Liam looking out past the mountains. The frown on his face gave her pause.

'What's his problem?' Janine asked, looking up from where she'd been digging next to them.

'No idea. That wind was strong, though. I hope the weather doesn't turn on us.'

'They don't seem too concerned,' said Patty.

She was right. Melissa was standing with Maxwell and Lucinda, helping them lay out their bivvy sacks. She didn't seem that concerned about things in the same way that Liam was. When Melissa caught Olivia's eye, she glanced over Patty's sleeping set-up and nodded.

She gave Melissa a thumbs up.

'You're good at this,' said Janine, raising an eyebrow.

'What qualifies an actuary to be so good at expedition life?' asked Patty.

Olivia smiled. 'Absolutely nothing! But I learned some things from my dad. He loved the outdoors. When he wasn't off sailing, he used to build snow caves in the mountains back home in Scotland.'

'You must be excited to tell him all about this when you get back,' said Patty.

'He passed away when I was young.'

'Oh, I'm so sorry. I didn't realize, so stupid of me.' Patty frowned. 'Look at us, grieving in our own way. I think we were meant to be in this cabin together. We should call ourselves "The Lost Girls".'

'Did Annalise lose someone too?' whispered Janine, though Annalise was digging with her earpods in, so there was little chance of her overhearing.

Patty sighed. 'I'm not sure she had anyone to begin with. She's a fighter. She's had to work for everything she's got. But she's proven herself. To me and anyone who knows her.'

Olivia took a few steps back from digging her bivvy shelter and surveyed their – well, mostly her – handiwork. Neat little rectangles in the snow, nice and flat on the bottom, with a small wall of ice they could duck beneath if the wind picked up.

It was as if the skills she'd learned from her dad had never left her but had become ingrained – part of her DNA, as effortless as the calculations she did at work. It was a comfort to know that part of him was still with her, even if she had buried it deep for so long.

'Nice work,' said a male voice from close behind her.

Olivia felt like she jumped out of her skin. Behind her was Maxwell, his arms folded over his chest.

'Um, thanks?'

He frowned, furrowing his brow. 'Why didn't you tell me you had it all along?'

Olivia blinked. 'Had what?'

He sighed, throwing his hands up in the air. 'The ring. I told you on that first day, Aaron owes me. He was sourcing this vintage sapphire engagement ring Lucy wanted and was bringing it to me so I could propose on the continent. You don't have it with you now, do you?'

'I-I don't know what you're talking about.'

He sighed and pulled out his phone. In a few clicks, he had a photo up on his screen, which he turned to show Olivia. 'This ring. That's the one you have in your safe, right? Cutler told me.'

Olivia could hardly believe her eyes. But on the screen was a photo of the ring she'd found in Aaron's jacket pocket. 'Your idiot boyfriend was supposed to give it to me on the first day of the cruise but then he never showed. Do you know how much I paid him for that? I thought he'd completely ruined my grand plan. But if you can get it to me when we're back on the ship, I can still do it while we're in Antarctica.'

Gone was the threatening Maxwell she'd been wary of. In his place – a romantic whose main concern was that his proposal had been foiled.

So Aaron hadn't meant to ask her to marry him. She'd just made a massive assumption, and she felt like a giant ass because of it.

'I didn't realize,' she said. 'Of course I'll get it to you as soon as I'm back.'

'Great,' said Maxwell, sighing with relief. He returned to Lucinda, wrapping his arms around her waist as they stared out at the ever-changing sky.

What a fool she'd been. She looked back at the *Vigil*. Maybe she'd got everything wrong, all the assumptions she'd made – about Sergei, about Pierre, about Maxwell, about Liam. The only things she knew for sure were that Aaron hadn't made the boat, people had died – Jay, Christa, Stefan – and that she had escaped from harm twice – with her life-jacket cord and in the sauna. Who was behind it?

The truthful answer was that she had no idea. She shivered, staring down at what she'd built.

She couldn't help but wonder if she'd just dug her own grave.

40

They spent the evening listening to Dr Vance telling stories of the ice. It turned out, when he stopped speaking in scientific jargon, he was a superb storyteller, a true historian of the glaciers. Maxwell had his arms wrapped round Lucinda, and Olivia felt ashamed for leaping to conclusions about the ring and foiling Maxwell's romantic plan. Still, they didn't seem to mind. Janine set up her camera to take a time lapse of the white night sky, while they listened out for the ethereal cries of the Weddell seals, the occasional puff of a breaching humpback whale, and the wind rushing down the mountains.

As the sun set, the colours grew more vivid – almost violent in their intensity, brilliant reds and purples, before settling into a lavender haze. It was almost eleven p.m., but there was plenty of light to see by. Still, as the sun dipped below the horizon, the temperature began to drop and the exhaustion of the week's events soon caught up with her.

She nestled down into her bivvy sack, amazed at how warm she could feel while the cold air nipped at her cheeks. The hole of snow she'd dug around her – the shallow grave in the ice – was no longer so ominous now that she was actually in it. It felt more like a crib for a baby. She felt like she'd just entered a new world, and it was scary – but here, in her cradle of ice, she was safe.

She had a sudden pang for her mother. She knew that

if her mum were seeing this, she would be inspired to recreate the landscape with her oils, and with her talent she would create something truly magical. Just like Yennin, she would be inspired.

This trip had given her a deeper perspective on what had happened to her mother. Graham Campbell's death had been a calving of her mum's life. Part of her world had come crashing down, and with it her mum's confidence and vibrancy. What had been left of her mother was glacial and cold, fearful – fear that she passed down to her daughter.

Olivia had been desperate to try to keep the rest of her mother together, but it was too big a job for one person. She'd felt her control over her own life slip away since her mother's diagnosis, the pressure mounting with every passing year as her mum got worse and Olivia's financial situation became more precarious. Meeting Aaron, throwing herself into side projects, increased stress at her day job had all brought her mental health to boiling point. Taking some time off was supposed to have made things better. But instead she'd spent so much of it being afraid.

Eventually most people settled into their bivvy sacks, and she heard them shuffling under their covers, coughing, even snoring. She was amazed what people could sleep through. Reaching inside her bag for her bottle of water – their only permitted provision – she looked over to her bunkmate. Janine seemed deep in thought, wisps of her copper hair escaping from beneath her black beanie.

'Would you like some?' She waggled the water bottle in Janine's direction.

The young girl took a moment to answer, blinking back her thoughts before nodding. 'Sure, thanks.'

Olivia passed over her bottle. 'Penny for them?'

Janine smiled. 'This landscape is just wild, isn't it?'

'I was just thinking the same thing. How inspiring it is. I can see what drew Yennin to paint here.'

'Even the sounds were based off recordings he made down here,' Janine said.

Olivia tilted her head. 'You've heard them?'

Janine shook her head. 'No – I wish.' She smiled. 'I was chatting to Lucinda at the showcase and she knew all about it. She played me some of them on her phone. He really changed your and Aaron's life, didn't he?'

'In so many ways. Thanks to his artwork, I've been able to take some much-needed time out . . .'

'You can live this incredible life, all thanks to his death.'

Olivia shivered. 'What? No – it was a huge loss, not only to us and his family and friends – but to the wider art world. And my life is not so incredible.'

'What do you mean?'

'Just before coming here, I had to leave my job. I destroyed my closest friendship, pretty much ignored my mother in her care home. I fantasized about hurting myself so I no longer had to go into work. More than fantasized actually.'

'What do you mean?'

Olivia blew out a long sigh. 'It's a long story.'

'And? It's not like we have anything but time here!'

'That's true.' Still, something held her back. But Janine remained quiet, and Olivia found herself opening up. 'It was actually the night of the big Yennin auction that it happened. I had to work that day, but I was feeling extra anxious because I needed to leave early to get ready. Aaron had only asked one thing of me: that I pick up Yennin and take him to the auction.' She paused, taking a breath. The guilt was so overwhelming; she could hardly speak. She took another sip of water. 'It had been a bad year for me in general. I'd failed the final exam I needed to qualify, which meant I lost my promotion. I had some demanding clients I was trying to please, alongside my boss and Aaron too.

'That day in particular, though, I'd dropped the ball on one of my biggest clients, and my boss had given me an ultimatum – step up or lose my job. I've never faced anything like that sort of pressure at work before. Aaron was also blowing up my phone, messaging me in a panic, saying how he couldn't get hold of Yennin, how he was convinced he wasn't going to show up at the auction, and that he needed me to go get him right away. I hadn't realized until this cruise, in fact, just how much he had on the line. How much he needed the auction to be a success. But I couldn't help him. He needed me, but I just wanted to lock myself away.

'I was being pulled in so many different directions . . . but I felt numb. I left work without telling anyone. I just walked out the door. I didn't even change out of my office clothes.

'I can hardly remember the next hours passing – I was in a daze. A dense fog that wouldn't lift. I knew I had to get to the auction, so I started walking towards Mayfair – in the pouring rain no less – but I was spiralling. All I kept thinking was that if I could have a bit of time off where no one could ask anything of me, no one could blame me for missing deadlines or not doing favours, then maybe I could get back on top of everything that was threatening to bury me.

'But how? A holiday wouldn't do it. I would only end up checking my emails anyway. I couldn't cut down my hours – I needed the pay cheque. Every penny. And a sabbatical? That seemed insane – I'd lose all the momentum I had with my career.

'I knew what would do it. An injury. Just something small. Something that would buy me time, but I could recover from fully. A broken leg? Everyone knows you need time off after that; no one thinks it's your fault. As I walked down to the Tube, I fantasized about taking a fall down the stairs.'

'Yikes,' said Janine.

'I didn't, of course. But then I got off the Tube, and I thought maybe if I was hit by a car? I didn't want to die. Only to be injured *just* enough . . .' Olivia drifted off.

'You didn't go through with that either.'

'No. But I really thought about it.'

She closed her eyes.

She'd exited the Tube station a few minutes' walk away from the auction. She wondered if it was a good idea to show up in her state. She'd flaked on picking up Yennin – hopefully Aaron had arranged a different driver, or he'd managed to get himself to the auction. She looked a disaster – her hair a bedraggled mess, her eyes swollen from crying, her carefully planned outfit still hanging up in her closet in her and Aaron's bedroom.

Everything felt wrong. The noises of the city – the rain pounding against the concrete pavement, the cars whizzing past, the sirens of emergency vehicles – all sounded too loud in her ears. The street lights seemed to throb; her senses were swamped.

She desperately needed the world to stop, just for a moment, so she could catch up. *Just a small bump.* The cars weren't going that fast here, after all, it was central London, not a motorway. All she wanted was some time. *Was that too much to ask?* She felt like a deer on the side of a country road, drawn towards the headlights – aware of the danger but unable to stop herself.

There was a gap between two parked cars. She stood in between them, wondering if she could go through with it.

Just a little pain. Then she could stop disappointing people.

Then she could rest.

'I spotted this car weaving its way down the road, driving erratically. I don't know, maybe the driver was running late . . .

'I wasn't thinking straight. I stepped out. I actually did it. I prepared for the pain. But immediately I realized how stupid I was being. I jumped back between two parked cars and up on to the pavement. A cyclist yelled at me – I'm pretty sure he gave me the finger. But I was safe. Unharmed.

'I knew then that something had to change, that I'd hit rock bottom. It was like all my senses switched back to normal at once. I managed to make my way to the auction after that – late, but I made it. I confessed to Aaron that I needed actual professional help. I was signed off with burnout and anxiety by my GP the same week and I took an official leave of absence from work.'

'My God. What a story.'

'I know. I can't believe how close I came to a seriously

bad decision. But it was the wake-up call that I needed. This cruise was supposed to be our fresh start, but it's just been a nightmare. Starting with what happened to poor Christa and Jay.'

'I know,' murmured Janine. 'That was awful.'

'Even worse, they know it was a poisoned champagne bottle.' She leaned closer, lowering her voice. 'Liam told me he was paid to bring it on board, so he's terrified he'll be accused of killing them.'

'Jesus. Did he say who paid him?'

Olivia shook her head. 'No. All he said was that it was a woman. But when I get back to Ushuaia, I have to go to the police.'

'Good plan,' said Janine. 'I'll be there to back you up — whatever you need.'

'I appreciate it.' Olivia looked up at the sky, clouds encroaching on the deep indigo sky.

She looked over at Janine, who seemed lost in thought. She'd sucked her bottom lip into her mouth and was chewing on it. She looked so young in that moment. Olivia was about to ask how she was feeling, when Janine reached forward to grab her shovel again. Her feet almost touched the end; she'd need more space to get really comfortable.

The crunch of boots on the snow and the bleep of a radio made them both jump. She didn't want to escape her warm bubble, but there was a shiver down her spine that she didn't think had anything to do with the cold. There was something in the tone of voice that carried towards her on the wind.

'Olivia? Can you come with me?' It was Melissa, standing at the foot of her makeshift ice bed.

'Me?' Olivia was surprised.

'Where are you going?' said Janine, standing up in her bivvy sack.

'I just need Olivia for now. We'll be back soon.'

'OK,' Janine said, hesitating, before settling back down.

Melissa led her down towards the pulk, which was loaded with emergency supplies. She indicated for Olivia to grab one of the ropes and help to drag it around to the back of where everyone was camping for the night. It was surprisingly easy to pull with the two of them, and they walked in companionable silence until Olivia couldn't hold it in much longer.

'Look, I wanted to say I'm sorry about the kayaking. For getting too close to the glacier. You saved my life.'

'Don't mention it. Since you helped unload earlier, do you know where the first-aid supplies are?'

'Oh, sure. They're in the third box from the bottom.'

Melissa kneeled down and began rooting through the pulk to the bright red first-aid box. 'It's not really protocol to take passengers on shore outside of the excursion hours.'

'Liam was doing me a favour.'

'Lots of non-protocol things happening. Crew changing ships halfway through a voyage? Unthinkable.'

Olivia tensed. 'What are you talking about?'

'The captain asked me to bring some luggage on shore that belonged to a former crew member for him to collect. Can you believe that? Aha! Here it is. Now I can give these to Mr Hughes and hope he stops complaining about his headache.' She waved a packet of paracetamol at Olivia.

'Wait, Melissa. Did the captain say when the gear was being collected? Tonight or . . . ?'

Melissa grimaced. 'I don't know. If you want answers, ask Liam – it was his roommate.'

Olivia's heart pounded. 'Where did you leave his things? Near us?' She didn't know if Sergei was the threat, but all she knew was that she didn't want him stalking their camp.

Wind blasted them both, forcing them down to huddle against the pulk before Melissa could answer. Her radio bleeped and she frowned as she listened.

'What was that about?' Olivia asked once she had put the radio back in her jacket.

'I'm not sure. But I think you better get back to your bivvy. And the gear? I'd left it right here. He must have collected it already.'

'Sergei's here?' Olivia whipped her head around, scanning the snow for a sign of him or his footprints. But she couldn't see anything.

Melissa furrowed her brow. 'I wouldn't worry too much about it. If he has any sense, he would've taken his stuff and headed straight to his new boat.'

'Why do you say that?'

'Because that's exactly what we're going to do. I don't think we're going to be camping here after all. We need to get back to the ship.'

41

Melissa strode back up to the plateau, leaving Olivia trotting behind her, struggling to keep up. Her heartbeat hadn't slowed since hearing that Sergei was on the continent.

She thought coming here meant she was safe. She'd even begun to relax into the experience of the night. But that was all stolen away now. He could be anywhere.

She needed to be with people. And when they got to the top of the mound, no one was asleep in their bivvies. Instead, they were up and looking out towards the water.

Olivia squeezed in next to Patty and Annalise. A gasp of awe went up from the far side of the crowd. It was yet another calving, Antarctica proving just how unstable the continent was. Huge chunks of ice were tumbling off the glacier, dropping with large splashes into the water. The sun was just below the horizon, turning the icy cliffs various shades of purple and blue, almost like they were bruised. Wounded by their presence.

'You just missed a big one,' said Patty. 'At first, a full-on waterfall spouted from the cliff. Then it's been shedding ice like crazy since then. It's amazing.'

There was another rumble like low thunder from the glacier, and beside them, Annalise squealed, scrambling to point her camera in the direction of the cliff. 'Do you think more of it is going to go?'

'Wait, look! Oh my God.'

A ripple of shock coursed through the group. Patty reached out and grabbed Olivia's wrist. The scene in front of them didn't look real. At first, Olivia doubted her eyes. A crack appeared near the top of the glacier wall that started to grow, slicing through the ice like a lightning bolt. A piece of glacier the size of a house broke away, shedding boulders of ice into the water, before the whole thing dropped into the sea.

With horror, they watched as the newest iceberg to be born into the Southern Ocean drifted with intent towards the *Vigil*.

'Fuck me,' said Dr Vance, sliding his knitted hat from his head and holding it against his chest as if he was in mourning.

Melissa was on the radio. She turned away from the group, but she couldn't hide the worry in her tone. 'I'll gather everyone up.'

Olivia could hear the resignation in the woman's voice. And maybe a hint of something else. Fear. When she turned around, she was frowning.

'Anyone seen Liam?' she asked the group. No answer. There was more scratching over the radio as Melissa pressed it against her ear to hear the reply. 'I got it,' Melissa replied into the mouthpiece.

The wind blew hard, and Melissa shielded her face with her arm. When it died down, she had a steely look of determination. She gestured to Arthur. The two of them talked, heads close, for a moment. When she turned back, they both looked grave.

'Sorry, everyone, we have to cancel the camping.'

'What?' shouted Robert from the back of the group. 'Because of all that ice? Surely not.'

Melissa exchanged looks with Dr Vance. 'No. While a calving that size is a sign of major instability in the area, we've just been informed by the captain that a storm is heading for the bay.'

Olivia gasped. It must be the same storm that the captain had been worried about in the Drake Passage. Had it changed course?

Melissa continued talking: 'Combined with the strong katabatic winds we've been experiencing from the interior ice caps, we could be at major risk of flying debris, severe temperature drops and sea conditions that would make it impossible for us to return to the ship if we wait.'

'We would be marooned here, without food or adequate shelter,' said Arthur.

'Why were we brought here in the first place if it wasn't safe?' asked Lucinda.

Maxwell wrapped a protective arm around her.

'This is Antarctica. The weather can change in an instant.' She clapped her hands and raised her voice. 'All right, everyone, return to your bivvy sacks and pack up as quickly as possible. Please don't leave anything behind. Then head to the Zodiacs so we can return to the ship.'

There was surprisingly little grumbling from the group, as the wind swirling around them grew in intensity. It felt like the continent itself was asking them to leave.

Olivia grabbed her sleep sack and began stuffing it into a dry bag. Patty was struggling, so once she was finished with her own, Olivia took over.

Annalise was moving much more efficiently but kept looking over her shoulder at Cutler. 'Do you think this counts as a scandal?'

'Surely not,' said Patty. 'Like that woman said, "This is Antarctica." Bad weather happens all the time. You have to be flexible. This is part of the adventure.'

'Here you go.' Olivia handed Patty's bivvy sack back to her.

'Thanks. Where's Janine?'

Olivia stared around her, but Janine was nowhere to be seen. Her things were missing too. 'She must've finished and gone ahead already.'

They were among the last to leave the circle of dugout camps, which looked like a desecrated cemetery. Melissa eyed the mess. Olivia wondered if normally they would fill the beds in – all in keeping with the 'leave no trace' ethos that the crew had spouted at them since getting on board.

She stamped her feet, jamming her hands into her pockets. Now that they had been standing for a while, she noticed how cold she was. Other people seemed to be feeling the same way, their shoulders hunched over and shivering as they trudged down the hill.

She fell in step behind Melissa as they headed back down towards the beach.

The *Vigil* glinted out in the bay. More worrying, however, was the huge iceberg, freshly born into the ocean, drifting towards the ship. It brought with it thick chunks of sea ice, threatening to block the channel between the beach and the ship.

'This isn't good,' said Arthur. 'If that huge chunk of ice stays there and those bergy bits surrounding it are too thick and clog our path, we won't be able to steer the Zodiacs through to the ship.'

'Bergy bits?' asked Olivia.

'Weren't you listening in my lecture?' His attempt at a joke fell flat, as he was unable to hide the worry in his brow. 'Those smaller floating bits of ice. Tricky to get through. Impossible if there's too many. They can get stuck in our propellers and break the boat.'

A woman screamed, and Olivia grabbed the professor's arm out of shock.

'Out of my way!' said Melissa, running in her big boots to where the woman – Lucinda – was standing by one of the Zodiacs.

A deep slash marred the rubber, and one side of it had almost completely deflated. Three of the inflatable chambers were ruined. Unusable. The Zodiac wouldn't be able to float.

'How on earth?' Arthur muttered beside her.

'Did someone do that?' Olivia asked, her voice shaking with fear.

Melissa ran to the next, and fell to her knees with relief. 'This one's OK! Everyone, leave the gear for now. Let's get in.'

She held one side of the rubber, while Arthur stabilized it from the other.

Cutler was first to clamber aboard. 'Anna, come on,' he growled, grabbing her arm and pulling Annalise on board. At least he showed compassion for the people he loved, Olivia thought.

Olivia helped Patty in, while Robert and Aida scrambled on the other side. Maxwell, Lucinda, Yara and Delilah had waded into the water, throwing themselves over the thick inflatable sides and on to the benches. Maxwell reached back over and gave a hand to Kathy, boosted by her husband Dave, before he jumped in as well.

'Dr Vance, your turn!' said Melissa.

She gave him a lift into the boat, before accepting help herself. She pushed through the sea of people to get to the engine.

'Wait!' Olivia said. 'We're missing Liam. He's not here.'

'He'll hear the engine and come running, I'm sure,' said Melissa. She pulled at the engine cord but was aghast when it came loose in her hand.

'It's broken,' she said, her tone grim.

Olivia's stomach dropped. That couldn't be a coincidence.

'What about the paddles?' asked Arthur.

'Right!' She dug around in the middle of the Zodiac, where they stored emergency oars in case of a broken engine. But there was no sign of those either.

'Everyone, back on shore,' Melissa said, her voice resigned.

'Melissa?' Maxwell's expression was grim as he looked down the side of the boat into the water.

'What is it?' she snapped.

He reached down and yanked something from the rubber. A knife – a jagged Stanley knife – was in his hand. 'Looks like someone tried to slash this Zodiac too.'

The confirmation that they'd been sabotaged rushed from person to person.

They were stranded.

42

They huddled together near the ruined Zodiacs.

'What's the plan?' Cutler asked.

Melissa spoke, but her words were whipped away by a sudden gust of wind that made all of them cringe down into their jackets. It seemed like the storm had gone from 'impending' to 'imminent' in an instant.

She pulled her radio from her pocket, trying to get in touch with the boat. 'Beach to *Vigil*. Our Zodiacs have been compromised. You need to send another to come and reach us.'

Olivia looked around the group. They were glued in place with shock. Liam was nowhere to be seen. Where could he be? The only reason she'd agreed to come on this camping trip was because he'd promised to protect her, and she knew only one person could be responsible.

Sergei. She had to let Melissa know.

Arthur was shivering, his teeth chattering as he watched Melissa repeat her call to the *Vigil*.

The sea was now a roiling grey colour, like molten metal, the wind whipping white caps on to the waves. The clouds were much thicker, obscuring the beautiful sky of a few hours ago. Now everything was an ominous grey monochrome. Not night, but an even stranger half-dark, almost unearthly.

'Who would have done this?' asked Cutler, looking at

the two Zodiacs. The one with the slashed sides looked like the deflated carcass of a beached whale.

Melissa had taken custody of the knife, putting it inside her backpack. Olivia ran to her side. 'I have an idea of who it could be.'

'You do?'

'Sergei. The crew member whose luggage you delivered . . .'

'Impossible,' she replied. 'There's no way a crewman would do this. Excuse me, I need to talk to the group. OK –' Melissa raised her voice – 'I want to do a head-count.' She gestured for everyone to come close.

Olivia bit her lip, angry that Melissa wouldn't take her seriously. She looked around for Janine and thought she spotted her at the edge of the group, the hood of her jacket up over her head so that barely the tip of her nose was visible.

All of a sudden, lightning flashed, followed by a roll of thunder so loud the group cowered. Lucinda screamed. Greg dropped to his knees, covering his head with his hands, and Tariq comforted him. Fear was contagious. No one knew who to trust, but they all could sense the danger from the environment.

'All right, all pax are accounted for, except Liam. We need to get to some shelter.' Melissa gritted her teeth.

'He's probably hiding because he did this!' Cutler gestured at the Zodiac.

'That's enough,' snapped Melissa.

'Where is he then?'

No, not Liam, Olivia thought. *Sergei*. She was certain.

Melissa's radio bleeped. She tilted her ear and, as she listened, her face fell. 'What are you talking about? That can't be right. We won't . . .' She stopped talking as she looked around the group.

'Spit it out, woman!' said Cutler.

Melissa glowered at him. Olivia stomped her feet against the ice, trying to get some warmth into her numb toes. As she did, she stared at the other guests. Fifteen suddenly seemed like a lot of people to manage.

Robert had dug out a pair of binoculars from inside his jacket, scanning for signs of rescue from the *Vigil*.

But Olivia returned her gaze to Melissa. Her brow was still knitted together, her lips moving like she was trying to figure out a plan but was too afraid to say it out loud. The only time she'd seen that look before was when she'd flipped from her kayak. That's when she knew.

They were all in the water this time. And she didn't know if Melissa had the power to save them.

Melissa swallowed and when she spoke, her voice wavered. 'OK, everyone, more bad news.'

That got their attention. They huddled close, trying to hear over the wind. 'I've spoken with the captain. The berg from the glacier calving is approaching the *Vigil* fast and it's blocking the path from the ship. The wind is almost at forty knots, so they're not able to launch a Zodiac to collect us this evening. He may even have to move the entire ship as the storm is getting worse in the bay. They're considering heading back to Neko Harbour. They'll come and get us tomorrow, first thing in the morning, when it's safe.'

There were horrified gasps in the crowd.

'And what are we supposed to do in the meantime?' asked Cutler.

'We'll head back to where we dug our shelters and

build them up higher to protect from the wind. We'll hunker down for the night until it all blows over and then we'll come back to shore in a few hours. Then it will be back to the ship for hot chocolate and pancakes.' She tried a light-hearted smile but it didn't reach her eyes.

Now the shouting began. 'There's a knife-wielding maniac on the island and you expect us to stay here?' shouted Cutler.

'We'll freeze to death first,' said Maxwell.

Olivia's mind raced. The Zodiacs were out of action. No rescue was coming from the *Vigil*. They had no tents and the bivvy sacks weren't much protection against a storm. They hadn't brought any food. Maybe there were some emergency-only rations on the pulk. If this didn't count as an emergency, she didn't know what would.

'What if they can't come tomorrow?' Olivia blurted out, before she could stop herself.

Melissa paused. 'It won't come to that.'

'But if it does?'

'Then we'll go to them. We'll walk to Neko Harbour.'

'Across the peninsula?'

'Exactly.' Her lips were set in a thin line. 'We have to find Liam. He will have a plan. He's the expedition lead.'

Large flakes of snow were beginning to fall from the darkened sky. Olivia raised her hand to catch some of them. Antarctica was meant to be one of the driest places on the planet. If this was being blown in from the mainland, they were about to have a big problem.

She felt a pull deep in her gut. The thought that Sergei was out there somewhere, sabotaging their attempt to leave, was terrifying enough. Adding a polar storm on top? It was unfathomable.

Melissa dug a couple of torches out of one of the Zodiacs, but there weren't enough for all of them.

She handed one to Arthur. 'I'll lead us back up to the campsite. Quickly. You stay back and make sure there are no stragglers.' She raised her voice again. 'Everyone buddy up. No one goes anywhere alone.'

Janine grabbed hold of Olivia's arm. 'Can I stay with you?'

'Of course.' Olivia patted her gloved hand. 'Patty and Annalise?'

'We're right behind you,' said Patty. 'Do you think we'll be safe?'

Olivia didn't know how to answer.

'We have to be,' said Annalise, her voice laced with quiet determination.

'Melissa, is there really no way for the *Vigil* to send another tender to pick us up?' Patty asked.

She shook her head. 'Zodiacs are dangerous in rough seas. Anything could happen – one of you could fall and break something, go overboard, or get crushed against the ship trying to get on board. No, the captain is right. We'll be safer on land.' She continued to trudge forward.

It took them much longer to make it up the hill to the campsite battling against the wind. On the plateau the gusts were even stronger, and the snow was falling thickly, making it hard to see. They stuck close together. There was not much in the way of natural shelter, so they set to work deepening the holes in the ground.

Janine retreated into the hood of her jacket, her shoulders hunched. She was pacing from foot to foot.

'Hey!' said Olivia, waving her glove in front of her to

305

get her attention. 'Why don't you grab a shovel and see if you can start connecting these holes – we'll need walls of ice and snow around us.'

To her surprise, Janine didn't argue. Greg and Tariq picked up shovels, and together they started to dig.

Once Arthur had caught up and confirmed there were no stragglers, Melissa raised her voice again. 'I need to send out a search party for Liam,' she said. 'We need to find him. Cutler, Greg, Janine, come with me. The rest of you stay here under the guidance of the professor. He has expedition training too and can supervise building the shelters.'

'Is she serious?' asked Annalise. 'They can't just comb the ice looking for him. Where the heck could he have gone?'

Patty slumped down inside the tunnel of snow holes they'd built. 'This is hardly better than being exposed to the elements.' She'd pulled on a life jacket she'd taken from the Zodiac – Olivia didn't know how much that would help, but she supposed it might keep the woman a little bit warmer. Maybe it was the illusion of safety she needed. Like wrapping herself in the life jacket might be a signal to the universe. Olivia could hardly blame her. She wished she could cling to anything that might stop her from sinking deeper into the mess she'd found herself in.

But there was no life jacket for bad decisions.

It was sink or swim.

'It might help to have the pulk over here too,' Olivia mused out loud. 'Professor?' She waved her arms to try to get Arthur's attention.

He trudged over. 'What is it?'

'The pulk – Liam left it on the other side of the camp. I can go over and get it but I might need a hand.'

He nodded. 'Good idea. Robert, why don't you go with her?'

She stalked off towards it before the storm worsened their visibility. Robert jogged to catch up with her.

'Come on, Liam . . . where are you?' she muttered under her breath, scanning the horizon around them. The cloud seemed to have closed in on them, making her feel as if her eyes were wrapped in cotton wool. Her feet swum in her oversized boots, and she struggled to see much further than the sleeve of her crimson jacket. She couldn't believe that only an hour ago she'd felt safe, staring up at the sky of a clear white night.

She was almost there. She could see the outline of the pulk now, with its bright red plastic base. Then she frowned. There was a splash of red on the snow, as if some of the paint had leeched from its surface.

She felt her stomach drop, her body knowing before her head caught up with what she was seeing. Blood.

She didn't want to, but she took a step closer to the pulk.

And then she screamed.

43

Robert was only a few steps behind her.

'Holy fuck,' he said.

Olivia was on her knees, a pool of vomit next to her. She still couldn't lift her head. That would mean seeing it again.

Liam, dead, his body lying across the pulk broken and bloodied.

She didn't need to be a medical professional to know that Liam was gone. There was no chance of reviving him. Half his face was caved in.

Janine was next to reach Olivia, but Olivia stood up then, catching Janine in her arms, stopping her before she could see the horror. 'We have . . . we have to get the doctor.'

'Holy fuck, holy fuck . . .' Robert appeared to be in some kind of trance behind her, unable to process what was happening. She didn't need that. She grabbed the sleeve of his jacket, shaking at his arm until he turned around.

'Get yourself together. We need to find one of the crew. Tell them what we found.'

'What did you find?'

Melissa came running up behind them, and Olivia had never been more grateful to see anyone in her life. She held her arms up for the rest of the group to stay back as she approached. Robert ran back to his wife.

Melissa's eyes were fixed on Olivia's. 'I heard somebody scream . . .'

'It's Liam. He's . . .' But Olivia couldn't say it. She
knew it would do no good for her to completely fall
apart. She took in a deep breath, but still couldn't trust
herself to speak. Instead, she gestured with her head.

Melissa stepped past her and let out a low guttural
moan when she saw. For a moment, there was silence.
Then she jumped into action. She leaped to the man's
side, shaking his upper arm. 'Liam? Are you OK?' She
looked up at Olivia. 'Have you checked his pulse? What
about this bleeding . . . can we stop it? Why has no one
done anything?'

Olivia swallowed, but no one else was moving. She
kneeled down next to Melissa. 'You can't save him. He's
gone.'

'No. He can't be . . .'

She was shaking. Olivia had to turn away.

'I just can't believe it. I just . . . I don't know what to
do any more.'

Olivia couldn't look, but the image remained burned
into her retinas. The wound on his head. There was no
chance that was an accident. With her head bowed, all
she could see were his hands. There were cuts on his
palms – defensive wounds.

A shiver travelled down Olivia's spine. He'd tried to
fight.

'Melissa, someone did this to him. Someone killed
him.'

'Who would do this?'

'I told you. Sergei. His roommate.'

Melissa looked like she was about to interrupt but

309

Olivia kept talking. 'Listen to me. He was caught stealing from our cabin and was supposed to be locked up, waiting to be handed over to the police. I don't know what he said to the captain to be allowed to leave the ship, but he's dangerous. This proves it.'

Melissa's eyes searched Olivia's face. 'Then we're all in danger. But—' she grabbed Olivia's hand. 'We can't let the others know. We need to stay calm, not spread panic. That's how we'll be safe.'

'But what if Sergei isn't finished?'

'Then it's more important than ever that we all stay together. Help me cover up his body. Let's get him on the pulk and we can use the spare blankets.'

She began without her, struggling to move Liam's legs on to the sledge. Olivia's mind was a blur. 'He must have sabotaged the Zodiacs too, you know.'

Melissa tensed. 'Who else has seen this?'

'Robert. And probably Janine too.'

Melissa looked over her shoulder. 'Then we might as well tell everyone the truth. I need people to trust me. But they don't have to look at him like some animal at the zoo.'

They moved quickly until his body was fully on the pulk, and Melissa covered him with the blanket, tucking it under his head. Watching his face disappear – even with tenderness – made Olivia want to be sick once again.

Melissa handed her the ropes to the pulk. By then, the rest of the group joined them, brought together by the commotion. Melissa raised her hands, attracting all their attention. She was their leader now.

'Everyone, gather round.' Melissa shouted to be heard

above the wind. Olivia stood slightly behind her, scanning the crowd, expecting to see Sergei lurking in the background.

'You found Liam?' Cutler asked.

'Yes. But I need you all to stay calm. I'm going to be honest. There has been an accident. Liam is dead.'

A shriek ran through the crowd, and Olivia stared at Melissa in surprise – she hadn't expected her to be quite so direct. Patty looked like she was about to faint, clutching at Annalise's arm. Aida was weeping, Robert trying to comfort her. Maxwell was gripping Lucinda's hand, but her face was stony, her lips set in a firm line.

'This is fucked up,' shouted Tariq. His typical reserved nature out of the window.

Greg touched his arm. 'Honey, calm down.'

'Don't tell me to calm down.' Tariq wrenched away, but then tears streamed down his face, and he allowed Greg to fold him into a hug. Everyone was distressed, and the group threatened to fragment unless someone took charge.

'What do you mean? What kind of accident?' Cutler stepped forward.

Melissa held up her gloved hand. 'It means we have a new plan. We can't—'

'I demand to see Liam. I am the CEO of Pioneer Adventures and I have a duty of care towards my employees.'

Melissa stepped forward to meet him. 'You might be the CEO but while we're on this ice, I am the leader. And what I am saying is that we cannot stay here. It is too exposed. We need proper shelter.'

'Finally you're speaking sense!' said Cutler.

'We're going to walk to Brown Base. It's not occupied at the moment, but there might be food provisions.'

'Do we really have nothing to eat?' asked Janine.

Melissa shook her head. 'We don't have time to keep discussing this. We need to move, now. If we keep the shore to our left, we won't be able to miss it.'

'How far?' Maxwell asked.

'If we move now, it shouldn't take more than an hour. I'll lead the way. Dr Vance, can you manage the pulk? Make sure no one is left behind.'

The professor looked pale, but he nodded. Melissa strode off into the snow in the direction of Brown Base.

Olivia hesitated. She hadn't relished the idea of sleeping in the campsite with Liam's corpse – and with a killer on the loose. But at least here they were all together, and could keep an eye on each other. Keep watch. On the move there was a chance they'd get separated. Lose the pack. Luckily a few others felt the same way. 'We've just spent an age digging out these bivvies and preparing the walls here,' said Robert at Melissa's back. 'I can only barely hear you above the wind as it is – and you want us to go out in this?'

Cutler looked as if he was about to protest too, but when he stood up to lift his head above the parapet they'd made he was smacked in the face with a gust of strong wind. He trudged after Melissa.

Once he was moving, there was a moment's pause with the rest of the group. Annalise was next to step forward, running up to be alongside the CEO.

That got the rest of them moving. Janine grabbed hold of Olivia's hand, and they followed.

'Can I walk with you two?' Patty came up beside them. 'I think I lost my buddy.'

'Of course,' said Olivia. She bent her head close to Patty's. 'Did you know those two were close?'

Patty scoffed. 'Close? I wouldn't say that. But maybe being stranded in an Antarctic storm is enough to bring father and daughter together.'

44

'Annalise is Cutler's daughter?' Olivia blinked back her surprise.

'She thinks I don't know, but I've worked for Pioneer my whole life. I figured it out. I know she'll take over one day, but I respect her wanting to learn the business from the ground up.'

'Wow. I got the complete wrong end of the stick. I thought they were dating.'

That made Patty guffaw, and Olivia laughed too. Janine frowned. She was right; it was a strange – totally inappropriate – reaction to their situation. They sobered up and kept walking.

According to her watch, it was past midnight.

As Olivia had feared, the group spread out as they hiked to Brown Base. Melissa broke the trail in front, Cutler and Annalise, Robert and Aida and the couple whose names Olivia had already forgotten were close behind. Delilah had huddled together with Greg and Tariq. She'd snapped at Yara for continuing to film their desperate situation. Maybe she was hoping to go viral. Maxwell and Lucinda held hands as they walked in eerie silence, focused on the goal of reaching the shelter.

As for cabin twelve? They'd fallen to the back of the pack. Adrenaline was the only thing keeping Olivia moving at this point. It coursed through her veins, somehow propelling her legs forward even though every muscle screamed in pain. So much had happened, her mind was struggling to contain it all.

And underneath everything, there was fear. Fear that Sergei would leap out at them at any moment, crush her skull the same way he killed Liam.

She looked behind her every few steps, her eyes constantly scanning the horizon. But there was no sign of him.

She also kept an eye on the professor. As the minutes ticked by, it was clear he was struggling with the pulk as they headed down the hill towards the beach. It was too heavy for one person to control.

'Melissa!' Olivia called out.

The expedition leader looked over her shoulder, then jogged back to help. The rest of the group ground to a halt. 'What is it?'

'It's Arthur – I don't think he's able to pull the sled much longer.'

Melissa nodded. 'OK, I'll take over.'

'No you bloody won't,' said Cutler. 'You're the one who knows how to get us to the shelters.'

'I can help him,' said Olivia.

'You sure?' Melissa's eyes searched her face. Satisfied, she nodded. 'I'll assign someone to replace you in five minutes. Take it in shifts.'

'Got it.'

Arthur looked relieved when she came up and tapped him on the arm. He gave her one of the ropes, and she slung it over her shoulder. Together they managed to stabilize the pulk's weight and slide it down the hill.

Even with the two of them, it was hard to drag it through the snow. The rope bit into the outer shell of her jacket, and she struggled to keep a grip through her ultra-thick mittens. The undulating landscape worked against them, even small mounds feeling like mountains.

The professor stumbled, slipping on to the ground. Janine took up the other side.

'Let me take that,' said Cutler, gruffly to Arthur.

'Melissa sent us back to help,' said Annalise. 'Shall I take your side?'

'I'm OK for now,' said Olivia. With Cutler on the other end of the pulk rope, they were able to move more easily again.

Patty took the professor by the arm, propping him up. Along with Annalise and Janine, they walked ahead, tramping down the snow to make sliding the pulk easier.

Cutler narrowed his eyes. 'We're losing the others.'

Olivia looked up. Between the thick snow and the wind, even though the sun was back above the horizon, she couldn't see more than a few feet ahead of them. Even Patty and Arthur's bright jackets were no longer visible. She felt like she was back in the Hunt Gallery, although stripped of all its artwork. Just a blank, white space – a maze – just as terrifying as complete darkness might be. There was no point of reference, the sky and the ground blending seamlessly.

She swallowed. 'We can't be far from Brown Base now. Melissa said an hour's walk. We've been on the move for, what, forty-five minutes now?'

As she said it, she was shocked it had been that long. Why hadn't Melissa sent anyone else back to take over from them?

'Let's keep going then,' he said.

'Thank God I found you,' Annalise appeared, walking

316

towards them, dragging Dr Vance behind her. 'I stopped to help Arthur and I lost Janine and Patty. I've been retracing our footsteps hoping I'd come across them – or you.'

'Professor, are you OK?' Olivia asked.

'I think he hurt his leg on the way down the hill. He's not walking well,' said Annalise. 'But we're close to the base. I saw it.'

'Get him there,' said Olivia. 'We'll be close behind.'

'And the others?'

'We'll find them. They can't be far. They're probably already there too.'

Annalise nodded, throwing Dr Vance's arm over her shoulder and hobbling off towards the base.

'There we go – we're close,' Olivia said to Cutler. 'We have to get inside. Before . . .'

'Before what?' he asked. 'Tell me. What happened to Liam?'

Olivia kept her mouth shut, pressing forward.

'There's someone dangerous out here, isn't there? Someone killed that man.'

A scream sounded from behind them, stopping Cutler and Olivia in their tracks. They looked at each other, his eyes widening. He dropped the rope and ran, following in the direction Annalise had gone.

Olivia was tempted to follow, but she recognized the voice that made the scream: Janine.

She couldn't leave her all alone.

She ducked down beneath the pulk, using it as shelter as she tried to figure out what was happening. Shielding her eyes against the snow, she thought she could make out two figures: one in a red jacket, and another in black.

The pair stumbled closer, Janine running towards the pulk, still screaming her distress. In a few steps, the black jacket caught up with her, and Janine beat her hands against her attacker. The hood of the black jacket fell back as the two of them struggled, his hat falling to the ground. The man was tall, with a shaved head. Sergei. Sergei had found them.

Her instincts had been right after all. It had been him all along.

'Get off me!' Janine screamed again.

Olivia had to help her. She couldn't allow Sergei to claim another victim. She grabbed one of the shovels from the pulk, trying to ignore the wave of revulsion that rose up as she brushed against Liam's dead body. Then she ran towards the pair, brandishing it high.

The element of surprise was the more effective weapon. She swung the shovel but it didn't make contact – all it did was shock Sergei enough to let go of Janine's jacket. She swung it again, but it was so heavy. It clattered against the man's leg, and he cried out in pain. Olivia dropped the shovel, grabbed hold of Janine's arm, and pulled her away.

'We have to run!'

'Wait, Olivia!' shouted Sergei, stepping forward before grunting in pain again.

But she didn't wait. She ran, dragging Janine behind her, as fast as she could. She didn't know if she was headed in the right direction. All she knew was that they had to get away.

'That guy is a psychopath!' said Janine, panting after every word. 'He came out of nowhere looking for you. I tried to stop him. But now . . . where did he go?'

'I don't know. But he's going to follow us. That much I'm certain about. We have to keep moving.'

A huge black boulder disrupted their path. They ran around it, leaning up against it to catch their breath. Olivia chanced a look around it, but couldn't see any sign of Sergei. From the other side, she could see they'd run perpendicular to one of the red metal shacks of Brown Base. They could make it there in a few minutes if they ran.

'Look, Janine, we're so close. We can make it.'

She grabbed her friend's arm, but there was a wild look in her eyes. The poor thing was terrified.

'Come on, we have to get to the others.' Olivia took a step, but Janine had hold of her sleeve. Then Janine dropped to the ground, picking up a rock the size of her fist.

'Good idea,' said Olivia, grabbing a rock too. She didn't know what good it would do, but there were two of them against Sergei. Maybe with an extra weapon, it would be enough.

The snow had eased, though the wind still roared. But she was surprised by how much she could see in the eerie light.

But if she could see, that meant Sergei could as well. It meant they wouldn't be able to hide from him. Not until they could get into one of those buildings.

Then she saw him. He was staggering towards them.

'He's found us!' she shrieked. She grabbed Janine's hand and forced her to bolt.

45

To her relief, Janine ran, useless shards of rock in hand.

Olivia glanced over her shoulder. Sergei was limping towards them, but they were moving faster. The base itself was on a rocky promontory into the bay, with a big hill rising up behind. The path towards it was littered with boulders, mounds of snow and penguin guano. It was undulating and uneven – she hoped the terrain might slow him down.

She stumbled over loose rock, cursing her own carelessness even as she wished it on him.

There were several buildings making up the base. 'Let's go here,' Olivia said, pointing at the closest – which looked more like a shed. 'If they're not there, we'll move on.'

There was a bang from inside the second shed. 'Did you hear that?' Janine asked.

'OK, that one first then.'

They headed over to the next shed, battling against the wind – stronger now they were right next to the water. She tugged at the door, which caught for just a second before flinging open.

Despite the ambient light outside, it was pitch dark inside the shed, any windows covered in thick black material. 'Melissa?' Olivia shouted inside.

'Olivia? You made it!' said Annalise.

Janine fumbled in her pocket for her phone, then pressed the torch button. It illuminated Annalise, Patty and Cutler huddled in a corner – behind them shelves and racks piled high with different tools, some electronic equipment, ragged-looking down jackets – things a team might need to survive a summer in Antarctica.

'Thank God. What happened? Did you find the others?' asked Patty.

'No, haven't you seen them either? Liam's roommate – Sergei – attacked Janine,' said Olivia.

'Olivia saved my life,' said Janine.

'Are we safe?' Patty asked. 'What if he tries to come in?'

'Maybe we can barricade the door?' Olivia suggested. 'But really we need to find Melissa.' She looked around the room, testing if any of the cabinets would move – but everything was bolted to the floor. But she could see tools – hammers and screwdrivers – things that could potentially be used as weapons.

'This is ridiculous,' said Cutler, stamping his feet and blowing into his mittened hands. 'This should never have happened.'

'No one could have predicted the storm would be this bad. I spoke to the captain – if he'd had any inkling, he wouldn't have allowed it,' said Olivia.

'The weather is one thing, but the sabotage? What happened to that Zodiac . . . ? My wife was right. We never should have come on this trip.' He turned to Annalise. 'I wanted a chance to hand things over properly. And I've dragged you into this too.'

'Hand things over?' Patty asked.

Cutler snorted. 'Doesn't matter who knows now, does it? Four people dead. Some madman on the loose. The deal isn't going to happen now. Pioneer is finished.'

'Your wife told me you were selling off the business even before all this happened,' muttered Olivia.

'Oh, she told you that, did she? Yes, well, Annalise was going to take over the online business, but, yes, we were going to shut down everything else. There was no point flogging a dead horse.'

Annalise shuddered inside her jacket. 'I hadn't said yes yet actually, Dad. You sprang this on me.'

Cutler shrugged. 'You are ready. We both know that.'

There was a sharp intake of breath from Patty. 'You were going to close my branch?'

'The business is completely broke, Patricia. We tried to keep it going as long as we could.'

'You knew about this?' she asked Annalise, her voice breaking with emotion.

'He only told me a few days ago. I had no idea, I swear.'

Patty turned back to Cutler. 'You lied to us. My Karl gave everything to you.'

'Patty . . .' Annalise moved towards her.

There was a scraping sound from the cabinet.

Janine shone her torch in the direction of the noise.

The light illuminated Patty's expression: a blankness, as white as the landscape outside. Her mouth was set in a grim line, her eyes hard.

And in her hand: a wrench, taken from the counter.

Janine screamed and dropped the phone, and then Patty rushed towards Cutler, the weapon held high.

46

'Stop!' Olivia screamed, as Patty lunged towards Cutler, swinging the wrench down as he tried to scramble away.

Annalise flew forward, trying to block Patty's path, but it was too late. The wrench connected with the back of his head with a sickening crack, made worse by the agonizing cry that Cutler let out.

'Patty, no!' screeched Annalise.

Hearing her name seemed to snap the woman out of her daze, and she blinked rapidly, waking up to the realization of what she'd done.

Olivia rushed to Cutler's side, helping him to his feet.

'He destroyed everything! Everything Karl and I built together. He's going to leave me with nothing.'

'So you thought you would kill him?' Olivia's voice was shrill.

Patty turned to Cutler, still high on her own adrenaline. 'You never wanted to save the business. You think this is your company, but this isn't anything to do with you. We all work our asses off for you. I've worked my entire life for you. Karl worked himself to death. And this is how you were planning to repay us?'

She took another menacing step forward, but both Olivia and Janine screamed. The wrench clattered to the floor, and Janine kicked it away. There was something behind Patty's eyes now. A sheen of tears.

She turned and ran, heading out of a door at the other

end of the shed. Annalise screamed her name and chased after her.

'Where's Cutler?' Janine asked.

Olivia groaned. 'For God's sake.'

The man had stumbled out of the shed, lying prone in the snow. She glanced from side to side, but there was no sign of Patty – or of Sergei. Her head was spinning with the danger all around them. 'Cutler? Can you hear me?'

He didn't respond. She took off her glove with her teeth and tried to lift his head, but her fingers came back red with blood. 'Shit.' Her hands were shaking, yet she managed to trace down to his neck, to feel his pulse. There was one, but it was thready and weak. He was alive – but barely.

Olivia had no idea what to do. She was no doctor, no adventurer. She'd worked in an office her whole adult life.

Even though she had no idea if he could hear her, she kept talking. 'We can't stay out here in this weather. It's too dangerous. We have to find the others.'

All the money in the world couldn't buy Cutler help in that moment. They'd paid for the privilege of visiting one of the most remote places in the world. But Antarctica was wild. Untamed. It was the ultimate leveller. No helicopter was able to swoop in and help him. The doctors were trapped on the ship. Olivia almost laughed, despite herself. Was that supposed to be part of the appeal of coming here? The same reason so many of these billionaires attempted to go to space – so they could truly get somewhere that money didn't matter.

A place where money couldn't solve problems.

All day she stared at problems that could be fixed by

money – moving it, counting it, acquiring it, giving it away, storing it, investing it – anything but losing it. But out here it was so much more elemental. She literally had blood on her hands. It put the entirety of her world into perspective. She'd run away from her job, from her friends, her family. What was a lost qualification compared to this? She'd run from responsibility, ever since her dad had passed.

She didn't want to have more horrors on her conscience. She had to get Cutler inside alive.

'Cutler? Are you still with us?'

His skin looked grey and clammy. She tucked his hood up as tightly as she could, after having reassured herself that he was still breathing. He was shivering violently – shock and the extreme cold. They didn't have long.

'Can you see if you can find Melissa?' she called out over her shoulder to Janine. There was still no sign of Patty and Annalise. 'Tell her to bring Robert and Maxwell. We'll need help if we're going to get Cutler inside and warm.'

When she didn't get a response, she glanced backwards. Janine was walking towards them, the bloodied wrench in her hand.

'What are you doing?' Olivia's breath hitched in her throat.

Another sound broke through over the wind. Engine noise. Janine's eyes widened. 'Evidence. I thought we'd need the wrench to show what happened to Cutler.'

'Good idea. But I think rescue is here,' Olivia said.

Janine ran towards Olivia. A boat – a small black Zodiac – was pulling up to the beach, struggling against the waves.

'Over here!' Olivia cried. Someone had been able to get to them from the *Vigil*. It was a miracle.

But as the boat drew closer, she frowned. The crewman driving it wasn't in a standard *Vigil* blue jacket. In fact, he was in a fancy khaki parka reaching down to his knees, with a fur-trimmed hood up shielding his face. He jumped out of the Zodiac with practised ease. Her heart beat fast. She clutched Janine's hand and stood as the second man approached.

'Thank goodness I found you.'

Olivia stepped forward.

The man lowered his hood.

Her heart pounded as she recognized him. 'Pierre?' Her voice cracked as she spoke his name.

Any relief she felt drained away, replaced instead by a jolt of fear.

She thought she'd flagged down their rescuer. But instead, she might have waved over more trouble than ever.

47

Pierre stepped towards them, but Olivia held up her hands.

'Wh-what are you doing here?'

'I came for you. Come on. The storm has abated but not for long. We have to get to my yacht.'

'Who is that?' asked Janine, grabbing Olivia's sleeve.

'It's . . . Pierre Lavaud.'

'The billionaire guy?' she whispered, and Olivia nodded.

'Come on,' he said. 'We don't have much time.'

Olivia gestured to Cutler. 'This man needs help.'

Pierre nodded. 'I have a doctor on board.'

A strong wind blasted Olivia from behind, battering her almost to her knees, proving Pierre's point that the storm wasn't done with them yet.

'There's more of us,' Olivia said to Pierre. 'Shouldn't we go find them first?'

Pierre kneeled down next to Cutler. 'Is this Mr Hughes?'

Olivia nodded.

'He's not going to make it if we wait much longer,' he said. 'Where are the other passengers?'

'They took shelter somewhere in the research base. But we don't know in which building.'

'I will return for them. I promise. If they're in the base, they'll be sheltered for now. But we need to move.'

Cutler let out a guttural moan. He needed a doctor. The questions she had swirling around Pierre's appearance would have to wait. Between the three of them, they managed to get Cutler to his feet. Just. He swooned and groaned, his feet dragging.

'Is it safe to go out there?' Olivia asked, as they headed down the beach towards the tender. While the storm had lessened, she still didn't like the look of the waves in the bay, topped with chunks of ice. Only a highly skilled pilot could navigate it successfully.

'I've been waiting for the right conditions to come ashore. My yacht is anchored in a small inlet, so while we are cut off for now from the Lemaire Channel, we can still access the beach. We heard the distress call from the MS *Vigil* on our radio and I came to see if I could find you. *Bien, on y va.*'

Between them, they got Cutler into the bottom of the Zodiac, then Janine followed. As Olivia reached the inflatable boat, she hesitated, still wary of Pierre, her eyes hardly believing he was there, in Antarctica. Wasn't Sergei working for him? The madman they'd been running from?

But then why was he being so kind? If he wanted Olivia dead, he could have left her to the elements – or to Sergei. At that moment, the will to survive overtook all other fears. Pierre wouldn't capsize the tender with them all in it, so that meant he really was taking them to the *Clarissa II*.

One step at a time. She could figure out what to do next once she was on the boat. At least Janine was with her. Together the two of them could look out for each other.

The Zodiac crunched through the thick slushy water, bouncing over rogue waves. The journey was mercifully short, but it was clear why the *Vigil* hadn't been able to send a rescue. The nose of the boat rose over the waves before slamming down like an unbalanced seesaw, and Olivia cowered, clinging on and trying not to wince every time Cutler cried out in pain.

Freezing-cold droplets stung the exposed skin of Olivia's face, and she fumbled the hood of her jacket tight around her cheeks with her free hand – but it wasn't enough. Each blast was a shock that stole her breath from her. Each wave made her tighten her grip on the inner safety rope, not wanting to think for a moment of what might happen if she should get swept overboard into the churning icy water.

The lights of the yacht loomed red through the stormy haze, and Pierre navigated them with ease. A figure stood on the stern of the ship, waiting for them. He caught the rope Pierre threw to him, securing the boat. It was hardly an easy transfer. The waves tossed the Zodiac around, bashing it against the yacht's loading dock and then pulling it away again. She remembered Melissa's warning, that she risked being crushed, or falling in the water. The man reached out an arm to Olivia. 'Let's go!'

She paused at the very edge of the Zodiac, still clinging on to the rope. The man on the yacht shook his hand at her again. She took it, sailor's grip. He gripped her wrist; she gripped his. 'Ready?'

The swell rose up and the man pulled, yanking her on to deck. Her foot slid on the slick wooden floor but she just about managed to remain upright. 'Get inside! Now!' he shouted.

She scrambled for the door. Once she was inside, she paused at the window, watching as Janine jumped on board, then Pierre wrangled Cutler's body on to the yacht. He was looking extra pale except for the dark matting blood on the back of his head.

'Let's get him below,' said Pierre. He switched then to rapid French to the man on deck. Soon another crew member joined them, and the two of them balanced Cutler's enormous broken body, his arms draped over their shoulders, and disappeared down the stairs.

He was going to be treated by a doctor. They had done all they could to get him to safety. She sighed with relief, almost swooning with exhaustion.

'Well, well, our doctor is going to be busy tonight.' Pierre entered the small wet room, smoothing his hands over his neat silvery-grey hair. He stepped up to her, kissing her on both cheeks. 'I cannot tell you how pleased I am to see you, and looking well. We have been worried.'

She tensed. 'Where's Aaron?'

Pierre didn't answer her. 'Please, come inside. Make yourself comfortable. I have a small weather window to return to the shore to fetch your other stranded passengers. But first, this is important. Is there anyone in the group you are afraid of? Someone I should keep from you?' His eyes searched her face.

'Sergei,' she said immediately.

Pierre shook his head. 'He works for me. He's been trying to figure out who is targeting you, not the other way around.'

'What?' Olivia could hardly think straight. She was cold, wet, her system crashing from the adrenaline spike. 'Then . . . no. I don't know.' She thought about Patty, the wild look in her eyes – but she was a threat to Cutler, not Olivia. She might have said Maxwell, wanting to collect on Aaron's debt. But that was before . . . what about one of the others? What about the double take Liam had done when he'd seen Delilah in the long, dark wig, only to find himself dead a few hours later?

Pierre read the indecision, the uncertainty in her expression and shook his head. 'I will return soon. We have much to talk about. Don't leave the lounge.'

After he'd left, Janine lowered her hood and craned her neck to look around the cabin. 'Wow, this is some yacht.'

Olivia hadn't even taken it in. But Janine was right; as they moved from the practical wet room into the main body of the yacht itself, they found themselves in a breathtaking lounge – a huge space with polished walnut walls and pristine soft white-leather sofas, a large William Morris-patterned oriental carpet on the floor. A huge dining table, with room for ten people, ran along the back wall, fluffy, monogrammed towels neatly folded on its top. All the accents were marble and polished gold, but the opulence turned her stomach. The finishes reminded her of the original *Clarissa*, so much so that she practically expected her dad to walk in from the cockpit and give her a hug. Now any doubt that Pierre – a man who'd been her client most of her working life – had owned that boat too was gone. She was on its next reincarnation. If there wasn't a storm raging outside, she would beg to leave.

Janine passed her a towel, and she wiped the sea spray from her face.

'I can't believe you know this guy,' said Janine.

'Sort of. I mean . . . he's a client of the actuarial firm I worked for. And in a way, he introduced me to Aaron – he was the one who asked me to look into art investing for him. But I never expected to see him here.'

'I think he cares about you. He seemed to have been looking for you.'

Olivia frowned. 'I don't understand it.'

'I guess we'll find out when he gets back. I don't know about you but I'm starving. I'm going to see if I can get us some food somewhere on this super yacht,' said Janine. She ventured towards the back of the lounge, then disappeared through a sliding door.

Olivia slumped down on to the sofa, the towel in her lap. She felt overwhelmed with adrenaline and emotion. She still couldn't get her head around what she'd seen Patty do. The hurt and anger in her new friend's eyes. She thought of the rest of the group, huddled some-where on Brown Base, and felt guilty that she was now somewhere safe and warm while they were out there in the storm. And what about Sergei? Did she trust what Pierre had said?

Her body didn't. A man walked past the window, and the silhouette made her immediately stiffen. He was limping, favouring his left side. He stopped outside the door to the lounge.

'Psst, Olivia!'

She turned around to see Janine gesturing at her to come, her eyes wild with panic as she pointed at Sergei outside the lounge door. 'That's the man who attacked me! We've got to get away. We're not safe.'

The handle to the lounge jiggled, and that was enough for Olivia. She didn't want to be alone with Sergei, no matter what Pierre said. She followed Janine as she ran down a set of stairs. 'I just found one of the cabins. We can hide in there.' Janine stopped in front of one of the doors, pushing it open with her hip. When they were both inside, she locked the door behind them, then grabbed a chair, propping it up against the handle.

'There. He won't be able to get through that easily,' she said.

Olivia paced across the plush carpet in the centre of the room. 'Pierre said Sergei is working for him. Maybe he's not the threat we think he is. But regardless, we won't leave here until Pierre returns with the rest of the *Vigil* group,' she said.

'Oh, Olivia,' said Janine softly, 'you won't be leaving here at all.'

48

Olivia stopped pacing. 'What did you say?'

Janine smiled, but it didn't put Olivia at ease. In fact, her body tensed even more, a coiled spring. 'When Pierre found us, I thought my luck had run out. I'd been waiting to get you alone on the ice. I almost had you too. It would have been so much more perfect to kill you there. But this works. Especially after you told me what happened on the previous *Clarissa*.' From behind her back, Janine pulled out a long kitchen knife. 'It's surprisingly hard to find a weapon on board that isn't nailed down, but the galley provided.' She checked the blade with the edge of her finger, pulling back when satisfied it was sharp.

'Janine, what are you doing?' Olivia tried to keep her voice calm, even though fear pulsed through her body. Her eyes flicked around the room but there was little she could use to defend herself. The only exit was the one Janine barred. There was a set of sliding doors leading to a balcony, but beyond that was only the freezing, stormy sea . . .

'You don't feel an ounce of remorse, do you?'

'For my father? Of course I do. I think about it every day—'

'Not your father. For Kay.'

Olivia paused, staring up at Janine's face. There was real anguish there, deep pain she'd kept hidden, now rising to the surface. The hidden underside of her iceberg, pushing through the woman's skin.

'I'm sorry, Janine. You have the wrong person. I don't know who Kay is.' She paused. 'Wait, are you talking about your boyfriend? Who you broke up with?'

'I didn't break up with him. He's dead.'

'Oh, Janine, I'm so, *so* sorry. But I don't see what that has to do with me . . .'

'Don't be stupid!' Janine slapped the knife against the nearest wall, making Olivia jump. 'Why do you think I'm in Antarctica? To make you all pay. That disgusting man Stefan profiting from his legacy. Aaron drugging him into a mania. And you – you killed him.'

Olivia choked, her throat closing. 'Your boyfriend was Kostas Yennin?' she managed to say. She thought of Stefan swinging from the curtain rail. She knew it hadn't been suicide. But Janine had mentioned Aaron too. 'Wait. What . . . what did you do to Aaron?'

'Murderer,' Janine growled.

'Murder? I don't know what you're talking about!' Olivia almost screamed it. It was so absurd. Her mind couldn't reconcile the gentle, friendly Janine from her cabin with the wild-eyed woman in front of her, snarling with rage.

'But you do. You've told me yourself why you did it. Your burnout. Stepping out into the road. But that wasn't the whole story, was it?'

Olivia swallowed. Janine was right. It wasn't the whole story.

After she'd jumped back on the pavement, she realized how stupid she'd been. What an awful mistake she'd almost made. But she was safe. Unharmed. She'd stopped herself before there could be any terrible consequences.

No. Not quite.

Almost immediately a horn blared. Tyres screeched on the road, brakes squealing in protest. Then a loud bang resonated through her body. The car that had been driving erratically had swerved into a lamp post, smashing into it at speed. The cyclist who'd given her the finger had stopped, scrambling around for his phone. A black cab pulled up just behind the scene of the accident, a woman rushing out to check whether anyone in the car was hurt. Olivia had heard her anguished scream when she must have seen he was. Other drivers, on both sides of the road, stopped their cars, getting out to check on the crash. So many people with their phones out, dialling 999, alerting the authorities.

She thought about calling the police too but she caught sight of the time – she was already so late to the auction. She had about a million missed calls from Aaron. There were enough other witnesses around. A man shouted that he was a doctor. She felt sure that whoever was in the car would be getting the help they needed.

It wasn't until hours later that she made the connection. Once she had heard the full police report from Aaron, she suspected – and when he told her the name of the road, it was confirmed. Yennin had been in the car. He had passed away on impact.

If she hadn't been in such a bad way, if she'd picked him up like she had promised Aaron she would do . . . it never would have happened.

She didn't think anyone knew she'd been there.

And yet now she was staring directly into the pain-filled eyes of someone who knew.

Janine whimpered but held the knife firm. 'So you do remember. You ran away. But you knew you had caused the accident. And then you benefited from his death. My Kostas.'

'But I didn't cause the accident.' Olivia's mind was spinning. 'I was there, yes, but the car was already swerving all over the road.'

'Don't lie!' Janine shouted, tears filling her eyes. 'I was following in the black cab behind. I saw you step out into the road in front of Kostas. I saw you. He *had* to swerve to avoid hitting you!'

'No, that's not . . .'

But Janine wouldn't listen. 'He'd almost made it. He was so close. If it hadn't been for you . . .'

'Janine, please. You have to know – I'm so sorry for your loss. I hardly knew him but Aaron was absolutely devastated when he heard Kostas had passed. The police said he was high when he crashed? That's probably . . .'

'Yes, on drugs that Aaron gave him!'

Olivia shook her head. 'I know Aaron. He would never have given Kostas drugs. He wanted him clean.'

'Oh, you know Aaron, do you? Is that what he told you? I bet he conveniently left out the fact that he'd visited the studio that afternoon, didn't he? Kostas was painting – as always – even though it was the night of his big auction. Aaron made it clear that this was Kostas's last shot. If he didn't attend, and if his painting didn't sell, he'd be dropped as a client. How cruel is that? He only ever saw Kostas as a money ticket – not for his talent. But Kostas didn't care about schmoozing with buyers or being represented by some dealer. All he wanted to do was create.

337

'I left to get us some food. It was always a struggle to get him to eat when he was in his creative flow. He didn't like seeing anyone at that time either. That's why I was surprised to see Aaron's car leaving the driveway. When I got in, I knew something was wrong. I walked into the studio and that's when I found him.'

Her eyes welled with tears. 'He was acting strange, erratic. But he'd been sober for so long; I didn't think . . . then I saw his eyes. His pupils were all dilated and weird. He was so far gone I barely recognized him. I didn't think he should go to the auction in that state but he insisted. Now he was all amped up and excited – exactly Aaron's intention.

'He insisted on driving, even though I didn't want him to. Begged him not to. I don't have a licence or else I would have done it. He wouldn't let me get in the car with him, though, so I had to follow behind in the cab. If you hadn't been so stupid, stepping out right in front of him, he would have made it. And you just ran away. The police didn't even question you. No one even knew you were there!'

Janine clenched her jaw. 'But it was worth it for you, wasn't it, when the auction lot sold for millions . . . ? The rumours around his death were exactly the extra-special magic that Aaron needed. Do you think Kostas's family saw any of that? No. What about the foundation he dreamed of starting? Not a penny. After his death, all the profit from his sales went directly to the Hunt Advisory. He'd signed over all his copyright. To you and Aaron.'

'But, Janine . . . Aaron couldn't have known Kostas would die that night.'

338

'He might not have known your role in it. But he knew what the drugs would do to my sweet Kostas. I told the police that I'd seen you, but there was no way of finding you. Even then – seeing you behind bars wouldn't be any sort of punishment. Not for how you went on to profit from his death. When I heard about this cruise ship deal, I couldn't believe it. Mass-producing his beautiful art, watering it down, wringing as much out of his work as you can. But I was never going to let you get away with it.'

Janine's voice was full of raw emotion, and part of Olivia wished she could reach out and hug her. In so many ways she agreed with her – the showcase, as it had happened, wasn't what Kostas would have wanted. It wasn't what Aaron had wanted. But there was no way Janine would listen in her current state. In the next moment, Janine jabbed the knife towards Olivia's chest, snagging it on the material of her parka. Olivia yelped and took a step back.

'I booked my passage on the ship, so I could get to you all,' Janine said. 'Aaron was the easiest. I've been threatening to expose him for months with footage of him giving Kostas the drugs. Leaving him notes. Text messages. Never letting him forget what he did, not even for a moment. All I had to do was lure him off the ship then kill him in the hotel room. I was back on board before anyone noticed.'

Olivia let out a cry that barely sounded human. Aaron was dead? All that time she'd spent being angry at him, cursing him, then wanting to make him proud . . . and Janine had just coldly confessed to his murder.

'I thought you would be easy too – you'd drink the spiked champagne I had Liam put in your room and that would be it. Two down. But you didn't drink it.'

'The . . . the couple. The honeymooners. You killed them? And then you just carried on with the cruise?'

Janine's eyes flashed. 'How was I to know you would switch cabins? At least I'd taken Aaron's phone before I left him, so I could throw you off the scent. Then I saw that Art Abroad guy utterly ruining Kostas's vision. Luckily he was such a small man, I didn't have any trouble staging his death either. And after Liam told you he had been bribed to put the bottle in the room – I couldn't risk him telling the police when we got back. Now . . .'

Olivia's mind was spinning. Janine had killed Stefan and Liam too. She thought of Stefan hanging from the window, then Liam's body that they had dragged together on the pulk.

The extent of what Janine was capable of was sinking in. The body count she'd left in her wake. If Olivia didn't get out of here quickly, she was going to be next. But she could hardly see through her tears, hardly think through the fog of grief that had descended. Aaron, gone. She thought she was going to be sick. 'Janine . . . you're right. I am to blame.' Olivia sucked in a shuddering breath. She dropped her head in her hands. 'I blame myself. I should have been the one driving Kostas that day. Aaron had asked me to pick him up, and his social media assistant. That was you, wasn't it? Although obviously you were so much more than that. I am so, so sorry. But don't think I don't hate myself every day for my part in what happened.'

Janine blinked. For a moment, Olivia wondered if

by accepting some culpability, she had got through to her.

'I thought we were becoming friends,' Olivia continued.

'Your apologies are not enough,' said Janine. 'I have to finish what I started.' She took a step forward.

Olivia recoiled. Janine might be grieving, but she was also a cold-blooded killer. She'd proved that. It was all so senseless. Yennin's death was an unspeakable tragedy, and she knew she'd played her part, but it didn't warrant the murder and carnage that Janine had wreaked.

'You won't escape the police just because we're in Antarctica. You won't get away with any of this. But if you let me go, I'll make sure Yennin's art – his legacy – is respected. You know him best. Whatever you think he would want, whatever his family wants, I'll make sure it happens. I'll start the foundation in his name. He loved this environment, didn't he? He'd want to help preserve it. We can do that.'

Janine shook her head. 'I know what you're doing, Olivia. You're trying to logic your way out of this. Figuring out a way to manipulate me. I've done my research on you. I know you're a fixer. And you know both sides. The art and the money. I'm sure you've always found a solution for everything. But let me tell you something. There are some problems you can't solve. No matter what clever solution, what workaround you present to me, there's one thing you can't change. You can't bring Kostas back.' Her voice cracked then – she was on the brink of tears. 'You can't change the fact that he's dead. And because of that – you need to pay.'

49

She lunged at Olivia then, thrusting the knife. Olivia shrieked, throwing her arms up over her head, trying to defend herself. The knife slashed the fabric of her jacket, creating a gaping hole.

She scrambled back against the desk. There wasn't much that wasn't nailed down – Janine had been right about that – but she threw whatever she could at her attacker – a pen, a book. Not much connected, but they threw her off just enough to not get in a fatal thrust.

There was a loud pounding against the cabin door. Pierre's deep voice sounded through the walnut. 'Olivia? Are you in there?' The door handle shook.

The interruption helped. Janine paused for a moment, and Olivia went on the offensive, grabbing Janine's wrist and twisting it so she dropped the knife.

'Help!' Olivia shouted. She ran to the door, pulling the chair out of the way of the handle. But by the time she got to the lock, Janine had recovered. She grabbed her around her neck and yanked backwards.

They slammed against the bookshelf, Janine twisting at the last minute so Olivia's shoulder bore the brunt of the force. Glass shattered around them as they were flung up against a cabinet in the struggle. Olivia dropped to the ground, groping around her, trying to find something that she could use as a weapon, but she only succeeded in cutting herself. She barely felt any pain, because the blows from Janine were constant.

She could feel herself slipping away. She wasn't a fighter. And Janine was fuelled by anger and desperation.

The blows let up, and Olivia's eyes cracked open. Oblivion wasn't hers just yet. But Janine hadn't stopped because she was giving up. Quite the opposite. In her hand now was a shard of glass the size of her forearm, jagged and sharp. So sharp it was causing Janine's hand to bleed as she held the end of it, the blood trickling down her wrist, into the cuff of her jacket.

She raised the glass over her head, kneeling on Olivia's chest, aiming it at her heart.

'This is for Kostas,' she whispered, before bringing the glass down.

Olivia's arms flew up to protect her face. She felt the shard dig in above her wrist, and she cried out in agony.

Maybe she deserved this. She'd fantasized about escaping her life, hadn't she? And she had played a part in the events leading to Kostas's death. It would be easy to let Janine take her revenge. Aaron was gone. So many innocent people, dead. There was a sick poetry to it. Dying on board the next iteration of the ship that had killed her father.

But these past few weeks had changed Olivia. Unearthed memories she'd buried deep inside. Her dad would have urged her to fight. She wanted the chance to reconnect with her mum, bring her down to the water and watch her smile again.

She wanted to live a different kind of life. But in order to change her future, she had to be alive to see it. And someone needed to get justice for all the people who had died.

Loud banging on the other side of the cabin door made Janine hesitate. Someone was trying to break down the door. Olivia only had to last a little longer and help would be there.

With the shard lodged in her arm, she gritted her teeth against the pain. Then she kicked out, connecting with Janine's knee. Now it was Janine's turn to cry out. Her hand flew open, and the glass shard dropped. She dripped blood as she grabbed at her leg.

Olivia rolled on to her front, scrambling to her feet.

She heard shouts. Pierre's face appeared in the split cabin door. 'Stop this!' Pierre tugged at the door, but the mechanism hitched. 'What the hell is going on?'

Janine's arm hooked around Olivia's neck, and she pulled her backwards, towards the balcony door. She threw it open with her free hand and Olivia felt a blast of freezing air against her back.

'Let her go,' Pierre said, having finally flung open the door. Pierre and Sergei rushed into the cabin now, but slowed as they approached the two women. Olivia felt frantic, desperately searching for a way to break Janine's grip. They were about equal height, but Janine was so much stronger.

They were backed up against the balcony railing.

'Don't come any closer,' said Janine.

Pierre's hands were raised, palms facing out. Sergei tried to step forward but Pierre shook his head. It was obvious where all Janine's anger was directed.

'Whatever you want – money, freedom, escape – we'll give it to you,' said the Frenchman. 'Just let her go.'

But Janine just pulled Olivia tighter to her chest. Olivia could barely hear Pierre, the rush of blood pounding in her ears was too loud and the wind was howling across the water.

'There's nothing you can offer me that will stop this.'

'Then you leave me no choice. Sergei?' Pierre gestured to him with a head tilt. Sergei stepped forward, removing a weapon from his belt. It looked like a gun encased in yellow plastic. He pointed it straight at Janine.

To her relief Olivia felt Janine loosen her grip. The woman's body dropped, like she was sinking into the deck. Olivia took her opportunity, stumbling forward a few steps. Sergei continued to aim the weapon at Janine, while Pierre reached out his hand to Olivia.

She almost had the chance to take it.

But then she felt a tug on the hood of her jacket. Janine used the momentum to slam Olivia back against the railing. Then, with a scream of agony from pushing against her injured leg, Janine boosted Olivia up and over the balcony railing.

Olivia didn't let go of her grip on Janine's jacket. For a moment, they were caught in limbo: if Olivia let go, she would fall in the water. If Janine tried to break her hold, Olivia could scramble back on the balcony.

Janine chose a different option. She pushed off the balcony.

The men rushed forward, watching her plan unfold.

But it was too late to stop the inevitable.

Janine and Olivia plunged into the water.

50

The water enveloped her and she felt her lungs constrict. Her breath was stolen away by the cold.

She wasn't in a drysuit this time. Now she felt every drop of freezing water through her clothes, the weight of it dragging her down even deeper below the surface. Her muscles constricted; she lost her grip on Janine. The pain was far more intense than when the glass shard had sliced her arm – it felt like she had fallen into a pool of broken glass, and every which way she turned, the pain intensified.

Then, almost as quickly as it came, pain left her. So did panic and fear. She was floating in the deepest, coldest darkness. She wanted to fight, but her mind was shutting down.

Thankfully her body had other ideas. Her muscles spasmed, her mouth and throat desperately fighting the urge to gasp for air. *Stay calm, Olivia.* Her dad's voice. It was as if she could hear him right next to her. Her eyes flew open, searching for him, but all she could see was the green-black water.

Which way was up? It was too confusing. She squeezed her eyes tight shut again. The desire to take a breath was almost overwhelming. She needed to kick, to surface. But which direction?

With one desperate plea from her brain, she opened her eyes again. She saw a blinking red light – the ship? It was her only chance. She kicked towards it, arcing her arms in a breaststroke.

With seconds to spare, she burst through the surface, and now she gasped. Her arms and legs flailed; some part of her knew that she should try to stay calm but she wasn't in control.

There was no sign of Janine, but the water was thick on the surface with a slurry of ice, those bergy bits she'd seen from the shore, dragged out into the bay by the calving from the glacier. The wind whipped the waves up, so she had to expend even more energy to keep her head up.

She tried to cry out, but there was no power in her voice. Her entire body felt heavy.

'Over there!'

'Quick, throw it now.'

A splash close to her. An orange life ring. She tried to swim towards it, but the weight of her drenched clothes and the tightness of her muscles made it almost impossible.

One more push. Somehow she got an arm around the ring and clung on out of desperation as she was dragged back towards the *Clarissa II*.

Strong arms grabbed her jacket, pulling her up on deck and immediately wrapping her in heavy towels.

She couldn't stop her teeth from chattering, violent shivers taking over every part of her body.

'Where's – Janine?' she stammered out.

No one looked at her. She stopped moving on the outer deck, spinning around to stare at the water. She scoured the ice-strewn waves, trying to spot a sign of the girl.

There was nothing.

'We are watching for her,' said Pierre. 'I swear it. Now get inside.'

She nodded, then once they were in the lounge, Melissa helped peel her jacket and boots off. Olivia blinked up at the expedition leader. She was on board. Was everyone safe? She wanted to ask, but every time she opened her mouth, nothing would come out.

'I'll find her a change of clothes,' said Pierre. 'Take her into my cabin. I'll get the galley to send up a warm drink. Get her dry and then we'll meet in the lounge – it's warmest in there.'

Olivia's legs weren't cooperating, but somehow – with Melissa's help – she stumbled into the master cabin.

Strangely the first thing that struck her was the sound. A hum reverberated through her body, the frequency signalling her stressed-out body to breathe deeper. She recognized it immediately.

She looked up and her feet almost gave out from under her. An enormous painting hung on the far wall. *nemiga*. The original Yennin that Pierre had bought at the auction.

The reason she was in this condition: soaking wet, freezing, cut, bloody and bruised. Now she wondered if she'd died in the icy water. Was this a dream? Was she slowly slipping into hypothermia and this was her body's way of comforting her?

Pierre knocked on the door. Melissa took the clothes and waited for Olivia to dry herself in the bathroom. She didn't even feel that cold, but that could also be a symptom of severe hypothermia.

By the time she'd crawled into the soft cashmere

clothes that Pierre provided, she felt her skin beginning to tingle, her senses coming back to life.

Melissa placed a blanket around her shoulders, rubbed at her hands, then looked with concern at the cut on her arm. 'We should have the doctor look at that.'

'You guys made it. Is everyone OK?' Olivia asked through chattering teeth.

Melissa furrowed her brow. 'Don't worry about that right now. What happened?'

'It was Janine. She . . . she killed Aaron before he could get on the ship. Then she murdered the couple in cabin sixteen thinking it was me, and Stefan, and Liam . . .'

'Janine?' Melissa gasped. 'But why?'

'She blamed me for her boyfriend's death. He's the artist from the showcase.'

'My God.' Melissa gripped the edge of the sofa. 'We need to get a message to the captain. Let's get you back to the lounge and find you a warm drink. Then we can sort everything out.'

Olivia nodded, pulling the blanket tighter around her shoulders.

'Wait, Melissa . . . how is Cutler? And what about Patty?'

Melissa turned her face away, so Olivia couldn't read her expression. 'Cutler will live. Patty . . . she's the only one still unaccounted for on the mainland. It's too dangerous for us to cross the water again, but when we can, we'll look for her again.'

In the lounge, Pierre was sitting on one of his sofas, staring at his laptop. He looked every inch the billionaire explorer in his black turtleneck and khaki slacks. He smoothed down his silver hair as she entered. 'Please, come sit. I have hot cocoa on the table for you. And an excellent whisky if you would prefer that.'

'Janine?' she asked.

Pierre shook his head. 'We spotted blood on the hull. There has been no sign of anyone on the surface. We think she must have hit her head on the way down. Besides, it's been far too long now. She is gone.'

Olivia closed her eyes, and for the first time allowed herself to cry. She knew how it must look, crying for someone who had tried to kill her. But before that Janine had been her friend. The shock was too great to reconcile.

Sergei stepped into the room. 'The rest of the passengers are warming up in the galley. Mr Hughes's condition is stable, but he will need further medical assistance.'

'And your leg?' asked Pierre.

Sergei grimaced at Olivia as he spoke. 'It will heal.'

'I . . . I'm sorry for being so suspicious of you,' said Olivia. 'But after I saw you in Ushuaia and then later on the ship . . .'

'Sergei works for me,' said Pierre. 'Initially I wanted a man on board the *Vigil* to keep an eye on Cutler for me. You know LUJO is set to acquire the Pioneer fleet? Anyway, it was a good thing he did. Aaron was supposed to keep me informed on all the details of the showcase, so when I didn't hear from him on the day of the ship's departure, I was concerned. Then Sergei sent a message back that Aaron hadn't even made it on to the ship.

'My suspicions were confirmed when the police found Aaron's body a few days after the ship's departure.'

'What . . . what did Janine do to him?' Olivia could hardly bear to ask, but she had to know.

'She was clever, I give her that. She'd rented a room and asked them not to disturb or clean it for the duration of the stay. The hotel found him when the room was supposed to be handed over. The police determined he had been poisoned. Injected with something.'

'Liquid MDMA?'

'How did you know?'

'That's what she spiked the champagne with, which killed the couple who I had switched cabins with.'

'I knew then that you were in truly grave danger. And since you hadn't responded to my radio call or any of my emails—'

Olivia blinked. 'But I didn't receive anything. In fact, I sent *you* emails. Several.'

'I know, I received them,' said Pierre. 'But it was clear that you were not getting my replies. That's why I realized perhaps you were in even more danger than I previously suspected. I asked Sergei to keep an eye on you from a distance. I didn't want to alarm you. But I set sail for the continent immediately, hoping I could intercept you before it was too late.'

'Why didn't you just come straight to me and tell me all this?' she asked Sergei.

'I told him not to,' said Pierre. 'Until we knew who was behind the attacks; it felt pointless to panic you. And if your attacker knew you were being watched, they might have changed their plans, and then she would have got away with it all. I couldn't have that.'

'I only realized it was Janine when I was back on board the *Clarissa II*,' said Sergei.

'Yes, look at this.' Pierre pressed a discreet button chiselled into the wooden top of the coffee table. On the far wall one of the walnut panels slid open to reveal a high-definition television.

He pressed another button on a remote and the screen jumped to life. It was a collection of photographs and social media posts relating to Kostas Yennin – including a selection of the threatening messages Aaron had received. Seeing them in black and white – knowing what the person who sent them was truly capable of – made her throat close up.

'Sergei had asked Stefan if there was any reason Aaron would be in danger, and he mentioned the threatening emails and message – these are just some of the tweets we found online. We tried to trace who was sending them, but it was almost all from anonymous accounts.

'Still, I was at a dead end until Sergei came on board. So maybe it was a good thing she had you kicked off the *Vigil*.' Pierre threw a sidelong glance at his right-hand man. 'When he embarked and saw this board, he recognized something. Or, rather, someone.'

Olivia stood up, approaching the television. Something stood out to her too: a photograph of Yennin in his studio, taken for a profile on him in the *Guardian*. In the background of the photograph someone was standing just off to one side, their phone up – maybe filming or taking a photo. A young woman with long dark hair. It was not immediately obvious. But when you looked closer, it became clear. It was the same person. Without the copper-dyed hair.

'Janine,' Olivia whispered, reaching out and touching the screen.

'She went by Nina, but, yes, she was his social media

manager, and his long-term girlfriend. She'd been on the scene too, the night he died.'

'When I realized you would be on the continent with her, I knew I had to get back to the shore – or else she would kill you,' said Sergei.

Olivia swallowed. 'She almost managed it.' She closed her eyes, still struggling to come to terms with everything she'd been through. 'All this scandal, all this death . . . your deal with Pioneer must be over.'

'I don't care about that,' scoffed Pierre. 'It's you I was concerned about.'

'Me? You went through all of this to look out for me?'

'I have been looking out for you for a long time,' Pierre said. 'Ever since what happened to your father.'

51

Olivia felt as numb as if she'd been plunged back into the water outside.

Pierre poured himself a dram of whisky, knocking it back before continuing. 'Your father was one of the best sailors I'd ever met. I would have trusted him on any of my fleet. He helped choose this vessel too. He always talked about captaining a yacht capable of sailing in the most extreme environments – like the one we're in now.'

'I remember,' said Olivia quietly. She didn't sit back down on the sofa, but leaned against the wall, still feeling weak.

'After the accident, we did a lengthy investigation into what happened. We had put in a new collision-avoidance system just before your voyage. State of the art. But it hadn't been installed properly. There was no alert when that idiot speedboat driver fell asleep at the wheel. He had no lights on either. No way for your father to avoid it.'

She shook her head. 'It wasn't my father's fault. It was mine. I was on watch that night. I missed it.'

'Oh, child. I know you blame yourself. But I know, as your father did, that no system is truly foolproof. You didn't see the boat coming, but the alarm should have sounded. It didn't. I have never forgiven myself.'

'You don't understand. I fell asleep during my watch. It was only for a few seconds but it was long enough.'

'But you weren't the only one on watch. Your father

wrote in his log that he was awake that night. He was doing circuits of the deck every few minutes, making sure you were OK. That's why he wasn't down below that night. Why he fell overboard when the boats collided. You both missed it, and the technology failed. You weren't to blame. And you were far too young to lose your father. I felt it my duty to keep an eye on you and your mother.'

'There was no secret savings account, was there? You helped us with the moving costs. And then later on with my university fees.'

'Yes. Your father didn't have life insurance and I knew you needed help to get on your feet. Up until you graduated, I took care of you. But then your mother abruptly cut contact with me. I got the sense my help was no longer welcome. But still, I kept an eye on you. When you started as an actuary, I was so proud. It was natural for my company to use your firm after that.'

'And then all those years as my client, and you never said anything . . .'

'I didn't want to overstep or go against your mother's wishes. I already felt so wracked with guilt that your father had been lost on my boat. Besides, you seemed to be doing so well. I ended up trusting you as I did your father.'

She sipped at her hot chocolate, the cup returning sensation to her fingers. Her mind struggled to turn over the implications of Pierre's words. She'd asked to see the results of the inquest into her father's death and the collision, but talk of it was always shut down quickly. If her mother had stopped refusing Pierre's aid after university . . . that coincided with the start of her

355

illness. Was that really what her mother had wanted or was it the disease?

Pierre had been their secret benefactor.

Then she had another realization. 'Aaron knew,' she said. 'That you had a special connection to me.'

'Well, I did specify that I would only come to his gallery at your recommendation. Your mother and I had once had long conversations about art, and like I said – I had come to trust you. And I'm glad I did. Once again, you didn't let me down with your evaluation of this investment. Yennin was a wonderful, gifted artist and I am proud to own one of his originals.'

Olivia felt a chill return. She'd always wondered why Aaron had pursued her so persistently. Now she knew. It had never been about *what* Olivia could bring to the table. Only who. She was his key to Pierre. And Pierre was the missing mystery buyer in the Pioneer sale equation. Aaron needed to keep Olivia happy at least until that had closed.

Had their relationship even been real? The engagement ring hadn't been for her. When she was back on the *Vigil*, she'd return the ring to its rightful owner. Maybe the doubt that had niggled her stomach – that sense things had moved way too quickly, that it was all too good to be true, even Trish's instinct that things might not be as they seemed – was what had been real.

She shook herself. It didn't matter now. Janine had robbed her of the ability to ever find out. And whatever Aaron had felt for her, her feelings for him had been real. She'd loved him, and he was gone. Now she had his family to think of, his friends and loved ones to explain to about what had happened.

And a legacy to protect.

'Do you have a laptop I can use?' she asked.

'Absolutely,' replied Pierre. He gestured to one of the sideboards, where a slim MacBook was plugged in and secured with clamps, so it wouldn't slide off.

Olivia turned it on, opening a browser, amazed at how fast the connection speed was.

'We have excellent satellite Wi-Fi on board. One of my requirements. In the meantime, I will go check on our other guests.' He paused. 'What happened to Mr Hughes, by the way? His wounds did not look . . . natural.'

Olivia grimaced. 'They weren't.' Then she looked over at Melissa. 'It was Patty. But please find her. She . . . she was blindsided.'

'We will look for her,' said Pierre. 'Please, can you stay and look after Olivia?' he asked Melissa, who nodded.

Olivia returned her gaze to the computer. She logged into her email, where there was still no sign of any emails from Pierre. Had he been lying to her?

She checked her trash folder. Nothing. Then her spam. Also nothing. But there was a second folder labelled *Spam*. Or – not 'spam' but 'sparn'. At a glance they looked the same.

She opened it to see a string of emails from Pierre – but also from Tricia. Someone had set up a filter on her account to send all non-marketing emails to a place she never would have known to check.

Janine. She must have accessed her email while they'd been on board. Another ploy to make Olivia feel even more isolated and alone.

Pierre, true to his word, had replied to every email

she'd sent since they'd left port. He'd told her he was coming, to save her from Aaron's attacker.

And Tricia. She didn't hate her. She had been worried about her. Her emails had become more confused and frantic in their tone, hoping that nothing bad had happened.

She opened a window to reply, but had no idea what to say, or how to explain.

She started with: *I'm alive.*

Then it hit her. But Aaron wasn't. She would never see him again.

'Everything OK?' Melissa asked.

Olivia reached up and touched her cheeks. She'd been crying and hadn't even realized it.

'Hello?'

Olivia looked up sharply, startled by the voice. It was Annalise, her eyes red-rimmed and raw. Melissa stood up and gestured for Annalise to come in. 'Sit. Make yourself warm by the stove.'

To her surprise, Annalise rushed over and hugged her. 'I'm glad you're OK. We heard you went overboard.'

'I think she's had enough polar plunges to last a life-time,' said Melissa with a wry grin.

'Me too,' said Olivia.

Annalise dropped her head in her hands.

'Patty?' Olivia asked. She knew by Melissa's grave expression, and Annalise's sob, that she was right. 'She could still survive, right? She could be out there still.'

'Maybe. But I saw it in her eyes. She didn't want to survive. Not after what she did,' Annalise said. 'It didn't have to come to this. I hadn't known the extent of my father's plan until this cruise. We'd talked about me

358

leading up the digital side of the business. I was ready for that. But I didn't know he meant to close the rest of it, make everyone else redundant.'

'Pierre has gone to talk with him now.'

Annalise shook her head. 'I've just been to see him. My arrogant, headstrong dad. He's in no condition to make any decisions. We need to get him to a hospital.'

'I'm so sorry, Annalise.'

'I've lived most of my life without him looking out for me. It wasn't until I developed this aptitude for business that he showed any interest at all. I just hope Ingrid and the boys will be OK. What happened to you?'

'Janine. She'd followed me and Aaron here to kill us.'

'Jesus! Does Pierre have her locked up somewhere?'

Olivia shook her head. 'She went overboard with me. But they didn't find her.'

Melissa reached out to the centre of the table, and poured a generous dram of Scotch into three of Pierre's heavy-bottomed fancy crystal tumblers. They caught the light like chips of pure ice off a glacier. She passed one to Annalise, and one to Olivia.

'Drink,' she said. And Olivia was glad for the smoky warmth of the whisky's burn.

52

Olivia watched from the bow as the *Clarissa II* pulled into the port of Ushuaia. Her wrist still throbbed where the knife had sliced her. She'd been neatly patched up by Pierre's doctor, but she'd need the stitches looked at in the local hospital.

She would have company there. Cutler had woken up, but he needed proper medical aid. They'd kept him on the *Clarissa II* as well, the yacht faster and more nimble than the *Vigil*. He was down below, preparing to be rushed into intensive care.

The crossing had been so different. Subdued, peaceful, the Drake Lake this time, showing just how calm the waters could be when they wanted to.

She raised her binoculars, training them on the harbour entrance. There were police cars and an ambulance on the road nearby – waiting for Cutler – but there was someone else there too. Her breath hitched. Someone she recognized on shore was waiting for her.

The person raised their hand, tentative at first.

Olivia lowered her binoculars, then waved back.

Tricia. Her best friend had come for her.

Olivia rushed inside, wanting to be at the gangway the moment that they docked. She bumped into Annalise, who hadn't left her dad's side.

'How is he doing?'

'He'll survive,' she said. 'And the word is that the *Vigil* should be docking a few hours after us. I'm sure Ingrid and the boys are anxiously awaiting an update.'

Olivia patted Annalise's arm. 'You're doing the right thing.'

'I hope so. For Patty's sake.'

The *Vigil* – led by Melissa – had sent out search parties for Patty and brought Liam's body on board. They hadn't found her.

Annalise had been distraught – almost inconsolable. But when she recovered, she spent hours negotiating with Pierre, trying to come up with a plan to save the life of the Pioneer business. She offered to lead the expansion of a new LUJO adventure travel arm, so that hundreds of people wouldn't have to lose their jobs.

She wasn't the only one to be offered a new career. Pierre had spoken to Olivia too. 'Are you certain you don't want a job with me?' he'd asked. 'There's plenty of room in my company for a talented actuary. You wouldn't have any more financial issues.'

But Olivia shook her head. 'I think I have to find my own path.'

'Are you sure? It didn't seem like you were happy at Pendle . . .'

She'd shaken her head. 'No, I won't go back there either,' she said. 'But I have another plan that you could help me with.' Despite everything that had happened between her and Janine, she hadn't been able to get away from what she'd said. How there might be a better way to preserve Kostas Yennin's legacy, which honoured his art and the environment he loved so much. The Hunt Advisory could be part of that. A foundation in Yennin's name. She could make it happen.

'I'm all ears,' Pierre had said.

The yacht pulled up to the dock.

'You'll take care of yourself?' Annalise asked.

'I'll try. You as well, I hope.'

The two women – the survivors of cabin twelve – embraced.

Then Olivia ran down the gangway. At the bottom she waved her arm. 'Trish!' she shouted.

Tricia turned around, and her face lit up with relief. 'Liv, thank God.'

'What on earth are you doing here?' Olivia asked.

'Are you kidding? You've been sending me these weird emails and clearly not receiving my replies. I've been so worried about you. I flew out here as soon as I could and I've just been waiting for your ship to return.'

'I'm so glad to see you. When I didn't receive anything I thought maybe I'd lost you too.'

'Never,' said Tricia, a fierceness in her voice that Olivia had sorely missed. 'So not the burnout-recovery trip you'd been expecting?'

'Not exactly.' She looked over at the Argentinian police gathered just outside the gate, waiting for her to walk through.

Tricia followed her gaze. 'I'm so sorry about what happened to Aaron. That's so awful.'

Olivia took in a deep breath. 'At least I can tell the police what happened and hopefully give Aaron's family some peace. Along with Jay, Christa, Stefan, Liam . . .' Her voice cracked as she went through it all. She thought she'd come to terms with it enough to talk about it without crying. More likely she never would.

'Whatever you need, I'm here for you.' Trish grabbed her arm, holding it tight.

Olivia took one last look back over the Beagle Channel and the sparkling sea. The sun was high in the sky, so bright it was almost blinding. She closed her eyes, allowing the last few moments of it to shine on her face.

No more hiding from her problems. She was going to stay facing the sun.

53

She helped her mum down into the sloop. At first, it looked like she was going to slip with the unsteady motion of the water, but she reached down to grab the rope with practised ease and settled into position.

Olivia breathed a sigh of relief and jumped into the boat alongside. She had already checked over her mum's life jacket ten times, but now they were on the water, she checked it again. Every knot and tie was secured, her own the same.

'Checks done?' She didn't know if she was asking her mum or herself. Her mum smiled, and it was answer enough. 'Let's dive in.'

Before she could change her mind, Olivia released the ropes tying them to the dock, navigating them out towards the open sea. The water was deep blue, the breeze gentle – just enough to fill the sails and get the boat moving. Perfect conditions for her first sail as captain of her own ship.

'Isn't this glorious?' Her mother shouted to be heard over the wind. She closed her eyes, tilting her head back and allowing the sun to hit her, the breeze lifting her hair from her shoulders. 'I used to do this every year with my family,' she said. 'My favourite time.'

'Mine too,' said Olivia.

She tightened the sail sheet until it stopped luffing, allowing it to take full advantage of the wind. The sloop picked up speed and skimmed across the waves. Beside them gulls squawked and a gannet dived into the water.

Olivia's heart pounded with adrenaline, her attention sharp to every whim of the wind. But she'd done it.

'Pinpoint the feeling, Mum,' she said.

There was a moment's pause, as her mum turned her face to catch the sun's rays, the breeze tickling the hair that framed her face. 'Happy,' she said.

'Me too,' whispered Olivia.

They were free.

Acknowledgements

In February 2016, I was staying in a hostel in Rio de Janeiro, Brazil, when I overheard two fellow backpackers talking about how they'd travelled on an expedition ship to Antarctica at short notice. Immediately I knew it was something I wanted to do too. I asked them for their secret, and they gave me the name of a travel agent based in Ushuaia who specialized in filling any empty berths at highly discounted prices. Only a few days later, I was on a plane to Ushuaia ready to board the MS *Expedition* – and to begin my own unexpected solo voyage to the final continent.

I don't know what I expected, but Antarctica blew my mind: the abundant wildlife, the extreme beauty of the ice and the gripping history of this vast, dangerous and remote place. It was impossible not to be inspired as we visited the famed 'Penguin Post Office' at Port Lockroy, or thrilled as I took the polar plunge in the freezing waters off Deception Island beach. There's no doubt that my visit to Antarctica on the eve of my thirtieth birthday pushed me out of my comfort zone and ignited a love of adventure that would only grow from there. So my first thanks has to go to the place itself: to Antarctica, and to the passengers and crew of the MS *Expedition* who made my visit so special and memorable.

Writing this book has been its own adventure, and I'm forever indebted to my first readers: Kim Curran, Lizzie Pook and Saara El-Arifi for their insightful notes and unwavering enthusiasm. Also huge thanks to the numerous authors who have supported me as I have made the transition to being a thriller author: Claire Douglas, Gillian McAllister, Stacey Halls, Abigail Dean, Nikki May, Nita Prose, Samantha Bailey, L. R. Lam, Sarah Pearse, Christie Newport, Amie Kaufman, Charmaine Wilkerson, Ally Wilkes, Lucy Clarke, Juno Dawson, James Smythe and Laure Van Rensburg. How lucky am I to know you all!

My incredible agent, Juliet Mushens, as always has been integral to making this book a success. Along with the rest of the team at Mushens Entertainment – Rachel Neely, Liza DeBlock, Kiya Evans, Catriona Fida, Den Patrick – and with Jenny Bent of the Bent Agency in the US, I always feel like my books are in such good hands.

Supporting me through numerous drafts are my three incredible editors: Joel Richardson of Michael Joseph, Edward Kastenmeier of Anchor Books and Lara Hinchberger of Penguin Canada. I couldn't ask for a better or more thorough editorial team to guide me through the process of bringing this second book to life. Also huge thanks to Jennie Roman for her eagle-eyed copy-edit, and the production teams on both sides of the pond for managing schedules and moving deadlines for me! There are huge publishing teams on both sides of the Atlantic, with some of the most passionate and dedicated book lovers in the business working behind the scenes to get this book into as many hands as possible – people like Ellie Hughes in MJ's publicity team, and Stella Newing at Penguin Audio who produce such brilliant audiobook editions of my work. Thank you so much for being in my corner.

A special shout-out to Victoria Snowden, who talked to me about life as an actuary. Any inaccuracies in the text are my own, but it was great to talk to another Antarctica fan too!

So many thanks also to my parents, Angus and Maria McCulloch, for their early reads and name suggestions. I couldn't do this without you. To my aunt Diana Barnes and uncle Malcolm McCulloch for inspiring me with their tales of sailing around the world.

And none of this would be possible without the best partner I could ever hope for – Chris, our adventures have taken us to some incredible places, and I'm so grateful you're the one by my side.